SURGING TIDES

BOOK 1

girl
SUBMERGED

AVARA YARON

Printed in the United States of America

First Printing, 2018

ISBN 978-1-7320797-0-0

Published in 2018
by What's Next Publishing

www.whatsnextpublishing.com

Cover art by Kelly Carter.
Cover photography by Claire McAdams, courtesy of Shutterstock.
Author's portrait by Alina Vlasova.

Dedicated to the wondrous Bali sunsets that arouse romance in the most jaded soul.

girl SUBMERGED

I am falling, plummeting, gaining speed as I sink, out of control. I have had the same repetitive dream since childhood, awakening to the bleak, terrifying sense of being alone in the world. Sometimes the imagery changes: I have fallen out of the upper story of a skyscraper and descended into a dark, watery abyss; or most often, I have just begun to drop off to sleep when suddenly and rapidly I am hurtling through space, into a black hole, and awaken with a start, breathless and unsettled.

In an effort to connect, Jorge and I are drinking shots of tequila. We began discussing our increasingly tight finances after dinner, but didn't get farther than Jorge's liquor cabinet. Alcohol doesn't soothe me and the slightest drop makes me sleepy, but I am desperate. The tension between us has been escalating lately, the pillars of goodwill and trust teetering more precariously each day. We are on shaky ground with each other and it feels like the plates of the earth are shifting beneath my feet.

"Be honest for once," he demands of me, curling a lock of my long mocha brown hair around his finger. He is acting playful, but his gaze is ruthless. "What really turns you on?"

I look him directly in the eye and, wearing a mask of seductive confidence, slowly mouth, "Size matters." Immediately I wish the words back, not even sure I mean them or why I've chosen to jab this sore spot in Jorge's psyche. He won't ever let this one go.

The Brazilian hip hop he likes fills our loft and we dance, Jorge imposing his rhythm against my body while his fingers stray under my shirt and fist my hair, on a mission. He yanks off my clothes more roughly than usual and pins me against the couch. I have been missing his attention lately, but the harshness of it makes my chest tighten while the mixed cocktail of raw emotion and impending separation fuels our passion. He fumbles at the moment of entering me, making up for it with deep, forceful strokes. Then abruptly he pulls out and walks off to the kitchen.

"Am I not satisfying your hunger, Jorge?" He doesn't usually wander away before his own grand finale.

"Actually, I plan on satisfying yours."

I crane to look, but his head is lost inside the refrigerator.

The night ends with Jorge penetrating me with a condom-covered, oversized cucumber. "Maybe this will get you to open up. Size matters, right?"

Moaning, tears streaming down my face, I am awash in a confusing mixture of shame, pain and arousal, at once electrifying, horrifying, and strangely familiar. Jorge plays oblivious to my emotional soup, removing the cucumber and drunkenly finishing himself off.

I lie there, the mere receptacle for his release, wondering how have I managed to put myself in this situation. I haven't worked in months, my credit cards are maxed out, and my boyfriend has somehow become my opponent. I hardly recognize my increasingly round body, nor my collapsing life. Jorge is snoring but I am wide awake, estranged, heaviness crushing my bones.

When I finally sleep I have the dream again. I am alone on a sailboat, mercilessly tossed about by waves that threaten and taunt, ominous clouds darkening above me. Attempting to hold down the mast, my hands clench as I realize I don't know how to sail. Gale-force winds smash the head-sail into me, and I look up into a towering wall of seawater forcing me overboard. I sink quickly, clawing at the water in panic, when a mysteriously dark and powerful force passes overhead. Massive black wings soar through the water, encircling me, and as if someone has pulled the bathtub plug, my fear slowly drains away. I awaken with an uncommon tranquility, weight sunk deep into the sheets.

Dragging myself out of bed, I am relieved to find Jorge has already left for the station, and even more so that he will be gone until tomorrow. I used to yearn for him during his long shifts, fantasize about running my fingertips across his chiseled muscles, miss laughing at his silly jokes as we improvised in the kitchen. Now I am glad to have a break from the highly-charged tightness that fills the molecules between us. Except that I have to make my own cappuccino this morning. When he isn't off fighting fires, Jorge moonlights as my barista.

Early morning rays of sunshine streak muted highlights across the loft wall and spill their friendly announcement onto the floor. I sip my coffee as the subtle gradations of light seduce my eye, pondering an essential difference between Jorge and myself: Jorge is fire and I am water. A bundle of sizzling energy and flammable Brazilian genes, he needs to push everything to the limit, from his passion for karate and welding metal, right down to his career, dancing with a fiery grave.

He used to have a fire burning for me, I think, descending into my familiar cesspool of gloom. I get lost in watery emotions, vulnerable to shifting tides and the occasional tsunami, a sea creature more mermaid than woman, a mystery to myself. A multi-layered watercolor beside Jorge's bold graphics, I attempt to stabilize my emotional currents by anchoring in my intellect, while Jorge stokes his fire through perfecting his physical form.

One of my earliest memories is of water. I am three years old, busily stacking brightly colored toy cups on the baking concrete. They wobble, full of water, balanced at the lip of the swimming pool. I pour the liquid onto the hot pavement, fascinated by the droplets shrinking and disappearing as they evaporate in the sunshine. When all the cups are empty, I lean over the side of the pool to refill them just as my older brother, Barrett, dashes past me at full speed, knocking me over the edge and into the blue.

At first I am too flabbergasted to be afraid, but plunging downward terror flashes through my chest like lightning until a certain excitement overtakes it. I don't know how to swim, but feel natural in the water and am curious about the way the world looks underwater. Lines of sunlight make repetitive, strobing patterns that bounce as I move. My hands in front of my face grow large. It seems like a long time before I bob to the surface and sputter, gulping air. I look for faces, hands reaching out to me, anything, but there is only pool and sky.

I drop down again, but not as far this time and with more ease. Swishing my arms and legs, I realize I can propel myself through the water. This is the precise moment I learn to swim, and it is as if I already knew. The tiled wall comes into sharper focus as I draw myself closer. Somehow I make it to the edge and grab ahold, my plastic cups strewn nearby on the ground.

Across the yard I see my mother, my aunt and their friends at a table under an umbrella drinking cocktails, gray cigarette smoke curling above their heads. Barrett finally points to the pool, shouting, heads swivel in my direction, and there I am, clinging to the concrete, wet and calm, watching. In a flurry of exclamations my mother rushes over, the other women on her heels, multiple hands reaching for me, everyone asking questions at once. My brother remains silent as my mother wraps me in a beach towel and rocks me in her arms. I feel neglected and cared for, frightened yet awake to an entirely new world.

My phone vibrates, jolting me back to the present as I polish off the last lukewarm sip of coffee. Must be my agent, I convince myself, wanting that idea to mold itself into reality.

"Hey babe, pay that stack of bills you've been avoiding." Jorge's demanding tone has a good-humored veneer, probably due to the company of his co-workers.

"I haven't forgotten."

"I didn't say you forgot. I said you've been avoiding 'em."

"I don't need the nudge, Jorge."

He chuckles, then muffles his voice privately into the phone, "But you like it when I push against that cushy ass of yours, baby."

I hear jostling in the background, male rowdiness, firefighters with too much time on their hands. A sharp thunk precedes chair legs scraping and scuffling sounds.

"Gilbert can't keep his hands off me," Jorge grunts before his voice grows distant. "Punch me again and I'll take you out. And get your grubby fingers off my mozzarella." The phone fills with laughter and catcalls, quieting into background din. "Still there, Sirena?"

"Don't you guys have anything better to do on the taxpayers' dime?" His workplace seems more frat house than firehouse. I can't believe he gets paid for homo-erotic wrestling and playing Julia Child.

"Heroes have to eat." I hear his grin. "I have a lasagna to finish. Pay the bills, or we'll be sitting in the dark."

I stare at the phone in my hand long after the line has disconnected. We are already in the dark, he just doesn't want to admit it.

The stack of bills leers at me from the desk, but paying them will drain my account. I like the belief I still have a reserve in the bank, even if it's just an illusion. Jorge and I have an agreement that for now, until I get back into the flow with my work, I cover the general living expenses, the household bills, the groceries and such, and he covers the mortgages. Plural.

Not that long ago we were earning, saving, and mostly debt-free. Then last year Jorge's buddy Matthew, the workaholic real estate agent, convinced us we couldn't pass up this investment 'deal of the century', a duplex in a section of Culver City on the brink of a boom.

"This neighborhood's the next ultra-hip spot," Matthew gushed conspiratorially when we came to view the building a second time. The place was shabby, but Jorge's eyes glimmered with the enthusiasm of a real estate mogul.

Sitting in Lexi, my sporty new Lexus, we discussed our options away from Matthew's big ears and fervent promises.

"This stretches us too thin," I shook my head, fingers twisting the trim on my shirt.

"Don't bring the energy down, Reni. This is our chance to pump it to the next level."

"I like to dream as big as you do. But when you're out of touch with reality it forces me to be the grumpy, practical one. I just bought this car, you're helping support your mom… we don't have the cash."

"Doll, the bank is throwing cash at us," he asserted, tossing his fist against the glove compartment in demonstration. "Since the first time Matt showed us this place I've had three lines of credit offered up to me on a silver platter."

"That's not cash, Jorge," I hedged. "That's debt."

"Billionaires carry towers of debt. They got where they are using other people's money. We have great credit, that's all the banks care about."

"It feels like gambling," I frowned.

"Life's a gamble, baby. You wanna live large, you gotta take a risk."

Jorge is a fireman, not a business man, and I'm an artist with more knowledge of cameras and lenses than real estate deeds, but we plunged in and took the chance. We purchased the building with every scrap of cash and credit we could scrounge together, grasping at visions of full occupancy and passive income. I could have refused, but I do want to live large, even if it gives me a queasy stomach. I'd rather err on the side of too much experience than backing off and having too little.

While the building was in escrow we received more offers, the banks indeed tossing bouquets of credit our way. Already committed up to our eyebrows, we accepted another loan and renovated the property. Matthew — his commission happily squirreled away — offered the name of a contractor to oversee the project. On his days off Jorge welded modern, angular metal and glass shelving units, and I managed the interiors, recruiting my mom's design assistance and overhauling the lighting, my forte. I enjoyed the creative process, and we signed tenants into leases straight away, but I was less than thrilled to now own the most attractive building on a dated, somewhat scruffy street.

Bit by painful bit things turned sour. First our tenants walked out without a word, breaking their lease. We took them to court and won, but still ended up with nothing except legal fees. Then, at my bleakest moment, a big job offer — my very first feature film — leapt from the abyss, finally launching me out of the world of industrials and advertising, only to fall apart a short time later.

My slick-talking agent had skillfully put together a package deal with a popular director, tagging me on as the director of photography. For a female cinematographer with zero feature film credits, the break was nothing short of miraculous, but the movie required a percentage of underwater shots and that's my specialty. It seemed too good to be true and it was. When the tabloids filled their front pages with photos of our director caught in Mexico with an underage (very underage) girl, the studio decided to shelve the project and that was that.

I fell into a funk after the deal evaporated. Truthfully, it was a full-fledged depression. I felt betrayed by a hostile universe that dangled fulfillment of my dream before my nose, teasing me, then cruelly ripped it away. This devastation was something I had sensed within myself before, but hadn't been able to touch the core pain lurking beneath it. Some mornings I stared at the ceiling, sifting backwards through the years, searching for the moment I became damaged, but the answer lingered just beyond the farthest reaches of my memory. I did, however, stumble upon clues.

The third grade is assembling single file for P.E. class. Up and down the line kids are roughhousing while the prim substitute teacher, cardigan buttoned up to her neck, struggles to make order out of chaos. A boy behind me, Bradley, bumps into me hard, on purpose. I don't like body slams or Bradley and his visible ear wax, and turn around, giving him the evil eye. "Stop it," I hiss.

"Sirena," returns a shrill voice. "Please stand next to me until you learn appropriate third grade behavior." Of all the rambunctious, misbehaving children I, the do-gooder, get reprimanded.

Bradley smirks at me and the rest of the line sobers as we leave the classroom. Our regular teacher always accompanies us, but the sub remains behind. I imagine her seated at her desk, head in her hands, crying into a monogrammed handkerchief. The temptation of the empty hallway proves too great; soon the kids at the front of the line are speed-walking and falling out of order. As we round the corner for the final stretch, pandemonium strikes and the class makes an explosive dash down the hall.

The gym door swings open before we reach it. Mr. Jones, our tall, stern, African American athletics teacher, has heard the stampede and is not at all pleased. With one look from Mr. Jones the atmosphere shifts and the entire third grade skids to a halt, falling into a hush.

"Sit in your lines," he commands, standing before us with his perfect posture, and we instantly obey.

Mr. Jones paces in the loudest silence I have ever experienced. I wish he would speak, even yell. Instead he stops and glares at us for an eternity. Finally, with gravity and disgust, he asks, "Do you like yourselves?"

My classmates blink up at him in confusion at the degree of his punishing tone, but my private response is immediate. *No*, I think silently, *I do not like myself*. And I know my answer has nothing to do with Mr. Jones or third grade.

I rinse my coffee cup and make room for it in the packed dishwasher. The stack of bills remains ominous, untouched. I contemplate a workout at the gym, but can't motivate myself to do that either. Instead I curl up in a chair with a cinematography magazine, trying to ignore the invisible pressure steadily deflating me.

The brightness of a ringtone interrupts. Reading my mother's name on the caller ID, I resist answering. I find it difficult to be honest with my family about my emotional state, and equally difficult not to be transparent. When she calls a second time, I give in and pick up the phone.

"Hi Mom." I pull at threads dangling from my worn sweatshirt.

"Oh Reni," she emotes, "you don't sound like yourself. Work stresses?"

"Maybe if I had any work to stress about."

I hear her pause on the other end, knowing she's deciding whether to console me or offer advice.

"What if you try something else in the meantime, just to take the pressure off?

"Such as?…"

"You could do some filing in Dad's office."

Anything but that, I groan to myself. I worked in my father's accounting firm when I was in film school, performing tasks a trained monkey could have managed. What a horrifying step backwards that would be after scrambling long and hard to make it as a cinematographer. My father has never been supportive of my career choice, and I can picture his *I told you so* expression, eyes peering at me over the top of his reading glasses.

"Thanks for offering, but I really want to find something related to my field."

"Then how about shooting an interior I renovated? It's a lovely condominium in the desert."

I bite the inside of my lip. This is probably a hand out; my mother's small interior design business doesn't have a marketing budget. The job will not solve my financial crisis, but the gesture touches me.

"Sure, I'd be happy to shoot some stills for you. Thanks, Mom."

She launches into a mostly one-sided conversation about the furnishings of the remodel while I absent-mindedly straighten up our galley-style kitchen counter and leaf through Jorge's gym bag.

"If you can get a few shots of the exterior, too, that would be super. Could you drive out there soon? The desert air might do you good."

I tell her I will while unconsciously sifting through the bag's pockets. It's not like me to go through Jorge's things, but it has been days since he went to the dojo and the interior is musty. Once I start, I find myself opening them all.

"You'll like the cactus garden," she says cheerily, "the diversity of textures. It will make a dramatic backdrop..."

As I voice my agreement, sickeningly-sweet floral perfume rises from the musk of old sweat and damp clothes.

"Okay," I say, wrinkling my nose. "I can shoot the gardens right before..." My fingers discover a lacy envelope and trace over the handwritten message. "Before sunrise. I mean sunset."

"You always capture wonderful photographs, Reni. I'll leave it up to you."

My heart thumps a ragged rhythm in my chest. "Can we talk a little later, Mom? Something just came up." I am staring at my hand holding the card. It is shaking. I haven't yet focused my eyes and allowed the flowing script to shape itself into words.

"Call me when you can, sweetie."

The moment I set down the phone, the text leaps off the card and the words slice into me like a blade.

You're the sexiest guy in this place.
Let's have tea together sometime.

Anyone could have slipped this into his bag, I assure myself, but the sting of Jorge holding onto something this overtly flirtatious incites me to hunt further. I turn up a second envelope in the same pocket.

I'm fantasizing about our next private lesson. I still need to perfect that half-moon stance, and show you some more tricks of my own....

S pinning with vertigo, nauseous and stirred up, I flee. My parents have a condo in Palm Desert, their occasional vacation getaway and part of their real estate portfolio. I have a key, but don't often use it; most of the time the place sits vacant. I don't really like the condo, but the empty isolation of the desert is the only balm that comes to mind. I'll go mad sitting in the loft waiting for Jorge's return.

I toss a few articles of clothing into an overnight bag, wondering what it might be like to pack up everything I own and simply vanish. Instead I artfully arrange the cards and their envelopes across the uncluttered kitchen counter where Jorge won't miss them. It isn't until I am walking through the doorway that I suddenly stop and backtrack for my camera gear.

Taking refuge in my speeding car, the concrete and congestion of the city gradually dissolves into numbing, endlessly similar outlying suburbs with their sprawling automobile dealerships, cemeteries and malls. The landscape whizzing by, I dial Mom and am relieved to get her voicemail. Using the most neutral voice I can muster, I leave a brief message announcing that I have hit the road, without mentioning what prompted my quick departure. I habitually keep a cautious distance from both of my parents, throwing on a guise of all-is-well, unable to trust them with my deepest feelings without being sure why.

Neither of my parents ever thoroughly embraced Jorge. Dad finds him rough around the edges and they only connect over sports. Mom has more affection for him, but still seems to harbor an unspoken belief he isn't the right fit for me. I'm sure they would rather see me with a buttoned-down, white-collar professional, but they never interfere. Right now I wonder if the reason for that is they don't truly care.

Driving feels powerful, the momentum invigorating. Housing developments give way to straw-colored hilltops dotted here and there with an oddly-shaped church, or triple-decker billboard. The white, vaporous heat of the sky beckons with an empty hand. In my head I am ranting, rage mounting into something dangerous, explosive. I picture his hands on her supple, perfect body and poisonous darts of jealousy and betrayal inject their toxic stream into my nervous system. Lexi's engine screams down the freeway while I howl at the top of my lungs, erupting past rows of wind turbines standing tall against the rugged mountains like an alien army rooted in the sand. My cries morph into sobs, the sobbing into half-crazed laughter.

13

How bizarre my own life looks to me. Where did the polite good-girl, over-achiever disappear to?

Needing a break and refreshment, I pull off the highway onto the palm-lined driveway of a date farm Jorge and I once visited. On the way out a vintage poster on the wall, a line drawing of a smiling couple in love amidst a grove of date palms, captures my attention. *The Romance of the Date* I read in blocky typography splayed across the top, desperately wanting to empty the date milkshake in my hand over the top of Jorge's unfaithful head. I dump the cup, untouched, into the trashcan and return to my car full of ache and longing. For what, I am not exactly sure.

The condo is sterile, its expensive furnishings failing to prevent a mood of hollowness. For an immeasurable length of time I sit on the stiff couch and stare at the wall, expecting its cream-colored paint to crumble and decay like everything else in my life. Instead the space starts closing in on me, my lungs tighten and I struggle for breath, afraid of suffocating. I can no longer live inside the gloom I have been carrying; it's strangling me. A dark foreboding has long been lurking inside a mysterious corner of my psyche, but is no longer neatly tucked away on a back shelf. It's running the show.

I am alone. Starkly, menacingly alone. I thought I could trust Jorge, but he was never truly there for me. He doesn't have my back; no one does. I crave affection and tenderness, but can't manage to give or receive either one. I want understanding, but have nowhere to turn. Why haven't I kept up with my college girl friends? What happened to my gym buddies? The realization of how I have isolated myself increases the constriction. Despite carrying a philosophical stance of independence, focused on a thankless career in a man's field, I have still made Jorge the center of my life, my closest friend, my only true intimate. I shared everything with him, but it has all been a lie.

I roam the condo in a daze, room to room, ending up absent-mindedly leafing through clothes in the guest bedroom closet. My blank stare stalls on a blue wool letter jacket belonging to my father, fingering the dense fabric, occasional whiffs of scented stationery ricocheting mockingly through my brain. Something more vast than Jorge has stampeded across my existence with uncaring hooves. I sense that actually I have somehow done this to myself, but have no idea how to prop open the walls of my mind to keep them from flattening me.

The wool of the letter jacket. My fingers know its felted surface. It's my freshman year of high school, and I am wildly attracted to Kenton, a popular football player undeniably out of my league. One night at a party Kenton sidles up beside me and I assume it's accidental until he invites me outside for a walk. I am flattered, flustered, and scared stiff.

We sit on a rock wall together without finding much to say. He stretches his jaw, glancing at me sideways, then suddenly turns and kisses me. For exactly four weeks, Kenton and I are an item, at least in my mind. We occasionally stand next to each other in the hallway at school and he calls me each Friday afternoon to see if I am going to any of the weekend parties. At some point during the sweaty dancing or clustered conversations over loud music, we lock eyes and duck outside to make out.

On the fourth week Kenton notices me shivering in the autumn wind and drapes his letter jacket across my shoulders. I remain on a lounge chair, buzzing with anticipation, as he returns inside to find something else to wear. The gesture elevates my status and confidence until the wait grows long. Slipping past a window I see Kenton pressing a girl up against a bedroom wall, his mouth moving against hers. I want to crawl in a hole and cover the top with soil, but instead ditch his jacket on the chair and find my friend Trudy.

As we walk home, she asks me, "What's wrong?"

"Just chilly," is all I admit.

I don't recall walking out the door, but somehow find myself rummaging through the condo garage. In a metal cabinet I discover camping equipment and, acting on raw inspiration, toss a sleeping bag into the trunk of my car. I drive into a state park just a few miles away, passing every designated camping area, drawn to the wild, untouched expanse of desert sand, rock and Joshua trees silhouetted against the twilight. By the time I choose an isolated spot to park, the last remnants of daylight have deepened into blackness.

Stepping from the car, I find the air particles humming with life. The monotone landscape seems naked, empty, but the sky is teeming with stars. I tilt my face up at the luminous sparkles as if seeing them for the first time. This city girl never knew there were so many. Beneath infinite starlight I feel transported to a new planet in a friendly galaxy devoid of stimulation.

The longer I lean against Lexi, drinking it all in, the more I sense an unspoken invitation drifting through the dry night air. With only the sleeping bag under my arm, I head into the night, walking into the landscape as if entering a painting. Eventually I find a fairly flat spot, spread out my bedroll, and climb inside it. For hours I lie under the zoetic stars watching them blink, simply breathing, my imprint pressing into the sand. I become enlivened with each moment, with each inhalation of the cooling night. The vastness of the universe stretches above me, brimming with life I sense but cannot see.

I awaken to the distant howl of a coyote. Fear registers in my body, but not enough to motivate my sleep-sluggish muscles to bolt for the car. My eyes flicker closed and, suspended between worlds, rhythmic drumming rises from beneath the desert floor, sounding like the heartbeat of eternity. Life is more than I have been experiencing, more surprising, more mysterious.

I dream I am walking along a lonely, unpaved road. Somewhere up ahead I hear a faint, percussive throbbing. Abruptly the path ends, and as I plow through thick brush the pulsating beat increases in volume. The foliage parts, revealing a group of dark-skinned people, naked from the waist up, singing and dancing in an undulating ceremonial circle. Their intense movements broadcast aliveness. An elder, seated in the central position of honor, has an indigo symbol across his shoulder muscle. I step closer and see it is a bat, or perhaps a manta ray. He turns to me, his severe face looking directly at me, through me, eyes gleaming in the firelight.

D awn is just beginning to creep into the sky when my lids open once more. I watch a shadowy Joshua tree coming into focus, knowing something has shifted in me that I cannot define.

For hours I roam the sand. The sun rays scorch everything in their path, heat penetrating the desert floor. Ducking beneath the shaded overhang of a rocky outcropping, I remove my clothing and sit in the sobering stillness. My thoughts, calmly contemplative, return to Jorge. He has chosen another woman, violating the trust between us. Still, we are knotted together by cords of companionship and dependency. I stretch out, naked to the full exposure of the sun, until beads of perspiration form on my brow and roll down my neck. I want to sob, but the desert sucks all moisture dry.

B y the time I drive back to the condo, last night's panic has dulled. I am pulled together enough to call Mom and arrange our photo session.

"Darling, I didn't realize you'd be ready so soon. I'll make a call to get the property unlocked."

"I decided to jump on it," I explain, filling a glass of water and chugging it in one go. It's a relief when she doesn't question me, the delicate fibers of my current even-stasis threatening to unravel at any moment.

Mom calls back and directs me to a housing complex of identical, meticulously-groomed, Mediterranean-style units. The unlocked door glides open on smooth hinges. Natural light floods the condominium's great room with its expanse of sandstone, marble, and blonde hardwood flooring. Everything from drapery to couches is bone white as if the desert light has bleached it clean. I leave my shoes at the door, wondering how anyone can live in this pristinely immaculate setting; one spill and it's over. Even breathing carefully, I tiptoe through the rooms with my camera and tripod, shooting every possible angle.

Sliding glass doors open to a celadon pool and stylized desert garden. I wait for that magic moment before sunset when golden honey sunlight glazes every surface, and click away at the basket-woven lounge chairs and multi-textural cacti. Watching the sun disappear behind distant jagged mountains leaving only a deepening russet backlight, my stomach grumbles and I realize I haven't eaten all day. I am running on empty in more ways than one.

Back to the condo or the loft? Both options are abysmal, but despite his affair — more of a fling, I console myself — I am not ready to cut Jorge out of my life. Not yet, not without some discussion at least.

I find Jorge sitting on the couch with the cards in his hands, miserable, embarrassed, barely able to meet my eyes. He apologizes, professes his love and brushes off the encounter with *that girl* as insignificant. He says she threw herself at him at every chance, and eventually he caved. I know his words are honest, yet I sense other truths as well, the ones he is not mentioning. *She compliments me, Reni, in ways you no longer do… She's young and fit and takes care of herself… Being with her is light and breezy…*

Somehow we keep going. We don't harp on the floral-scented issue looming between us, but I find myself watching him closely each time his phone rings and scanning his body when he comes home from the dojo. My imagination continually compares me with *that girl* in all the ways that matter — she's more attractive, more fun, more responsive — and I come up lacking every time. I fume if Jorge gets distracted while I'm speaking, but keep it to myself. The more distant he grows, the more I mope, and the more I mope, the more irritated he becomes. We are entangled rather than connected, our exchanges bearing specks of broken glass around the edges.

Aunt Libby and I are eating lunch on a terrace overlooking the eighteenth hole of the golf course. Libby has been a fixture my entire life, yet as I bite into my Cobb salad I realize we hardly know each other. Libby and Mom have long been the example in my mind of what I refuse to become, their identities wrapped up in the success of their husbands. I am a fish out of water at her country club, but she has invited me here to offer me a job.

The little vanity video Libby hires me to shoot of her husband, my mother's revered and accomplished older brother, is not what I consider real work, more snack than meal. Her payment will not cover my expenses, but something is better than nothing.

I take a modicum of enjoyment in following Uncle Carson around his medical office and the hospital for a day, filling in with footage on the golf course, tennis court, the weekly card game with my parents, and dining at his home, both my aunt and uncle beaming for the camera. Even though I can't imagine who will want to watch this piece of self-indulgence, when I deliver the edited video I have a momentary thrill receiving Libby's check.

I spread out a stack of bills before me. Embracing the fresh, new morning, I tell myself I am grateful for them rather than resentful, but it's phony. Turning from the pressure held inside each envelope, I check online job ads for my fall-back: still photography work. Disappointed, spiraling downwards, I stray into office-temp listings and sink into a tailspin.

My cell phone rings, buried somewhere in the distance, its melodic tone full of false cheeriness. Certain it is only Jorge, I ignore it. Rather than paying bills, I'll go grocery shopping; it is counterintuitive relief, but I enjoy buying food and need to get out of the loft. As I head for the door, I hear the landline ring, but let the answering machine pick up.

"Sirena, I have something for you. You're going to like this one."

That stops me mid-motion. It isn't Jorge, but Gregor, my hot-on-it agent, who talks a good number but has been missing in action lately. "Why on earth are you not answering any of your phones? You told me you're sitting around every day waiting for my call."

A little spark of life dances in my heart as I dash to the phone. "What do you have, Gregor?"

"Oh, there you are, Breathless," he sings out. "This is exciting."

We both know how badly I need this, but I keep my voice light. "Care to explain?"

"Well, you love to travel, and you've wanted a longer piece…"

Optimism leaps, but a snarling skepticism tracks it. I find myself nibbling on a cuticle. Why is he buttering me up? "Is this an industrial shoot for the whaling industry?"

"Don't be cynical." He winds up a big breath like a game show host. "You and Miss Piggy are going to Indonesia."

"Indonesia?" I'm not exactly sure where that is. Somewhere in the Pacific? I do know if we're employing The Pig, our nickname for the underwater camera I favor, chances are this is a cheesy shoot for some fancy beachside hotel.

"I thought you'd be hugging me through the phone. You haven't been working, Sirena…"

"I noticed."

"…and the longer you're out, the harder it is for me to sell you."

I am a few years his senior, but somehow feel like the junior partner here. "Okay, okay… tell me what you've got." Holding the receiver between my ear and shoulder, I dig my cell phone from my purse for a quick search online.

"It's a new production company…"

Groan. "Not a documentary on spec again?"

"Film schools are churning out DPs left and right. Rather I pass this off to someone else?"

"Sorry, Gregor. I'll behave."

"It's a new company, but they're well funded. The film is about color in nature, and plenty of the action takes place where you like to hang out... under the waves."

A tingling flutters through my belly. "What are they paying?"

"Now we cut to the chase," he huffs. "They're paying scale."

My enthusiasm starts a slow tumble and my teeth sink into my lower lip. "I was afraid you were going to say that." It's income, hard to argue with that. Scale will cover my bills, even if it won't pay down our debt or pad my account while I find my next job.

"It's work, Sirena."

"I'm looking at Google Maps. Indonesia's thousands of islands. Which one are we talking about?"

"They're sending you to Labuan...bajo," he sounds out the words. "Western Flores. Some of the world's best reefs. Think of it as a paid vacation."

Tell that to Visa and MasterCard. "I'm in." I do a little dance in place.

"One more thing. They want you at the beginning of December."

"Less than a month?"

"You had other plans?"

I ignore him. "I guess I wasn't exactly their first choice."

"They're choosing you now." His exasperation crackles through the earpiece. "They have a couple of Indonesian operators and want you as lead. They loved the underwater footage on your reel."

One phone conversation and my life has returned. My spirit wants to lift, but I hold myself in check, afraid to trust, afraid to succumb to happiness and then lose it.

I download Indonesian gamelan music as I pull on a sports bra and dig through my drawer for exercise gear. If I'm going to hang out with The Pig in Indonesia I need to get in shape and the clock is ticking. Piggy is a hefty girl, and even with the water helping buoy her, she requires brute strength and stability to maneuver. And I haven't been at my strongest lately.

At first the percussive clash of metal instruments seems atonal, structureless, rambling, but the longer I listen, the more I grow enchanted. The sounds are lilting and intriguingly exotic, the trancelike music gently prying open my grip of doubt. As I pull on a tank top, some of the tension across my shoulder blades recedes.

The members of my inner city gym are a mixed stew of working-class ethnicities. I like this place. Swinging the glass doors open, I wonder why have I stayed away so long.

I put the gamelan music on repeat before stretching and using weight machines. It seems natural to listen to Indonesian music here, but its languid pace is not going to motivate me into the necessary aerobic frenzy. Shifting to dance tracks, I will myself onto the treadmill, starting out at a brisk walk and gradually picking up the pace to a full run. At the fifteen-minute mark my heart rate abruptly spikes and, sweating profusely, I find myself struggling to breathe. I must be more out of shape than I thought.

I ease off the treadmill to catch my breath, but my pulse refuses to slow. The room spins. Somehow I slouch onto a bench near the free weights, my heart slamming at a furious pace. Sweat pours from my forehead and trickles down my neck while my stomach clenches with nausea. In my terror I am immobilized, overcome with the sensation of tumbling chaotically through space, blood pounding, my dreams suddenly come to life.

"You alright?" A large, bald African American man grasps my shoulder. As if my atria and ventricles had stalled between gears, this man's empathetic touch eases the cogs into place, and they creak back into motion.

"Just a bit winded," I deflect, not in the habit of opening up. He remains in front of me, warm brown eyes peering directly into mine and beyond, through skin and tissue, right into my organs. I have trouble meeting his gaze, and when I do my eyes well up.

"Need me to call a doctor?"

"Really, I'm okay." I push away the thought of rushing to an emergency room. My medical insurance expired months ago and, anyway, my pulse is relaxing now and I can breathe again.

"Make sure you let out what you need to," he says and slowly returns to the bench press. It seems an odd thing to say, but I am too rattled to question him.

Jorge is thrilled when I tell him about my job, carefully omitting the treadmill incident. He will only insist I see a doctor and going to doctors is something I avoid, insurance or not. Besides, whatever is troubling me has been there a long time and I sense it may only be partially related to bodily mechanics.

With little time remaining to prepare for the shoot, I force myself to return to the gym. After a circuit of weight machines, I busily pump free weights. I am stalling and I know it, afraid of approaching the treadmill.

"Lovely lady, step over here and work some rounds with this dignified gentleman." It's the man who approached me during my… episode, today crooning his words in a jazzy baritone, gesturing to the bench press and taking a theatrical bow.

"You look dignified, but we'll wait and see if you're a gentleman," I smile, moving towards him.

His hand moves to his chest in mock offense, and thus begins my unofficial training with Oscar. During the following weeks he whips me back into shape with less angst and more humor than I could have conjured on my own, and more honesty than I am accustomed to, from strangers or friends.

"You been deprivin' yourself, sweetheart." Oscar's melodious voice sugarcoats the sting of his message.

We're doing flies with free weights, Oscar standing behind me, gently keeping my arms in position, ensuring I do all the work without hurting myself. It's true; I have let myself go.

"I've kinda been in a dark pit lately," I admit, raising the dumbbells overhead.

"Girl, you been backin' off from life," he agrees. "Don't let your elbows drop…" His fingertips press them upward and I wince with the strain. "You got a fine shape, well proportioned. And don't get me wrong, I like me a woman with some meat on her bones, but you be usin' this padding to keep everybody away."

Bull's eye.

With more than a little trepidation and my coach's promise to stand guard while I run, I return to the treadmill. No more heart palpitations. Oscar hoots, cheerleading more than coaching, and I blush, trying to ignore the curious eyes around us.

The gym becomes my daily regimen; fear eases, muscle memory returns, and my spirit elevates. I am thawing. Like an ice floe melting, my dark thoughts begin breaking into smaller fragments, some neutral space left between them.

By nightfall, my body is gratifyingly exhausted and I want to cozy up with a bowl of fresh popcorn and a movie. I put coconut oil in the pan with the corn, afterwards adding sea salt, a sprinkle of nutritional yeast, and a drizzle of truffle oil.

For some people songs are their place holders, symbolic of an era, but I tend to comprehend the world through film. Jorge and I met during my *Like Water for Chocolate* phase when I must have watched that movie twentytwo times. It's not lost on me that the couple goes up in flames at the end.

Jorge opposes television in bed. "Beds are for romance," he insists, but it is late and he is away on duty at the station. Needing to fill the emptiness, I begin an old documentary series I discovered called *Ring of Fire*, and once I start I cannot stop, consuming all five episodes in one sitting. Two brothers from England venture into the lesser-traveled regions of 1970s Indonesia, carrying a camera, some 16mm film and little else. They encounter sea pirates, erupting volcanos, Komodo dragons and various forms of human sacrifice. One island has an annual ritual involving spear fighting on horseback, ending when the first man dies. Stunned by the adventure before me, I write myself a to-do list with entries such as *canister of mace*, then laugh at my worry about becoming some tribe's exotic soup ingredient when I've never carried any weapon through the jungle that is downtown Los Angeles.

An email arrives from Rupert, the director I will be working with in Flores. His compliments on my headshot, sent by my agency with my bio, make my skin crawl. I am struggling to come up with a suitably cool response when I think I hear a knock at the door. We live at the very top of a converted warehouse on The Nickel, as Fifth Street is not too affectionately called, home to street vamps, transvestites, homeless people, Chinese toy merchants and alternative artist types like me. The lobby has a serious lock system and our building manager closes down the freight elevator after dark. No one just wanders upstairs. Ever.

Hearing sounds in the hall but no voices, I creep down from the bedroom, wishing for one of those hotel room peepholes. Ear to the door but afraid to open it, a familiar, wrenching distress splashes through me that someone will invade my home, someone male and menacing. I return to my bed, uneasy.

In the morning I find a note neatly tucked under our doormat from the building manager. A television crew will be shooting on the rooftop and utilizing the freight elevator for the next two days. I chastise myself for my nighttime panic, while resenting that it won't be me behind the lens for a shoot in my own building.

With only a few days left before departure, I get organized. I like the orderly act of packing: carefully selecting layered outfits that suit weather fluctuations; rolling my clothing to avoid wrinkles; fitting everything into the suitcase just right like a three-dimensional puzzle. Between trips to the closet I pause to try on an old bathing suit.

I have further to go, but have lost weight, toned my muscles, and my true shape is quickly returning. I break into a spontaneous, giddy dance on my way to my toiletries cabinet, digging out from the back of the shelf a basketful of health products I have ignored lately; multivitamins, olive leaf capsules, grapefruit seed extract and non-refrigerated probiotics to deal with foreign bacteria. Being thorough, I check and recheck my scuba gear, telling myself I am organized, efficient, professional. Then I catch sight of myself in the bedroom mirror, sunhat in hand, and the look in my own eyes stops me dead in my tracks. Like a dog, I smell fear rising off of myself and react. In my face is something tangible yet unnamable, something hardened, fierce and terrifying. I continue staring, but no answer comes and I brush it off, adding another bikini to my suitcase.

The night of my departure Jorge prepares a farewell dinner. In his chef persona, apron around his waist and a battery of implements at his disposal, he whistles while mincing garlic. His wooden spoon doubles as a percussion instrument as he stirs a saucepan. I sneak my finger into the pot, tasting the sauce, and he shoos me away.

"You have to wait for the final presentation."

"When will you be ready?"

"You can't rush magnificence."

Magnificence is no exaggeration. As a starter Jorge places before me baked crisps of shredded Italian cheeses topped with chopped tomato, Kalamata olives and fresh basil, accompanied by a frisée salad with balsamic-glazed figs and pecans. We eat facing the downtown cityscape, but aside from my copious compliments of Jorge's dishes we are not finding much to say to each other. The evening sniffs of desolation beneath the flavors, of an unspoken finality that frightens me.

Finally, I cannot hold it inside any longer. "I know it's ridiculous, but I have this feeling I'm not coming back from Flores."

Jorge drops his fork in irritation. "What's that supposed to mean?"

"I don't know," I shrug. How can I describe what I don't understand? "But it makes me afraid to go."

Jorge's jaw works hard as he chews. "I have no idea what to say when you come up with shit like that, Sirena. Can't you find a way to appreciate that you got a job doing what you want to do? Doesn't anything ever satisfy you?"

I regret speaking up and wish I knew how to be as easy going as he wants me to be. I sip my water, feeling more remote from him than ever, a fish in my own aquarium, a pane of glass separating us. "Sorry. I'm just trying to share something with you."

We eat in silence and I know he has reached his limit with me. I am not leaving a day too soon. As Jorge moves to the kitchen for our next course, I hear the disgust in his footsteps. Out of nowhere it occurs to me that in my absence he will have oodles of time for outside activities and a sludge of jealousy mixes distastefully with the meal. How have I managed to hide the obvious from myself?

He returns wearing oven mitts, and sets a piping-hot lasagna on the table before removing them from his hands with a flourish. "My monumental work of art."

"Smells better than art," I tell him, picking up a knife.

"Not yet." He places his hand on top of mine. "It needs to settle." He leaves his fingers there for an extended moment, surprising me. We look at each other, eyes expressing the words we cannot seem to find. I kiss him tentatively and he kisses me back. It feels real enough.

Silently, we climb the stairs to our bedroom. Words have not been serving us. In the generosity of bodies and desire we offer each other what we have left to give.

"I guess the lasagna has settled," I say afterwards and we laugh.

Back at the dining table, I lean over Jorge's masterpiece and take a strong whiff before making the initial cut, inhaling a heady aroma of wine and something earthy reminding me of soil scraped from the forest floor. The lasagna holds together in perfect squares as the knife cuts into it. Beneath a rich topping of Pecorino Romano is a lacy-edged weave of thick noodles layered with spinach and a plethora of wild mushrooms. Jorge brings out a side dish of young French green beans lightly sautéed in olive oil and garlic.

I close my eyes, taking in a bite, savoring every flavor. "Beyond art, Jorge." He is pleased.

Having polished off my lasagna, I set down the fork. "Now I don't have to worry about dysentery in Indonesia. I won't need to eat again for a month."

"You need to eat more. Right now."

"Jorge, I can't." I slump back in my seat, removing the napkin from my lap. "I think I just put on every pound I've lost recently."

"I have one more course, lighter than the last one."

"Anything is lighter than lasagna," I groan, hand on my belly. He gives me a look that says my comment has registered as a complaint. "It's all been unbelievably delicious," I cover.

"Just try this." He brings out two halved, frozen lemons filled with citrusy sorbet and a little sprig of mint on top. "I know you love chocolate, but I didn't want you buzzing all the way across the ocean, baby."

Our approaching separation hangs in the air unacknowledged. Discouraging Jorge from parking and joining me inside the airport, I dodge a prolonged goodbye and hop out curbside. While I gather my carry-ons, Jorge lifts my luggage from the trunk.

"Farewell, my love." I mean to sound cute, but it comes out clunky and final. Instead of reacting with anger, Jorge frowns sadly and looks at his shoes.

"You're still mad at me, aren't you?"

I study his face, trying to find the right response. This is the first mention of his infidelity since that day I returned to find him on the couch.

"Not angry really, more hurt about how distant we've become."

One burst of truth-telling does not bridge the gap. "Are you going to drive Lexi while I'm gone?" The sudden image of him using my car with *her* is revolting.

"Do you want me to take her out for a spin?" he asks, as if he's doing me a favor.

"No, I'd rather you didn't." The firm tone, far from my norm, hushes us into silence. We stand at the curb in our own private malaise while hundreds of late-night travelers swarm around us, dragging suitcases and pushing luggage carts. He makes no further move towards me and, not wanting to draw it out, I kiss him and walk away, willing myself not to turn around. As I enter the building, I sense a large vacuum suctioning Jorge backwards, away from me, belly-up, far into the distance.

Midnight in an international airport is a lonely time to be hanging out with strangers. Around me everyone is sleepy, eager to board, already weary of their proximity to unknown fellow-travelers. I am tired just thinking about being in the air for nearly a day, flying through Taipei to Jakarta to meet the crew.

The economic hierarchy is starkly apparent as first and business class passengers settle into their relatively luxurious berths with reclining seats. *Oh well*, I tell myself, squeezing into the aisle seat beside a middle-aged Chinese couple. Someday Gregor will negotiate business class seats for me.

I fall asleep right away, only to be awakened with the rest of the plane an hour later for meal service. How can I eat plane food after Jorge's feast and who is hungry at this hour anyway? I try returning to sleep, but the cabin lights are on and my cramped legs shift repeatedly. Apprehensions flicker through my mind: uneasiness about my first gig with a foreign crew; uncertainty that this job will lead to more work; worry that my career isn't leaping forward. There's the director's vaguely slimy email and Jorge's failure to promise he'll be faithful while I'm away. The trail of doubts leads me nowhere I want to go, but I don't know how to find a more optimistic stream of thought. I have sprung a leak in my confidence container and my sense of succeeding in the world is draining out all over the grimy aisle floor.

The Taipei airport is an architectural wonder of glass and steel. We have crossed the international date line and, as if traveling by space ship rather than airplane, have catapulted two mornings ahead. I drag my wheeled carry-on bag and my sluggish, sleep-deprived body down the mostly vacant terminal hallways, finding an open coffee shop. After a few sips of my cappuccino I notice a tightening in my back and a dull pain below my left shoulder blade. I must have slept awkwardly on the plane.

If Taipei was Asia modern, Jakarta is Asia in transition. The terminal is crowded, men smoking cigarettes line the dingy hallways, and the warm air is thick with humidity. A wall mounted television blares the call to prayer as a feral cat furtively roams the lounge floor. Only two immigration counters are open, servicing mile-long queues that appear to stand still. Unconcerned immigration officials contently chat in groups while those of us in line wither. Eventually I make it past an unsmiling official with a stamp on my passport, fatigued, unsettled, sticky with perspiration.

Outside the terminal I learn the muggy airport was actually air conditioned. I have stepped into an oven. A crowd of taxi drivers aggressively approach, but I have the name of a driving service prearranged to meet me. When I fail to find anyone holding a sign with my name, I wait impatiently on a nearby bench, swatting perspiration from above my lip. Just when I'm considering hiring one of the persistent cabbies, my driver finally arrives, apologizing for his tardiness in broken English.

Following a long ride through gray, seemingly endless stop-and-go traffic, I arrive at my hotel. The bland lobby smells strongly of smoke, as does the hallway to my nonsmoking room. As soon as I am resting, wrinkled and bleary on my bed, the phone rings. An energetic Australian voice inquires after my flight, expressing his happiness at having 'a sheila amongst the blokes'. The director, Rupert, suggests a swank bar for the crew meet-up in an upbeat manner that instantly irritates me, but maybe I'm just exhausted.

Unable to sleep, I attempt unsuccessfully to shower off the jet lag, then venture out on foot to explore. I am an oddity on the street, a dazed, light-skinned, sleep-deprived foreigner stumbling over broken footpaths, and receive numerous blank stares. Spotting a vendor pushing a cart of tropical fruits, I point at what I want to sample. He peels and chops with brisk efficiency, ladling a mysterious condiment into a small plastic bag. My mouth burns from the spicy-sweet dipping sauce, a delicious counterpoint to the crunchy fruit. My taste buds are dancing, while my insides are jumbled and disoriented.

The afternoon heat and smog rise like crematorium smoke and I duck into a bookstore. Walking through the doorway, air conditioned coolness hits my face like the plunge into a pool. Hip Asian lounge music fills the sleekly-modern store interior and I want to lie down on the cool smoothness of the polished concrete floor, but restrain myself and scan through art books. The work of an Indonesian artist captures my attention, particularly one intricate, anatomically correct painting of a human heart, arteries flowing into jungle rivers, waterfalls and mermaid ponds.

Moving to the periodical shelf, I am flipping distractedly through a European fashion magazine when my eyes fix on the image of a male model walking a runway in a dark suit, dreadlocks woven into a crown atop his head, eyes shining brightly, and a chill shudders through me. I have the distinct sensation he is looking right at me, but glancing at a clock on the wall, am startled to realize I'll soon be late for the crew meeting and abandon the periodical. Long flights and time zone changes have altered my perception of time.

Back in the hot grit of the street, a smoky haze hangs in the air as I hail a taxi. The driver nods his head, affirming he knows the location, and the car inches through snarled traffic. Without awareness that I have drifted off, I awaken to the cabbie politely nudging my shoulder. For a moment I cannot remember where I am and fumble with the new currency. The man's eyes widen at the tip I press into his palm, and I belatedly wonder how much I have given as I climb out, turning at the last moment to grab my bag.

The restaurant could be in New York or LA; exposed brick, sandblasted glass, stainless steel, a backlit bar. It's easy to spot Rupert holding court, his loud Australian accent projecting over a table of men who obviously started drinking long before my arrival. He hoots at me from across the room and my first inclination is to turn on my heels and head for the door. Reaching the table, I admit to myself that Rupert is more charismatic than I imagined, tanned, well-muscled, and sure of himself. From our correspondence I was expecting someone more run-of-the-mill, chain-smoking, with a beer gut.

"Welcome to the crew, Sirena," Rupert booms, his friendliness reeking of pomposity. "Mates, this little honey is our mermaid with a camera."

Thus begins the least professional introduction of my career. I have dealt with predominantly male crews for years, blatant comments and unspoken slights are de rigueur, and still this scene screams of a bygone era. Bone-tired and flustered, I give up on a quick retort and instead look at them all in exasperated disbelief.

Unaffected, Rupert pulls out a chair for me beside his and throws an arm around my shoulder.

"Bring this young lady some amber liquid," he orders the waitress.

I don't drink beer, but it doesn't seem in my best interest to refuse. He introduces the crew, a ragtag collection of Indonesians who, under the influence of alcohol and Rupert, exhibit cocky smiles and lingering glances. Since we will be working together I do my best to remain good-natured.

"So, how does a chick your size manage that behemoth of a camera?" Rupert drawls.

"I work out, so... I can handle it," I say, cringing at the double entendre.

"I bet you can," he retorts, raising his eyebrows.

The moment is thankfully broken by the arrival of steamed dumplings, stacks of samosas surrounding mango chutney, stir-fried rice noodles topped with paper-thin strips of fresh vegetables, and cubes of tandoori fish beside garlic nan. The platters seem to tame the wild beasts. The assistant director, Joko, seated across from me, talks about his large family in central Java and tells an endearing story about mixing up his identical twin sons when they were young. I find myself genuinely smiling for the first time all night.

Excusing myself from the table, I push back my chair.

"You're not shootin' through?" Rupert asks, his eyes following me.

"Just on a brief adventure," I try to play along, a smile stitched onto my face.

Escaping to the washroom, I sink into the small stall, head spinning. I have only consumed a few sips of beer, but my jaw is tight, my breathing shallow. Desperate to calm myself, I take a deep breath, but something indescribable is whirling within me as if the Indonesian 220 volt electricity is passing through my American body wired for 110. Worried I might pass out, I drop my head between my legs. Will someone find me, unconscious, sprawled on the commode with my drawers at my ankles? Eventually the intensity subsides and I can stand. I take my time at the sink splashing water on my face, preparing to return to the table.

As I open the washroom door I walk straight into a wall of muscle. Looking up, I lock eyes with Rupert, but instead of stepping back to make way, he forces his body against mine, crashing me backwards against the bathroom sink while he kicks the door shut. The scent of booze and aftershave rushes my senses, one of his arms closes in around my waist as the other reaches behind him to lock the door. I am too shocked to do anything but attempt squirming away. My voice has vanished; I cannot access it. His thighs lodge me against the wash basin and his chest crushes the breath from my lungs.

"Don't," I manage to gasp, as his foot knocks my legs apart. A beefy hand digs under my top, but when I push it away, he grasps my wrist, overpowering me.

His sour mouth whispers, "Relax mermaid, let's have some fun."

Then everything goes spotty, silent, blank.

The next thing I know Rupert is holding me up, his hands under my armpits, and now he looks scared. I think I only fainted for a

33

moment; I still have all my clothes on and so does he. As I find my balance, he backs away and turns to open the door. Without even looking at me he says, "This didn't happen," and walks out. His words ricochet through the tiled room, through my braincells, the whole incident too surreal to be reality.

I am still leaning against the sink, stunned, when the door opens again. A startled woman sees me jump and apologizes, quickly shutting it. I imagine walking up to the crew, punching Rupert squarely in the jaw, and cruising out the exit. Instead, I return to the table, carefully avoiding eye contact, and make an excuse about jet lag before scurrying out and hailing a taxi.

My head throbs, feeling like it's spinning in circles as I sit in the cab unable to remember the name of my hotel. Digging through my purse pockets, I find my room key fortunately printed with the logo. The panic that has been bobbing and submerging is now awash in my veins. I have nothing to diffuse it with, nothing to clutch at, nothing to hide in. I am halfway around the world, appalled and terrified, humiliated and disgusted, unable to do more at the moment than sit trembling. Something is profoundly wrong with me, probably always has been, is the thought that slugs me in the gut and sobs erupt from me, heaving, gasping wails beyond my usual decorum. I see the driver's worried eyes shooting glances at me in the rear view mirror, but I cannot restrain it.

Somehow I get to my hotel room and double bolt the door. I consider calling Jorge, but phoning has become a gargantuan task and anyway, how could I explain what took place without getting into murky territory? I imagine Jorge's voice insinuating that in my determination to be one of the guys I may have given Rupert the wrong idea, and my hands and feet tingle uncomfortably, my breathing labored. Propped against the pillows on the bed, too drained, too astounded to resist any longer, I let go into the harrowing, shadowy mystery. I can't keep fighting this, whatever it is.

Within a millisecond of surrender something cracks, little fissures spreading in all directions. The straightjacket eases and I witness the delicate birth of a new awareness. Even in the midst of this chaos, I am okay. I care about myself. I still do not understand what is happening to me or why — and I fear it deeply — but a resolve to face it emerges. Beyond the panic and woven through the anxiety is some kind of crazy beauty. The air particles vibrate, gradually fading into blankness as I drift to sleep.

A dark void fills my dream. Abruptly a window I hadn't noticed flies open and a powerful force draws me into the night sky, high above the Los Angeles cityscape and beyond the gravitational pull of the earth. Floating through the inky-black weightlessness, a school of angel fish cross before me in a flurry of group activity, then dart away. Two massive manta rays swim directly at me, their fins undulating like wings, and it seems we will collide. I tense, but they part as they approach, gliding smoothly around me. The enormous dark eye of one manta looks inquiringly into mine before vanishing into the depths.

I awaken before the sun, silent and blank. Soon memories of the previous night flood back and acidic anxiety washes through me again. I consider fleeing and blowing the whistle, but if I return to LA and report Rupert to the production company, I'll only damage my own reputation as an unreliable hire. In the film world *the show must go* on isn't merely an expression, it's sacrosanct. I will have traveled halfway around the world for a bizarre attempted assault only to return home without a pay check. I am not confident that Jorge, Gregor, or anyone else will understand.

The ping of my phone announces an email from Mom asking if I have arrived safely. She writes that she is proud of me doing what I most love. My eyes well with tears; how I wish that were the case. Beyond that, I wish I could tell her the truth.

I decide to march on, refusing to return home defeated and

empty-handed. I have always been capable of toughening up and tending to business, muscling through life like training at the gym. I can work with these guys, if I keep my wits about me. Slipping into a practiced professionalism, I check my equipment, repack my bags with the few items I have used, check out of the hotel and climb into a waiting taxi.

The crew gathers at the gate before the flight to Labuanbajo, Flores. One or two at a time wander off for coffee, cigarettes, or newspapers, and Joko plays the sheepdog, herding the pack. As expected, Rupert behaves as if nothing unusual has passed between us and so do I. He is all business this morning, the creases of his pants neatly pressed and a notebook in his hands, mentioning to me within earshot of the others that he'd like to go over the locations and shot list on the plane. I simply nod.

I have scored a seat on our small flight several rows away from the other crew members. When I spot Rupert making his way down the aisle, I close my eyes and tilt my head back. His penetrating gaze attempts to rouse me, but I don't budge and the welcome sound of his retreating footsteps follows. Soon enough we are landing.

The crew filters through the tiny, sweltering airport, and loads into waiting bemos, ancient looking vans, part taxi, part tin can, painted in bright colors. Like boats, each vehicle has a name stenciled broadly on the side, and fetishes or trinkets hanging from the rearview mirror. I opt to travel alone on an open bench in the equipment bemo, busying myself making notes on my laptop.

The driver starts the engine, and just as he shifts into gear, Joko hops on board through the open, sliding side-door. He nearly gets tossed out as our vehicle bumps and bounces down the pockmarked road until he shoves a few bags aside to make seating room. I sense Joko's eyes watching me, but avoid him, focusing on my computer.

Finally he breaks the silence. "What are your thoughts on the schedule?"

I look up, feigning surprise, and shrug. "Seems ambitious to me, for the number of days allotted."

"Always that way, isn't it?" He laughs, his natural geniality encouraging me to lift my eyes from the screen. "Squeezing a month into two weeks. Everyone complaining when we go over schedule and over budget." We exchange knowing smiles, then fall back into silence. Out the window are small villages of timber houses on stilts, bright blue, red or mint green paint peeling off the sides. The driver swerves around children and dogs playing on the muddy road.

"Everything good with you, Sirena? I'm worried you aren't… comfortable."

I swallow through the initial flush of being discovered, and try to smile. "Just jet lagged, Joko. But thanks for asking."

"It must be tiring for you, working with so many men."

"I'm used to it." I laugh, but it rings hollow.

Our humble hotel sits high on a hill. A large concrete slab with wooden picnic tables and a plexiglass roof offers a stunning view of the gleaming ocean. Two older women run the kitchen, observing us with mild curiosity as we sit at the tables waiting to check-in, the crew ordering beers and smoking cigarettes. I luck out and am first to receive my key.

The room is musty, but clean. Bouncing on the faded polyester bedcover I find the pillows and mattress are as mushy as my thoughts. I yank the bedspread off and direct the rusted pedestal fan towards my sticky-as-molasses skin, but it only blows around the hot air.

A knock at the door disturbs my rest. Fear surges through my bloodstream, tasting bitter on my tongue. Whomever is there needs to go away. The knock comes again, more emphatically.

"Who is it?" I call, voice cloudy.

"Sirena, open up." I recognize Rupert's muffled voice.

"I'll be out in a bit." I aim to sound casual, but firm. There is no way I am opening that door for him.

"Just give me a few minutes," he insists. When I don't respond, he lets out with, "Open the bloody door," mouth pressed near the frame.

The longer he stands there, my fear converts to anger. I want to open the door alright, so I can clobber him. "As I said, I'll be out when I'm ready."

Sensing his retreat, I peek through the drapes at my front window. In the distance, Joko is watching Rupert leaving my door. The two confer there on the walkway, Rupert's sweaty back to my window, his cotton shirt sticking to his skin.

When I have showered and dressed in fresh clothing, I check through the drapes. The doorway is clear. Emerging from my room, I squint into the blazing-hot sun, finding Rupert and Joko still in the same spot, chirping about logistics.

"You wanted something from me, Rupert?" I don't sugarcoat my words and notice Joko taking in my tone.

"Perfect timing, Sirena." Rupert is slick. "Joko and I would like to meet with you and the two other cameramen." He grins. "Or should I say camera people?"

I ignore him and scan the seascape, a much more pleasant view. Miles of aqua coastline stretch to the horizon without even a fishing boat in sight, sunlight bouncing off the placid surface. The two Indonesian camera operators wave us over to join them at a table with sodas and snacks of freshly fried peanuts and *krupuk*, rippled crackers. I begin relaxing once we are discussing shot lists, lenses and lights for a cave shoot. Concrete technicalities are grounding for me. Organized for our big first day of shooting, I slip back to my room.

The relief of isolation is short lived. Why haven't I made any move to contact Jorge since I left LA? I don't want to admit what happened with Rupert, but I can leave that part out. Looming behind that question is a larger, lonelier one: Why hasn't Jorge contacted me? What — or who — is keeping him busy? The silence between us is stark and ominous, full of murky places I would rather avoid. I want to eat potato chips or chocolate. Or both.

I rifle through my carry-on for the 79% chocolate bar I stashed away in case of a chocolate emergency. Starting out biting slowly, I savor the rich, musky, bittersweet flavor, letting the bites melt on my tongue, but my neediness is too great. I take bite after bite, chewing and consuming every last bit of the entire bar, wishing I had another. When the momentary chocolate rescue is over I am left with an empty wrapper and a dark pit in my gut. A knock at my door puts me instantly on alert again, but Joko's kind voice, inviting me to dinner with the guys, is a solace.

A pair of bemos deliver us down the steeply curving slope and cruise past a single row of seaside restaurants, the full extent of the commercial district. After a dinner of *nasi campur*, a combination plate of Indonesian rice, vegetables, fritters and fried fish which I hardly touch, I leave the crew to their beers and wander the seaside shops just as the ocean swallows the setting sun, converting it to liquid fire.

The relief of being on my own soon collides with the anxiety of my separateness, heightened by the open stares following me with each step. I am a stranger in this new land and a foreigner in my own skin. Immersed in a thick malaise, I wander the full stretch of the road and back again, inhaling the scent in the air of sea salt, sewers, and frying oil.

Seeking distraction, I peruse sarongs and rubber flip flops in a tiny shop, carefully observed by three generations of females watching me with undisguised interest beneath the light of a naked fluorescent tube. The grandmother and mother wear headscarves, but the bright-faced little girl's head is bare. She shyly flashes luminous smiles at me whenever our eyes meet and I buy a pair of flip flops out of appreciation for her warmth.

Turning to leave, the sight of Rupert lurking at the open storefront stops me in my tracks. He is draped in darkness, ordering something from a street vendor, but I can still detect his eyes burning with intensity when he glances my way. Is he stalking me? He bites into the food in his hand as he steps towards me. I stumble back.

Just then the bemos pull up to the curb, stopping Rupert in mid-motion. Joko agilely hops out and ushers Rupert into a vehicle. As the first van departs, Joko opens the door of the second one. Did he separate us purposefully? I barely have a chance to ponder this before our bemo stalls at the foot of the incline. The driver is unable to get it restarted, and we decide to hoof it up the hill to our hotel. The exertion leaves me struggling for breath, heart thumping in my chest. Something is wrong, but I can't tell if my body or my mind is the culprit.

Back in my room I notice my cell phone on the bedside table and stare blankly at the missed call from Jorge. I contemplate calling him, but instead ease back onto the doughy pillows stacked against the headboard.

I awaken with the soft light of dawn filtering through the thin, floral window dressing, fully clothed, and only minutes for showering and breakfast before the first day of work. The crew is joking in an early morning, grumbly sort of way, but none of it strikes me as funny. I am nervous. The veins in my arms feel electrically charged, setting me on edge as I lift my gear into the bemo.

Four outrigger boats await us at launch point. The local drivers look like fishermen, wiry, lean, and salt stained, loading our tanks and cameras on board with quiet competency. Now the camera crew is on task and all about business; it's showtime. I gather and check my equipment, synchronizing my underwater computer watch with Joko's. As I remove my shorts and top, revealing my swimsuit underneath, I see Rupert's eyes dart in my direction. Turning my back to him, I pull on my rubbery wetsuit, tight as a second skin, and load my personal equipment onto a boat.

The water is choppy, but the expanse of sky is clear. I pull in a deep inhalation of sea spray and some tension lifts from my shoulders.

After all, this is a wonderful project for me. Our focus is on lyrical visual imagery, capturing the color and dance of nature underwater. Since we are all hired guns, the political pressure is not as great as it would be if we were shooting some producer's pet project, but the technical pressure is still enormous. We have only so many minutes we can stay below the surface, find the marine life we seek, and meld with the environment so as not to frighten off our subjects before the camera starts rolling.

The boatmen kill their motors above a reef they appear to know well. I put on my trusty BC vest, tank, fins, snorkel and mask, routine for me, yet my fingers are trembling. Rupert shouts the order for all in and I enter the ocean backwards off the side of the boat, flipping in a somersault until I naturally bob to the surface. One of the crew helps ease Miss Piggy into my waiting arms.

With the push of one button I drop into a dark, dreamy, mysterious world, cool even through my wetsuit. I usually like to hear the meditative whoosh of my breath through the regulator, but today it sounds raspy. Right away we encounter five sea turtles, beaks nipping at the soft sponges on the colorful reef that sways a gentle hula. With single-pointed concentration I capture the intricately-patterned, mosaic-like, spotted-leather of their flippers and their graceful movements as they swim away.

During our second dive, we happen upon nudibranchs, frilly sea slugs in jaw-dropping colors, their shocking-red, fluorescent-orange, and day-glow blue tentacles waving in the current. Few people actually get to observe these little guys in their natural habitat and our footage will share with others the thrill now delighting my eyes.

The packed, first-day schedule includes a shallow sunset dive, gearing up at dusk, diving only a meter down before we spot an abundance of tiny, neon mandarins, their squiggly stripes looking like the artwork of a psychotropic, plant-consuming tribe. We follow a female mandarin, using a red, gel-covered light so as not to disturb, until a large male swims along, initiating his courtship ritual. I keep the couple's vivid blue maze of markings in my viewfinder while they chase and play. Finally the female rests on the male's pelvic fin, the pair bobbing together above the coral, cheek to cheek, directly in front of me. A cloud of fertilized eggs explodes in the water before they dart back into the darkness. Caught it. This is diving at its spectacular best.

That night as we watch the dailies, the crew's enthusiasm and confidence in the footage puts a genuine smile on my face, but the day's work is not complete. One of the assistants helps me clean salt and sand off The Pig to ready her for another round tomorrow.

After breakfast — and another night of ignoring Jorge's call — we head out again on the boats. Routine has not yet settled in and jittery prickles run down my arms. Did I drink too much of the hotel's muddy coffee? The crew slides Miss Piggy into the water and we patiently search out an encounter with mola mola, the massive but elusive sunfish, occasional visitors of our location.

Without warning, I am moving swiftly. The most powerful, unpredictable current I have ever encountered sucks me away from the boats with a force beyond my control. I know to remain calm, but as the seafloor rushes below me, fear leaks into my wetsuit, into my pores. My jaw tightens and aches, my fingers and toes tingle. The invisible current is sweeping me away, and as I struggle to hold onto my equipment, I realize I am struggling even harder to breathe. Feeling faint, I hear myself say, "Oh my," as my fingers let go of the camera.

A massive, undulating creature rapidly approaches, wide as two cars, flapping its graceful wings directly towards my limp, floating body. My camera sinks away from me into the watery depths as the manta ray slowly circles beneath me, its flattened body supporting me from below. In the background I hear the faintest beating of a drum. I am keenly present yet removed, viewing every detail from somewhere outside, above, beyond. It is as if I am floating in a vast, limitless ocean containing within it what I used to understand as ocean. I can clearly see Joko and three others swimming towards my body, can read their alarm, yet I am completely tranquil, a witness without a desired outcome. Two divers capture my camera while Joko and another lift me in stages to the ocean's surface. I witness as if watching an underwater film in a movie theatre, only everything is vibrantly aglow and expansive.

Simultaneously, I am observing Jorge in his own watery environs, showering in our LA loft. He is not alone; a young, lithe, long-legged blonde is soaping up the dark hair on his chest. I watch free of animosity, with love, while simultaneously witnessing the boat crew hauling my body on board an outrigger, and removing my diving equipment with terse, efficient motion.

Beyond us, something else is capturing my attention. I see myself in a bathtub, only it is not me as I am now; I am a small child, and I am not alone. A man holds me on his lap while rocking his naked body against mine, parting my legs with his large hands.

Amorphous, angelic presences, so massive they dwarf me, seek my attention and beckon me toward a gateway. Somehow I always knew this moment would arrive. I hold myself back, uncertain, until a conscious choice to surrender arises within me. Instantly I am gliding through the opening, floating effortlessly in a vast, dark tunnel, joining others floating there with me in immeasurable peace. I sense rather than see them, wordlessly absorbing their complete support. We are distinct yet interconnected, formless yet richly present. What I have thought of as me is no longer, yet I am more aware than ever. Velocity increases, gliding farther and farther away, at the same time traveling into boundless depth, into particles, into the molecular structure of life, into the sparkling, invisible essence inside the inside of atoms, until there is only a brilliant, golden glow of love and beauty. Only exquisite, sustained tones reverberating outwards. Only the loveliest chorus singing my name without words.

"I'm not getting a pulse. I think her heart has stopped."

"She's turned blue. Breathe, Sirena. Breathe."

Like a thunderbolt, I pop back into my body. What a shock. It's as if I have been in a vivid dream and suddenly an alarm clock is shaking me awake, snapping me back into routine consciousness, the dream fading, receding, vanishing. The faces of the crew encircle me in grave concern, yet I recognize only love in each expression.

"Holy Mother of God, she's back." Rupert's voice is drenched with fear and relief.

I do not share his dread, nor his consolation. Freshly returned to my body, my focus remains on the infinite brilliance within me. Silvery particles of life still vibrate at the edge of the seemingly solid world surrounding me.

The boatmen are speaking back and forth in rapid-fire Indonesian. Motors roar to life and we speed to shore, bouncing across choppy waters.

"Her color is returning."

"You breathed life into her, Joko."

I listen to their conversation without desire to interact, my nostrils filled with a tantalizing fragrance I can't quite place. Two men carry me off the boat to a waiting car. Still in my wetsuit, I sit up and begin to unzip, but they dissuade me, insisting I remain supine.

"Are you in pain?" Joko inquires.

"Not at all." I grin widely and he looks at me as if I have sprouted a second head.

Joko slips hurriedly into the front passenger seat and we race off, rumbling over potholes, kicking up a cloud of dust. From my position lying across the back seat, I drink in the eggshell-blue expanse of sky, elongated, marshmallow-puff cloud formations, and feathery-green tops of palm trees fluttering in the breeze. More relaxed than I have been in ages, perhaps ever, the colors look more vibrant, their mere existence awe inspiring.

"We're airlifting you to Jakarta." Joko adjusts to speak to me over the front seat. "I'm sorry I cannot accompany you. If we both leave, this shoot will be over. I'm arranging your way there."

"I'm fine. I don't need to leave."

"You almost died, Sirena. I think you had a heart attack. You need proper medical attention."

"I think I did die." Suddenly I am laughing and it is an entirely new kind of laughter, a rich belly laugh lifting out of fathomless parts of me, tickling unobstructed through my entire body and my whole being.

Joko watches me, unsmiling, his forehead creased. "Do you remember where you went?"

He asks with such earnestness, with such genuine need to know, that it ripples through me. Tears stream lightly down my face, and we hang in a wordless space together. His eyes fill, too.

He blinks and looks away. "My wife died two years ago."

It would have seemed farfetched to me just yesterday, but I feel her presence wrap around the car like a soft, silk shawl.

"I left my body, Joko, until I didn't exist any longer. And I felt more alive than ever."

"Thank you," is all he says, eyes shining, and turns to face the road.

Our car pulls directly onto the airport tarmac, and instantly waiting medics load me onto a gurney. I smile at everyone whose eyes meet mine, an ambassador of goodwill from a distant land, not halfway around the globe, but halfway across eternity. Joko assures me the hotel staff packed all my things, my suitcase is going into the cargo hold, and my carry-on luggage is following me on board.

"I'm sorry I can't escort you," Joko apologizes again, and I start to wish he was. Our eyes lock and I can feel him offering a silent prayer for my journey as his image shrinks, the gurney wheeling me backwards, away from him, to a waiting plane.

My attendants carry the stretcher with me on it up the stairs. Curious eyes follow me to the row of seats and I transfer love to each person who meets my gaze. Well, I got a first-class reclining seat after all, I smile, stretching out with a full row to myself. The words *heart attack* reverberate through my mind. Isn't that something that happens to pot-bellied old men who smoke cigars and drink whiskey? I am in such a high degree of acceptance that I almost giggle.

In the Jakarta hospital a woman identifies herself in English as my cardiologist, Dr. Wulandari, and explains she will be conducting a coronary angiogram, inserting dye into the main artery in my leg to capture a picture of the interior of my heart. The procedure will require me to remain completely still for the next twelve hours.

A male attendant hooks me up to a heart monitor while another takes a blood sample from my arm and a third man removes my bathing suit. He gives my pubic hair a lopsided bikini shave, and injects me with a sizable needle. I am already sedate, I think to myself, but am grateful for the anesthesia when he inserts a long, thin tube into the right side of my groin. A warm sensation flushes upward from inside my leg.

After a time Dr. Wulandari returns to my side with a roadmap image of my heart, the rivers of arteries and veins as pristine as a newborn baby's, she informs me, except for the one tiny artery with a blockage resulting in a heart attack. Somehow I have always known I was holding something in a dark corner of my heart. As the artery is too small to surgically insert a stent, she is prescribing heart medication I will need to take for the remainder of my life. *We'll see about that*, I think to myself, but I am not disconcerted; this is simply another thing that is happening.

In the Intensive Care Unit a nurse named Angelina — how perfect — lets me know she will attend to all my intimate needs, as I must remain stationary. I am not allowed visitors in Intensive Care and I assure her I do not know a single soul in all of Java. Two female orderlies wearing surgical scrubs and head scarves, their faces innocent as school girls, give me a sponge bath with great tenderness. They do not speak a word of English, yet their empathy is clear. I am in good hands.

Once I find myself alone for the first time since my life turned on a dime, a wave of fatigue overcomes me. Without a single window in my room, I have no idea what time of day it is, but am eager to return to the tunnel of light and the song of eternity. Closing my eyes, I am there again, sustained musical notes reaching into the beyond.

I am floating in immeasurable bliss when something jarringly interrupts my serenity. Thick fingers trail down my belly and lower, until I am squirming in alarm. The someone is a man and he is familiar to me. I cannot see his face, but sense his anxiety, his hunger, as his fingers prod. I am just a little girl and every sensation has tremendous impact, imprinting my cells. He forces something big and rigid into my mouth, and as his need intensifies I start to choke, but he pushes in farther. Pain scorches my throat and I cannot breathe. I am aware of his yearning and his guilt, his longing to tap into something pure in me and his absolute disregard of my feelings. I want to scream for help, but my breath ceases and my terror becomes panic as I pop out of my body. I know I have chosen this life, it has only barely begun, and yet here I am, floating in formless space. With my whole being I choose to return to life and instantly I am shivering in a towel, clutching my stuffed giraffe, awash in the devastation of being completely alone in the world. More than anything I want my mother, but she is not there.

Awakening in my coldly-sterile hospital room-cave, I want to tell myself this is only a dream, but cannot. I have never been able to dismiss the potency of my dreams, but have kept myself wrapped in a protective bubble of incertitude, unsure how to interpret their intense content. Now my firm grip of control has loosened to no grip at all. I have no resistance, no defenses left to insist the secret remain captive, and I give way to a volcano of rage, betrayal, and abandonment. The feelings are overwhelming, but I allow them to inundate me.

I know that man's hands. I know his scrubbed-clean scent. I can no longer deny I know, but still cannot determine his identity.

For years I thought if I could only figure out where things went wrong with me, I would be healed. Now the sword of truth is bringing its stroke of clarity, but I do not feel restored. The pain is stark and raw. Out of the very center of me bursts a commitment to myself: so help me, I will allow the identity of this man to come forward.

With that revelation, old mysteries start unraveling in my mind. So this is why Jorge says I won't open up to him, why I can't. This is why I dodge the most intimate moments, and why I don't trust men, or anyone really. Why I have kept a lid on my sexuality, and it has always seemed dangerous. Why I get a tightening pain in my throat when I want to ask for help, and why I never tell my parents what is really going on in my life. Why I have always felt, deep down, that something is wrong with me. Each realization rolls over me in one devastating wave after another, and I allow them to pummel me. Like sea glass, my rough edges are rounding out, softening.

When a nurse finally removes the catheter, I find shades of purple, green, and yellow spread across my upper thigh form a seascape of bruising. From my bed I recognize the familiar sound of my ringtone, muffled within furniture. Newly liberated from the tubing, I embark on the journey across the room to find my phone. Inside a drawer, beside my purse, I discover Jorge has found me. For an elongated moment I contemplate closing it and walking away, but as the phone rings on, my fingers accept his call.

"Hello Jorge."

"Reni, it's you," he breathes heavily. "I've been worried. The AD called and said you almost died."

"Not almost…I did die, Jorge. But I'm back." *I tried to tell you before I left, but you wouldn't listen.*

"Oh babe, I can't believe it. He said you're at the best hospital in Indonesia."

"I'm getting good care. The people here are kind."

He expresses his shock at the heart attack diagnosis, and as we speak for a few moments I cannot help but notice he is making no mention of rushing to catch a plane to be with me. I let a long, fat silence sit between us and then I say it. I thought uttering these words would require a face-to-face encounter, but I cannot hold back the tide.

"Jorge, there's no need to pretend. I know."

He pauses. "What, baby?"

"I know about the woman in our shower." His guilt seeps through the echoing phone line. He doesn't know how I've discovered the truth and chooses not to ask, or present any kind of defense. "I can't live like this anymore," I say calmly, but resolutely. It is literally killing me.

Jorge is speechless, shocked I suppose. "Come home, Reni, and we'll work it out," he finally offers.

"There's nothing left to figure out, nothing at all."

Tears roll down my face as I end the call and close the drawer. One of the orderlies finds me motionless beside the cabinet and gently encourages me to return to bed. I tell her my boyfriend is having an affair, knowing she doesn't understand my words but can read my tears. She sits with me as I cry, her arm around my shoulder. My tears become unrestrained sobs of release, transforming into soft laughter. The young orderly and I laugh together. It is the new sound of sudden weightlessness.

For three days I do nothing but lounge in my adjustable bed, shifting from elongated periods of utter calm to trembling rage at Jorge's betrayal. Empowered thoughts of striking out on my own arise, doused by fears of no longer having a partner at the epicenter of my orbit. At times I sit caught in wonder at what an amazing, blessed thing it is to simply breathe in and breathe out. Joko's resuscitation has taught me to appreciate each gentle inhalation, and the relief of a long, relaxing exhale, simple yet essential things I once took for granted. The grace in each breath is so vast it holds everything without collapsing. Even the intensity of my realization about my sexuality — which heaves through me like a rip tide periodically throughout the days and especially the nights — eases as I sit and breathe. I am alone in a country I hardly knew existed just months ago, but I do not succumb to my habitual worry. The cloud of gloom that was my constant companion is dissipating.

Despite my practiced feminist stance, I realize I have stayed in a relationship long beyond its expiration date because of some inner need to have a man beside me justifying my existence. Even more horrifying than that realization is the one that follows: what if I have fostered Jorge's infidelity, replicating the betrayal that haunts me from childhood? Now that the betrayal has occurred, and my memories are no longer a toxic cesspool buried in my subconscious, I keep asking myself, *what would make my heart sing?* I don't yet hear an answer, but I like the question.

M y phone rings and, lost in thought, I answer without looking. "Sirena, it's Dad calling," he announces in his no-nonsense voice.

I freeze. I don't feel prepared to address my parents nor capable of subterfuge.

"Jorge told us you've had some kind of incident there in Indonesia. Are you okay?"

"I'm more than okay. I'm fine."

"If you had a heart attack, you'd better get proper care here in the States, somewhere reliable like UCLA."

Returning home is the logical next step, but I find myself assuring him this hospital's cardiology department is state of the art.

"Well, I'd like Carson to have a word with your doctor."

Dad and Uncle Carson are practically inseparable, and he thinks Carson is the final word on anything medical, yet the mention of his name leaves me feeling skeptical. "Carson is an orthopedic surgeon."

"He'll still be able to assess the situation and determine if the doctor there knows what he's doing."

"My cardiologist is a woman and she went to school in Ohio. I'm sure she'd be happy to speak with Uncle Carson."

Dad doesn't sound convinced, but something in the background diverts his attention and he removes the phone from his mouth. "What? Jeepers, hold on." Returning to me, "Sirena, your mother is eager to speak with you. She won't stop fret…"

"Reni darling?" Dad's voice disappears as Mom's interrupts. "I've been worried sick."

I repeat my story about the quality of my hospital care. She implores me to come home where they can ensure I'll be safe, but home and safety have never really gone together for me. "I just need to rest here a while."

"Oh darling, I wish I could help. I feel so far away." It's a familiar pattern for us, even when living in the same city.

If asked a week ago, I would have said sexual abuse was an impossibility in my family. No way. Never. My relatives are prosperous, upright citizens, homeowners, taxpayers, who attend dinner parties and contribute to charities. The warm familiarity of Mom's voice has me wrestling with my own knowingness. Could I be inventing all of this? It wouldn't be the first time I have fallen prey to my dramatic temperament.

Mom continues voicing her concern, but my attention is on the woozy sensations coursing from my belly to my throat produced by questioning my own perceptions. These memories are horrifying and unthinkable, yet they make sense of what was previously, gnawingly, confusing. Floating outside my body, I knew the truth of what I was seeing, free from any trace of doubt. When I told Jorge I knew about his blonde, he denied nothing.

Ending the phone call, my mind freely hunts for the missing file. Whose greedy hands were touching me? The information is right there, yet I can't access it. Where were my parents while this was happening? Could the man be my father? Dad has always paid closer attention to his work, and to a lesser extent my brother, but I know he loves me, too. Who was it then?

No one protected me from those hands and what they did, no one comforted me. A cataclysmic abandonment drags me into a murky pond of sadness and I allow it to drown me. Still the grace holds me in my devastation; it resides in a place within me that has somehow remained unmarred by the past and supports each cell of my body with its invisible force, coaxing me into a love of myself in and through and beyond the pain.

On the sixth morning of my rebirth, as I've decided to term it, a knock at the door presents two visitors. The hospital administrator, a formally dressed, fully made-up woman, is collecting payment for the many procedures I have already received. It's odd that I have not considered how I would pay for my hospital stay, nor the price tag. The second visitor is Joko, carrying a large flower arrangement and a magazine. Before I can address my bill collector, Joko speaks to her in Indonesian and they move into the hallway for a discussion. Joko returns alone.

"May I put these here?" he asks, setting a ceramic vase overflowing with red and yellow tropical flowers on top of a small dresser.

"Sure. They're gorgeous, Joko." I sit up taller in bed and pick up the magazine. "Thank you."

"It's in *Bahasa Indonesia*," he smiles, "You won't be able to read it, but there's a photo essay about diving I thought you might enjoy." He sits in a chair beside the dresser. "I had already informed the hospital that the production company is covering your bill. The woman was coming to verify that."

"That's a relief," I say, knowing somehow it would work out.

"I hope it's okay... I spoke with your doctor. I was concerned about you."

"What did she say?"

"She is happy with your progress, but she thinks you are in denial."

A small giggle escapes me. I have been in denial since I was three, and this is me finally coming out of it. "She sees me as damaged by this experience, in need of medication for the rest of my life, but I see myself as liberated by it. So you see, we have a difference of perspective."

"Indeed," he chuckles.

"How did the rest of the shoot go?"

"We have some great footage." Hands on his knees, he leans forward in the chair. "Do you remember the manta rays when you passed out?"

His words trigger a hazy recollection of horn shaped paddles and dancing wings, briefly mingling with flashes of intense dark eyes and the sound of drums. "Did they return?"

"They stayed with us for days, the black and white stars of our color movie," he laughs. "Their undersides have such distinctive markings that we got to know them individually. One in particular loved to perform for the camera."

"I'd like to see the footage."

"Of course." His eyes twinkle, then darken. "The company is afraid you're going to sue them. They want to cover your hospitalization and pay your salary, although you did not finish your contract, in exchange for signing a waiver." He produces a piece of paper from a briefcase while I gleefully bounce on my bed.

"Are you supposed to be that active?" Joko asks with caution.

I assure him that I am supposed to be this happy, and to have things work out nicely for me. "I've been reborn," I tell him, and his concern begins to melt away.

Joko hands me the waiver and a pen, and while I sign with panache, he adds, "The doctor said they are releasing you tomorrow. You are ready to travel. I'll rebook your flight and take you to the airport."

Something airborne in my spirit takes a nose dive at the suggestion of departure. I watch my toes wiggling under the sheet, the joy draining away from me. "Yet another long flight," I cover, handing over the document.

After Joko leaves, a dank weight tugs at my bones. Having floated, suspended in grace, for nearly a week, the contrast is wrenching. How do I maintain my newfound buoyancy in the hustle of Los Angeles? I don't think I can.

I flip through the Indonesian magazine Joko gave me, skimming over pictures of a Jakarta fashion show until I reach the article about a local dive spot called Nusa Dewi. The empty white sand and turquoise water fills me with longing, but I resign myself to returning home.

In the morning I replace my hospital gown with street clothes, the medical team releases me with a set of prescriptions I have no intention of filling, and Joko drives me to the airport.

"I transferred your salary today," he says, handing my luggage to a porter.

"Thank you." I express my gratitude for all he has done, including saving my life.

"I doubt that was my doing," he says bashfully. "I think you made your own decision." He extends his hand, but I pull him into a hug.

The glass airport doors open automatically and the porter follows me through, then unloads my luggage at the zig-zagging maze of travelers before the check-in counter. The swarm of people and possessions inches forward, as does my apprehension. Grimness is setting in and I resent its presence.

What awaits me at the other end of all this? First thing I'm going to do is insist Jorge moves. No, the thought of staying in that downtown loft alone makes me shudder; I'll find a cute little place by the beach. Who am I kidding? Cute little beach houses cost a hot fortune. Shoulders slumped, claws of tension tightening around my throat, I slide my luggage forward, listening to the sunburnt family in front of me squabbling over the window seat. I fight the urge to scream at the top of my lungs, to explode, to bolt.

Nothing about Los Angeles is calling me home, not Jorge, not my family, not my work. I feel worn to threads from scrambling for jobs and fighting to prove myself, banging on doors nailed shut. My heart pounds with the mounting pressure, building steam, and heat stings at the back of my eyes. The airport is no place for a breakdown, I firmly reprimand myself, swatting tears away.

Finally I reach the head of the line, nerves twitching. A woman behind the counter nods for my approach. Stepping up to the desk, my hand quavers as I hand over my passport. She asks me a question, but I can't think straight. Somewhere in the background a young child shrieks, and the ear-splitting cry rattles me like a bomb going off. I glance over my shoulder, eyes darting in search of an escape route. I can hear the agent saying something, but the only thought my mind grabs onto is the need to flee. *Be real*, I chide myself, *you don't have anywhere to go.* But I only just received my new set of wings, I argue back. Already my old life is clipping them, plucking out feathers by the fistful.

The agent offers my boarding pass, but I make no move to take it. Instead I blurt the words, "I can't go," surprising myself even more than the puzzled woman.

She frowns. "Would you like to rebook?"

"Yes... no, not now." I am already striding away, a volcano of power activating my limbs, when an older gentleman in line grasps my arm and directs me back. He recoils from the fierce wildness flashing in my eyes, and I manage an apologetic smile.

"Your passport and luggage, ma'am," says the agent.

I take my belongings and dash away without any idea of what follows. Nabbing an abandoned cart, I throw my luggage onto it and wheel with adrenaline-fueled speed far away from the counter, escaping as if someone might give chase and drag me onto the flight. Eventually I sink onto an available bench, head tilted to the ceiling, catching my breath. Close call. I almost gave up my new life.

My desire for freedom is practically splitting open my chest and flapping restlessly into the atmosphere. I am half liberated, half trapped. My credit cards won't approve a purchase the size of an airline ticket, and my pay needs to pass through agency channels before landing in my account. I am in a terrible bind. If I call my parents for help, they will convince me to return. Only one person pops into my mind as a solution.

"Sirena?" Joko's concern pulses through the phone. Instantly I feel guilty for demanding more of his time, but aim for humility rather than humiliation.

"Where is Nusa Dewi?"

"It's a tiny island off the coast of Bali. Why? Is something…"

"Is it easy to get to?"

"Yes," he answers, confused. "Good diving, too."

I'd guessed as much, based on the pictures in the magazine he gave me, but the thought of returning underwater makes my muscles tighten. It's not fear exactly — fear seems to have fallen away from me — but a hesitation nonetheless. "I guess at some point I'll be ready to dive again. It's one of my favorite things."

"When you return to Indonesia, let me know. I'll go with you."

"Thank you," I whisper.

"*Sama sama*," he says. "You are welcome."

I close my eyes and take a deep breath. I'm unaccustomed to requesting help, but I must.

"I have a huge favor to ask." The pause that follows is heavy and I rush to fill it. "Could you buy me a ticket to Nusa Dewi and I'll pay you back as soon as my pay arrives?" I am astounded at my own audacity, assuming this man has the money, and is willing to risk it on me. My old life is absurdly bankrupt. There is no going back.

Joko assures me he is happy to be of service. He is driving, but will book the flight as soon as he arrives home. When he phones back, I have a plane ticket to Bali, transit to a speedboat, and a hotel reservation. The ease with which it unfolds feels like grace itself rolling out the red carpet. I fall over myself thanking Joko for his assistance, but he brushes it off as nothing.

With time before my flight I find a cafe with an upholstered chair and free wifi. I send Mom a simple email explaining my decision to recuperate longer in Indonesia, away from the frenetic pace of Los Angeles. I begin composing an email to Jorge as well, but my desire to elude direct contact with him is just plain chicken. It's late night there, but I catch him on Skype, looking tired. When he hears I'm at the airport he brightens, saying he'll be waiting for me at arrivals.

I sit up taller. "Jorge, I'm not coming back."

"You don't mean that." His lips purse. "Are you going to your mother's?"

I shake my head, unwilling to share details. My life is no longer his concern. I want to shut my computer, closing this chapter, but I stick it out.

"You're being dramatic." His hands rub through his thick hair. "You can't just throw everything we've built together in the trash. I won't let you."

"You've already trashed it quite thoroughly by sneaking around behind my back. But it's not about her, Jorge. It's over. We're done."

I end the call and this time don't shed a tear. Much is left to discuss, a whole life needing to be exhumed — possessions, properties, memories — but I have moved on and there's no turning back.

I board a flight to Denpasar, Bali, the Island of the Gods. Bare-breasted women on terraced rice fields fill my mind, but I figure that must be an idealized fragment of history. I have no idea what to expect. I am on an adventure, the fresh taste of freedom on my tongue as if I was newly released from captivity.

Driving through the streets of Denpasar, I try not to form hardened opinions. I like the gritty earthiness of developing countries, but cannot wait to depart the crowded capital and make a beeline for the oceanside. While we wind our way through grimy, congested city streets, my personable driver describes the Balinese custom of stealing their brides, his family compound (where twenty-two people share one bathroom), and his passion for wood carving and mask making.

The sprawl behind us, we arrive at a beach without marina or dock, and I board a speed boat tethered to a post in the sand. The sparkling aqua surface of the ocean softens my initial impressions; when I am on the water my heart sings. Still, I cannot help noticing all the other travelers are couples or in groups. I am profoundly alone. Isolated. Penniless. Directionless. It all seems destined for failure, but something urges me on.

A smiling young man approaches me once the boat lands on a new island. He holds an umbrella against the delicately warm dusting of drizzle.

"Ibu Sirena?"

I like the sound of my new title. "That's me."

He says he is taking me to Crystal Beach. Will I find a crystal ball there helping chart a new course? I can only hope. Sitting on his motorbike, the umbrella now in my hands and my luggage strapped onto a second bike, we rumble along narrow and bumpy country roads. Eventually I fold down the umbrella, welcoming the soft droplets. The veil is thin again and I sense life all around me that I cannot see, life full of love and intelligence. Existence is more complex than I previously knew, or perhaps far simpler. Big city life was a competitive assessment of how I measured up to others, constantly putting forward a good appearance. Now I am carefree, laughing as the increasingly wet breeze dampens my hair and mists my face, little streams trickling down my neck and pooling on my clavicle. I let the raindrops fall in my mouth and they taste exhilaratingly of aliveness.

Stunning my mind whispers as we arrive at Crystal Beach. Huts line a berm above the beach, modeled after traditional rice barns with wooden bases and strongly curved, thatched roofs. In front of them is a two-level infinity pool facing an empty stretch of white sand and an endless swath of turquoise ocean. I no longer need a plan; I'll stay forever.

Days pass in a lazy blur of shifting clouds, ecstatic sun bursts, and papaya, tangerine, and ginger juice blended with ice. For a week I wander only from the pool to the beach, and from the beach to my hut. In the evening I watch the sunset until every last petal-pink hue filters into starlight-sprinkled ebony. So much is happening on the inside I cannot do much on the outside, watching as others go to practice their yoga or take diving trips. Alone, I discover the wonders of the original Indonesian fast food: a whole young coconut served with a papaya-stem straw and a spoon, both a drink and a meal. In fact, I am on my first ever, unofficial coconut fast of a sort, as I can't seem to get enough of them and the other food, mostly fried rice or noodles, feels too heavy.

Here I have no distractions from the pain of my failed love life, or the childhood memories that have, with one swift motion from the sharpest of blades, sliced open that dark little place in my heart, setting my previously-trapped demon of insecurity loose. Can I survive on my own? Will anyone else ever truly love me? Even in my sleep, a recurring nightmare has me running desperately through a jungle, hounded, a figure chasing me and getting closer every night. The terror does not dissipate in the daylight, but the intensity of the tropical sun and the rhythm of the waves pound away at the fear and the pain, breaking them down into smaller particles, just as shell becomes sand.

Only Joko calls to check on me, and I tell him he has saved my life a second time. He seems to know I am working through something, and it takes some convincing to assure him I am well. I invite him to Crystal Beach for a visit, but he is already working on another film.

I am not surprised my father hasn't called; he never phones to chat. It puzzles me, though, being halfway around the world on a remote island after a nearly fatal heart attack and not hearing from Mom. Reaching out requires an effort I am not eager to exert and I don't feel prepared to discuss my memories with her. Mom's distance, I realize, is part of the equation. Her comfort was not with me when these early memories took place. Where was she?

Asleep in my hut on Crystal Beach, I have the dream again. Feet trampling jungle vines, heart palpitating, I explode through the darkness as the thrash of my pursuer grows louder. I risk a glance over my shoulder just as a massive male lion springs forward, tackling me to the ground. Shocked motionless, the scene instantly transforms. The lion and I are huddled together on a darkened, sandy beach beneath a blanket of twinkling stars. He sets an enormous paw upon my chest, and I relax against the thick wool of his fur surrounding me.

My eyes blink open, but for once my breathing pattern is slow and steady. I linger in bed, luxuriating in my newfound freedom. Suddenly it dawns on me, with the weight of a revelation, that I have chosen my life. This life. I never previously viewed my life as a choice, more of a sentence really, or a happenstance at best.

At breakfast I fall into a conversation with a Dutch acupuncturist, Mila, staying in a hut down the path. Traveling alone through Asia, she landed on Nusa Dewi weeks ago and knows far more about the place than I, in my reclusiveness, have discovered. I am not talkative, but her gregarious chatter draws me in.

"Sirena, come for yoga this afternoon by the beach," Mila presses.

I feel my eyes roll before I can stop them. "Yoga is for skinny, bendy, Cirque du Soleil types." I speak as if I am still well padded, even after shedding almost all my excess weight. As soon as the words leave my mouth I hear my gym buddy Oscar questioning why I am shielding myself.

"These do yoga," Mila tells me, pointing to her sizable but shapely thighs. She is an Amazonian beauty, tall, blonde, buxom, and statuesque.

"What are they feeding you on the European continent these days?" I frown, feeling frail and petite in her presence.

As if reading my mind, she pats me on the head. "Trust me, you need to come to yoga. The teacher is a dreamboat." She fans herself from the heat of her thought. "Ricardo is the real deal."

"Tell me he's not Brazilian."

"He's from Planet Hot, Sirena. So hot I slide off my mat every time I get a look at him." She sweeps her hand down her ribs. "Abs to die for, and dreadlocks as long as his body." I wrinkle my nose, skeptically humoring myself by picturing long dreads dragging dust bunnies across the floor. "After class he plays his guitar on the beach," she sighs, oblivious to my reaction. "His voice is like palm sugar." She gives me a look that says I'd be a fool to refuse.

"Fine," I huff. "I'll check out your yoga-rock-star-sex god." Even if the class is boring, I could use the entertainment of an impromptu concert by the water.

M eandering down the beach several hours later, any enthusiasm has waned. Without yoga clothes or a mat, I approach the open pavilion clutching my hotel towel like an imposter. A sense of obligation is seeping back in, and I tell myself I should be doing something practical like working, or at least calling my agent, instead of chanting *om* and folding my body into origami. The reality is, however, I couldn't match the rigor of a film shoot in this condition even if I wanted to. The income from this last contract will only last so long, but I must trust that the answers will come.

I arrive to find most of the floor space already covered with yoga mats and people quietly stretching or talking in hushed voices. In an open spot, too front and center for my liking, I stretch out my towel. The teacher is working the room, greeting each student, and I can't help but notice him hugging many of the women. Mila was right; he's gorgeous, but obviously a player. Jorge's face flashes to mind and I swallow my grimace.

Despite my agitation, or because of it, I keep glancing at the instructor. He has a captivating presence, and I wonder why he is on this tiny island working for donations when he could easily be on a runway in Paris. His tall, strikingly powerful frame moves with natural agility, his muscles thick and defined without being bulky. I bend at the waist, stretching, and catch a glimpse of him framed between my calves, his skin the color of sun-warmed dates, his dreadlocks wrapped around his head forming an elegant turban. I have the feeling I have seen him before, somewhere.

Ugh, I sigh, straightening once more. He has probably been adored and idolized his entire life, and I resolve to ignore him. I slump onto my towel just as he turns and our eyes meet across the room. Something in his face makes me pause, his eyes so intense I check over my shoulder to see if he could be staring at someone behind me. When I turn back, his attention has diverted to Mila, who is fluffing her hair with her fingers while asking him a question.

The teacher is hot, but he's not a pretty boy; his face at rest is somehow fiercely and beautifully exotic. If not for the dreadlocks, I might have mistaken him for a Lakota Sioux warrior. *What he looks like is trouble*, I tell the sensations ricocheting through my body.

Closing my eyes, I attempt meditation, and when I open them again he is squatting before me on his heels. I almost choke at his proximity, and immediately wonder what I am doing wrong. How could I mess up sitting down and breathing? I dart a look at the other students, my pulse pounding in my ears, but they are sitting cross-legged and silent, just as I am.

"I'm Ricardo," he says in an East Coast voice faintly tinged with a Spanish accent. His walnut-brown eyes meet mine with confidence and perception that rattles me, his gaze a beam I cannot meet. Flustered, I look away.

"I'm Sirena."

"Pleased to meet you, Sirena." When he smiles, his eyes seem to brighten with sunshine. "Are you new to yoga?"

"Total beginner." I try to return his smile, but I think the signals from my brain are misfiring. Instead I grimace, fingers twisting my towel.

"It's an honor to introduce you to this ancient and sacred practice." He has a warm, welcoming demeanor, but I catch him looking me over. When his eyes linger on my chest, I blush. Womanizer.

"You have a lion on your heart," he says and I am almost disappointed to realize he is, in fact, staring at my tank top.

I am wearing a tee my mother gave me after I signed my first — and only — feature film contract. At the top is the graphic image of a lion with a wild mane. Underneath in small print are the dates for a Leo birthday, July 23 to August 22, and beneath it reads, *Leos have the power to make just about anything happen.* After the deal fell apart, I put the shirt away and never looked at it again. Until I packed it for this trip.

"You're a Leo?" He asks.

I peer at the people around us, their eyes closed as they quietly breathe in and out. Isn't it time for him to start the class? "Yes, the first day."

"Me too, on the last. We're bookends."

He starts to move away, then hesitates. "You'd better borrow my yoga mat. You'll be sliding across the floor on that towel."

He takes his mat and hands it to me, then sits on the polished bamboo floor, folding his long legs easily into lotus position, his spine as straight as a telephone pole. He is the picture of poise, and I know he won't be slipping anywhere, even after sacrificing his mat.

I attempt to emulate him, putting one ankle on top of the opposite thigh, but there is no way I can achieve the same with my second. My eyes close and I breathe. I can do this. I don't wish to run away. I hear the distant sound of motorbikes approaching, feet stepping, and yoga mats unfurling, but I stay focused within myself. I am actually enjoying keeping my eyes shut, free of distractions, plus my emotions are so raw that everything I have been through recently must be written all over my face.

Throughout the class Ricardo speaks repeatedly about the unity of our movements linked with our breath. I discover that the more consciously I move, the more it is like swimming through air. Swimming is something my body understands. Some of the poses are difficult for me to hold, but he encourages us to relax into our resistance and breathe through it, assuring us yoga nurtures our capacity to ease into tight places inside ourselves. Now that my breath is my new best friend, that kind of makes sense and is even intriguing. I don't recognize any of the poses as he calls them out by their long Sanskrit names, but everyone around me moves with a practiced assuredness. Ricardo describes the ideal positioning in intricate detail from the inside of our flesh; I am getting to know myself anew as bone and muscle and fascia. His recorded playlist includes everything from exotic Arabic music to hip hop, the beat helping me stick with the discomfort of bending my body in new positions. We finish in corpse pose, stretched out on our backs, the music fading until the only sound is the soft lapping of waves on the shore. I lie prone, a trinity of corpse, adult woman and newborn child.

I open my eyes to see the teacher has returned to full lotus position, straight body silhouetted against the sun sinking into the horizon. The moment is rich, and the experience has unexpectedly cracked me open. This practice is far more than physical exercise, I realize. A tear trickles down my cheek and I don't even know why. Others start to unfold their legs and stand, and I sense Mila join me on my borrowed mat. She rests her arm around my shoulder, not asking any questions. Some of the yoga students filter out, buzzing away on motorbikes while others sit on the floor near us, chatting with Ricardo. An attractive woman kneels behind him and drapes her arms across his broad, sculpted shoulders, her long hair falling across his arm as she whispers into his ear. She must be his girlfriend, or one of them, I suppose. The moment passes, and soon I'm standing, rubbing my eyes.

Mila draws me onto the beach in the final tangerine glow of twilight, and as we migrate across the powdery sand more musicians arrive, mostly Indonesians. Soon a full-fledged jam session, surrounding a bonfire, rocks the shore, guitars, drums, and even a violin filling the damp night air. A crescent moon rises above the tree line like an off-kilter smile, moonlight reflecting across the flat sea, reminding me I am in the southern hemisphere, far from home, and even the heavenly bodies have a new orientation.

After the drummers have built the rhythm up to a frenzy, the pace tapers down. Ricardo sings a melodic song in Spanish, his voice smooth and resonant. I try to study the faces around the circle, but in the firelight his high cheekbones and full lips are too compelling. My eyes eventually settle on the fire, but as he sings the chorus I have the strangest sensation he is looking right through me. A shudder courses down my body, but I refuse to let my eyes leave the flames. This man obviously thrives on attention, and I refuse to join his little harem.

Mila invites me to accompany her for dinner, but I have lost my appetite and am happily anchored in the sand. I don't want to leave the enchantment of the beach or the music, but the thought of Ricardo assuming I am hanging around for him, drawn into his vortex, repels me. I wave goodbye to Mila and walk away from the circle, glancing back over my shoulder despite my better judgement. Ricardo catches me looking, and I've already started to spin away when he raises his hand in a graceful goodbye gesture. I've half seen it, half ignored it, and flap my hand at my side so as not to appear entirely rude. I must be the most awkward person in history.

The next day I am restless, and pour my excess energy into a spontaneous art project on the beach. I collect seashells, pebbles and bits of broken coral, hunting for exactly the right sizes and colors, and arranging them in a series of long, waving, serpentine shapes. After several hours my seemingly abstract design has taken the shape of a lion's head, a plethora of undulating serpents radiating outward as the mane.

Three young Indonesian boys watch me from a distance, inching closer even as they pretend to focus on their game of kick the soda can. The friends range from about five to seven years old, perhaps eight. Eventually they grow brave enough to squat in the sand beside me, following my hands fluttering over the shapes. We do not have a common language other than our appreciation of the beach, but without uttering a word they understand what I need and run to look for shells, chattering together incessantly. As the afternoon heat increases, two of the boys scamper off, but the oldest remains, quietly watching.

My mind is uncluttered, letting the flow of creation have its way. As I focus on my curving forms, the boy delivers a handful of lavender cowrie shells. One shape wants to curl into a spiral, and my new helper places the perfect piece of sea glass at its center.

A waterfall of sweat pours from my brow under the broiling sun. I pantomime for the boy to wait and scoot to the bar, returning with treasure: glasses filled with water and ice cubes. We sit together in silent companionship under the patchy shade of a palm grove, condensation from the glasses dripping onto our knees. I have long felt an aversion to young children, but today is a new day. Drink finished, my friend smiles goodbye and trots away.

Some time later, I rest on my haunches to enjoy my lion in all his colorful glory. When a small wave nips at my heels, I jump. The tide is rising. I dash to my hut, grab my camera, and head back out the door to document my artwork before the water steals it away.

I am rushing past the palms when I see someone standing on the otherwise empty stretch of sand, scrutinizing my arrangement of shells. He is not facing me, but I recognize the broad, brown back covered by ropes of dreadlocks tied in a knot. Immediately my heart speeds up. I think about waiting for him to go away, but the water edges ever closer, and I am annoyed at myself for being overly sensitive. *Enough skirting around other people*, I lecture myself, and stroll toward him even as I consider racing back to my room for a cover-up to throw over my bikini. I brandish my camera like a shield as I walk across the burning sand, watching him sink to his knees to scrutinize my art up close. He is wearing only a pair of board shorts that hang just right on his slim hips, the muscles in his back and arms flexing as he braces himself on the sand. Darn it, Mila was right, his body is from Planet Attraction, and that thought makes me nervous and annoyed in equal measure.

As my shadow falls across the shells, Ricardo turns his head. I see recognition in his eyes and something else, a kind of questioning I cannot interpret. He stands to greet me and I am now facing the utter perfection of his half-naked, toned, beyond-distracting torso. It is totally unfair that he looks like that on my beach, checking out my artwork, making my body clench and flush. He simply oozes masculinity, and although I am trying to clamp down my response, I am jumpy and eager. Far too eager.

"Hi Ricardo," I say as indifferently as possible. The hand on my hip drops to my side when I realize I'm posing, but that feels awkward, too. I cross my arms over my chest, camera shoved under my armpit. Somebody shoot me.

"Did you create this, Sierra?"

"Sirena," I wince, wishing a sudden tsunami might wash me away. At least his voice is rich with appreciation, and I find myself smiling. "I did. It was cathartic."

I try to ignore him as I shoot images of the lion from several angles. Retreating behind the sanctuary of the viewfinder, my nerves begin to melt away until I feel his eyes on my body. I suck in my stomach and keep snapping, daring to steal some shots of his stunning face. He doesn't seem to mind.

"I was going for a run on the beach," he stands up and pantomimes, "and I saw something out of the corner of my eye. At first I thought it was alive." He halts in mid-motion, narrowing his eyes in confusion. He's kind of a ham, but a cute ham. "I stopped to take a look and..." He kneels again near my art piece, peering up at me. The look in his eyes is so unguarded it pierces something in my chest and suddenly I am dizzy. I must have been in the sun too long, and sink into the sand to regain my equilibrium.

"This may sound strange, but I felt like your art piece spoke to me."

His eyes are too clear, too intense, speaking a fire language, an underground lava field that burns into me. I can't hold his gaze for long and look away, adjusting the position of a shell beside my foot and tugging at my bikini top. "What did it have to say?"

"That's what I was trying to figure out."

We sit at opposite sides of my creation, looking at the shells as if they might magically relay a message. Even in easy silence the magnetic pull he has on me throws my orbit out of whack, my body draws towards his, my cells attuned to his every breath and the occasional flicker of his dark lashes.

"I have a thing about lions," he admits softly. "These undulating shapes you made in the mane…I've seen them before." He skims his hand over the subtly shifting colors merging from peach to cream and violet, and I shiver as if his hand is moving across my skin. "Clam shells into cowries…" he murmurs. "Must have taken you a long time to do this."

"I started this morning."

Just then a strong wave comes up faster and farther than any before it, overtaking the design and splashing us. We both leap up swiftly, Ricardo graceful while I scramble, instinctively raising the camera above my head, both of us laughing in surprise. Ricardo gets speckled with flying droplets, but I am thoroughly inundated with saltwater, foam, and sand.

"I'm eating grit," I exclaim, wiping sand from my lips.

"Hold still a sec." He steps close enough that I smell the woodsy scent rising off his skin, close enough that I hold my breath. "Close your eyes."

With the focus and precision of a surgeon, Ricardo brushes grains of sand from the fold of my eyelid, and they dust my cheek like the lightest of kisses. The tender warmth of his fingertips sweeps lightly across my face. I wonder if he knows what this is doing to me, but then another big wave comes in, drenching us up to our knees. My seashell lion is gone.

"You spent so much time making it and now you're offering it to the ocean. Just like a Tibetan sand painting."

I do my best to act nonchalant as he describes monks utilizing colored sand to create intricate mandalas, chanting mantras as they work. Every detail is exacting and takes weeks, he says, and when their masterpiece is completed they sweep every grain into a bottle and release it into a body of water.

The process sounds fascinating, but I'm only half listening, my body leaning toward him in an unconscious effort to close the distance separating us. His feet remain firmly planted, and I swear I see a glint in his eye revealing that he knows his effect on me. Both my hunger and his confidence leave me biting my lip in irritation. He is talking about monks and ceremonies while his eyes sparkle with life and sex. He must slay every woman he meets with that megawatt smile. I draw shapes in the wet sand with my toe, dodging his influence.

"I think the Navahos and Hopis do something similar with sand," I offer. "And the Aborigines in Australia."

"And now you," he replies, leaning closer as he says it.

I lift my eyes. The air between us is charged, the molecules rearranging. It's as if someone is seeing me, truly recognizing me, for the very first time. I can't figure out how he does that, peering inside my psyche. Or does he have the same effect on every woman he encounters?

He tilts his head, giving me a sheepish look. "Did you like the yoga yesterday?"

"More than I thought I would," I concede, trying not to like him at all and failing miserably.

"Will you try it again tomorrow?" His voice makes that one simple question seem like an invitation for so much more, and I find myself nodding like a child offered a triple scoop ice cream cone. Internally, I roll my eyes. Playing hard to get has never been a strong point of mine.

"I hope you do, Sirena."

Zing. The words reverberate through my hesitation, and my spine lengthens. For an instant his eyes drop and I feel them sweep my body, singeing every place he looks, and firing off my nervousness all over again.

"Would you like to come up to the pool for a swim?" I ask. Why on earth am I extending an invitation, convinced as I am that he's a total playboy with a new yoga student in his bed every night?

To my embarrassment Ricardo's face grows taut, as if I just asked him to move back to LA with me for a big white wedding. He must have a girlfriend waiting at home.

"Thanks, but I gotta finish my run," he says, eyes fixed on the horizon. "Hope I see you tomorrow." He flashes his brighter-than-the-sun smile, and I watch with a mixture of confusion and relief as he lopes gracefully down the beach like a gazelle.

Saved. I almost got in over my head. He is merely a distraction from everything that has happened recently, and nothing could be more ridiculous right now than setting myself up for a short-lived affair, or worse, rejection.

To my great frustration, brown muscles and dark lashes flit through my mind throughout the evening and into the next day. I don't want to think about him and ruthlessly banish the thoughts. He is like honeycomb with thousands of females buzzing around him, and the last thing I need is that kind of complexity in my life. Besides, he can't be truly interested in me. I am certainly not interested in him. It's a diversion.

I take myself for a swim, losing track while counting short laps in the pool. While gliding through the water, I work out the mathematics of how long I can afford to hide out on this little island before I'm footing Joko with a bill I can't pay back. An idea pops through my anxiety like sunshine bursting through clouds. Jorge can buy me out, owning our properties outright. I think he'll like that. I like it. He won't have a lump sum for me, but he can pay installments into my account. Maybe he can get a loan and pay it off in one fell swoop. He likes loans and I like payments. I can even ask him to sell Lexi; that money would go a long way here. Maybe I'll open a dive school on Nusa Dewi and videotape tourists underwater.

I am still dripping wet when I dart through the hut door and pick up my phone, taking action before over-thinking can siphon away my conviction.

"Hello Reni."

"Glad I got ahold of you," I pant, "with the time difference and all." Dripping a puddle onto my floor, I return outside to the porch.

"How are you? You sound out of breath."

"I'm really well. How are things in your world?"

I hear annoyance in his exhalation. "Look, how about we cut the bullshit. What's going on? When will you be home?"

"I've given you my answer, Jorge." I sit on the front step facing the ocean, and holding my ground.

"You belong here, not running away from home like some pissy teenager."

I brush away grains of sand stuck to my feet. Is this a lark, hanging around on the beach in Indonesia? In some ways I do feel like a teenager with a fresh lifetime of possibility spreading before me, but is starting all over again a huge mistake? Despite the barbs Jorge is tossing, for a moment the familiarity of home and the sincerity in his voice sink hooks that tug at remnants of the closeness that once existed between us, but I know better than to be lured in by that.

"I can't help but notice, Jorge, that you didn't rush to Indonesia to be by my side when you learned I'd had a heart attack, died for a moment, and wound up in intensive care."

"I'm working here, Sirena. You know that," he says quietly, tinged with guilt.

"Yeah, I know you're working hard. And with whom." I pause for a poignant beat, and he doesn't deny anything. Full speed ahead into my new life. Time for my sales pitch.

"I have an idea that benefits us both and I think you'll like it."

He meets my opener with stony silence, but I barrel on. "I think the fairest way forward is if you buy me out of our properties." I hear a disgruntled sigh from his end of the line. "You'll own them outright, and we know they're appreciating in value," I rush on. "Maybe you can get a loan for an initial lump sum, and then we'll agree to a payment schedule."

I bite both my lips at once, not uttering one more word. Gregor taught me the best way to close a deal is to make your pitch with pizzazz, then don't say a thing. The next person to speak loses.

"I can't believe this." I hear Jorge's sniff of indignation, and for a moment I feel responsible for his discomfort. Then I don't. "I need some time to digest what you've said. You've just deserted our life together… massacred it."

"I'm not the one with blood on my hands." My tone is harsh, and I feel Gregor shaking his head at my approach. "Look, I'm presenting solutions," I offer more softly. "Separating from you hurts me, too, but being with you hurt me more. I can't do it any longer." My heart literally will not allow.

He doesn't, can't, respond. In a hush I say goodbye and hang up. Tears come, but a sense of excitement follows. My impossible future suddenly has a potential foundation.

Throughout the day I carefully ignore the women walking past in their yoga leggings, and the purple mat Mila has lent me while she visits a nearby island. Even so, I find myself walking down the beach in the afternoon sun with the neatly-rolled foam under my arm. Refusing to appear eager, I arrive at the last minute, finding most of the space already taken, and Ricardo in meditation at the front. I spread my mat in a back corner, grateful for its anonymity.

After a few minutes of chanting together, Ricardo is on his feet, giving poetic instructions in intricate detail for each movement. He speaks of *ahimsa*, the Hindu and Buddhist principle of doing no harm to any living thing, encouraging us to bring this gentleness to our body as we practice. Midway through class our eyes meet, and I see a flutter across his face. His expression reaches out to me across a sea of bent backs, and that one look undoes me. I am an undeniable puddle of arousal. He coaches the class in linking breath to movement, and boy do I need to focus on my breathing. Concentrating on a sun salutation, I pretend not to notice as Ricardo gradually makes his way to my corner of the pavilion.

"Hiding in the back?" The grin in his voice is loud enough for those around us to hear. "I hope you're not avoiding me."

I can't believe he is openly teasing me, and try to swallow my smile as I hold a warrior pose. "This was the only available space."

As if these postures were not difficult enough, how am I supposed to balance in a lunge while his chocolate-brown eyes are staring at me like something he wants to devour? I take a quick peep at those around us, but they seem to be studiously focused and ignoring our interaction.

"I thought you'd be at the front with me like last time." He places his hands on my arms, gently but firmly turning the muscles into an outward rotation. His touch is attentive, sensitive, and sparks of heat radiate from each point of contact. My traitorous body swoons, and a moment later his hands are on my waist, steadying me. I nearly collapse with relief when he wanders off to assist someone else.

Throughout the class Ricardo repeatedly drifts to my spot in the back to correct my technique. Clearly I do not know what I am doing. He adjusts the poses of other students as well, but seems to show me special attention. Or am I reading into his diligent teaching style?

At one point we are belly down on our mats, chests lifted upright by our wrists. Ricardo asks us to reach around with one hand, catch our foot and pull it towards the back of our head. This seems an advanced pretzel pose to me, which must be evident from my facial expression. Standing at the front of the room, Ricardo holds out a cotton yoga strap and asks, "Sirena, *quieres?*"

I don't speak much Spanish, but having lived in Los Angeles my whole life I understand enough to know he is asking me if I want the strap. What unnerves me is, if I answer that I want it — and I do — will it sound like innuendo?

"*Quiero.*"

He raises his eyebrows quizzically, waiting. Apparently the word has barely made it past my lips. This private, yet quite public exchange tickles me, but I refuse to repeat myself louder. No doubt my awkwardness is only drawing more attention to us, but I can't seem to act composed around him. When he tilts his head, full lips curved into a mischievous smirk, I bend my forefinger and mouth, *please?*

He brings me the strap, held loosely in his fingers, with a little rascal of a smile. "What's this?" he asks, mimicking the gesture of my forefinger beckoning him to me. "Calling your servant to your side?"

The man is toying with me. Blatantly. Publicly. My body responds with pleasurable, nervous jitters as he slips the strap around my foot, his strong, well-groomed fingers bringing both ends to my palm. Carefully, his grasp atop mine, he helps me draw my toes back farther than I thought was possible, bringing me to the edge of what I can do and not beyond in a delicious stretch slightly tinged with discomfit. I love it.

By the time *savasana*, corpse pose, comes along, I am pleasantly tired and astoundingly relaxed. Unlike the muscle exhaustion after a tough workout at the gym, this relaxation reaches into the center of me. Flat on my back, eyes closed, I drift into the place between sleep and wakefulness, sensing the beat of a drum and seeing flashes of magenta light behind my eyelids as Ricardo's voice sings softly in Sanskrit.

After class a number of students approach Ricardo, mostly women with a post-yoga afterglow and lots of questions about form, technique, and what their dreadlocked idol eats for breakfast. I take my time getting off the mat, rolling it, collecting my things, aware of Ricardo chatting up his admirers and giving goodbye hugs. Deliberately aloof, I head into the soft violet hush of dusk, unrolling Mila's mat on the beach beside the drummers and a didgeridoo player. Ricardo makes his way to the drum circle with a small group of followers, and soon the jam session is in full swing, the crowd swelling as passersby join in, dancing in the sand.

It has grown dark by the time a group stands, preparing to splinter off, Ricardo among them. Disappointment floods me, although I probably have no right to feel irked by him not acknowledging me. I dig my toes into the sand, lecturing myself to relinquish this outlandishly teenage infatuation — Jorge would surely agree — and return to the safety of my hut. Turning my back to the crowd, I roll up Mila's mat and walk away without so much as a backwards glance this time. The drums decrease in volume as I retreat, but soon another beat replaces them, growing faster and louder, footsteps in wet sand.

"Hey, wait up."

I turn and there he is, face etched with surprise. Just like that I feel him in every corner of my body, and an undeniable tremor moves through me when I meet his eyes.

"Can I walk you home?"

I am half-crazed in his presence, maybe three-quarters. A thump audibly hammers in my ears, my brain scrambled so I can barely speak. "Sure," is what comes out.

The farther we sink into the empty darkness ahead, away from the music and the crowd, the more at ease I become. I tell him about diving in Flores, leaving out the almost-dying part, and Ricardo describes seeing orangutans in Sumatra. At the steps leading to the pool, I hesitate. What comes next? Nervous prickles antagonize me all over again as I turn to face him.

He remains in the sand a step below, gazing up into my eyes. The tip of his tongue passes across his full lower lip, and it might be the most sensual thing I have ever seen. "My guitar's still at the jam circle…" he starts, and I nod quickly, not wanting him to catch my disappointment.

"How 'bout we meet here at this spot tomorrow night? Want to?" He makes the offer lightly, so I couldn't possibly refuse. He's good at this. Too good.

"Okay," I say quietly, while my central nervous system screams exclamation points inside my head. "When?"

He looks at his watch. "It's 8:15. Let's meet at the same time tomorrow night and pick up where we left off."

Which is where exactly? A conversation? A seduction?

"Alright."

He lifts an eyebrow at my monosyllabic communication and starts to leave, only to stop, turn, and flash that dazzling smile of his before blending back into the night.

He didn't walk me to the door or kiss me goodnight. I didn't even get a hug. I'm relieved, right? Shoulders slumped, I enter my hut wondering if the attention he gave me during the class was an illusion.

I spend much of the next day debating with myself whether or not Ricardo could truly find me attractive. While grateful for the vacation this inner tug-of-war provides from processing my recent traumas, I am aware this is not a particularly confident way to prepare for seeing him later. The possibility that he might, maybe, perhaps be interested in me, that the outrageous chemistry I feel around him might possibly be mutual, puts a pleasurable swing in my full hips. The dormant seedlings of my sensuality, long left in the dark, are wiggling their little roots and sending up fresh shoots. I jiggle my shoulders and finger comb my hair. Maybe it doesn't have much to do with Ricardo at all, simply me returning to life.

The day is languid and long, and the hours after sunset crawl by even more slowly. This isn't a date, just a friendly get together I assure myself, all the while knowing that a gorgeous man on a starlit beach pretty much tops the romance charts. No way am I dressing up, I hedge, even as I carefully shave my legs, just throwing on something casual, unpremeditated, as if that nullifies a whole day spent obsessing.

After sunset I am pacing the porch and checking the time so frequently I embarrass myself. Desperate for diversion, I visit the hotel restaurant and chat up Alit, an amiable young waiter who has never left tiny Nusa Dewi. I describe for Alit the vastly different world of downtown Los Angeles, painting a portrait of the flamboyant transvestites, graffiti artists, and street dancers who congregate outside my building. He is particularly interested in the dancing, and I have some fun doing my best to act it out.

As I am spinning my spine around in circles on the floor, I hear Alit say, "*Malam*, Ricardo."

Instantly I turn to a pillar of lead, blood climbing up my throat. Legs in the air like a dead bug, hair in my face, I look up into Ricardo's eyes peering down at me sporting a bemused smile. "Taking up break dancing?"

The jitters make the craziest things fly out of my mouth. "Checking out the electrical wiring," I mutter, pointing to the lighting fixture on the ceiling, then glaring at Alit for not providing adequate warning.

Say, a tsunami siren, for instance.

I sit up, and Ricardo extends a hand. His grip is firm and assured, and merely touching his hand sends quivers all the way up my arm. He's wearing a simple pair of shorts and untucked button down shirt, but looks like he stepped out of a magazine.

"Sorry I lost track of time," I apologize as we walk to the beach together, tremulous butterflies knocking around in my stomach.

"Looked like you were having too much of a good time to stop." I am not sure how to interpret his words. Is he super calm, or indifferent?

On the sand are two yoga mats side by side facing the shoreline, and a guitar case resting alongside them. We sit on the empty stretch of beach, alone under a canopy of stars and slice of moon. In my nervousness my lips remain sealed, fearful of what might pop out. Ricardo doesn't fill the space with idle chatter, but takes up his guitar, softly plucking at the strings, humming almost to himself. I watch the horizon, fidgeting with my shorts and stealing glances at him, until surprisingly, as the moments pass, I feel increasingly natural.

While occasionally strumming, Ricardo describes his day as the visiting instructor for a yoga teacher training. "They brought me in as a yoga before-and-after story," he explains quietly, adding that he taught "all kinds of inversions, head stands, hand stands, shoulder stands, that sort of thing." When I admit I find the acrobatic aspect of yoga intimidating, he smiles and says, "Sometimes you gotta get upside down to see the world from a different perspective. It opens up the possibility of radical change."

Radical change. Just a few weeks ago that term would have been an abstract mental concept, but has become familiar territory. "You've been through a big change?" I ask.

He plucks a few notes, then turns towards me, his direct gaze full of candor. "I did an about-face."

"What did the before part look like?"

He bites his bottom lip and I guess he's deciding how to answer my question. "I grew up on the streets of Brooklyn." His face grows pensive, a different man than the one I've witnessed playing music and teaching yoga. This guy looks haunted. "One of those neighborhoods where you hear gunshots most nights and walk down the street with eyes in the back of your head. I hung out with some rough dudes and did things I shouldn't have to fit in." He laughs. "I actually learned yoga in detention."

I sense he is sharing something he doesn't speak of often and bite down on my desire to pepper him with a million questions. "You seem to have moved beyond all that."

He blows air through his lips as he plays a few intricate riffs on the guitar. "Moving beyond... that's a long process, if it ever happens. Always seems to be more."

We fall back into silence, much left unsaid. Ricardo improvises on his guitar and it seems he's working something out through the music, letting me into his inner realm with notes rather than words. When he sets the guitar in its case, he puts aside the ruminative mood that's swallowed us both up. I look into his eyes and see them ignite with secrets I am yet to discover. Sparks fly rapid-fire between us, the atmosphere shifting in an instant. My entire lower body clenches and I brush the sand from my thighs to busy myself, not knowing how to handle him, not even sure that I want to.

He reaches out, his knuckles graze my arm, and he places his palm on my shoulder, subtly drawing his thumb across my skin. This one little movement is enormous for me, the warmth of his fingers launching a wildfire that races downward. The instantaneous impact scares me and I have to keep from wriggling away.

"How about a change of venue?" His eyes lower, masked by thick lashes. "Let's go back to my house."

Warning alarms flash, and a flood of panic extinguishes the flames. I can't go to his house. I couldn't hold him off, and I am far too fragile right now to be another of his conquests. I pull away and spring to my feet, his hand left dangling in the night air. "Thanks, but I have to go."

"Sirena, wait," he calls after me, and I stop at the steps, turning to him. "Can we do something else? Go for tea?"

His look is open, but he feels too dangerous to me now. I need the security of my own room. "I really have to go."

"Then meet me here again tomorrow night. Same place, same time?"

I nod quickly, agreeing in order to leave faster. Something tells me Ricardo isn't going to let me walk away without extracting some sort of promise.

"If I can't find you I'll check all the suitable break dancing sites."

That makes me laugh and I smile my way down the path.

In my hut I turn on the fan, climb in bed and pull the covers up to my chin, listening to the chorus of insects and frogs. Ricardo is dignified, funny, respectful — the polar opposite of Rupert — but he scares me just as much. More. Thinking about him makes all my body parts feel like they are trembling, and it unnerves me that I have lost control of my own reactions. I am in hot water.

A mental wrestling match consumes much of my day. Is Ricardo genuinely interested, or is it the chase he enjoys? Maybe I'm the first woman who hasn't thrown herself at his feet, and the challenge alone is seductive. If I took our flirtation to the next level, only to watch him repeat it with the next lonely woman to walk into his class, my little slice of paradise would become a living hell. Distracting myself with a swim, I promise not to think about him. And fail.

That night I get to the beach early and wait seated on the steps, inhaling the saltwater scent in the sultry air. The gentle crash of waves massages my nerves. Ricardo arrives right on time with yoga mats and guitar, wearing a faded pair of jeans and a solid gray T-shirt showing off all his cut muscles. Despite my better judgement, excitement swells at the sight of him and bobs around in my belly. He doesn't try to hug me, just offers his illumined smile as he unrolls the mats. When we sit, he takes out his guitar and sings an entire song in Spanish. His voice is intoxicating, and I lean back to stretch my legs, stargazing, absorbing the sensitivity he reveals through his music. I don't understand the words he is singing, but I can tell he delivers each one with sincerity.

Lightning bolts flash offshore without a cloud in sight, releasing electrical energy into the atmosphere, each one momentarily brightening the beach like a strobe light. Ricardo finishes his song and I sense him turn to observe me in silence. Feeling on display, pins and needles tingle through my limbs.

"I like watching your hair billowing in the breeze." His words, his voice, his eyes caress me, while all I can do is sit there, paralyzed.

He returns to the guitar, strumming casually, and tells me about the day's adventure with his yoga group. They worked on back bends, *heart openers* he calls them, and one student had a big breakthrough, moving from tears into laughter. "I've had that experience on the yoga mat more than once," he admits, before we fall back into silence.

"I've been wondering…" He glances at me, then out to the horizon, "why d'ya run away last night?"

The words hang there, huge and unavoidable. I know Ricardo is not the kind of man who will accept a lame excuse; truth is at the heart of what he says and does. I don't understand him, nor entirely trust him, but his honesty is clear.

"I didn't want to be…" I shrug, "some yoga conquest. Another notch on your bamboo bedpost." I was aiming for nonchalance, but it comes out sounding presumptuous to the point of being rude. My face prickles with embarrassment, and I'm hoping it's too dark for him to notice.

He nods his head, sucking in his bottom lip, and looks at me sideways. "Pretty sure you have me figured out, huh?"

The way he says it cuts through the subterfuge, not only revealing there is more to him than what I have seen, but that he recognizes my fears and sees right through them. Feeling horribly judgmental, I bury my face in my arms. "I'm ridiculous."

Warm fingers nudge my shoulder playfully. "You're many things Sirena, but ridiculous isn't one of them."

He improvises a jazzy riff, his fingers dancing down the strings. My legs shift, trying to find a comfortable position. Admitting my fears has dissolved some of my anxiety, but I am nowhere near acclimated to the constant pulsation surging through my body whenever I am near him. He sets down the guitar, lounging beside me, when a bright meteor with a long tail rockets across the midnight-blue sky before us.

"Make a wish," Ricardo encourages.

Words whisper through my heart so quickly I almost miss them. *I want to feel safe.* The complete support I experienced as my body submerged underwater in Flores showed me what is possible. I long to embody that depth of security while here on earth, alive.

"What did you wish for?"

I frown at him. "It won't come true if I tell you, right?"

"That's birthday candles," he smiles, an expert on wishes. "I'll tell you mine if you tell me yours."

I am unaccustomed to sharing this kind of thing, but what do I have to lose? When I tell him, his extended pause makes me wonder if I should have kept it to myself. "Hey, you said you'd tell me yours."

He is looking out to sea, but when he finally turns towards me he looks conflicted. I see heat in his eyes, and concern. "My wish was to kiss you."

He watches me, waiting for my reaction. I am holding as still as I possibly can while all the blood in my body rushes south, my every muscle tensing as if I am readying to launch myself at him.

"But I want you to feel safe." He leans closer to me on his elbow, his warm breath against my ear, "Do you feel safe with me?"

Yes.

Instantly I chide myself; I barely know him. And no, I have not been feeling the least bit safe around him, swinging from wild excitement, to insecurity, and back again. How has he managed to immerse himself deeper under my skin in just three days, than Jorge did in as many years?

"I…" Flustered, I can't find the words. "I'm afraid of you," I confess, releasing some tension that's gripped me. "But it's really a matter of me feeling safe with myself."

"Good answer," he says as his fingertips slowly, exquisitely, journey from my temple to the rise of my cheek, his gaze never once leaving me. I swear every pore in my skin wakes up just to drink his caress.

He holds the side of my face in his palm, his touch somehow tender yet firm, inquisitive yet sure. The sensitivity of the moment moves me, pries open my armor, and a teardrop rolls from my eye straight into his fingertips. I'm not even sure why I am crying, but wish I wasn't. Jorge would be groaning at this point and hightailing it out of there.

"I never used to be such a crybaby."

"There are all kind of tears," Ricardo whispers, running his finger along the single wet stream on my cheek. "Tears of sadness or joy, tears of awakening…"

"Mine are all of those."

"Something cracked you open recently?"

"It's that obvious?"

"With eyes that can see." His fingertips trail from the plane of my face to my neck, and I'm certain his fingers have sensors reading everything about me. With a delicate, reverent touch, he repeatedly strokes my temples, making me feel like a treasure and I want to believe he means it.

I roll onto my side, a gesture of acceptance, and his hand drops to the space between us. *Kiss me*, I silently implore him, too afraid to close the final gap between us. Ricardo looks deeply into my eyes, before leaning forward and pressing his full lips to mine, leaving them there only a few beats before pulling back and caressing my face, my neck, my hair. His eyes are the deepest brown, flecked with glowing highlights, and they face me, unblinking, welcoming. He's either one smooth operator or the most genuine person I've ever met. Or both.

"What opened you up, Sirena? You can tell me."

Really? Already? "These pressures were building up in my life," I sigh. "They all fired off and erupted at the same time."

He takes my hand and squeezes gently. "Care to be more specific?"

His fingertips dust across the back of my hand and up my arm, his every contact with my skin dissolving my resistance. He strums the same spot from last night, the touch that sent me running, but tonight I run right into him, a torrent of words spilling out. Aside from Joko, I haven't had anyone to talk to since my life turned on its head, and once I get started, I don't stop. He listens attentively, constantly touching me — and he knows how to touch — as I share a fairly uncensored account of my life with Jorge, the bankruptcy of our relationship reflected in the financial strain, all the way to Rupert's aggression and the cinematography job in Flores. I stun myself with how much I tell him.

"While we were filming underwater I had what the medical world calls a heart attack, but I'd rather call it a heart experience. I stopped breathing, left my body and…" I trail off. It's overwhelmingly intimate to recount, even for myself. I look away.

"Did you float in the tunnel, into the light? Did you hear the chorus?"

My eyes dart to his, widening. How could he know that? Gazing into each other's eyes, we take in this new level of connection beyond the visible world and something in me exhales for the first time in his presence.

"I've been there, too." He cups my shoulder with his palm. "Please continue."

How much do I say? I have told him plenty, but haven't ventured into the darkest places. Having already behaved erratically, I don't want him to see me as an emotional basketcase, or worse, damaged goods.

"I was watching everything from above my body, saw the film crew trying to help. At the same time I could see my boyfriend — former boyfriend," I quickly amend, "in LA with a woman in our shower. And I saw something from my childhood, something traumatic." It is the first time I have spoken the words out loud and they sour in my mouth.

"Someone hurt you?"

"I was very young. I couldn't see the face of the person who was doing things to me, but I sense it was someone I knew well, touching me inappropriately."

His fingers return to my cheek and jawline with such empathy that I think I might start crying again. "It's hard to talk about. It's hard for me to even think about it."

"Thank you for telling me," he says with tenderness, near my ear and I find myself leaning into his touch, his breath.

"I was in a formless place. Not me the way I am now, but somehow more alive. I was happy to stay there, but I popped back into my body."

"I'm glad you did." His fingertips slowly glide from my shoulder down my arm. "When did that happen?"

I shrug. It feels like recent and ancient history at once. "Maybe a couple of weeks ago."

"Ahhh. You're a newborn." Ricardo caresses my forehead, my eyebrow, my eyelid, my cheek, and skims over my lips to my chin, thawing me further, liquifying me. He gives me a soft, sensual kiss, drawing my lower lip into his mouth. When he breaks away, I am breathless. "Welcome back to Planet Earth."

"Had I known you'd be the welcome committee I might have floated back sooner."

Now he kisses me in earnest, his tongue slipping into my mouth like hot silk. Is this really happening? He tastes like heaven, and as my tongue dances with his I understand why I have been on guard around him. He is totally intoxicating, and everything he does makes me want more. My head slants and I open further, but a moment later he leans back, lips raised in a half smile. Am I coming on too strong?

I focus on the ocean, trying to still the crash of my heart against my ribs. "Will you tell me your story?" I request, breaking the moment.

He pulls in a breath, and I can practically hear the thud as his shield comes down. "Let's save it for another time. It isn't pretty."

My shoulders hunch at his attempt at dodgeball. I just told him everything: death, betrayal and incest, and he's holding out on me because *his* story isn't pretty? "Seriously?"

Ricardo rolls onto his back, storm clouds shifting across his face. His arms fold under his head and, staring up at the sky, he sucks in a huge breath, sighing it out in one long, loud exhalation. Starting slowly until he gets rolling, he explains about growing up in the Dominican Republic with a habitually-drunken Hispanic father and young Jamaican mother, how his sailor dad had women in every port, and skipped out when he was young. His mom took another lover, ending up with two more kids to raise.

"My mom's big dream was to make it as a singer in America. She moved us to Brooklyn when I was twelve, but it didn't turn out like she hoped. We lived in a rough neighborhood, and I ran with some foolish and dangerous kids, got arrested, sent to juvie."

He peeks at me, determining how much to say. But he already told me that part, and I know there is much more. "Keep going."

He nods his agreement with the faintest hint of a grin. I think he likes it when I see through him. "This angel of a woman, covered in tattoos, came to teach us yoga. Darcy's a New Yorker through and through, bull dog on the outside, cream puff on the inside. She saw something in me, gave me a kind of attention no one had before then." He stretches his long arms above his body, muscles rippling. "She taught me real yoga, the philosophy, not just how to move my body."

He explains that William, Darcy's father, runs a prominent talent agency in New York City. When he got out of detention, William set him up with a photographer and head shots. Soon he started working as a model, bit jobs at first, eventually runways, all the way to international campaigns.

"I knew it." The words burst out of me. "You don't seem like an ordinary person."

He grimaces. "So what am I then? A cliché?"

When I start apologizing he laughs it off, and I realize he's teasing me.

"It happened fast. Connections, exposure, parties, more cash flowing than I'd had my whole life. William tried to mentor me, but I was just a kid, and aside from him and Darcy my only role models were street thugs and characters from television shows. I was in magazines, on billboards, flying around the world, but something inside of me didn't feel completely deserving." His face looks young, pained, and I rest my hand on the firm length of his pronounced bicep.

"You don't seem to feel unworthy any more."

"Well, not at the moment." He sends an erotic smile my way, but it fades into a serious wrinkle across his otherwise smooth brow. "At the height of my success I became a runaway train, and didn't know how to slow it down. There was always booze and dope at parties, in the bathroom wherever I would be working. I needed to find myself in the midst of the storm, but instead of meditating I went from pot and alcohol to cocaine, and then it got ugly. When I got addicted to coke, I crashed and burned fast. Lost everything I had built up. I got desperate and screwed over William, the person who had helped me so much."

He covers his eyes with his arm for an elongated moment, then brushes it across his forehead and turns to me with such openness my insides twist. "One night I was knocked down in a fight. I had to literally reach rock bottom — much of the blood in my body pouring onto the street, dead on arrival at the hospital — before I could turn things around."

I sit entranced as Ricardo describes hovering over his body just as I did. He was watching the medics work when he felt a fatherly presence. "I didn't know him, yet somehow I did. He was loving me deeply and directly like I'd always craved as a kid. That moment my whole relationship with myself turned around, and I knew I wasn't finished."

I stare at him in awe, convinced that nothing short of a miracle has led me to this man, on this beach, on this night, just weeks after my own experience.

"They shaved my head to stitch the wound, and I haven't cut my hair since. The hospital hooked me up with a twelve-step program. First I got sober, then I got clean by making reparations to every person in my life, especially William. It was painful, but he was gracious with me. Still, it took time to rebuild the trust." He sighs deeply. "Darcy brought me to Bali to assist with my first yoga retreat, and I keep coming back."

We lie side by side in silence. "Thanks for sharing that with me," I finally say.

"I'm sorry, Sirena. This is probably the worst date you've ever had."

Something inside me thrills at his words. This is a date. "Don't worry, I've had dates that would make your skin crawl. This isn't so bad."

I stroke the smooth, solid, caramel-colored muscle of his bicep all the way to the perfect arc of his forearm, enjoying the contrast of my olive skin against his, touching him as slowly and sensitively as he touched me.

This time I lean over and kiss him. His lips are full, full of magic that is, drawing me into a trance. My breasts press against his chest in a delicious contrast of hard and soft, until I sense him pulling back. This level of intimacy is stretching me to my edges, and my nervous system is hyper-sensitive due to all the recent commotion. I bottle up into protective mode instantly.

"I left something out," Ricardo says, face tensing.

Every muscle in my body freezes as my eyes dart between his, trying to read his closed expression. Already disappointment is sweeping through me. It was too good to be true, I knew that. He's married, or still struggling with his addictions. He's not interested in anything long-term. Bombs drop, one after another.

"I took a vow of celibacy when I went clean," he confesses, eyes downcast. "And I've managed to maintain it for five years."

The disappointment I felt a moment ago is nothing compared to the wave that crests and crashes through me now, quickly followed by a dash of anger. Why has he been kissing and touching me like this if he's celibate?

"I was addicted to sex as much as I was hooked on cocaine, he explains, reading the mixed emotions on my face. "I was using it like a drug, and hurting people."

I feel myself shift back from him slightly, my mind trying to grasp what he is saying. To think all this time I believed he was the local Don Juan, when in reality he's a monk. I feel used and misled, caught by an irrational desire to punch his beautiful face. It's great that he's found a healthy way to live, but how could he do this to me? Sure, I'm being unfair, but I can't help it.

"I'm sorry. I didn't really know how to tell you that part. I'm not proud of the way I used to be."

He goes to take my hand, but I pull it away. "Am I some kind of experiment?"

He thinks before he speaks, and I wait impatiently. "If you mean am I using you like a thermometer to test where I'm at, then no." He pauses, measuring my words and his. "I felt undeniably drawn to you from the first time I met you. I wanted to kiss you that day when I brushed the sand off your face," he admits, stopping to look at me, his eyes moving to my mouth. My lips part in response, but I purse them into obedience. "Everything sexual was tainted before, drug hazy. But I've gotten clean and clear. And now you're here. And I want to kiss you. So is that an experiment? I guess... sort of..."

When he rolls onto his side and drops his lips to mine, I meet him slowly, tenderly. I am still shocked by what he has said, and rocked by his implication that I am the first woman in five years to make him feel this way. Our breath mingles and soon the full stretch of his body is against mine. An instantaneous flood of sensation causes a gasp of pleasure to escape my mouth. I press my thighs together, heat rushing to my core which pulses like it has its own heartbeat. He is barely touching me and I am more turned on than I have ever been. I suppose he is somehow moving his energy through me, but I can barely comprehend breathing at this point, let alone energy fields. My head is turned off, my body turned on, and desire is rolling through my entire being.

"You're like music," Ricardo whispers into my ear, kissing my neck and humming against my throat with a thousand mind-numbing vibrations that oscillate through my entire body unlike anything I have ever felt. Are they orgasms? Heart-gasms? Oh, who cares. This is delicious.

We kiss sensually as we talk, without groping body parts or tearing off our clothes. We just stay there, truly with each other, not running away or towards anything, until the moon has set, early morning dew has fallen, and I am yawning.

Ricardo walks me across the empty hotel grounds. At the door of my hut, he lifts a long necklace from his chest and drapes the end over my head. We stand together, eyes locked, bound by a ring of small timber beads. "I've been praying with this mala for a long time. Keep my prayers around you." He removes the end from his neck and it comes to a rest between my breasts. "Will you see me again?"

I do my best not to snort. Is he blind to the effect he has on me? I don't have an Indonesian phone, but he takes my LA number and email, then gives me a final, scrumptious, spine-dissolving kiss.

Alone in my hut, I do a sleepy jig around the room, inhaling the intoxicating pine-forest scent of Ricardo on my skin. I feel alive. I haven't stayed up this late in ages, but as my head nestles into the pillow, I don't immediately fall asleep. I remember my parents taking me skiing as a child. After a day on the slopes, I would feel the motion of turning downhill around moguls even while in bed. Now as I stretch out to sleep, I still sense Ricardo's body beside mine, as if my every cell has a light switch in the on position. Is this what I was afraid of? I laugh at myself, drifting off to sleep.

I dream I am walking through a dense, moist, towering jungle. Drooping branches of elephant-ear leaves shift in the breeze, murmuring messages I can almost comprehend. Catching a glimpse of Ricardo up ahead, I run towards him, but foliage in my way causes me to stumble, losing sight of him.

I awaken covered with sweat, my hut baking in the midday heat. Still dog-tired, I turn on the fan and return to sleep, reentering the same slog through muddy footpaths of overgrown foliage searching for Ricardo. Dragging vines aside, I spy him in the distance encircled by seductively dancing women. His eyes meet mine. I let the branches fall back into a barrier between us, and dash away into the jungle. Ricardo calls my name, but I run harder. His powerful body tackles me and we tumble downward, endlessly it seems, landing in a hillock of feathers.

By the time I awaken it is mid-afternoon. I breathe deeply into my cotton top. A whiff of musk, pine needles, and tree bark lingers. Perhaps our night of pure magic on the beach wasn't a fantasy after all. Desire bubbles up like holy water from a deep aquifer and I sink back into the mattress. It might take months for Ricardo to decide to end his abstinence, if ever, and I don't have the right to rush him. Still, I have no idea how either of us will resist the magnetism, or whatever it is happening between us.

For the first time since my heart incident, I am hungry. I find Mila at the Crystal Bar, attempting to get Alit to create a custom smoothie for her. She asks for pineapple and mango blended with mint and spinach, and although I wrinkle my nose suspiciously at the unusual combination, request the same. So far, trying new things has been working out splendidly for me.

"Just wake up from a nap?" she asks with a silly mock yawn. She is such a natural beauty that her goofiness is surprising, and likable.

"Just woke up." I don't embellish. "How was your adventure?"

"We went to an awesome cave temple. But today I'm feeling a little funny." She places a tan hand over her belly.

"Oh no. Do you need anything?"

"Just coconut water, this green smoothie and some rest. How was yoga?" She chooses a table and pulls out a chair, stretching her long, shapely legs into the sun.

"It was lovely." I remain on my feet, focusing on a couple strolling down the beach. "The class was packed."

"I bet. Ricardo's a babe, isn't he?"

I shrug as if I have barely noticed, and thank Alit as he passes us the bright green concoctions. I wave goodbye and head back to my room, calling over my shoulder, "I have your yoga mat for you. Feel better."

The drink is delicious. As I walk away sipping, I feel a twinge of guilt for eluding Mila, but can't lie to her face, and the last thing I want is to fuel this tiny island's rumor mill.

Part of me — a big part — still refuses to believe Ricardo is for real. He could have any woman, so why me, and after so long? One thieving thought leads to another. Am I the canary sent into the mine of his celibacy to test for life? An easy exercise, before he takes on bigger game? Besides, isn't it too soon after leaving Jorge to start in with someone else? Shouldn't I be in mourning, or at least getting to know myself, before giving my heart to someone new? Thieves of insecurity be gone. Swinging gently in the hammock on my porch, I close my eyes and the ghost of Ricardo's fingers on my skin strokes the doubts into silence.

Needing a change of scenery, I bound into the ocean, leaping at each wave like a child at play, my first full entry into the sea since my heart incident. When I finally return to the hut, dripping and refreshed, I check my phone. No calls or email from Ricardo. Just like that the thieves return. I allowed myself to fall under his spell and now I want him. I toss my phone on the bed, cursing my naïveté.

I slip into the shower anyway, optimistically focusing on girlie grooming, shampooing twice, slathering on a deep conditioner, and scrubbing my skin with a sea salt exfoliant. Under the shower head I touch my arms tenderly, slowly, the way Ricardo did, finding — what do I call it? — that feeling of yum. Being alone isn't terrible; I can find pleasure in small moments, even if they are haunted by a pair of chocolate-brown eyes and luscious lips.

I towel off, shape my eyebrows and apply mascara, a first since arriving in Indonesia. A rose-scented lotion seeps into my pores as I rub it on my sun-drenched skin. Sifting through my suitcase, I choose a lacy black bra, matching boy-cut panties, a flowing claret skirt and a clingy little top. The combo suits my mood, and for the first time in ages, I feel attractive. Evaluating the end result in the full length mirror, I am surprised at how loose the skirt is over my hips, and spin in a circle, light enough to float away.

All dressed up with nowhere to go, I slump onto my bed and watch the approaching sunset through my window. The sight always fills me with a strange sense of happy-sad, and I try to breathe through the uncertainty that grows as the shadows lengthen.

Someone raps twice, strongly, at the door.

Is it him, or just Mila claiming her yoga mat? When I pull the door open, I am faced with my lion, his crown of dreads backlit in a blaze of golden light. He is wearing loose pants of nubby natural silk, a long tunic, and a look of expectation. His elegant sexiness slays me and instantly I am mere mush. Without words or hesitation, he scoops me up, one arm around my waist, one hand holding my neck, thumb along my jaw. This is not the soft or tender kisses of last night. This one burns with need, with unapologetic, erotic fire. His tongue seeks mine and I am defenseless, unable to control my hips as they surge into him, or my hands as they run up the strong cords of his back to explore with a mind of their own. After a few moments we are breathless.

"Miss me?" he smirks.

"I hoped you'd come over." I deplore the neediness in my voice, and know he's detected it when his expression falls.

"I'm sorry I didn't call. I thought I'd surprise you. All I've been doing is getting ready for you, and I wanted..."

I silence him once more with my lips, my gratitude at his understanding this thing I do, doubting myself, too great to express aloud. "You don't need to apologize," I finally murmur.

He holds me at arm's length. "You look radiant. Wanna come with me, see what I've been preparing?"

I take a deep breath and blow it out, staggered by his presence.

"I'll take that as a yes," and he leads me out the door, hand in hand.

We pass through the restaurant to enter the parking lot. Mila is still near the bar, playing a card game with another guest. She catches my eye as we pass through and the cards fall from her hand. When she mouths 'wow' and pretends to do a slow clap, I laugh, even as my blush spreads all the way to the tips of my toes. This cat's out of the bag.

Ricardo sits astride his motorbike and tells me to hop on, patting the seat behind him. Unsure how close to sit and where to put my hands, I keep space between us and grip the metal handle behind the seat.

He reaches a muscled arm around me, drawing me tightly against his body. "Don't get shy on me."

In the final, slanting rays of sunlight, we speed along the dusty road to his house, my hands linked tightly around his torso, hyper-aware of every point of contact between us, my thighs against his, my breasts pressed into his strong back.

Soft lights illuminate a footpath made of stone slabs set into manicured grass. When we get closer I see the glow emanates from candlelight diffused by translucent cylinders of banana fiber held in place with toothpick-fine wooden slivers. Did he roll and place each one?

I follow him across flat boulders forming a walkway through a pond, past towering pink lotuses and persimmon flashes of koi fish darting through the shallows, to a wide and breezy veranda. Stepping inside the house, enchanted yet on alert, my eyes shift around the airy, high-ceilinged, sparsely-furnished space taking everything in. He watches me closely. Sexy lounge tracks are playing softly in the background. A cluster of various sized candles shines on a low wooden table, with colorful cushions stacked on each side and two place settings.

"I made us dinner," Ricardo announces.

I smile and sink onto the cushions as he moves off to the kitchen, returning with a ceramic platter of food and a large, tamarind-wood bowl.

"Such vibrant colors. What is it?"

"Raw Asian lasagna and Chinese vegetable salad."

I seem to draw men who cook lasagna. "Raw lasagna?"

He disregards the quizzical squinting of my eyes and dishes us both up platefuls of his culinary creation. "I spent time in San Diego with my mom's cousin while I was cleaning up my act, using food as medicine to repair some of the damage I'd done to myself."

A bit of salad falls off the serving spoon and he scoops it up with his fingers, popping it in his mouth casually, as if we ate together every day. This small action stirs another level of relaxation within me, as he somehow becomes more familiar.

"I took classes at a rockin' spiritual center there. Those folks are living the love day by day you and I had to jump out of our bodies to find."

"I live in LA. You mean it was just down the road all along?"

He arranges the food on my plate, framing the lasagna with a salad of shredded napa cabbage, carrots and herbs I am yet to recognize, placing each spoonful thoughtfully.

"I read a quote once about God speaking to one man with a shout and another with a whisper. We get the message when we can hear it, the way we can hear it."

When he has scooped himself up a plate — albeit with slightly less consideration — I take a bite, savoring the explosion of flavors, and murmuring in appreciation.

"I think God is singing to my taste buds. This is the best food I've had since..." I'm about to say Jorge's lasagna, but stop myself. This is far better than that, for reasons that surpass flavor alone. "Since ever."

He drops his chin with a humble grin, explaining how he uses a mandoline to slice daikon radish into noodles, and soaked sunflower seeds blended with Indonesian spices, fresh turmeric and ginger become the filling. He offers me seconds and although it's delicious, this is a dense meal compared to my coconut regimen. I watch him eat another huge plateful with gusto and tease him about his appetite, my toes poking his under the table. Even that simple contact stops the food halfway to his mouth, and when he drops his fork and places both hands on the table, I feel as if I have just provoked a wildcat someone has foolishly released from its cage. When he springs around the table and pins me down I shriek, dissolving into giggles as he straddles me, a forkful of lasagna hovering against my lips until I cave and take another bite. He growls when my mouth accepts the food, and just like that, everything changes.

Up close I absorb every feature of his face; his large, expressive, melted-chocolate eyes looking right through me, thick eyebrows, prominent cheekbones. My eyes trail down the strong line of his chiseled jaw, finding the faintest shadow of a goatee framing those two lush, kissable lips. I like how small I feel beneath his powerful form, yet that anticipation is exactly what undoes me. I am jittery, an army of ants crawling over and under my skin, the electricity dissolving me, liquifying me, and I give in to it as best I can. A tiny smile curls at the edge of his mouth and his eyelids grow heavy as he dips closer. My breath becomes shallow, my nose drinking in his woodsy scent of essential oils and something essentially Ricardo that transports me to a cool, old-growth forest. His large frame surrounds me, his hand shimmering down my ribs, lips brushing my forehead, hot breath on my skin, inhaling me, possessing me. My body responds, pulsing a rhythm that radiates heat from between my thighs. Somehow, with his animal instinct, I sense he knows this. Our bodies seem to speak a common dialect and the sensations are building with increasing intensity, tremors vibrating through both of us like a tuning fork, and we aren't even doing much more than breathing one another in.

"Sirena, you're changing my whole world."

That is when he does the most surprising thing. Ricardo rocks back onto his heels, bows his head in a manner that seems almost ceremonial, and asks me to cut off his dreadlocks.

"But they're beautiful," I protest. "You're beautiful with them." Why would he ask such a thing?

He is looking at me with such earnestness, with more naked candor than I have ever experienced. "Sirenita, I want to make love with you."

I lie there, speechless. Obviously all this deep breathing and heated staring could only end up with us in the bedroom, but what does that have to do with me as his barber?

"I started growing my locks when I got clean," he explains, taking my hands. "They're my transformers. They grew long because I've been channeling all my unused sexual energy into them, learning much about myself in the process. But they've served their purpose. I had a dream that a lioness would come into my life and cut them off. Soon as I saw you, I knew you were the one. You were even wearing a lion on your shirt."

What I used to trust as the floor beneath me is now spinning, the earth fallen from its axis. I guess I comprehend it, sort of, the lions connecting us through the dreamtime. Instead of sharing how profoundly honored and moved I am by his words, I just gape at him.

Ricardo disappears into another room and returns with a pair of scissors. I'm almost expecting a sword or saber; plastic-handled shears don't seem special enough for what is to come. He deserves something more regal. I get the cushions from around the table, stacking them in the center of the room. Finding a basket near the couch, I place it beside his feet and form a circle of candles around him.

Ricardo sits cross-legged, elegant, courageous and vulnerable, his back ramrod-straight. I have never seen anything like it. Stepping inside the circle, I kneel beside him, shaky, timorous from the level of intimacy and responsibility. I untie the knot of his hair, and see the full length of his dreadlocks for the first time. The last time.

I caress the soft cords, saying goodbye, and look into his eyes.

"Are you sure?"

He nods.

Holding one rope from near his tall, proud forehead, I kiss it, thanking it for the work it has done, snip it close to the scalp, and place it in the basket. I do the same for every lock until they sit like a precious sacrifice at his feet.

"I didn't think it was possible, but you look even more handsome."

His eyes sizzle in response, burning through me, tongue wetting his full lower lip. My fingers run across his scalp and I trim any uneven bits they discover until he has only a close-cropped cover of hair. Setting down the scissors, I kneel before him, unsure of what comes next. He draws me onto his lap facing him, a startlingly open position, my skirt hitched up to my thighs, my entire lower half throbbing. I rub his newly-shorn head and his body shudders in response, something thunderous and fiery reverberating between us. When I dare look into his eyes, he locks me into his dark gaze and our breathing deepens, synchronizes. His hands grip my hips, anchoring me to his hard, muscled torso as he rises smoothly to his feet. I think we're headed into the bedroom, but he passes that door and continues to another.

We enter a partially open-air bathroom with its own tropical garden, votives glimmering along the periphery. Delicately he sets me on a teak bench beside a tub hewn from one enormous piece of natural stone, rough and raw on the outside, smoothly polished within, and big enough for two. Reaching across me, he turns on the faucet. On the bath's ledge, beside another grouping of candles, is a plate of chocolates. He has thought this through.

"Sirenita, my lioness, welcome to my world."

With that he pulls the tunic over his head and the sight of all that toned flesh, strong and tender at once, sends another heatwave through me. My fingertips are hungry to touch him, but I don't dare move or utter a sound, silently gripping the edge of the bench. Without hesitation he tugs the drawstring of his pants and they drop to the ground, revealing a pair of gray, stretch-cotton boxer shorts, tight around his muscled thighs with a sharply-defined ridge curving up to his stomach. He pulls off the boxers in one slick motion, and stands there before me in that same elegant, courageous way, nothing to hide. I can't help it... my eyes just go there of their own accord. I am seeing his penis for the first time, and he's watching me look at it. Oh my. What was that theory in physics about anything observed being affected by the observer? His cock seems to thicken, tall and proud as he is, as I stare, hypnotized. Hands down, he is the most erotic thing I have ever seen. His eyes are on me, they don't leave me for a second, following my every reaction, a slight smile appearing on his lips, exuding confidence and raw sexuality.

"I guess we don't need to be concerned about you suffering the same fate as Samson," I say, thinking of the biblical figure whose locks and strength fell prey to Delilah. "I'm getting the impression your power comes from elsewhere..."

"You need to catch up with me," he says, taking slow, purposeful steps closer. I wait as he reverently lifts my top from my belly, then higher to reveal my bra, and over my head. I do not have the confidence about my body that he has about his, and of course he knows this, too. Thank goodness I had the foresight to pack black lace undergarments for a work trip. He crouches to remove my skirt and slowly drags it down, fingertips reverently grazing every millimeter of hip and thigh, calf and ankle. He strokes the outlines of my underwear, and although I am nervous, his touch is mesmerizing, fingertips drawing up my sides until he stands again.

"I love your curves," he says as if divulging a secret, palms tracing over my hips and down my thighs. "Your little waist and this round part here," he emphasizes by grabbing my ample ass firmly, and a deep, guttural sound emerges outward from his chest that is pure want and need in a single note. His fingers comb through my hair and glide a trail from my neck to my shoulders, strumming my collarbone, and finally coming to rest on my heart. I feel wanted, honored, and cherished with each caress. An unfamiliar relief unwinds the clenching in my muscles and I realize I am experiencing a small taste of the confidence he embodies every hour of every day. Something wonderful happens to my insecurity; it vanishes.

Ricardo ever so slowly pulls down one bra strap, then the other, his careful attention making the smallest movement tantalizing. *"Mi tesoro,"* he whispers, lifting my breasts over the top of the cups, holding the weight of them in his palms as if cupping a treasure, pulsing them, spending time on each as if they alone fulfill his desire. Tossing the bra to the floor, his fingers circle lightly, then pull more firmly without letting go, until my nipples point outward and a muffled moan pours from my mouth. I am already lightheaded when he reaches for my underwear. Slowly he drags the lace over the curve of my bottom, leaving it suspended at the top of my thighs, and caresses the two roundest places before letting his fingers drift towards the cleft, barely pulling apart. I can't help but gasp. He places a gentle kiss between my shoulder and throat, removes my panties, and leads me to the bath.

Entering the water for a cool-down phase at opposite ends of the tub, I realize Ricardo likes to fire things up, step back, then fan the embers into flames again. Unlike the instant gratification I'm used to, he leaves me groaning with a pang of impatience while at the same time intriguing me, not knowing what he will do next. What he does is splash me. I splash him back.

"Not on the chocolate," he reprimands, setting the plate on a window ledge and sending a tidal wave my way, laughing at my outraged spluttering.

I am about to seek retribution when he reaches for a piece of chocolate and places it in my mouth. I let the bittersweet richness of his peace offering melt against my tongue and lean towards him on my knees, nipping lightly at his lower lip before allowing him to taste me. He wraps an arm around my shoulder, drawing my body in against his, and the kiss extends. My hand finds the nape of his neck as his mouth moves to my cheek, then laps my earlobe, his erection pressing against my hip, lightning-rod hard. My hand strays there of its own accord, holding him, and his abdomen clenches instantly.

With that small movement my own body tightens and when our eyes meet I sense him struggling to hold back.

He kisses me while rolling away, steps out of the tub, and reaches for my hand to pull me out. We wrap up in fluffy towels and he leads me into his bedroom. It's the moment of truth and I start to clam up. I don't want to, but I just do. My body has been responding to his every move, but my fretful mind has its own agenda. Ricardo reads the subtle shift immediately and gently draws me onto his bed, stretching out beside me.

"What is it? Tell me," he breathes soothingly into my ear.

"We haven't done the practical things people are supposed to do, like getting blood tests and buying condoms." I doubt after five years of celibacy he has a stash beside the bed, but it's actually the unarticulated concerns bubbling underneath that are troubling me.

He strokes my arm all the way to my hand and his fingers clasp mine. "That's true. But I had all manner of tests when I got clean and I haven't been with anyone since. You just came from the hospital, and I know how they love to draw blood. Are you worried about birth control? Are you using any?"

I grimace like a teenager caught breaking the rules. "I have a cervical cap, but I didn't bring it to Indonesia." The truth is I hate it. "I mostly used condoms, but I don't have those either." Gloom is seeping in, familiar as an old shirt, but more restrictive than ever because I hoped I was finally free of it.

"Holding and kissing you is more than enough for me," he says lightly. "But I want you to know I'm not afraid. I trust the signs and symbols as they show up in my life. You're my lioness," he purrs in my ear.

Ricardo doesn't get irritated with me like Jorge would when my fear arose. Instead he offers slow, reassuring kisses that begin loosening my contraction. We are lying on our sides, facing each other, legs and arms entwined. He is hard against my belly and my reserve is melting. I drape my leg across his, opening to him, and then I see it. How could I have missed it? Where his right leg and hip meet is a tattoo of a lion's head, the mane radiating outward. It is my shell arrangement on smooth, brown skin. No wonder he stopped to study it.

Tears pool in my eyes and it is as if I am underwater, or soaring through the tunnel toward the light, the air around us rarified. I have heard this before, this subterranean rumble of drums. A soulful song is playing from Ricardo's speakers, but this beat comes from somewhere intangible, loaded with significance.

I tell Ricardo about my dream from hunted prey to the lion's embrace. He pulls our already flush bodies even tighter together, voice filled with awe. "You see, you dreamed it, too. You're my lioness and I'm your lion. That's the way it is."

I nod, wondering why I didn't tell him earlier. Something in me had whispered to hold back, to wait and see if our insane chemistry was just fanciful, my imagination twisting reality to fill the empty spaces. Now I can no longer ignore the signs. This man, flawed in his own beautifully perfect way, came to me for a reason. Everything, every betrayal and heartache, heart attack and heart opening, led to this moment. There is nothing left to do, not one single possibility, but to surrender.

Ricardo rises on his knees and parts my legs. Placing his palm against me he asks, "Lioness, I give myself to you. Will you give yourself to me?"

At first I nod, but from the tilt of his head I understand he wants to hear my confirmation spoken aloud. "Yes," I whisper, but suddenly the simple word carries the weight of an oath.

He slips a finger between my folds and glides across my clitoris in slow upstrokes. A low moan breaks from my throat and my knees fall open, but the only thing I want right now is him inside of me, as deeply connected as possible.

"Now," I insist softly.

He lowers himself over me and, looking into each other's eyes, our hips tilt until his warm, broad head is pressing at my entrance. And there it is, the first moment of entry, the moment when time stands still, the moment so full of poetry and potency that nothing else matters, our two bodies merging like voices in a single song.

He barely enters me, slowly in, partially out, getting to know me in this way, letting me get to know him. We have each other's total attention. Eyes locked, mouths falling open, he drives deeper, then deeper still, what's left of my resistance dissolving with each long stroke lapping within me like the tide at the shore. My very cells are embracing him, healing him, just as each slow thrust is recognizing me, honoring me, healing me. I know it as I know my own heartbeat gives me life.

Gentle movements grow stronger, his muscles flexing, mine melting, our eyes sharing every note of sensation. He unleashes a primal sound, spreading me wider, filling me, surrounding me, stretching me to my limit. I feel the weight of his pent up need like charges detonating, inciting me so I can't hold back any longer, my back arching and my fingers gripping his thighs. Without a thought in my head, only pure, undiluted, unrestrained desire coursing through me like a rushing river, I give way. It's as if a doorway flies open, the walls shove back and disintegrate, and a thousand clenched petals unfurl while one delicious stroke after another overtakes me. I hear a sound and realize my own voice is singing out the intensity radiating through my entire body. I surrender into the sensations, into the safety, into the beauty, until the room is bathed in light, endless waves of pleasure are rolling through me, extended notes like a song are emerging from my mouth, I am visibly vibrating, and I can't tell where my body ends and Ricardo begins. Even when the tremors recede, every part of me is still tingling.

I open my eyes and find him watching me, face aglow with a sheen of sweat. "You're remarkable," he breathes.

"That... was..." I blow air through my lips, lost for words. Glancing around the bed, everything looks different, as if the focus of my lens just sharpened. My hips shift slightly, unconsciously seeking more of the deliciousness, and discover he is still hard inside me. "Saving for a rainy day?"

"I've been practicing containment," he smiles, ever the master of control, "but you put me to the test."

"I couldn't contain a thing. You blew my mind." I can't even think, which is probably a good thing. Laughter ripples through me. "Is it bad that I want to blow your containment to smithereens?"

"You almost have," he says seriously, though there is a twinkle in his eye. "Besides, I can have orgasms without ejaculating." As if to prove his point he rocks his pelvis into me and my body pulsates in response.

"Of the mind blowing variety?"

"Let's find out."

With one swift motion he rolls me on top of him. I know it's politically correct for me to like this position, but it hasn't always been my favorite. Yet when Ricardo props a pillow behind his shoulders the angle shifts, sending me right back into the swirling tide pool of pleasure. Resting my palms on his expanse of smooth, toned chest, I ride the escalating waves while his curious hands explore everything within reach. Palming my breasts. Twisting my nipples. Squeezing my ass. Pulling me open wider. He plays me like an instrument, building up to a crescendo, getting caught in the whirlpool himself. His eyelids sinking heavy. Chest heaving. Muscles straining. Lips moving in a mantra I can't understand, some mix of Spanish and English and something else half-man, half-growl. The delicious tension climbs higher, rumbling like an earthquake. As I tumble down the other side in extended release, Ricardo's pecs tighten under my palms and every single one of his sweaty, perfectly-defined muscles follow in a chain reaction, his thighs clenching beneath mine, fingers gripping tighter, even his toes flex and seize. Abruptly he holds completely still, not even breathing, until he throws his head back and exhales a low, guttural cry, throbbing inside of me.

"*Alucinante,*" he exhales, eyes wide. "Mind blowing."

If he's surprised, then I'm stunned. "I think the sex of my past must have been half asleep, zombified." Suddenly that admission seems too honest, too exposed, and I pull myself off his body. I'm sure he experienced plenty of incredible sex; that kind of performance takes practice. Years of practice.

"If you were a zombie, I was a vampire," he says, fingernails lightly running down my naked back.

I'm starting to get up to go to the bathroom when he springs on me, pushing my belly to the bed, teeth pressed to the nape of my neck. I wrestle under his weight, but he has me pinned, thighs holding me in place, hands gripping my wrists above my head. His dominating prowess arouses me and while my bottom arches into his groin with a will of its own, my knee-jerk reaction is fear.

"Let me go," I say in a voice shrill with panic.

He loosens his grip, but keeps his hands where they are, fingers caressing my wrists. Easing his weight off, he slides beside me, pressing taut against me. "I was just playing. I didn't mean to scare you."

"I know." I twist away, pulling further into myself. After blasting wide open, doubt and trepidation creep back in, and my trapdoor slams shut. I have jumped into bed with a man I barely know and traveled with him to far reaches of the galaxy. How do I know I can trust him when I've been hurt by people much closer and more familiar?

"Please don't," he says, fingers reaching for my back. "Don't pull away."

"Sorry," I look up over my shoulder, "it's just... we don't really know each other and this is happening so fast." The twang of discomfort sharp, I sit up and pull my knees to my chest. "It's getting late. Do you think you could take me back to my room?"

I may as well have punched him in the gut. We were traveling beyond the speed of light and I have thrown the spaceship into reverse. His face tightens, crestfallen. "Think we might get better acquainted with you at your hotel? 'Cause I had the distinct impression we were getting to know each other right here."

"I have some things I need to do in the morning." The words are hollow, and I can't even look at him as I say them. He has shown me such kindness and vulnerability that I feel terrible for failing to do the same. It would be better to say what I really mean, but I don't dare. I am thrilled and astonished by what has transpired between us, but I need time alone to integrate the enormity of it. He touches me as if the meaning of the universe might be found beneath my skin, holds me as if he never wants to let me go. I can't help wondering if he isn't just making me his next addiction. What happens when he needs to give me up cold turkey? His urgency hums through his pores, his years of loneliness in each tug to keep me close, but I am coming from an opposite set of circumstances.

He takes a few moments to read everything woven through my excuse and is sharp enough to see the truth. "Okay. You need some time alone, right?"

I cover my eyes with my hands for a moment, embarrassed, lifting the hair off my forehead. I only just died and came back again. I only just broke up with Jorge. I only just had the most amazing sex of my life. "This is a lot for me to absorb."

He doesn't try to convince me. We dress, he drives me to Crystal Beach and walks me to my hut. Outside the door he asks, "When do I get to see you again?" When I don't answer right away he follows with, "Breakfast? Lunch?" I make a funny, exasperated face and he laughs. "How 'bout this, I'll come by in the late afternoon and take you to my favorite lookout point for the sunset?"

"Deal."

As he walks away I shake my head and wonder how I've come to find myself negotiating with a man like Ricardo. I should be on my knees begging him to stay.

Inside my hut I watch myself in the mirror while getting ready for bed. Something has changed. Moving close to my image in the glass, I stare into my own jade eyes. Light is pouring out of them, visible even in the darkness. For the rest of my life I want to do whatever it takes to keep them that way.

In the morning I wander along the water's edge. Scrambling over rock formations, I discover an isolated strip of beach. Sitting near the water I close my eyes, attempting to clear my mind, but my body won't settle. Instead I stand, toes in the sand, eyes shut, hips swaying like the tickling breeze. Soon my mind stills. Rocking to the subtle beating of an internal drum, my pelvis continues revolving while my wrists decide to swish gently back and forth. Eventually my arms rise, dancing fingers articulating an unspoken language. I cannot define exactly what is happening, but know it is meaningful. In allowing the authentic movements my body wants to express, I am beginning to know myself anew. Then from my center rises a sound at once a cry, a scream, and a song too long held within. My body is mine, the inner voice tells me. I reclaim it.

With a serious Ricardo hangover, I spend the rest of the morning rocking in the porch hammock, reeling internally, my psyche struggling to digest the apparent contradictions. He seems like a playboy, but he's been celibate. He's teaching yoga on a remote island, but he's a fashion model in New York City. He could be with anyone, but he's with me. He scares me so much I shake in my flip flops, and he has opened me to brand new doorways of pleasure.

I felt I had to get away, but even on my own I can't stop thinking about him. How could I focus on anything else? That was the most exhilarating sex I have ever had, and I can still feel him inside my body. No one before now has paid that kind of close attention to me. Equally, I have never allowed myself to be seen to that degree. Something else fascinates me, what Ricardo called the signs and symbols. How is it that the dream lions have charged into our lives?

I feel both safe and wildly vulnerable with Ricardo. The arousal rocks me, spins me out of control, and I can't wait for more. I stretch one leg over the side of the hammock, wrestling with myself, fidgety with anticipation.

Later I walk through the humble nearby village with my camera. Beyond a long, concrete wall bearing the words *room for rent* hand painted in bright blue, I happen upon my beach gang squatting at the entrance of their family compound, playing with sticks. Wordlessly I ask their permission to take a photograph and laugh as they strike stiff poses. It doesn't take long for them to revert to being their natural, goofy selves, leaping around and leaning against each other, faces open and without guile.

The children invite me through the gate where several simple, rectangular, concrete-brick rooms house an extended family. From the back of the property a bare-breasted elderly woman approaches carrying a wide basket on her head, unconcerned by my presence. She sets her load down and spreads its contents on a tarp to dry in the sun. The tan-colored, tuberous seaweed smells of saltwater and wet dog.

A pierced and tattoo-covered man in his twenties, emerging from one of the rooms smoking a cigarette, introduces himself as Wayan, the boys' uncle. In English he tells me the children want me to show him my photographs. "You are good with the camera," he acknowledges, looking into the preview screen.

I share my cinematography background, and Wayan informs me he has a small boat for guiding scuba trips. The boys watch contentedly while we compare diving experiences.

"Is it okay for me to photograph your grandmother?"

He makes my request to the elderly woman, and she responds with a toothless laugh. "She says she is not beautiful, but it is up to you."

"Tell her I think she is very beautiful."

The grandmother stands stock still as the boys cling to her sides. Every crease in her skin seems to tell a story. After taking group portraits, I manage to catch closeups of her marvelously wrinkled hands and face like a topographical map. Dipping to my knees, I capture the pattern of the worn sarong tied around her waist. The boys pull me away to cover a mock boxing match with Wayan as he humors them under the blistering sun. Sweat streaming down my face, I say goodbye and retreat to my hut to cool down.

Arriving at Crystal Beach, Mila waves to me poolside. The relentless sun backlighting her statuesque body transforms her into a Viking goddess. I snap a photo of her striking silhouette, one long arm extending skyward.

When I am satisfied with the photo, she crosses her arms and refuses to mince words. "So you've stolen Ricardo. What's going on with you two?"

"Nothing much," I downplay, smiling self-consciously, aware the light bursting from my eyes gives me away.

"Oh, I bet. Sorry, but I'm drooling." We laugh together, although I catch the disappointment flickering through her expression.

"I'd like to return your yoga mat."

"Do you want to meet me at my room? I need a break from the sun… and I have something else you might want to borrow."

The air conditioner hums above our heads as we lounge together on Mila's bed. I tell her about last night, avoiding details, concluding that Ricardo is coming back for me again this evening.

"Hmmm…," she offers with a suggestively raised eyebrow, and walks to her open closet. When she whips around she is holding a slip of gossamer black fabric at her hips. It has a slit up the side and looks almost liquid against her skin.

"This will cling in all the right places."

"No way," I gasp.

She rolls her eyes. "I wear it as a skirt, but you're shorter than me, and tiny. I think it will work on you as a dress."

I hold it up to my chest. "But the slit comes right to the top of my thigh." My eyes widen in dismay.

"Exactly," she smiles.

I agree to take the shred of fabric, secretly planning to ditch it in my room. Mila stretches her long body across her bed, and as I settle back against the headboard she describes her acupuncture practice in

Amsterdam. She frequently works with pregnant women and those trying to conceive, "probably because I crave a baby so badly."

I explain my film background, my focus on building my career rather than raising a family, and the recent break up with Jorge.

"Congratulations on the upgrade," Mila says.

I sense she'd like to talk more, but I need time to myself before Ricardo arrives. The mere thought of seeing him again sends an electric buzz through my veins as if I have chugged a liter of coffee. Mila thrusts the skirt-slash-dress at me and I pick up my camera, pausing to show her the photo I captured. She stares at the image, mouth pressed in thought.

"That's the first photograph of myself I've liked in a long time."

"You look like a goddess. I'll send it to you."

Back in my room I review the photographs I took during the day, realizing a photo essay is emerging. Inspired, I decide to give Gregor a quick call until I compute the time and realize it's the middle of the night in LA. Oh well. I am pleased with my newfound willingness to call him and even more with my nonchalance if I don't. By default I send him a casual email without mentioning anything about Flores, and discover an unread message from Mom. It's one of her usual family updates: my brother's clan is on a ski vacation; my parents are driving to Palm Springs for one of their periodic weekends with Uncle Carson and Aunt Libby, the men attending a gun show while the women luxuriate at the spa. I reply with my customary sarcasm about Dad's gun collection, blatantly dodging mention of my split with Jorge or meeting Ricardo. That requires a conversation.

Heaven knows how I will explain this to my family. Our lives run in a parallel but separate universe, always have. Dad never approved of Jorge, but he'll take my breakup followed by a quick hookup as a sign I've gone mad. That is actually a strong possibility. I have jumped into bed with a relative stranger and allowed myself to fall for him in ways I am not ready to admit. Strangely, I feel Ricardo already understands me better than those who have known me my entire life. More curious still, it seems we have known each other forever, although we just met.

I fold up my computer and move to the shower to wash my hair, giving it time to dry in the tropical humidity. Next I fill the room with music and, dancing to salsa, face the sad reality of my undergarments. I try on a few stretched-out items and reject them, finally settling for a leopard-print thong with brown lace which has seen better days. I forego the bra, and decide Mila's skirt-dress is better than the alternative: the hotel sarong and a tank top. It falls down my body like a little black negligee, and I dress it up by adding a delicate moonstone and gold necklace with dangling pearl earrings. After a quick shimmy in front of the mirror, taking in the total effect, I let out some silent screams, running in place at madcap speed to release my mounting anticipation. A dab of makeup and perfume leaves me ready with a full twenty minutes to go. What on earth was I thinking when I tried to delay our date? I can barely keep myself from breaking through the wall and jogging to his house.

Minutes drag like hours. When I stray to the door, I hear the soft lilt of Mila's accent somewhere in the distance. Beyond the palms and hedges, I spot her lounging in display beside the pool, back arched, one long leg extended atop her knee. She is everything I am not: tall, blonde, voluptuous, gregarious, overt. My muscles tense and I hold my breath, hoping it is not Ricardo in her sights, but there he is, standing on the path, chatting with her from behind a line of shrubs. I try not to prickle at the sight, and fail. When he waves goodbye and strides towards my room, I softly close the door.

His footsteps fall on the wooden porch, and my body tingles in his proximity. He knocks twice, and I pause a moment, catching my breath before opening the door. Devastatingly handsome, his worn jeans grip his slender waist, his caramel skin glowing against the open, white mandarin collar. I get the sense we are trying to read each other, and I force a smile at Mila when I see her over his shoulder, watching us.

"Would you like to come in?" my voice creaks, revealing how awkward I feel.

I stumble back from the doorway, and he takes a few steps into the room, directly towards me. He seems nervous too, saying only, "Sirena..." as he draws me into his embrace. My nostrils fill with the stimulating earthy-fresh scent of him, making my head spin, and I tremble noticeably in his arms, trying to contain the flash flood washing through me. He stays with the hug, probably the longest hug on record, holding his ground, holding me close, until we both relax. The hug is a warm bath seeping down like water into thirsty soil. Our bodies melt into each other, and my muscles soften as our breathing harmonizes. All I wanted was to be this close to him.

"I missed you," he breathes. "Let's go catch the sunset."

We drive only a short distance before Ricardo parks the motorbike beside a small roadside stand. "I thought we'd grab a few things to take with us," he explains, dismounting the bike.

Rustic baskets hold a variety of tropical fruits on the back of a pickup truck. Ricardo lifts a bundle of round, bright-red fruits still on their branches and holds them over his head, making a silly face. "Rambutan. Hairy fruit."

"You can wear them as a wig now that you've cut off your locks," I tease.

He leans in close to my ear. "You cut them off, as I recall," he says as if accusing me of stripping his clothing in public.

I am pretending to punch him when someone calls his name. Two scantily-clad young women sharing a motorbike have pulled up on the opposite side of the road. They seem to be waiting for him to approach, and when he doesn't they saunter to where we are. It unhinges me how these yoga girls stick to him like fly paper, and I wander off, suddenly fascinated by a pile of large, fragrant mangos. Out of my peripheral vision I catch him hugging them both as they question him about his new hair style, voices high with enthusiasm.

Irritated, I step farther away from the truck, a ripe mango pressed to my nose, inhaling the sweet scent, criticizing myself for my petty jealousies. Ricardo has not given me any reason to doubt him; in fact, he's the definition of consideration.

Nearby a dog snarls, and I stop in my tracks as the mangy creature emerges from under the truck, baring its teeth. Images of the rabies warnings at the airport in Denpasar flash through my mind and the mango falls from my hand, splattering against the asphalt. The dog tenses, but before it can lunge a barrier of white cotton and warm flesh slips in front of me. Ricardo's hand grips a rock and when he feigns throwing it, the dog slinks away.

I should feel relieved and protected. I don't. "I can handle a grumpy old dog," I say, crossing my arms and failing to sugarcoat my tone.

One dark eyebrow arched, he dishes it right back at me. "If the dog's no problem, why are you rattled by a couple of girls?"

My mouth pops open in surprise. It's the first time he's said anything less than how perfect I am, and annoyingly, he's right. The grin splits across my face before I can hide it. "I might be scared of how well you read me."

"Like a book, Sirenita," he smirks, pulling me into his arms.

His friends drive off as we purchase a kilo each of hairy rambutan and hard-skinned mangosteen the color of eggplants, covering the cost of the ruined mango already carried off in the jaws of my would-be attacker. Apparently the mutt has a sweet tooth.

Soon we leave the narrow paved road behind and turn onto a dirt single track meandering uphill. After a few abrupt switchbacks and the occasional grave-sized pothole, the path ends at a promontory atop a barren hill. Below us the sweeping curve of the coastline sparkles in the low-hanging sun.

Ricardo spreads a sarong across the weeds. We sit side by side, and he demonstrates how to open mangosteens by pressing the woody part at the bottom with his thumbs. He places the delicate, creamy, sweetly-tart sections in my mouth, explaining the cultural significance of this queen of fruit, a local treasure surpassed only by the stinky, spiky durian. When he describes the flavor of the durian as a blend of vanilla custard, caramel, onions and gym socks, I am not sorry it happens to be out of season. As he talks, he undresses me with his eyes, aided by the revealing slit in Mila's dress, and the longer we are alone, the harder it is to keep my hands to myself. I crack open the red skin of a rambutan, pop the lychee-like globe in my mouth, and spit the almond-shaped seed at Ricardo. I don't know why I enjoy antagonizing him, but it has become my new favorite sport.

"Do it again," he threatens suggestively. "I dare you."

"You're all talk." I peel another and, holding him in my gaze, bite the fruit in slow motion, licking my lips and swallowing. I open my mouth as evidence of my innocence — seed carefully secured beneath my tongue — and lean toward him for a kiss. His eyes are fluttering closed when the projectile shoots out of my mouth and bounces off his cheek.

I'm a giggling mess, scrambling away and shrieking, when his strong grip on my ankles wrenches me back. Suddenly I'm on my belly in the dust, his hot mouth on my neck, erection pressed against my bottom, full body pinning me to the ground. His fingers reach under the fabric of the dress, grazing my inner thigh and upwards. Already I am lit like a live wire.

"I want to take you right here." His words echo between my thighs, and I fight the desire to press into him, goading him on.

"Let's go back to your house," is what flies out of my mouth uncensored.

A moment later his warm heat is replaced with empty air. "Am I pushing you again?"

"I want to be where I can enjoy you properly."

He ponders this. "You don't want to wait for the sunset?"

I shake my head. "I don't want to wait at all."

The edges of his lips curl.

The motorbike winds downhill, my arms linked around Ricardo's torso, hair blowing freely in the breeze. I am brushing my lips against the side of his neck, savoring the freedom, when the zephyr of an old memory interrupts my pleasure. I see my mother's face chastising me for riding with my high school boyfriend on a motorcycle, sans helmet. I can only imagine what she'd think if she saw me now. It's one thing to act like a teenager while a teenager, but now that I'm supposed to be a grown up, albeit underemployed and practically destitute…? By the time we pass through the village and arrive at Ricardo's house, my self-judgment has left my libido, raging moments earlier, crouching in a corner. Like a sea creature poking my head out of the reef, fanning my colorful fins only to retract at the first sign of action, I am trapped in my inhibited hiding place.

As soon as we park I escape him, crossing the living room into the kitchen to wash my fruit-sticky hands at the sink, but he follows. Pressing his body into me from behind, he moves my hair aside to kiss the back of my neck while humming an improvised melody. Despite my reticence, everything starts shimmering once more from his attention. When his tongue reaches the side of my neck just below my ear, a shudder rolls through me.

"Found a button," he hums in a proud undertone.

"I won't be able to wash my hands if you keep that up."

"Good thing I like you better as a hot mess," he quips, lifting my dress to my hips and thrusting his hardness against my ass. "This dress is ridiculously sexy." The thought that it's Mila's makes me queasy, but he doesn't know that.

I spray droplets of water at him over my shoulder, but undaunted, he reaches a hand around and slips his fingers inside my thong, his wet mouth returning to the tingling spot beneath my ear. One finger strokes my slippery flesh from bottom to top, and I lean back against his body, arousal spiking. His other hand gets into the action, a finger pushing inside me, while the first continues its strumming. Right away my circuits start overloading. He feels delicious, but overwhelming, and the bizarre premonition strikes that I am about to blow a fuse.

Eyes closed in frustration and embarrassment about it, my hand flies out to grab the counter for support, but instead sends something flying into the stainless steel sink. The resounding crash makes me jump, eyes flipping open and darting around. Ricardo's fingers still, but he leaves them where they are, holding me as I try to catch my breath.

"Sorry about that." For both the breakage and the way I keep blowing hot and cold.

"It's just a glass," he whispers, withdrawing his hand and wrapping me tightly in his arms. Like the first hug of the evening, we breathe together and everything slows down.

"This intensity is going to take some getting used to," I admit.

"I'm overeager."

"No, you're wonderful." I don't want to do anything to interfere with the way he pursues me, I just need to get used to it.

"Let's play some music," he suggests.

Abandoning the glass shards, we shift to the corner of the bedroom where Ricardo has his guitar, mandolin and drum. He lifts the guitar, improvising something with a classical Spanish flavor. As I listen, appreciating the beauty he coaxes from the strings, I must acknowledge to myself that all I want to do is touch him. I know he feels it, too. Maybe I would be more comfortable initiating the pace, although his energy coming towards me is the most erotic thing I have ever experienced. It takes me into an altered state where I am so out of control I feel crazy. And I want it more than anything.

Ricardo's eyes track me as I take my turn slipping behind him. I drop to my knees, curling around his back, while he continues plucking the strings. As I massage his firm shoulders, my tongue draws a line down his delectable neck. He tastes divine. The notes he is playing fill the room, but when I gently bite the lobe of his ear they falter, and when my fingers brush up his ribs they stop altogether. His head bows in surrender.

"Sirena…" His voice is strained. "All I want to do is get back into bed with you."

I press my forehead into his back. "What if I fall into your bed and never emerge?"

He places the guitar on the ground and turns around, chest rising and falling with shallow breaths. When he pulls me into his arms we fall backwards in a tangle of limbs, knocking over the drum that comes down with a resonant thud. Ricardo laughs and bangs on my behind like a percussion instrument, shouting out a samba chant. My outrage inspires him to tickle me, and when he discovers my overly sensitive ribs and waist, I almost break his nose trying to squirm away. He wrestles me into submission, sprawled on my back, dress hiked at my waist, but a hesitation lingers at the edge of his actions. This time instead of panicking and retreating, I push myself up onto my elbows and press my lips to his. He groans against my mouth, ramping up the kiss as he spreads my legs with his knee, holding me in place with his body. We are writhing, hands gripping and seeking when he suddenly stops, searching my eyes.

"Do you trust me?"

The question is so loaded, I swallow my impulse to make some smart remark and nod instead, wondering what my real answer is.

"Let's get a mattress underneath us." He pulls me to my feet, taps on his phone, and the wireless sound system fills the room with another sexy lounge track.

It would be easy to surrender into his hypnotic dominance, but I have enjoyed my brief stint in the driver's seat and am not quite ready to give it up. I step back from him, eyes lowered as I glide the elastic top of my dress down my ribs, and cup my bare breasts in my hands. When I risk a look, I am gratified to see him moving backwards towards the bed, mouth parted, his eyes fixed on my body. I step towards him to the beat of the music, then with bent knees, dance my breasts down his torso. He fingers my hair, twisting a lock around his wrist and tugging slightly. My eyes blaze up at his, and he releases me, albeit with a reluctant smirk. My hands move under his shirt across the lightly-oiled skin of his washboard stomach, and he shivers as I find my way inside the waistband of his jeans. His fingers try to cover mine, but I pull away, insisting on setting the pace.

"You're killing me," he says, falling back onto his elbows but his eyes are smiling.

I stand and slip the dress down to my ankles. Ricardo scoots farther back on the bed, and I crawl across to join him. Our silence is thick, the newness is strong. I think we are both wondering if the phenomenal connection of the night before is replicable. I unfasten his buttons, drawing my hands over his chest as he shrugs off his shirt. My fingertips trace circles around his nipples and travel down past his navel, unfastening his jeans and discovering an enticing patch of darkly coiled hair. I tug the denim down and let him see me lick my lips as his cock bounces against his stomach, wanting to taste him with my mouth but hungrier to have him inside me. My thong flies over the side of the bed when I toss it, and I straddle him, gripping his silky-hard flesh in hand, and feeling him pulse his response. He whispers my name while, with excruciating slowness, I lower myself onto him.

"I've been thinking about this all day," he breathes, gazing directly into my eyes, fingers embossing their print into my thighs.

I want to tell him that I have too, all day, all night, and in my dreams, but I can't speak. The exquisite fullness steals away my words.

He clasps his fingers through mine, and I push against his grip, circling my hips. My eyes start to close, but his mesmerizing stare holds me, keeping me present, while his hands move to my hips to slow me, showing me exactly how he wants me to ride him.

When his body tenses, control slipping, he rolls me onto my back, taking back the command, pushing into me in a single, deep thrust. A flush of warmth spreads through me, and a spontaneous "Oh yeah," rolls off my lips as I happily yield to his power. We fall into a trance-inducing rhythm, and I liquify beneath him, the rigidity of bone melting, any hard boundary of will or fear falling away. His strokes escalate to relentless pounding, and he thickens inside me, filling me, taking me, owning me, ravishing me. This I have craved, though I couldn't have articulated the sensation of the music dropping away, the ceiling lifting, until all that exists is the contact of his smooth, brown skin against mine. A slow ache builds, an exquisite tension that rumbles through me and peaks, spreading across my chest, spilling through my quivering arms and shivering thighs. Bodies fused, we pulse together as the intensity flares, and tones from my vocal chords fill the room. It's happening again, the magic, the interstellar scrumptiousness, and I want to drench myself in it.

When the momentous sensations subside, we roll onto our sides, facing one another. Ricardo's knuckles caress the side of my face. "This is a huge power between us, Sirena."

This is the best thing that's ever happened to me, I think to myself. I'm unready for any such grand declarations though, still unsettled by the thought that if something seems too good to be true, it is.

Ricardo's stomach spares me from replying by rumbling loudly. The man has the appetite of two lions. "I need to refuel."

"Can I help you make the food this time? I'm a good sous chef. I'd like to learn."

"Cool. You're hired."

"Not afraid I'll destroy more kitchenware?"

"No, I'm afraid of doing something stupid, and you running for the hills." The honesty of that admission slices through the soft afterglow, and I want to reassure him that I'm not going anywhere. Before I can he slides to the side of the bed and pulls on his jeans.

"Come on sous chef, show me what you've got."

He starts to get up, but I throw my arms around him from behind his back. "I'm here. I'm staying."

"I really hope so."

Ricardo shows me how to prepare something he refers to as rice made from Indonesian *bankuang* — what Angelinos call *jicama* — pulsed in the food processor. We grind cacao, pumpkin and sesame seeds, chilies and garlic into a paste, creating a raw version of a Mexican *molé*. He drains sunflower seeds he had soaking and blends them with cilantro, ginger, and spices, his take on refried beans. Asian cabbage leaves substitute for taco shells. I have been a lifelong foodie, but have never eaten this way.

"You've taken the flavors of Mexican food, but... it's so alive."

We are sitting again at his low, teak table, eating by candlelight. "Try this." He tears a cabbage leaf, rolls everything together inside of it, adds extra chili, and pops it in my mouth.

I wiggle in my seat, shimmying my shoulders, tastebuds having a party. "Feels like all my cells are dancing and saying yes."

Beneath the table, Ricardo runs his hand up my thigh. "Keep saying yes," he smolders, eyes flaming, his hand brushing sensitive places. "Are you sore?"

I shake my head no. He pushes another cabbage taco into his mouth and licks his fingers sensually, hypnotic eyes on me. "Still hungry?"

I know he is not referring to food, and nod my head. Yes, indeed. We can't seem to keep our hands off each other, and a flicker of doubt curls through my mind. I want him because he's mouthwateringly delectable, but is Ricardo's wellspring of passion simply due to all those years of abstinence?

"Come here." It's an invitation and a directive. "Sit on my lap."

Something in me bristles at receiving orders, even as I gleefully comply, thrilled to find him already hard and ready beneath me. I settle on him, my back to the table, as he reaches around and lifts the remainder of the wrap from his plate. Slowly he places the flavorful leaf in my mouth, his fingers lingering on my bottom lip, milking the moment, keenly interested in the multiple flavors of sensation, his eyes never leaving me. I run my tongue across his fingertips before biting the little taco, one hand holding him through the fabric of his pants. This is, without question, my new definition of a Happy Meal.

I lick my lips and grip him more firmly. "You like feeding me?"

His eyes scorch into mine. "Exactly."

His hand slips to the button on his jeans, releasing it, giving entrance to my fingers. I roll my palm over the broad head and slide down the shaft, shivering as he reaches under my dress. I love the way his eyes broaden when he brushes against my bare bottom, discovering I have not bothered to replace my underwear. As he lifts my dress, I rock onto one knee and lower myself onto him. Here we are again.

His warm, sensitive fingers drift from my face to my chest, pulling down the top of my dress, thumbs skimming back and forth. "Want to try something different with me?"

Everything so far has been different, and I can't imagine what might constitute something new in Ricardo's book. "Such as?"

"Close your eyes." His hands cup my breasts, kneading softly. "Imagine your light coming from here," he gently tugs my nipples, "into here." He raises my hands and places them on his chest.

At first it feels forced, silly even, but I do my best to envision golden rays passing through my breasts and shining into his chest, certain I am pretending.

"I'm receiving all that juiciness of yours, merging it with my light, pulling it down my spine to here." He withdraws from me a few inches and places my hand on the base of his moist hardness. Ahhh. "Now I'm sending my light back into you…" While saying the words he slowly pushes in, and I tangibly feel his bolt of energy glimmer up my spine, back to my breasts. That charged, liquid-warm flush is not my imagination.

We breathe together silently, eyes closed. I take in his breath, then he inhales mine. The air flow through our lungs is our only movement, traveling the circuit of our merged bodies. Even without any rocking, the sensations build. His spirit tangibly surges through me with each round, opening some kind of channel. The dam blows, a deluge courses, and a geyser of light shoots upwards as a cry spills from my mouth. Our bodies reverberate like bells, everything trembling from the inside out. Even my skin seems to shimmy and I grow lightheaded. Ricardo's lap underneath me feels as solid as granite, anchoring me into the earth's core, as the tremors increase and my tones become uncontrolled laughter erupting from a buried source.

The moment I get scared, wondering if I will explode with this much energy surging through me, it subsides. Just like that.

I open my eyes expecting to find us floating in the clouds, but we are still sitting beside the teak table, candles glowing around us. How does he know how to do this? I wonder if I can handle the answer to that question. "Where did you learn...whatever that was?"

"I work with a Balinese shaman."

I almost choke. "Doing this?"

He chuckles at my reaction. "He gives me meditations to practice." Strong hands grip my bottom as his lips tug my lower lip. "Though it's much better with you."

"It is?"

"*Asombroso,* amazing to the max. I've been working with this energy a long time, building up for this. But you just dove right in without any preparation and went sailing."

"That was the wildest voyage I've ever taken."

His eyes are shining with pleasure. "Still want more?"

My mouth pops open, and I have to manually snap it shut. I can feel the solidity of his being, and how hard he still is inside me, while I am shaken beyond recognition. He has blasted all my doors and windows open, rocketing me into unchartered territory that is seductive and intense beyond measure. If I stay, will we continue all night long? I can't handle any more right now; my countless exploded particles need to resettle. And while he might be part sex god, he's still a man. If I make myself available to him constantly, he'll get tired of me, right? I lift myself up from him and lower my dress. "I'm ready to call it a night."

"You want to go?" He runs his fingers through my hair. "I'd love for you to stay."

I can't help but smile at his tenderness, followed by a laugh at my own caution and contradictions. I wait for him to demonstrate he wants me, then hide from his desire.

"I like the way you do that," he says, caressing the length of my nose with his long, graceful index finger.

"Do what?"

"Laugh at yourself, and me. When you do, you crinkle up this part of your nose." He traces the bridge down to my lips. I suck the tip of his finger into my mouth.

"You think I should stay?" I ask, holding his finger between my teeth.

"Please stay," he mouths so quietly I can barely hear the words, yet so directly each syllable sends a thousand feathery arrows into the center of my heart.

This time I stay. Before dawn, in that halfway place between dreaming and wakefulness, my body pulses with arousal. Ricardo is behind me, rocking inside of me. As if from a distance, I hear tones rising off my lips, waves spreading through my torso and across my limbs. Cocooned in his arms, his hand on my breast, I twist my neck, mouth searching for his, tongues hungry to taste each other. Waves of sensation roll through me, crashing unobstructed, dreamlike.

Later I awaken alone and find my lion engaged in his morning yoga practice in the next room. I think about joining him, but don't want to shift him into teacher mode. Tiptoeing to the porch, I cross the koi pond into the garden. Bare feet on the grass, I begin my meditation, hips swaying, antenna fingers relaying messages to the sky. When little bumps whisper down my neck, my eyes flutter open. Ricardo is sitting in an oval, wicker pod suspended from the ceiling, observing my every move from a respectful distance. Hyper-aware of his presence, I try to continue, but ultimately the allure of Ricardo is too great. I give up, climbing into the chair with him which swings from my weight, thrilled to be in his embrace again.

"Sirena, do you know what I think?"

"What?"

"You're a medicine woman."

I blink. His gaze holds mine with such certainty it floors me. I know I don't have a medical bone in my body, but he is talking about something else, something mysterious and mystical. I have never thought of myself that way.

"You're tapped in. You receive visions and you communicate through movement and sound."

I snuggle into him, trying to grasp his words. "Sound?"

"Last night and this morning. Your singing... the sounds you were making were like songs from another dimension, with meaning and wisdom in them."

My face prickles with embarrassment. "They were just coming out."

We are silent together for a long while. I watch two geckos playing chase across the rattan ceiling, tails swishing. While I drink in the surprises of our connection, Ricardo shifts gears. "When does your visa expire?"

Dumbfounded again. "No clue."

"Did you get it at the airport?"

"Yes."

"Then you have 30 days. When did you enter Indonesia?"

I struggle to pull the date from my memory bank, and he calculates in his head.

"*Perfecto.* Let's go to Bali together. I'm going to teach yoga at a retreat, and you can join in. We'll process a new visa for you along the way." He gives me a coy look. "You do want to stay in Indonesia longer, don't you?"

"There's nowhere else I want to be."

We kiss sensually, the first kiss of a new day. The magnetism between us is self-replenishing, if anything growing, rather than diminishing, as I give it space. My desire to pull away still crouches in its sneaky corner, but I seem to have it under control.

"Breakfast, a*morcita?*"

"Are you on the menu?"

Hand in hand we return to the temple of his bed. In the daylight I can see the entire room is set up like an altar. On the wall behind the bed is a hand-painted silk image of a sacred union in an enchanted forest. Tall amethyst geodes stand guard on either side next to potted orchids.

We kiss hungrily, lips crashing, tongues colliding, falling onto the bed, clothes flying off. Ricardo plumps up the pillows and places me against them, arranging my body until the position is just right, reclining but not supine.

"I want to focus on you, okay?" My heart glimmers at the suggestion, eyes bright. Can I allow myself this much attention? I can.

He lowers his face between my thighs and licks me slowly, savoring me like I am gourmet ice cream. I can't fall into my old habit of fantasizing — as I would with Jorge — because Ricardo is keenly present with me, watching me closely, tuned in to the volume of my arousal. His mouth becomes increasingly voracious, lapping and suctioning, taking me to the edge of release, then backing off.

When he does it a second time I burst out, "Are you trying to torture me?"

"Not at all," he smirks. "I just want to take you somewhere other than where you're used to going."

How could he possibly know what I am used to? Stirred up, for a crazed moment I want to punch him, or quit.

"Let me," he purrs, wet tongue insistent.

Slowly, unrelentingly, he continues caressing the most sensitive tip, and I relax into it. When I finally shatter, the explosion extends through time, one dam bursting after another. I am still moaning as the whitecaps slowly smooth into rolling waves, long after Ricardo has stopped touching me. I lie there quivering, as open as the orchids beside the bed.

"You're like... an eternal fountain." He nuzzles his head into my neck. "Still frustrated with me?"

"Yes," I say with a vengeance, but he knows I don't mean it.

He puts his palm on my sensitized flesh, the aftershocks continuing in tiny echoes. "I want to try something. But talk to me along the way," he encourages. "Tell me what you want, what you like."

Talking during sex has always been cringeworthy for me, and I swear he can read my body better than I can anyway. "I'll try," I agree.

He slips a finger inside me and curls it slightly, pressing against my inner wall in search of that textured patch of extra sensitivity. When he finds it, sparks glint through me, but behind the pleasure is something sly and foreboding. Suddenly I am on alert. His hand works steadily, firmly, and as yet another surge starts mounting, I begin to feel out of control, my body no longer my own. The intensity, whipping through me like a hurricane, fuels a terror that I am about to die. I am overloading. I need to make him stop, but my aching throat feels sewn shut, my voice trapped. I want to reach out to him, but my fingers and hands lock into frozen lobster claws curling inwards and I cannot unclench them. As the walls close in, I hear his voice, sounding far away, "Sirena, what are you feeling?"

I can't catch my breath, and the light is extinguishing. There they are, the gates, the entrance to the tunnel. "Don't tell anyone," a deep voice warns, as I go rigid and stop breathing. All is silent and blank.

Then images roll like a film reel. Familiar hands groping guiltily, fingers shoving into me, hurting me, an engorged penis pressing against me. I am only three years old, but a voice of steel says I am naughty for doing this to him. Uncle Carson spanks my bare bottom, puts his hand over my mouth and threatens, "Never say a word to anyone." The sword of clarity cuts through years of masking the truth from myself.

"Come back to me, Sirena. Breathe, *amorcita*."

Ricardo is pressing the full length of his body against mine, wrapping me in his arms, anchoring me back to earth. My lungs rediscover how to pull in air, but I have not fully returned. My hearing is muffled, my vision dull. I am in shock. Ricardo softly sings in Spanish, rocking me ever so slightly in his arms.

It is only after he has stopped and whispers, "You are safe with me," that the rainclouds burst. Sobbing, I grab hold of him, releasing the reservoir I couldn't let out when I was small, decades of trapped anguish.

"You are safe, *amorcita*. No one can hurt you now." I struggle against him, but he doesn't let go and he doesn't stop his chant. "Feel it all. Don't be afraid of the pain."

It seems like hours before the tears and fight are finally spent, and I go limp in his arms.

"Can you tell me what happened? What did you see?"

It is hard to speak. I have to remove Carson's miserable hand from my mouth, his domination from my psyche. Words emerging haltingly, I recount the memory to Ricardo in a hush. The telling of the story does not make the darkness dissipate. I am enveloped, but in contrast to the cruelty in my uncle's face, Ricardo's eyes are swimming with compassion.

"A bath? Let's wash it away."

My throat is sore from crying and too many years spent holding in the scream. Ricardo runs a bath and brings me a warm drink.

"You did the hardest part," he says, stepping me into the haven of frangipani-scented water. "Now let the pain and the shame wash away." He pours water over my chest with a ladle made from half a coconut shell. "You're so beautiful. Strong. Courageous."

I pull completely under, holding my breath and letting the water surround me. This is where I feel most at home, and I know what I must do. I need to be underwater. I don't think I could handle a full scuba submersion, but free-diving with my snorkel might work.

I tell Ricardo that I need to spend some time alone in the ocean, letting a big body of water surround me. I need the spaciousness of no one to talk to and nothing to distract me.

"Please don't push me away, Sirena."

I can see the rejection pulling his face taut, but the need to restore myself is overpowering. "I'm sorry," is all I can manage.

We ride silently on his motorbike the short distance to my hotel. When we arrive at my door, he doesn't come in.

"Take all the time you need. When you're ready for me, tell Alit in the bar. He's one of the drummers I play with and knows how to find me. Or just walk over any time. The door is always open."

I know he is really saying his heart is always open. I wish I could respond with the same, but I'm not ready and can't articulate a thing right now. "Thank you," is again all I manage.

His lips brush mine and then he's walking away, leaving me to wonder if he has finally awakened to the realization that I am too much work. Midway down the path he turns to me again. "I'm going to Bali the day after tomorrow. I hope you'll come with me, but if you can't, I'll take your passport for you and give it to my visa agent." I just nod and look down.

He takes another step and adds, "You're having a healing crisis. Please don't hold it against me for bringing it to the surface. I know this feels like death, but it's just the old crud falling away. It will all be worth it when you're free. I promise." I nod again and he leaves.

Shoving him away like this is tearing me to pieces. I am not angry with him, quite the contrary; I know he is helping me. In fact, he has only been downright wonderful, but I am still trapped behind an old steel door.

I lie on my bed wondering how many times have I done this, pushing love away. How many friends have I cut off? How many retaining walls have I built around myself? I do not want to live inside this cage for the rest of my life, a cage I have climbed into many times before, swallowing the key. *No*, I scream inside my head. No to the hand over my mouth and the invasive fingers leaving their scars in delicate places. No to saying this didn't happen. No to this being a script I must re-enact forever.

I spend the hottest part of the day alone on the beach, letting the sun bake the trauma out of me. Torch the panic I felt as a child, I ask of the fiery orb. Carbonize this rage at my uncle, this muzzle I have worn. Consume the mistrust of myself and everyone else.

Incinerate this insane cocktail of shame, arousal, and fear into ashes that drift away in the sea breeze.

Nausea hangs in my stomach all day, rising into my throat, as if my body is trying to metabolize poison. My mind needs to make sense of the three distinct memories that have surfaced, but sitting right beside them is disbelief. Uncle Carson's orthopedic practice is thriving, he has investments galore and sits on charity boards. Mom idolizes him and he's Dad's best friend. In fact, everyone admires Uncle Carson, and that used to include me as well.

Despite how close my parents are with Carson, I don't remember spending time alone with him. How did he have that kind of access to me? Questioning myself, the subtle hint of a memory flutters at the edge of my mind. My parents driving away, my brother and I left with our aunt and uncle. Where was Aunt Libby when these violations occurred? Why do my parents and Libby feel like collaborators? If there are more memories, do I have to recover every single one of them? The loathing that rises at that thought is suffocating.

Clearly these incidents have stained my emotional outlook, leaving me in a perpetual tap dance, giving the appearance all is well while vigilantly keeping a lid on the submerged trauma. This is the thief that has stolen my innocence and robbed me of my confidence. This thumbprint of worry was stamped into my psyche, the constant, exhausting fear of what dangerous thing might happen next. I will myself to do whatever it takes to cleanse this pain.

Alone, I still feel Ricardo near me, his weight against my body, the journeys of sensation he took me on, the constant liquid love in his eyes. I miss him as if he has been beside me for years, not days. But what is he thinking right now? Could he truly be interested in a maladjusted, emotional nightmare like me? At some point he'll realize that I'm only setting him back in his own journey, ten tons of dark baggage he doesn't want or need.

In the middle of the night I awaken with anxiety pumping through my organs. Cramps stab my stomach. The fullness of the revulsion I have long suppressed rises up and I dash to the toilet, clasping the cool, ceramic sides as I purge. I do not like vomiting, but tonight I am glad. Get this out of me.

I awaken before the sun, feeling safer and cleaner. At first light my dancing meditation pulls me to the beach, the sky a mass of moody, gray clouds. Afterwards, I wander a barren stretch of shoreline. The tide is low. When I squint my eyes, I make out a sandy reef in the distance, creating a warm wading pool between reef and shore. My feet have a consciousness of their own, guiding me through knee-high water. I stand for an immeasurable time gazing to the horizon, heart heavy, mind still. Taking a step forward, my heel catches the edge of something hard. My fingers reach down, and rise from the water holding a perfect, palm-sized conch.

At that very moment, something inexplicable and expansive opens, as if a veil that usually exists in my mind draws to the side, and a fogginess I think of as reality evaporates, revealing a sparkling clarity. I see the seamless connection between water, sky, shell, and pink palm cupping it, an intelligent presence permeating everything. The same grace I encountered during my heart experience is all around me and within me, only this time I am still anchored in my body. I hold the shell to my chest, knowing it as a gift too beautiful to comprehend.

As I sit listlessly in the sand, the threesome of little boys returns, scampering across the shoreline collecting shells for me. I don't know how to tell them I couldn't possibly orchestrate an art project today, but instead of waiting for me, they dive into a design of their own.

"*Barong*," they tell me, jumping up and down, growling, making their hands into claws. I can't tell what kind of monster a *barong* might be, but their enthusiasm is infectious.

The roles have reversed; I help the boys collect shells while they are in charge of placement. I fetch my camera, documenting the evolution of their artwork, and progressively it becomes evident they are creating a dragon of sorts. How perfect. Let the tide wash clean my demons. I add sharp fangs, and the boys laugh. When they are satisfied with the piece, they want me to teach them how to use the camera and I let them photograph the *barong* from every angle.

"*Es crem,*" they gleefully beg, limbs flying in all directions.

We escape from the blazing sun into the shaded hotel restaurant. Three bowls of ice cream appear, and the boys happily devour every drop. I click images of sticky faces and bursts of animated expression between spoonfuls. When my young friends finally run off for home, tumbling along and waving as they go, they have replaced the heaviness I once felt around children with levity.

Time to submerge. After trading my land camera for a waterproof one, I splash into gently-lapping waves, swimming with snorkel, mask, and fins past the break. Around a rocky outcropping, I enter the vastness of the sea, no human construct visible, not even a boat in sight, only sky, swiftly moving clouds, rocky bluffs, and the bouncing ocean. Down I plunge, flippers thrust into the air, holding my breath and clearing my ears, hovering above a thriving reef dotted with barrel sponges. A moray eel slithers out of its den, retreating as my shadow falls across it. After resurfacing to draw another deep breath, I dive again, passing neon sea anemones and a school of unicorn fish with Pinocchio noses. Up and down, the weightlessness of swimming massages the distress out of me.

From the distance a shimmering cloud of plankton rushes my way, and I spot something beyond it approaching swiftly like the dark hood of a car. My initial flash of fear at its enormous size and speed shifts into curiosity, then delight. The creature flies through the sea in an underwater ballet, gracefully chasing its microscopic banquet. I finally remember to bring the lens to my eye and snap a sequence of photos.

The manta does a pass-by as I bob to the surface, and we eye each other with interest, its enormous black eyeball conveying intelligence and understanding. As it circles me again, more shadows emerge from the deep blue to join in the feeding fest. The plankton are plentiful and the lagoon is shallow; when the cloud engulfs me I remain motionless and the giant sea eagles spiral around my clicking camera. Fat, slow raindrops fall, bouncing off the surface of the ocean like illumined globes and my tears collect at the bottom of my mask.

At sunset I ask for Alit at the Crystal Bar and learn he is not working today. I have no way to reach Ricardo. Crushed, I wonder how it is possible to fall so hard for someone and not even know their phone number. I head out on foot, but come to a fork in the road. Both times I've traveled to Ricardo's house, I have been immersed in the pressure of his back against my chest and the woodsy scent of his skin in my nose, and the world has gone past in a hazy blur. Dusk has already faded into darkness, and I realize that I now have to navigate my way back to the hotel without a flashlight. I slump dejectedly onto a sawed-off tree stump.

A headlight appears in the distance, and my heart swells at our psychic connection; I knew Ricardo would find me. As the figure gets closer, I note the narrow shoulders and short stature. An old Indonesian man drives past without so much as a side glance.

Disheartened, I stand up and dust myself off, heading back toward the beach. Alit will be working tomorrow, and I'll contact Ricardo then. Two steps later my sandaled foot slams into something hard, and it isn't a pretty little conch shell. I double over, cursing Ricardo, Alit, the stars, and my soft, silly heart. My fingers discover a splinter wedged into my toe, but my fingernails can't grip the sliver to remove it.

I must try to find Ricardo. It's all I want. Once more I turn around and stick to the left, walking a distance without noticing anything familiar. The road twists beside scruffy brush, and I'm convinced I've walked too far when all of a sudden I recognize the loose gravel of Ricardo's driveway.

The doors off the verandah are open wide, but the house is dark. When I call Ricardo's name, the resounding silence confirms he is not at home. I sit crosslegged on the porch, but the longer I wait the more uncomfortable I become. What if he doesn't come back? Worse yet, horror of horrors, what if he brings someone else home? My toe throbs.

A scratching sound behind me interrupts the unpleasant thoughts, revealing a small prehistoric-looking creature scrambling across the floor in my direction. I shriek and leap to my feet, startling us both. Instantly, the funny long nose curls into its belly like a potato bug, and all I can see is scaled shell.

"I do that when I get scared," I tell the little guy, backing up across the porch to give him an escape route.

The sound of a motorbike approaching brings the flash of headlights, illuminating the miniature, anteater-like animal as it ambles into the bushes. A solitary Ricardo hops off the bike wearing a mud-splattered sports jersey.

"Whatcha doin' out here?"

Unable to see his eyes in the dark, I'm unsure what he means. I swear my lungs sputter to a stop. "I…you said…" My hand waves half-heartedly. My fears were right. He's realized I'm a big bag of too-much-trouble. "You told me I could come over," I finish lamely.

"I mean here, outside, getting eaten alive by mosquitos. I went to play football, but left the doors open for you."

A few nimble steps have him flying over the pond, and a moment later I am engulfed in his sweaty arms.

"I was hanging out with a little scaly… creature."

I feel his cheek against mine as it stretches into a smile. "You saw the little pangolin? It shows up sometimes and helps with the ant situation in my kitchen." He pulls back, eyes serious. "You sound kinda shaken up. How's it going?"

I glance down, biting the inside of my cheek. "It's been rough." I glance into his caring eyes. "Kind of like I've been beaten to a pulp, but I'm still standing. I swam with some mantas though, which was lovely."

"Can I help?"

I sense him wanting to draw me in and am relieved he still wants to. "You already have. So much."

"Cool." He steps back to peel off his filthy clothing. "I think a shower might be in order."

"Can I watch?"

His smile is a flash of moonlight in the darkness, and I see how cautious he has been with me up until now. "My pleasure."

I limp behind him into the bathroom and shoo him away when he tries to fuss over my foot, quite tired of appearing wounded and refusing to be helpless. He gives me tweezers and antiseptic, and I studiously focus on the splinter while sneaking peeks at Ricardo's wet body under the shower head. The pleasure is actually mine, witnessing him sudsing his magnificent form with natural ease.

When his hands scrub over his skull I ask, "How did it feel playing football without your dreads?"

He shakes his head and pretends to go for a header. "I got a lot of razzing from my teammates about being bald and cutting off my connection to Jah. Then I scored a goal with a header, and that was the end of that." He shuts off the water. "I was definitely lighter on my feet. Those babies were heavy."

"Do you miss them?"

He's drying off now with a fluffy, white towel. "I miss being able to shake them like a dog and get you all wet." He grabs me in a bear hug, rubbing his wet head on me, while I laugh and wriggle to get away. "I don't miss the dreadlocks... because I know why they're gone." The potent look he gives me undulates through my body. Just that one look alone is as rich as hot fudge and as intoxicating as champagne.

"And you don't miss living like a monk?"

He steps toward me, pressing my hand against the bulging plush toweling at his groin. I go to tug the towel from his hips, but he distracts me with a passionate kiss. "I'm beyond hungry." He pretends to bite me. "Let's whip something up."

I like to chop, so out of the refrigerator I pull fresh corn, red and yellow bell peppers, Japanese cucumbers, ginger, little purple shallots, cilantro, chillies, and limes. Ricardo has some leftover red rice, and we concoct a cauliflower and long bean curry with coconut meat and lots of fresh turmeric. Every minute doing the simplest things together has a special elegance.

We have much sharing to do so our friendship can catch up to our level of intimacy. While preparing the meal, we compare our personal favorites in the all-important categories: film, books, and music. He favors action movies with chase scenes, the kind that leave me unsettled, but we both like foreign films, comedies, and documentaries. Ricardo gets excited that I know most of his reggae favorites, even old-school dancehall like Sugar Minott. He reads non-fiction and I like novels, but I forgive him for being boring and he pokes me in the side with a carrot.

After dinner and dishes, we stretch out on the couch, wrapped in each others' arms. Our bodies want to be close. More tranquil than I have felt in days, I am still plagued by a question that has nagged at me from the first moment Ricardo's lips brushed mine.

"Why me?"

He raises his eyebrows, waiting for clarification.

"Why did you break your fast with me, Ricardo? You're handsome. Charismatic. Talented. You could be with anyone…"

"What, like runway models?"

I nod.

"Hot yoga students? Or that blonde diving instructor at the PADI office?"

When he continues to list every attractive person he can think of, I wriggle my hand into the soft flesh over his ribs and pinch him, hard.

He almost falls off the couch laughing, and when he looks at me again his eyes are shining. "I've been with models, Sirenita, too many, in too many configurations. I used them," he adds quietly, embarrassed. "And I can't go there anymore — all beauty and no heart. I need both."

He can keep the details of those stories to himself. I take an audible breath, understanding his response but still not seeing how I fit into the equation.

"Need more?" He squeezes me, holding a long kiss on the top of my head. "I was locked up as a teenager, right, and it gave me this hunger for freedom. The first moment I could, I busted outta there and ate up every experience... until life started devouring me."

His broad chest slides away as he shifts to meet my eyes. "The way I am — it's my strength and my weakness — when I concentrate on something, I go for it, dive in headfirst. I have to be damn sure I'm focusing on the right things, and the puddle-deep stuff doesn't do it for me."

I watch his fingers link through mine, trying to believe all this is real, that I just happened to find the perfect man at the perfect time in his life, and mine. But as much as his words help me to understand, they also carry an inherent warning. With Ricardo's passion and gifts come the risk of a transience and sudden changes.

He pauses, his breath slow and steady. Through the stillness of his body, I absorb the depth of transformation he has undergone, but I am still uneasy and he knows it.

"I took all those years to find myself. Dug deep to fill up with me, not somebody else. I never told myself, bro, you're gonna be celibate for the next five years. Had I known it'd go on that long, I'd probably have picked the afterlife instead." His chest rumbles with laughter, but I'm too consumed with ingesting the arc of his journey to join in.

"Along the way I let myself dream of what I really wanted." He looks directly into my eyes, caressing the side of my face. "I think I conjured you up straight outta my imagination, *amorcita*. You're my lioness." He delivers this like it's an undebatable fact. "When you talk about yourself like you aren't beautiful, it's..." I feel his body tense, but the words don't come. "You're gorgeous, and you don't even realize it. You're kind of innocently oblivious to it." He runs his hand over my ribs and around my back to squeeze my ass while his mouth finds my ear. "This hot, curvy body of yours has me hard all the time," he says pushing the evidence up against my side.

I roll my hip against him even as my head grapples with his words. I have always thought of myself as deficient in the looks department, more nerdy than ravishing. It dawns on me how that belief helped keep my sexuality at bay.

I want to ask him why, if he believes his lioness has arrived, he is still beaming out his magnetism like a lighthouse signal. He is catnip to anyone with a pair of breasts, and it's not a result of his looks alone, but him; the kindness in his smile, the perceptivity of his gaze, the seduction of his silken voice. Will it always be like that, Ricardo transfixing the women around him? Around us?

"I have something for you," he says with a gleam in his eye, voice bright with anticipation. "Come with me."

I don't want to leave the warmth of his arms, but he leads me to the musical corner of his bedroom and we drop onto the pillows. While removing his guitar from its case, he flashes a look my way. "I wrote a song."

I settle back, eager to hear it, and notice something different in the tilt of his head and the slant of his eyes. Is Ricardo, yoga-dream-god-extraordinaire, capable of something as earthly as shyness? It's adorable.

When he starts to sing his voice is tentative, but after a line or two he gathers strength.

> *The first time I saw you*
> *Doors and windows blew right open*
> *And the treasures I had hidden*
> *Appeared in your palm*
>
> *The first time I kissed you*
> *Ancient mysteries unraveled*

As solid as the mountains
And as sure as the tides

Then we're flying through the night
Fly-y-y-ing through the night
Lions stalking
Through the dark of night
We're flying through the night
Jade eyes flashing
Through the dark of night
We're flying through the night
Through the night.

I listen, struck silent, as he repeats the chorus, fingers picking notes that dance and dip, circling back in a tale of their own. I am moved, stunned even, by the deeply masculine passion and sensitivity of his voice, and have to blink as my eyes grow glassy. While I was at my most vulnerable, crumbling apart, questioning his interest in me, he was here alone, turning our experience into music.

When he strikes the final chord, his eyes slide up to mine, and widen slightly as he catches my expression.

"Thank you," I whisper. "I love it."

"It's just the first verse and chorus," he says sheepishly. "There'll be more. But there's one thing I need to finish it..." He pauses, looking at me with a hint of mischief. "I wrote the song for you, with your voice in mind."

I can only imagine how ridiculous the shock on my face must seem because Ricardo bursts into a loud belly laugh. Singing in front of people feels more naked to me than being naked. From the time I was a child it has drawn teardrops to the corners of my eyes, evoking something mysterious I cannot put my finger on, something too revealing to expose.

I remember my dismay in sixth grade at my teacher assigning me to the choir. Walking to rehearsal, dread fills my steps as if my shoes are weighted with concrete. To make things worse, a local official has invited our chorus to sing at a community event in front of a huge crowd. The other kids are excited, but I am secretly terrified. During our weekly practices, try as we may, we continually mess up a section towards the end of our song, frustrating our choir director. In the back row, I sing my part in a barely-audible voice, letting out only a wisp of sound, but no one seems to notice. Then, on the day of the performance, we sing in front of the dignitaries and manage to get every part right. Our entire choir is beaming, but I have mouthed the words without singing at all.

"Ricardo, you may as well ask me to jump out of an airplane. Without a parachute."

"You have a mystical quality in your voice, Sirenita. You have a special ability. I know it."

I am stuck on tar paper, unable to budge, and Ricardo puts down his guitar. "It was just inspiration that I followed. I didn't mean to scare you."

"You didn't," I assure him. "I... I want to do everything there is for us to do. You're the best thing that's ever happened to me." There. I said it.

I can visibly see my words pass through his body, his chest rising and stilling.

"I want to earn your trust," he says.

How frequently Jorge would demand my trust, but did he ever say he wished to earn it? Never.

We are both breathing hard, hearts blasted open beyond where we normally reside. The guitar slides sideways as our bodies press together, exploring their common language. Breathing in each other's breath, my lungs learn the stillness of his lungs. Dancing forearm against forearm, my bones hear the music sheltered in his bones. Belly rubbing belly, we discover the integrity each other holds. Brushing cheek against cheek, we share each other's sorrow and ecstasy. Palm to palm, our arms float upward together and, although we are fully clothed, the circuit of energy circulates through us without consciously initiating it. We let it ride until it subsides.

"Thank you for my song. I'll sing it with you."

"Right now?" He's excited, but trying hard not to show it.

I nod yes. How could singing be any more intense than simply touching him? Ricardo retrieves his tablet from the bedside table so I can read the lyrics and, call and response style, teaches me line by line. I try not to focus on how my voice sounds, so of course I am thinking about the sound of my voice, but the melody is beguiling, the creative exchange between us is alive, and after a few croaked tones the song takes me in. Oh my, this is actually fun.

Ricardo picks up his guitar and I attempt to sing the entire song through by myself. It is hard to maintain eye contact with him, so mostly I look at the screen. The chorus is tricky, requiring a broad range, and on a high note my voice cracks. I freeze, mortified, but he patiently encourages me to start again. A few times I cannot find the right note, but he helps me. When we have gone all the way through the chorus, I meet his gaze again. He is so happy his crossed legs are bouncing like butterfly wings about to take flight.

"Did I massacre it?

"No, you killed it, *amorcita*, in the best way possible. *Baile conmigo.*"

He sets down the guitar and scoops me up, dancing me out the door and around the living room in a humorous tango. He has just thrown me into a dramatic dip when we hear someone on the porch.

"*Permisi*, Pak Riko..."

Ricardo lifts me up from my backbend and moves to the door where a young Indonesian man is waiting for him.

"*Maaf*, so sorry, Nyoman, I forgot to contact you. I got distracted..." and he shoots me a huge grin over his shoulder.

"What time you leave tomorrow, Pak?"

Ricardo turns back to me. "We're on for Bali tomorrow, right?"

"Right," I nod, simultaneously questioning if I can survive a retreat full of Ricardo yoga groupies.

He asks me if I need to check out of my hotel. I realize that I do, not having excess cash to pay for an empty room.

"We'll drop your things here, repack, and travel light so we can move around easily by motorbike. Then when we come back, you can stay with me." He has a twinkle in his eye with that last phrase and just like that we are living together. Sort of.

Ricardo returns to the man at the door, arranging the final details of our pickup and thanking him for coming by. At least, that's what I think he is saying; they speak in a quick flurry of English mixed with Indonesian.

Ricardo returns, taking my hand in his, the other arm around my waist.

"Where were we?"

"I believe you were swooning, Pak Riko."

"You like that, huh?"

He twirls me around, dips me low, and as I rise, he draws me in close, holding me tight. A big yawn escapes me.

"Clearly my erotic aura is underwhelming you."

I laugh, and admit I need to get horizontal.

"Then put your feet on mine."

"Seriously?"

"Put 'em on top."

Supported by his strong arms, I decide to humor him and together we waddle into the bathroom, laughing so hard we almost topple onto the slate floor.

"I don't have a toothbrush."

"I have one of those hard airline brushes in a box."

Out of a cabinet comes a brand new, extremely firm toothbrush with a miniature tube of horrible toothpaste.

"Any floss?"

"I use these."

He hands me a box of dental toothpicks with tiny brushes at one end, and I can't help smirking. "Part of your supermodel toiletry kit?" I tease, but glancing up I find the laughter has left his eyes. Oh no. What did I say? I want to rewind and take the words back. "I'm sorry. I was trying to be funny." I'm getting upset, although I'm not sure what I did wrong. Despite the lovely night together, I am still quite fragile.

"Don't get all worried," he says, nudging me.

"I don't understand."

He takes a deep breath and sighs. "Here I am preaching a life of meaning, but earning my bread being a pretty face in a narcissistic industry. It's hypocritical."

I shrug. "I didn't even realize you were still doing it. What about the yoga?"

"Modeling allows me to be here. Teaching yoga is for my soul. I do some retreats for pocket change. Then fly back to New York to make bank." His face is hard, his eyes darken. "I've been holding back the reins since my crash, scraping by. I could do more…" The thought peters off unfinished.

"Sounds pretty ideal to me."

"I rent out my pad in the city for more than this place costs, so I make money just being here. I have more freedom than any of my ancestors has for generations." He frowns and his brow furrows in concentration, much going unsaid.

"I could build my career up again," he finally adds, "if I let go of the brakes." He's staring at the wall, being hard on himself, but then something in him relaxes slightly. "I haven't been sure I want involvement in that world any more," he confides.

I think he harbors more there, a fear perhaps that he could slip back into old habits and let his surroundings get the better of him. The idea of Ricardo working in New York with scantily clad models leaves me feeling ill, but that's my issue, not his.

"I've been layin' low, working on the inside." He gives me a grin, but I can tell his mind is traveling, his mood noticeably heavier.

"Are you still going to want to dance with me after you see me brushing my teeth?" I attempt distraction by doing a comical curtsy while hiding my teeth behind my hand.

"Depends on what you do with your toothbrush."

So I have to squeeze the gluey toothpaste onto the brush and chase him around the house with it. He's much better than I am at leaping over furniture and escaping, but I am quite good at pretending I have given up and starting in all over again.

Eventually drowsiness overtakes me. "I didn't sleep well last night," I explain. "I was busy throwing up."

My head falls onto the pillow and Ricardo spoons me, stroking my hair as I drift asleep.

Towering plants in a lush garden sway through my dream. Tree branches above my head hang heavy with ripening fruit. A tiny fig blossom dangling before me matures instantly into fruit before my eyes, splitting its dark skin to reveal garnet jam. Reverently, I reach down and pull open my labia which swell into enormous petals in my hands, until my body becomes the stamen of a giant, pink flower, opening to the sun.

I awaken in the dark of night to the sound of my own voice moaning with need. Facing Ricardo, my leg draped across his hip, my pelvis circles against him. My mouth seeks his. Tongue in his ear. Fingers gripping his ass. Hunger pouring out. Trembling, I angle myself until he's pressed to my seam, slipping against me once, twice, then blessedly inside. Hand cupping his balls. His fingers squeezing my nipple. Nectar rising up my spine. Skin fusing to skin. Muscle singing to muscle. Legs shuddering. Figs bursting their skin. Seeds popping. Petals unfurling. Thrusting deeper. All in.

When we fall still, catching our breath and allowing the honey-thick pleasure to slowly ooze away, Ricardo presses his lips to my brow.

"I like the way you dream, *mi cielo*."

In the stillness of predawn, Ricardo sits in full lotus, eyes closed, his fingers working the mala beads in his hand. I toss a habitual glance at my phone and, hooray, an email informs me the agency has transferred my pay into my bank account. Next I open an email from Mom and immediately wish I hadn't. Her offhand comment about one of my uncle's real estate investments jumbles through my nervous system. His financial security seems unfair in contrast to my constant scramble for income, and although it's totally illogical, I almost feel he's robbed me twice.

Mom's next newsflash floors me: Jorge called her, informing her of our break up, supposedly concerned about my mental wellbeing. She doesn't let on how startled she was by this information, but wishes she'd heard it from me first. Jorge's manipulation makes me fume; he knows I don't involve Mom in the details of my personal life. I write a short note, assuring her I will call soon and explain everything, but when I consider mentioning my plan to visit Bali with Ricardo, my fingers hover over the keys, unsure. Now is not the time. I sign off and hit send.

Ricardo is still in meditation when I slip from the porch to the garden and plant my feet in the grass. I have my own practice to turn to, I applaud myself, not having ever stuck with one before now. I close my eyes and rotate my hips, one hand on my heart, the other on my belly. As my breathing smooths, my mind stills. Slowly, I spiral inward and calm returns. For now, there is only the movement, the breath and the aliveness in every particle.

Eventually the rising sun begins warming my skin, and I open my eyes to soft, pink light painting the leaves and bushes. A cobra, scaly and sleek, slithers along the garden bed, stopping to lift its head and look at me. Surely this could mean death in minutes on a tiny island with sparse medical facilities, but the alarm slamming through my veins is reined in by something greater than the both of us. "Good morning," I whisper, remaining completely still. The cobra eyes me for a moment, then gently glides away.

In a seamless flow, Nyoman picks us up, follows Ricardo's bike to my hotel, I pack my things and check out. I am about to leave when I pause at the pool overlooking the azure sea, heart filled with gratitude for the healing Crystal Beach has offered me. I will never be the same.

As Nyoman and Ricardo strap my luggage onto the two bikes, I run back to Mila's hut. My knock might awaken her, but I need to return her dress and say goodbye. She cracks open the heavy, wooden door, squinting sleepily in the daylight, and pulls me into her room. I tell her I am heading to Bali with Ricardo, and she sighs.

"I'm happy for you, but secretly I'm wishing it was me," she admits with characteristic directness.

"A month ago I was stuck in a life I hated," I say, squeezing her hand. "Just give it time."

At Ricardo's house we pack as cleverly as possible in one large backpack for the two of us. Half an hour later we are tasting saltwater spray on our faces as the speedboat cuts through choppy water. Disembarking on Bali, Ricardo has already established his favorite place to rent a motorbike, and soon we are on the road, surrounded by a swarm of scooters. The other drivers are bundled in parkas or jackets against the tropical heat, the women wearing knitted gloves to keep from tanning. A passenger beside us carries a full-sized, glass-paned door in his hands. On another motorbike rests an entire store of kitchen wares. I lean close to Ricardo's helmet to point the guy out and he laughs, nodding in turn at a family of five across the intersection. Mom and dad, two small children, and a baby in arms are all on one motorbike.

"They're not even wearing helmets," I gasp.

He shrugs. "Karma is their ultimate health insurance."

Our first stop is shopping in the southern peninsula. Apparently I need a white gown for the final ceremony of the retreat and I didn't happen to bring one to the film shoot. Not that I own one.

I discover Seminyak is Bali, Los Angeles-style. The little streets are crammed with fashion-conscious, upscale boutiques and crowded with cars, motorbikes and blue taxis trolling for fares. We cruise past batik bedding, silver jewelry, and teak lamps inlaid with mother-of-pearl, the Balinese craftsmanship merged with Western sensibilities stimulating my artistic eye.

Ricardo parks in front of a shop with mostly gauzy white garments. Hangers dangle from twisted wood, suspended from the ceiling on chains. Having traveled under the scorching sun, I wonder if I am too grimy to touch anything and appraise the racks with a helpless shrug. Shopping is not my strong suit. Ricardo gives me a taste of his fashion expertise as he steps forward and selects three dresses.

"Make sure you come out and show me," he insists.

The first dress is a silk, bias-cut, eggshell-white slip dress with a plunging neck line. Unfortunately, the fabric seems to highlight every bump and lump, and I suddenly regret my promise to stalk the catwalk. When I creep out from behind the curtain, Ricardo's eyes sweep up my body and settle upon my décolletage.

"It's sexy, for a nightgown. Next."

I emerge more confidently in a Latin-style halter dress, ruffles spilling from my hips past my knees, and sashay towards Ricardo, shimmying my shoulders. Behind him, I notice a man across the store, accompanying his girlfriend, staring straight at my chest. I look down to see that — like the last dress — my girls are on display, bouncing with each shake.

I raise a brow and turn to my stylist, hands on hips. "So you're a breast man?

He laughs. "Why not? They're smokin'." He approaches me, and I catch him glance into the reflection of the mirror, taking in the guy behind us. His hands cup me, squeezing lightly. "And they're all mine," he breathes in my ear, one hand dropping to my bottom. "This too."

The last dress features a classic circle skirt of two silky-white layers, the top one scalloped to reveal the lower one. A wide sash nips me in at the waist and a criss-crossing bodice reveals… yep, more cleavage. This is, by far, the most feminine dress I have ever put on my body, and I twirl around like an old-time Hollywood starlet, skirt lifting off my thighs. Ricardo's eyes are flashing as he takes me in his arms and pulls me against his body. "This one is definitely coming with us."

From the dressing room, I call to Ricardo for assistance. When he pokes his head around the heavy curtain, I yank him into the little room, my near-naked body shaping itself against him. He responds instantly, lips enveloping mine, tongue thrusting inside my mouth. As my knee slides up his hip, my hand crowns his close-cropped head. I'm already dizzy when he pulls away, stilling my hands as they grip his chest. "Behave, *amorcita*. I'm not walking around Seminyak pitching a tent."

At the counter Ricardo points out a display of handbags that look like portable shrines. The bases and handles are made of intricately-carved wood, the body constructed of embroidered silk. A handwritten sign refers to them as *Empress Bags*.

"You need one of these, Empress, so you can carry my phone and keys."

I give him a playful shove, but lift the closest handbag; it is surprisingly light. A design embossed with gold and cream chrysanthemums calls my name, and I place it on the counter beside the last dress.

When Ricardo takes out his wallet to pay, I fish quickly through my purse. "I'll get it."

He gives me a firm look and hands the salesgirl his card. "Let me get it for you. I want to."

"But you said you've just been scraping by."

He gives it right back to me, more strongly. "And you said you were broke."

I bite my lip. This is hard for me. It feels like an attack on my independence, even if it's not intended as one.

"Let me," he says again, voice and eyes delivering a bolt of masculine intensity.

"Thank you," I finally murmur.

"Thank you," he replies just as softly, but with the slight hint of a victorious smile.

We stroll along the sidewalk, deciding where to get a bite to eat, and have stopped beside the bike when my shoulder suddenly wrenches backward. I stumble, shocked to see a man on a motorbike driving off with my leather purse. I am too startled to utter a sound, but Ricardo, having witnessed the theft, immediately drops his backpack and guitar to the pavement. When he mounts the scooter and shoves on his helmet, my voice returns.

"Ricardo, no," I scream, lunging forward and grabbing his arm. "It's just a purse, let it go."

He barely glances at me as he thunders off on the bike, weaving through traffic in hot pursuit. What if the thief has a knife, or Ricardo gets into an accident? My hands are shaking as I scoop up our possessions and follow the road on foot, but it curves sharply and soon I've lost sight of him.

Afraid of getting disoriented, I return to where we started and set our things on the cement. My arms tightly wrap around my body. I could be angry at the thief who interrupted our lovely day, or at myself for not grasping my purse more firmly, but instead I'm boiling mad at Ricardo.

My errant knight returns with my purse under his arm. The smile of victory he wore earlier has vanished. When I see his expression, my anger fades. He parks and hands me my bag, instructing me to put the strap over my head. Massively relieved he is safe, I thank him for the rescue, but he is sullen. I don't utter a word of reproach, aware he is already taking care of that himself.

"What happened?" I ask gently, worried by the way he refuses to meet my eye.

"I caught up with him and…" He shrugs, looking up for the first time. His hand scrubs across his forehead and I notice his knuckles are speckled crimson.

"What happened?" I gasp a second time.

"I kicked his bike over," he says, creasing his brow. "And then I punched him."

"Was that necessary?" It's a ridiculous question, as Ricardo is clearly suffering from guilt already, but the words have blurted out before I can recall them.

"I wasn't thinking, just reacting. I was pissed off." He moves his jaw, and I see how tight it is. And just like that I'm looking at a much younger Ricardo, the one who used to walk down streets with two eyes in the back of his head.

"Let's get out of here," I say, slipping onto the bike behind him.

The ride to Ubud is long. We do not speak the entire way. Ricardo weaves around cars and trucks as we do the dance of the Bali roads. Traveling north the streets narrow, winding through small villages with family compounds packed close together, their red brick walls and multi-shrined family temples nearly identical, right down to the palm-leaf offerings at the doorways. An old man pedals carefully on a rusted bicycle that looks as ancient as he is, machete in hand, while a little girl does her best to balance on a new bike too large for her, ribboned braids blowing backwards. Groups of uniformed children walk in the street, laughing their way from school, expecting the traffic to move around them. We skirt endless piles of gravel and sand that take up half a lane on roads that can barely handle two-way traffic. Building projects dot the landscape like a rash, and long lines of women, mostly elders, carry baskets of rocks or cement bricks upon their heads. I wonder what happened to the tiered offerings of fruit, or the rice terraces depicted on postcards. Then occasionally we pass an area without buildings and the landscape opens up, revealing rolling carpets of emerald-green rice fields just beyond the busyness of the road.

As we approach Ubud the sweet fragrance of incense in the offerings outside every structure and frangipani flowering on the trees mingles with the acrid stench of burning garbage. Ricardo warned me we would need to do what he calls *Bali Pranayama*, the ancient

Sanskrit breathing technique of holding our breath when passing a truck belching black smoke or a burn pile incinerating plastic trash along with leaves.

We cut through tall trees in the Monkey Forest via a narrow path Ricardo skillfully navigates, dodging oncoming motorbikes, pedestrian tourists, and furry little bandits suddenly darting across the road. The monkeys have unfriendly faces, tufts standing on their heads like mohawks and long, ropey tails.

Ricardo's visa agent works from a bamboo cafe selling raw food delicacies. We find her seated at a table, busily explaining immigration logistics to a Russian couple. Behind them is a line of travelers, sipping green juice and attempting patience.

As we wait our turn, Ricardo hands me a slice of raw tamale pie and *jamu*, bright yellow turmeric juice mixed with lime and honey. He is still remote and the longer he stews, the less I think it has to do with the purse incident.

"Just tell me," I finally request. "Whatever it is, I'm sure we can handle it."

That earns me a crooked little smile, and my heart pings in response.

"I got an email from Zee this morning," he offers, then seeing my confusion adds, "My sister." He scratches his leg, looking down deep in thought, then glances up at me. "It threw me," he admits.

I listen carefully as he explains their brother, Manu, has been dealing drugs again. He has already been busted twice, and had promised he would stop the last time Ricardo bailed him out.

"If he's dealing again, he must be desperate, which means he's in trouble," Ricardo says. "I understand what it's like ruining your own life, but if he's putting Moms and Zee at risk…"

Shadows of emotion flicker across Ricardo's face, volumes of backstory he isn't sharing. He stares off into the garden. When his expression hardens, I'm tempted to ask what he's thinking, but leave it. He'll tell me when he's ready.

The visa line inches forward. Polishing off a slice of velvety, vegan chocolate cheesecake, we fall into conversation with a doe-eyed Romanian woman. She recently completed her first yoga teacher training course and, learning Ricardo has been teaching for years, complains of a certain pose hurting her back. The visa agent calls my name and while handing over my passport, my eye catches the Romanian woman lying down, right there on the restaurant floor. She folds her slender arms across her chest and Ricardo presses against them, adjusting her spine, causing her to gasp. I know he is altruistically being of service, simply doing his job, but it still irks me that he is hypnotizing one more woman into his sexual vortex.

Walking away from the café — my passport now in the hands of a total stranger — I am struck with the impression of stepping atop a lake, only the thinnest layer of ice covering a void of dark water beneath my feet. Under the broiling sun.

G iant tourist buses, out of scale with the diminutive streets, dwarf our bike, and I breathe a sigh of relief when we exit the town. Balinese villages and expat homes dot rice fields on either side of the road. We wind down a remarkably steep jungle ravine, tangled with vegetation, and cross a small river. A group of young boys play naked in the water beside two men, bathing and chatting, impervious to the splashing beside them or the traffic passing by.

After climbing the gorge, we pass an expanse of open fields so green it looks like the very essence of vitality, and enter a small village at the far end. Ricardo surprises me by parking in front of a Balinese compound.

"I need to make the retreat staff induction this afternoon, but we have enough time for a quick visit first," he says with the hint of mystery in his voice as he swings off the bike.

I squint at the compound, but cannot see beyond its high walls. "We're visiting someone?"

"My teacher," Ricardo says, his face still obscured, with thoughts of his brother, I suppose. "I especially want you to meet his wife."

It has already been a big day. Part of me longs to beg Ricardo for a little more input with the itinerary, but I seal my lips and climb the steep steps leading to an ornamented gate, curious about who is on the other side.

"*Permisi, Om Swasti Astu,*" Ricardo calls out.

A middle-aged woman, wearing a sarong and a warm smile, opens the carved doors, ushering us in. The compound is comprised of a temple, several one-room dwellings, and a covered, open-air communal pavilion in the center. We sit on a woven palm mat on the pavilion floor while the woman leaves to announce our arrival.

A twinkling little man with a long, white beard and remarkably-fit body bounds over to us. Ricardo stands to greet him, and I follow suit. They hug each other, Ricardo towering over him. The man's leathery hands reach up and give his pupil's shoulders an extremely firm massage.

"Pak Agung, I want you to meet Sirena."

The teacher turns to me, eyes bright as polished jet. His expression is stern, and I feel my face start to flush from the intensity of his gaze. When he takes hold of my wrists and silently reads my palms, his grip is so strong it almost hurts. I have to fight my impulse to pull away.

"Ah," he says to Ricardo solemnly, "*Dia sudah datang.*"

I lift my brows, looking to Ricardo for a translation, and he smiles so proudly my heart leaps. "Yes, she has arrived." He tilts his head down to his teacher. "Is it possible for Sirena to see Ibu Iluh today?"

"Ibu is already waiting," he states matter-of-factly, turning towards a small woman standing at the door of a nearby dwelling. She is about the same height as Pak Agung, but far rounder, wrapped in traditional ceremonial garb of sarong, girdle, tight lace blouse, and waist sash. My forehead pours sweat at the sight, but Ibu Iluh seems at ease with her world.

Her eyes silently take me in, and I am struck by her quiet dignity. She shakes my hand and touches her heart in a lovely gesture of greeting. As she guides me into the room, I look over my shoulder at Ricardo who is clearly not joining me. He just smiles, nodding for me to continue.

Beside a narrow bed hangs a painting of an androgynous Hindu deity. An altar below it holds an offering plate of woven palm filled with flowers and lit incense, a vial of holy water, and a bell. Ibu Iluh kneels, lips moving in words too soft to hear, not that I'd understand them, while I sit behind her, unsure of what I am supposed to do or even why I am here. She finishes and sits beside me, not saying anything at all, but I have the sense much is taking place.

"You pray?" she eventually asks.

"Sometimes." Rarely.

"*Meditasi?*"

I nod, snaking my hands as I try to explain my dancing meditation.

"Good..." she murmurs, looking deep into my eyes. "You see things?"

Her hands sweep above her head and I look up, baffled.

"Spirits?" she continues.

"I have powerful images in my dreams."

"Ah." She rocks her head, closing her eyes. "You left your body. In water."

My hands grow clammy against my thighs. "Ricardo told you about that?"

"No." She opens her eyes, but they have a faraway look. "I can See."

I sit there, digesting the inexplicable, as she tells me water is my element. Where I lack balance is with earth, air, fire, metal, and wood, but she can help me.

"You are ready." I can't tell if it's a question or a fact, but I nod my head, wondering what I'm ready for.

Ibu Iluh asks me to lie on the bed and kneels beside in prayer. After what seems an eternity, she sings out a chant and slips to the foot of the bed. I am half asleep when she takes my soles in her hands and a current that could probably light up the island of Bali flows up the length of my spine. When it reaches my head everything turns white, and my muscles tense in momentary panic. Is she sending me out of my body again?

Shifting now to the side of the mattress, Ibu Iluh places one hand on my heart and the other on my crown. Energy passes from her hands to my head, down my body, out my feet, and I'm swept up in the powerful sensation even as fear lingers at the edges. Behind my lids I clearly see the image of a mountain covered with exuberant, leafy growth from canopy to forest floor. A small river of pure water I can see through flows at the bottom of a narrow valley, forming a pool in one of its wide, lazy bends. Birds swoop in, drinking the sweet water, and as dreamy as the images are, I am sure this is an actual place. Above the river I glimpse a rustic timber and concrete dwelling, and drifting closer, spy an elderly woman stirring a smoldering cauldron over a fire pit near the house.

She turns to me with penetrating eyes and I know she has seen me. Her midnight black arm beckons me closer. "*Yuh belong here.*"

Her words are still echoing when I open my eyes and discover I am alone. For a brief, disorienting moment I forget where I am, and slowly push myself up to sitting. A longing for the mountainside pulses through every level of me, and although I do not know where it is, I am certain it is not in Indonesia. A horrifying question rips through me: What if I am not meant to be with Ricardo? Ibu Iluh's touch has jumbled my brain until I don't know what's what, and I shoot an accusatory glance at the thick coil of incense smoke, wondering if it's laced with something.

Opening the door, squinting at the splash of daylight, I find Ricardo sitting with Pak Agung and Ibu Iluh on the pavilion floor, all of them looking up at me expectantly. Pak Agung says something, and they laugh. Ricardo turns to me, translating, "Bapak says you look like a newborn baby."

That somewhat explains the preverbal state I am in. I join them, sinking to my knees in silence. I know they aren't laughing at me, yet clearly I'm the vulnerable one here, unsure how to interpret what just happened.

Pak Agung leans forward, resting both his hands on my knees.

"You born again. Lucky you," he beams, joyful as a skinny, brown-skinned Santa Claus.

The woman who first greeted us brings a tray with ginger tea and biscuits. Ricardo speaks with the couple, moving between English and Indonesian, while I sip my tea in swirling stupefaction.

Eventually Ricardo stands and takes my hands, helping me to my feet. As Pak Agung and Ibu Iluh walk us to the compound entrance, Ibu Iluh leans close to my ear, murmuring, "Go to the mountain. The birds and leaves will speak to you."

I want to ask her where the mountain is, but she is already laughing and pinching my arm, teasing Ricardo for not feeding me enough.

At the motorbike Ricardo hugs me in close. "*Asombroso.* That was amazing."

I blink. "I don't know what happened, so how could you?"

He doesn't seem to notice the edge to my tone. "Ibu said her guides instructed her to give you a full dose," he informs me with bright eyes.

"Dose of what?" I tug uncomfortably on the bra strap creeping up my back.

"She channels pure spiritual energy through her body. It's like an electrical charge. Didn't you feel it?"

Anxiety bubbles up in me. Everything so far has been revelatory and mystical, but the fear of losing dominion over my body — and everything else — drapes around the periphery. Jorge has interfered with my life at home, and here on the island Ricardo is whisking me from one mind-bending experience to the next, without any discussion or disclosure.

"Why didn't you tell me we were coming here?"

He starts to answer me but stops, seemingly lost for words. "I didn't think she would do that today," he finally explains. "Energy transfer usually comes after numerous visits, and a lot of meditation." He looks at me closely, head tilted questioningly. "Hold up, are you upset with me?"

Yes, is the short answer. Ricardo has pulled me onto his runaway train, but if the journey and destination are wonderful, does it matter? Maybe, something whispers inside me, because I might end up in a devastating crash.

"I'm in awe of what I saw. And confused." I look away, afraid to tell him the words I heard. "You took me for electroshock therapy without giving me a chance to think about it."

His face sets at my reprimand. "Do you regret coming here and experiencing it?"

I glare at him, unwilling to concede the point. Although I have no desire to emasculate him, I don't want to feel manipulated either. "I think you like to be in charge."

He shoots me a look, then shrugs it off and gets on the motorbike. As I climb on behind him, I admit with a huff that I'm overreacting, and he says he will try to reduce the surprises. Just like that, our spat is over.

I think we're about to leave, but he swivels in his seat, helmet in hand. "So what did you see?"

I close my eyes for a moment, remembering. "A distant place somewhere," I say, deliberately vague. "Ibu Iluh told me I need to go there. That the birds and leaves will speak to me."

"Birds?" Something has piqued his curiosity.

"Do you want me to tell you the whole thing right here?" On a parked motorbike in a Balinese village? In the distance I hear gamelan music similar to the tracks I listened to at the gym in Los Angeles. Two women sit near a shop beside stacks of pineapples and papayas, and a group of men are squatting across the road, eyeing us while stroking their roosters and smoking cigarettes. A troop of little boys dash by with a homemade kite. Not a particularly private setting.

"I'm game if you are."

He hops off the bike and back on, rearranging himself so I'm straddling his thighs, our noses almost touching. My reticence melts away in the light of his attention, his warm smile encouraging me to divulge everything. I tell him about the mountain with the forest, the magical pool at the bend in the river, the birds diving in for a drink. I can see my words are having an emotional impact on him, but don't understand why.

We sit for a moment in silence. "Something else. I saw a house made of wood, standing on stilts. Next to it was an open fire-pit with an iron pot. An old woman with dark skin was stirring something." I leave out the part about her beckoning me forward, and the certainty that the next step in my journey will take me there. With or without him.

I look up to find his eyes swimming, as if my words have grabbed him by the throat. He is looking at me and through me, all at once.

"You saw Granny."

"Your grandmother?" A filament of hope flickers through me that Ricardo is somehow connected to the vision.

"My mother's grandmother. She's an old-style herbalist living way up in the Blue Mountains in Jamaica. You saw her making *roots*, an herbal elixir." He shakes his head, blinking a few times. "I wasn't even sure if she was still alive."

"Really? Why don't you know?"

The gamelan intensifies in the distance. "I only went to Jamaica once when I was a kid. I felt I could be myself there, like I belonged to something. Granny had this white bird, she said it spoke to her. It was wild, but it would come and land on her shoulder. Sometimes it would stand on mine." His voice is tender, his face youthful. "My mom couldn't wait to get away from that place. When she had a falling out with her mother, they were both so stubborn they wouldn't patch it up. I never went back."

"What keeps you from returning now?"

"Nothing… except Moms wouldn't like it. Her falling out with my grandmother was over me."

"You?"

"Pretty much. Grandmother thought I was running with the wrong crowd in Brooklyn and needed to stay with her and Granny.

And honestly, I think my mom realized she was right, but was too proud to admit it."

"You turned out okay in the end."

He smiles, but it doesn't reach his eyes. "My grandmother died just after I got arrested, and it broke my mother's heart. She blames herself. And me."

I nod slowly, beginning to understand why he seems to feel responsible for those around him.

"So the storyline is, you mess everything up for the people you love? Then as payback you have to rescue them?"

"Something like that."

"Are you afraid that will happen with me?"

The question catches him off guard, fear and pain washing over his face. Wide-eyed, his lips parted just inches from mine, Ricardo is exquisite in his vulnerability. So much so it slays me.

"I've had a habit of destroying what's most precious to me."

"We're all capable of that," I breathe. "And you've changed since you were younger."

"Have I?" His eyes are dark as he stretches out his knuckles, examining the tiny grazes spattered across them. "Sometimes I'm not so sure."

My palm rests across the broken skin, holding him. "I am."

"I've tried my best to integrate the past before you arrived in my life." But worry is knitted across his brow.

"Well you're way ahead of me. I just figured out what's been driving me crazy my whole life and have barely begun to integrate even the idea of it."

"You know stuff will come up…" His voice sounds assertive, yet I sense him waffling. "Just did."

I share his concern, but as I watch the boys in the distant field launch their kite, I also sense something greater and stronger pulling us together.

"Let's make a pact, okay?" I let him go and clasp my hands together, eyes bright. "If our old issues get triggered and one of us takes a nosedive, the other person helps pull them from the pit. Only one of us gets to have an emotional reaction at a time. Agreed?"

"I like it."

"I should warn you that I only have experience with compounded emotional reactions turning into cyclones. I've been called… dramatic." I'm joking, kind of, but Ricardo's expression is earnest.

"We'll find our way through the swamp," he assures me.

"I want to say nothing disastrous is going to happen, but I have worries, too. I'm afraid something will take you away from me." Or someone.

There they are, our worst fears, splayed out on the side of the road in a tiny village in Indonesia. We press our foreheads together, the sun shining down upon our skulls. I could sit like this with him forever, but I know we have to leave.

"We need to see Granny at some point," I add as he turns around and brings the engine to life. Then I say it, the simple sentence that rings inexplicably with powerful truth, "*You belong here,* that's what she told me, Ricardo."

His brows rise behind his visor as he takes this in, then he flashes me a brief smile and revs the bike. Maybe I am supposed to lead Ricardo to his ancestral land. Except that is not exactly what Granny said. If I belong there with her, maybe Ricardo is the one leading me.

We wheel around a bend and suddenly before us looms a majestic mountain enshrouded in clouds, only its ragged peak visible.

"That's Mount Agung, an active volcano," Ricardo calls over his shoulder. Ring of Fire has new meaning for me now, riding across this island where powerful energy simmers just below every surface. The man pressed between my thighs is no exception.

Down another verdant ravine and up the other side, even the towering clove trees and the cicadas seem to breathe more deeply here. We ride along, weaving around potholes, passing rice fields and vegetable plots, thick arcing bamboo and clusters of coconut palms, encountering only an occasional farmer carrying a pole across his back balancing baskets of field produce.

Eventually we turn onto a dirt alley, ending at a gated driveway. Ricardo honks and a uniformed guard opens the entrance to a lavish estate. Ricardo insists on carrying both the backpack and his guitar, and side by side we enter the vast, open-air, tastefully furnished retreat building. Oversized vases of tuberoses perfume the air, circulated by ceiling fans. I pause near the dining table, made from a split tree trunk the length of a telephone pole, listening to the soft rush of water and taking in the sweeping view. Beyond an infinity pool and the rooftops of individual bungalows scattered down the hill, is the unbroken panorama of a jungle gorge.

I notice a group of trendy women lounging at the far end of the space on plush, upholstered couches, their stylish city clothing at odds with the earthiness of Bali and the girlish way they lean into one another. When they notice Ricardo they make a fuss, and one of them rushes to greet us. Older than the others, she is meticulously groomed and casually dressed in expensive materials with a slightly unconventional cut to them. Silver drips from her throat, wrists and earlobes.

"Darling, what have you done to your marvelous locks?" she asks, stopping just before Ricardo and then openly staring at me.

I swallow my uneasiness. Did he not tell her I was coming? Before Ricardo can say a word, the woman steps forward and pulls him into a tight hug, her bright-red nails slipping over his scalp, obviously quite familiar with him.

As she releases him, he smiles. "Time for something new, Talia."

Her vivid blue eyes slide over to me. "And this lovely creature is the something new?" She draws back, hand on hip, and scans me head to toe.

"Talia, this is Sirena."

"Welcome into the Harem," she says. "We can't wait to learn all about you."

Instead of feeling welcomed, I prepare myself for an oncoming interrogation. That should be no surprise. After all, I am the woman who finally cracked Ricardo, and a quick glance reveals I'm nothing special. Of course they're curious. I smile weakly at the women around us, increasingly apprehensive the next few days may be an ordeal.

Talia walks us to a polished teak bar. "Drinks? I know Ricardo will want something tame," she sighs, "but how about a little fun for you, my dear? Gin and tonic with passion fruit? That's what we're working on."

I've never needed one more, but I sense I'd better keep my wits about me. "I'll stick with the tame Ricardo drink."

"Oh, I'm sure you will," she says, eyebrow raised, running her fingers through her short, stylized, bleached-blonde hair. "Though I doubt drinking Ricardo is at all tame." She laughs at her own joke, but it comes off as crass to me.

She fills two glasses from a large jug. "Most women rake their nails across a man's back, but you pulled the poor thing's hair right off his head." I try to grin, but fail miserably. Where is my own witty repartee? I take forever to warm up around people.

"Don't mind me," Talia hands us the drinks and leads us up a spiral staircase to the second floor. "I can't help myself. Sometimes I think I'm a modern day Mae West."

Talia opens the door to our room, releasing a wall of cool air, and we step into a bygone era. An expanse of sliding glass doors opens onto a private balcony seemingly floating in the jungle canopy. High-backed, filigreed rattan chairs with tufted cushions face the view beside an antique Chinese pot used as a side table. To our left, a king-size, four-poster bed awaits, its impeccably-crisp white sheets and stacked pillows outlined behind gauzy mosquito netting. I run a hand up one of the carved wooden posts, already enthralled with the romantic setting. Talia swipes invisible dust from a bronze statue of a Hindu Goddess sitting atop a piece of handmade European lace at a highly-polished teak writing table. She looks up and plucks a wilted bloom from a pot of orchids by the statue. I recognize a perfectionist when I see one.

"The room is lovely, Talia," I tell her, my attempt at camaraderie.

"The colonial era…" she says, hand outstretched theatrically, "Deplore the politics, love the aesthetics."

Once she is certain we are comfortable, Talia leaves in a cloud of fine perfume and I turn to Ricardo, incredulous. "This is your retreat? A harem?"

He laughs at my surprise. "Talia's been doing women's empowerment groups for years. I'm the yoga teacher."

"Aren't men banned from this sort of thing?"

"Usually, I guess." He shrugs, still smiling at my reaction. "I think she keeps inviting me here to stir things up. Maybe it's easier to find your femininity if there's a masculine presence, too." I wrinkle my nose dubiously, and he adds, "She's really serious about encouraging women to love themselves. I've seen people truly transformed here, Sirena."

"So who are all the girls on the couches?"

"The inner circle. Audiovisual team, nutritionist, beauticians… they go all out."

"I thought harems were degrading of women." I am picturing a brothel with Talia as the madam, or Ricardo as an emperor surrounded by servants.

He has the gall to smirk. "Talia would say the word has been profaned. She's simply taking what used to be holy and resurrecting it."

"And you're the token male eye candy? An idol in their temple?"

He shrugs off my annoyance. "Talia likes to say I have generated enough feminine juju to enter the Temple gates. But I don't attend the ceremonies. Basically I teach yoga and keep to myself."

Somewhere in this conversation, at this remarkable estate, I have sprung a leak. Jealousy simmers beneath my words and my confidence is evaporating. Ricardo strokes my hair. "*Que lo que*, Sirenita. What's up?"

He has brought me into a coven of desirous women who have

made a career of harnessing their inner goddesses. "I'm out of my league."

"I'd like to get you out of something. Those clothes, for instance…" he lifts his eyebrow and then pulls back the fabric draping the side of the bed. "Any clue of my intentions?" Two long, brown fingers press the center of my chest, scooting me back until my thighs hit the mattress. "Come on, let's mess up the sheets."

He bounces on the bed irreverently, and when I try to make him stop — what if the women downstairs hear us? — he wrestles me on top of him. "You have nothing to fear, *mi tesoro*," he breathes up at me. "You may have only just discovered your gifts, but you'll explore them and grow confident. I'll help you."

He's enticing, his woodsy pine and amber scent mingling with the lemon of the clean sheets. Still, I press away from his chest and roll off. The more he intoxicates me, the stronger my resistance grows. "Maybe I need to do it by myself."

Ricardo pulls me back to his side and tugs my bottom lip with his teeth, tempting me, but I can't get beyond the vision of him wading through a sea of admiring females. He wraps his arms around me more tightly as his tongue captures mine and my hips instinctively curve into his, but my body's response only makes me more aggravated, resenting him for things he hasn't even done yet.

"Give it up." His words have a touch of laughter in them; he knows the power he has over my arousal. His hands insist on stripping away my reticence, one gripping my bottom and the other working its way under my shirt, finding my nipple through my bra. I arch my back, grinding against him, but my hands grip the sheets in frustration.

"I'm having an emotional reaction," I blurt, putting our pact to work already, a much better idea than socking him.

"I see that," he says into my mouth, kissing me until I moan into his. He runs his fingers up my skirt, tugging under the damp fabric of my panties. "How can I help?"

Before I can answer a knock at the door summons Ricardo for his meeting. He calls out that he'll be right down, but doesn't budge, breathing into my ear, "I'm not leaving until you give it up." The way he says it, full of raw, masculine, erotic power, wilts my resolve.

His fingers part my folds in one long, delicious sweep as a muffled moan escapes my lips. Feeling aroused and manipulated, I roll away from him and stand up. I know I am running from my own pleasure, but I can't help it, and stare him down, irritated and flushed. He stands and adjusts his pants.

"We're not done here," he says, voice gravely. "To be continued."

We descend the stairs together. Ricardo slips off to Talia's villa for his meeting, while I drift awkwardly toward the crowd of young hipsters on the couches, hanging at a distance, still spinning from the unresolved rupture with Ricardo. Although I sense my arrival as Ricardo's sidecar elevates my standing with this crowd, somehow it leaves me feeling diminished, a mere accessory. I guess there is going to be a learning curve with this man both in private and in public. His beam of light casts an awfully long shadow.

Feminine primping is taking place. A woman, with multiple piercings, dramatic bone jewelry, dyed-black hair and the look of a pirate, is clamping purple, blue, and turquoise feathers onto another woman's tresses. The longer I study my companions, most of whom have feathers dangling from their hair, ears or around their necks, my ease increases.

"Would you like to get feathered next, Sirena?" calls out the hair stylist with a British accent.

I'm not really the feathers-in-the-hair type, but suddenly I am a new person in more ways than one. A month ago if I'd been told a shaman would conduct electricity through my body and I'd speak to birds, I would have laughed — or groaned — so why not?

"What colors do you fancy?" she questions as I step closer and peer into her box containing every shade of the rainbow. "How about earth tones for your olive complexion? Browns, and a touch of this rusty one?"

Another woman opens a small suitcase on her lap, revealing the portable contents of a nail salon. "I'm Aurora, here to work on your talons."

"Heaven knows I need that." My mother and aunt with their immaculately-coifed hair and enameled nails would be appalled at my current lack of upkeep. "I've been on the beach for weeks. Thank you." I choose a glittery rust color for my nails, brighter than the feathers falling from my ear to shoulder.

When yet another angel appears with a makeup kit I decide that perhaps the retreat won't be so bad after all. While the three women work on me at once, I can't help wondering what Ricardo will think of the dolled up version of me.

A discussion of contraception techniques accompanies our beautification ritual. One of the young women is eager to be pregnant, but the rest of us are working hard to keep the babies at bay.

"I had extra-heavy bleeding with my periods and pain in my abdomen, but removing my IUD cleared that up. Guess my uterus didn't like living with a copper wire. Which is a drag, 'cause the IUD was easy."

"I use a basal thermometer to figure out when I'm ovulating and bar the door to the bedroom," laughs another, her hair bushy with feathers. "Such a drag… that's the time when my whole system screams, 'Now, lover,' but my little chart insists that's off limits." She looks wistfully into the distance, as if thinking of the man waiting for her at home. "I call it natural birth control, but it feels damn unnatural at three in the morning when all I want is to tackle him."

"I don't eat food sprayed with pesticides, so how can I put spermicide inside my yoni? No way."

"Yeah, we eat organic, but we're supposed to take pills with weird side effects to trick our body into believing it's already pregnant?"

"What about condoms? They're pretty harmless."

"Killjoys is more like it." Laughter all around. "My boyfriend calls it wearing a raincoat."

"And they aren't very green if you throw them away after each use.

Unless you wash and recycle." More laughs.

"What are you using, Sirena?"

Oh no. All eyes are on me. I have always been vigilant in the past, but now am regularly having crazy-delicious, unprotected sex. "I guess I'm still trying to figure that out..."

When the primping ends we pass around a gilt mirror and I take in the deep-claret lipstick, smoky eyes and tiny rhinestones sitting just above my lashes. A fawn-colored feather brushes against my cheek and an inexplicable shiver of excitement runs up my spine.

"How about breaking out the belly dance costumes?"

The pirate leads a raid on a nearby room lined with shelving and boxes overflowing with fabrics. I hesitate at the door, but Aurora throws her arm around my shoulder, drawing me along. Trying on various outfits, from hip-hugging, full-flowing skirts to sashes with dangling beads and bra tops covered in sequins and coins, I am beginning to realize how much Talia has invested in this retreat, and start to believe her motivations must be largely altruistic. From what Ricardo has told me of the costs to attend, I wonder if she is breaking even.

We help each other accentuate our finer points, accessorizing with belts, necklaces, and bangles. When each woman is sufficiently bedazzled, we return to the open lounge and blast poly-rhythmic, ethnic dance music from the high fidelity sound system, shaking our beads and sequins to the beat.

Spontaneously we form a circle, egging each other on as our hips swirl and breasts shimmy, smiling faces glowing with sweat. The bravest dancers sashay into the center to the cheers and clapping of the group, showing off their finest moves. I enjoy the dancing, but keep to the outskirts.

The music segues to a slower tempo and we return to dancing individually. More at ease on my own, I close my eyes and focus on dancing from the inside out, as I do during my morning meditation. My mind quiets, sinking, emptying, becoming trance-like. Time stands still. With my eyes shut, the women moving around me fade, and the music drops away until I'm standing on the mysterious mountainside I visited earlier with Ibu Iluh. A hummingbird with elongated tail feathers drinks nectar from red hibiscus flowers, then darts closer, hovering directly before my nose. It's wings are a blur, fluttering a soft wind on my cheek, yet the delicate bird is still. The tiny creature leads me to its nest full of colorful leaves and glistening gemstone eggs. The closest cracks open and rainbow light spills out.

When I open my eyes a prickle of awareness creeps up the back of my neck. He's watching me, I know it, somewhere beyond the swaying bodies. Turning slowly, I find Ricardo seated on the couch, leaning forward with his chin propped against his long fingers, hooded eyes following my every move. Talia and her organizational team, seated beside him, are also looking in my direction. Have they been talking about me? Am I missing something?

A new song picks up the pace and the belly dancers respond with raucous spiritedness, sauntering to the women on the couches, teasing and seducing in an attempt to get them to join the fun. I remain where I am, feet planted, eyes locked with Ricardo's. My attention is quick to respond to his presence, but I am doing my best to retain the quality of dancing from the inside out. It doesn't help that he is looking at me as if no one else is in the room, or on the planet, and I am meeting him there, all else dissolving into soft focus. We are not close enough to touch, yet my body moves as if pressed against his. I almost falter when I feel the laser beams of other eyes on me and realize everyone is watching us. Pirate winks at me. I guess this is what happens when you've nabbed the only man in the Harem, and that man happens to be Ricardo.

My head whips around as his tall, strong frame looms at my side. "We have business to finish upstairs. Now." He takes my hand and pulls me towards the staircase.

"Dinner is at 7, if you're still hungry," Talia calls out, and laughter trails us to our room.

"They all want to jump your bones," I can't help but groan once the door closes.

He's quiet, thoughtful. "Or they just want what we have."

The words warm me from the inside out. I glance at him standing by the bed, arms loosely crossed over his chest, while I move to the writing desk and examine the antique inkwell. Picking up the quill pen, I wave it at him, "How was your meeting?"

"Productive. Fun. Talia wants you to participate, by the way."

"That's kind of her." A small flash of guilt flickers through me as I think of the makeover and dancing I've already helped myself to, but it's quickly followed by a burst of pride. The old Sirena would have spent the afternoon hiding in her room with a book. "I kind of joined in already. Hope she doesn't mind."

"I mean she wants you to be a presenter."

"Me?" My nose crinkles in surprise, the feather pointing at my chest.

"She suggested you lead a dance meditation."

"That's why she was watching me?"

"That, plus you seemed to be in a trance."

Remembering, I meander towards the balcony and peer out into the ravine. "I think I was." Either that or I'm going crazy. Turning back to Ricardo, "I saw the mountain again."

He moves quite close to me, running his fingers through my hair, examining my new feathers. "What did you see?"

"A hummingbird with exceptionally long tail feathers. It showed me to its nest."

"Was it full of baby birds?" His thumb cleaves the soft pillows of my breasts, thrust high in the belly dancing bra.

"Gemstone eggs."

"Mmmm…" His palms brush down my exposed midriff, fingers splayed wide as they settle on the fullness of my hips. He pulls slightly on the skirt, taking in my costume, murmuring, "I love the way you move."

I lean into him but he retreats to the bed, and sinks against the pillows, his arms loose atop his stomach. Indolent lion. Every supple inch of him is languid and regal. "Dance for me," he directs. "Let me see you move."

His voice is thick with promise, and something in me stirs. Jorge would have loved a strip tease, but it always felt contrived and I was far too self-conscious. Perhaps it's the way Ricardo responds to my costume, or how hot he looks as he pulls off his shirt, keeping his eyes on me even as it slips over his head. I decide to tease him a little, sauntering to my phone as if checking messages when I'm actually selecting a seductive dance track. I feel him shift on the sheets, ready to jump up and drag me to bed, but when the notes start playing I turn and he's reclining once more as if he'd never moved.

It seems another woman, maybe a spirit from another era, enters my body as I begin rotating my hips, accentuating each movement. I sway closer to where he lies, time slows down, and something magnetic passes between our locked eyes.

"So, Your Highness," I climb onto the bed and sink back on my knees, torso slowly undulating. "Have you chosen me from among your harem?"

"I have," he muses, almost more to himself than me.

My hand slips over my rolling chest. "What do you want with me?"

"I want to capture you…" he says, unblinking. "Bind you to me forever. And set you free." My hand stills on my thigh, already held captive by the intensity of his voice. "I want you as my queen."

Stepping away from him, back to the floor, his eyes cover me, consume me, landing on my breasts. "Dance for me," he commands again, reaching for me, but I scoot backwards, unwilling to surrender quickly. Instead I swish around him, close enough to touch but far enough to move away, should he try. With my back to my raja, I slowly drag the skirt up my legs, arching as I glance over my shoulder.

"Show me what is mine." His voice is raw.

I release my breasts over the top of the bra, turning enough to offer them to his eyes, but not his touch, continuing to circle my hips.

His throat bobs as he swallows.

"Take the bra off," he demands, and I let it sail in his direction.

Teasing the skirt down, I carefully stretch the elastic waist from one side, then the next. I look up to see he has slipped his hand inside his pants and is holding himself as I move. He may as well be stroking me; the sight sends a bolt of heat between my bare legs. My thong is all that blocks his complete view, until I bend over and drag that down, too.

"Here. Now," he orders, and I move toward him, almost afraid of the intensity as he looks at me. Ricardo's passion is palpable at the most relaxed of times, and I can't imagine the strength of his desire when deliberately provoked. I've gone and jabbed the hornet's nest.

I'm barely on the bed when he lunges forward, much faster, stronger, and agile than I am. Instantly my back is against the sheets, my wrists pinned above my head and legs spread by a single, powerful thigh. My body sizzles with heat, paralyzed, as his hand moves down to adjust himself at my entrance. I am eager for the long, delicious stretch as he fills me, but instead he holds himself back, staring deep into my eyes.

"Want me?"

I nod my head, but that isn't enough. His lips against my ear are wet and hot as he draws a breath. "Say it."

"I want you more than I have ever wanted anyone, or anything."

For a fraction of a second I think he is taken aback by my response. He was probably only looking for a simple yes. Then he drives into me with one swift thrust, his mouth consuming mine, his hands pawing at me, a lion mauling its prey. I am just as wild, bucking at each thrust detonating inside me, dragging my nails across his back as he drives into me harder, faster, and deeper than ever before. He is taking me, devouring me, capturing me as he said he would.

His large hand grips my thigh and draws my leg onto his muscular shoulder, and I am filled so full I wonder if he'll split me in half. Still he pushes in farther with his turbo charged body, groaning, "Take it all."

And I do, allowing him in, even like this, even this far, all the way in, surrendering into the sudden gush of pleasure, the warm jet of liquid spraying out of me like a dark geyser of love. I shudder and explode, then fall back to earth like a dying star.

The sheets are soaked and I blink, dazed by what we've done, but he is not finished with me. Shifting me to the edge of the bed on my hands and knees, he stands behind at just the right height for full command. Grasping handfuls of my bottom, he slides deeply in and most of the way out, winding us further into the intoxicating web we spin together. His thumb draws some moisture from the hot, juicy place where we merge to the tightly-puckered flesh above. His finger caresses in a circular motion and I surprise myself by pressing back, leaning into the sensation, foreign as it feels. In one explosive move, he pulls himself onto the bed and my back heats as he curls over me, pressing in harder, pumping faster, hungry, voracious, his teeth on my neck.

"I want to fuck you in the ass," he grunts into my ear.

He hasn't used the f word until now. And this is how he chooses to use it. It is so real and raw and strongly male that my body is quivering and I feel myself melt, a swamp running down the inside of my thigh.

"I don't know," I gasp, wanting it, but afraid. "How will you fit?"

"Step by step," he says, pulling out of me.

I am suddenly bereft, hot, soaking and on all fours, perched alone on the side of the bed. Over my shoulder I see Ricardo lifting a small bottle from his backpack.

Something shifts in the brief downtime, and I start to cool off, though I don't want to. Then he is standing behind me, the smell of coconut filling the air as his fist moves up and down his glistening cock, his other hand massaging oil onto my ass. He pushes his finger inside the tight, tense entry and a short stab of pain ricochets through me.

He freezes. "Are you okay, *mi tesoro?*"

His hands spread across my back, and he pulls on my shoulders until I'm sitting upright, against his torso. His hands sweep down my arms, soothing me, as his lips nuzzle my cheek.

"I hurt you, didn't I? I got carried away."

I relax into his hold, even as I wonder why everything has come to a grinding halt. I didn't want him to stop.

"I liked it. You were wild. I finally started breaking through all your self-control."

He sinks onto the bed beside me, pulling me into his arms. "It was amazing, but… " His broad chest moves in and out in a slow release. "Something wasn't right, wasn't pure."

"Are you kidding? You were pure passion."

His eyes are wide, but conflicted. "Your dance was so hot and that fountain that came out of you was beyond sexy." He makes his eyes widen. "Thing is, I dig playing the role of your king, but I wrestle with that old-school, dominant thing in me. You're right, I do like being in control, but for the last five years I've been trying to eliminate the machismo. Actually thought I'd gotten rid of it." He grimaces. "When I act like that, all I see is my stepfather."

My fingers trace the outline of his lion tattoo. I don't know how that man abused Ricardo, but I can tell he is deep under my lover's skin.

"Something happened, didn't it, with your mom's boyfriend?"

He knows what I'm asking, but erects a barrier of silence. After everything I have exposed about myself, his unwillingness to open up to me stings.

He pulls in a huge breath and blows it through his lips, but when his eyes meet mine what I see there makes me want to cry. He looks young and broken, a world away from the adrenalized, powerful, relentless man of a few moments ago. Now he is unable to hold my gaze. I want to scoop him up in my arms, but don't dare move.

"I've talked to my sponsor about this, but only vaguely. I've never told anyone the whole story."

His words suck the air from the room. Out of the silence I ask, soft as down, "Will you tell me?"

The mix of innocence and sorrow that flashes across his features reminds me of something I read scribbled on the blackboard of the restaurant washroom earlier today. Was it only this morning?

Everyone you meet is fighting a struggle
you know absolutely nothing about.

Tenderly, one hand on his heart, I feather a kiss on his forehead. I want so much to stay by his side, comrades in purging our ghosts.

"He would use his belt on me. A lot." The words hang there, ugly and brutal, and I wince. "Sometimes he hit the little ones, but mostly it was me. I was older and I wasn't his kid. He'd pull my pants down and whip my bare ass," he continues, looking miserable. "One time I was watching television with him…"

He leaves the sentence unfinished and stares down at the sheets. I recognize the war waging within him, the need to get the words out and the overwhelming fear that keeps them in, the wellspring of anger that it all still has such vast power.

Gently, I urge him on. "What's his name?"

After a long pause, he lets out a pained sigh. "Herman."

Judging by his disgust, it's been a long time since he last uttered that name. "Where was your mother?"

"At work." He goes on to explain that his little brother and sister were with an auntie when he came home from school. They were watching TV when Herman told Ricardo to go to the refrigerator and fetch him another beer. "It was the middle of the show and I didn't want to leave, so I said no." As he speaks, I can feel the surprise radiating off him, as if all these years later he is still startled by what happened. "He blew a fuse. Flung me on the couch, yanked off his belt, pulled my pants down and went crazy on me. Then he was fumbling with his zipper, pinning my head down, and pressing his dick into my ass…" He tapers off, unable to look into my eyes or continue speaking.

I lie there, horrified, indignation ripping through my stomach. I had no idea he also carried this kind of trauma. "He raped you, Ricardo."

"Yeah. I wanted to punch his lights out, but he was much bigger than me. Even now I get mad at my own paralysis." His fingers flex, and I can almost see the fumes rising off of him.

In stunned silence, I take his closest hand and press it to my cheek. My eyes, squeezed closed, paint tears on his fingers. When I lift my eyelids, the look of pain on Ricardo's face claws at my chest and I see his discomfort with my sadness.

"He would beat my mom behind closed doors, but we could still hear everything." Ricardo's voice hardens, recounting how one night Herman started wailing on his mother, worse than ever. When she finally ran out into the living room to get away, nine-year-old Ricardo snapped. "I grabbed a frying pan from the kitchen and told him to lay off my mama. He turned on me, but he was drunk and I was fast. I whacked him as hard as I could. He fell to his knees, and with one more swing he was on the floor. My mom rushed me to the neighbor's apartment, and they helped her send his ass packing."

"Sounds like David and Goliath."

"It's hard to feel victorious when your mother is sobbing like she's lost everything."

He can't speak right away and rolls onto his back, rubbing his eyes and staring at the canopy above us. "Somehow this is the worst part," he tells me without adding anything more.

I wait, the extended silence straining like a guitar string stretched taut. Ricardo is completely still, gaze far away. I've lost him. I know I mustn't prod, but after awhile the stillness is too much for me. Delicately, I drape my body next to his, being there without pushing.

The movement jars him, his eyes jerk to mine, and he spits out, "I'm so fucking tired of this plaguing me." His hands curl into fists that slam against thigh, then his forehead. I know the feeling, the urge to beat the memories out your body, but the sight of him hurting himself burns through me like a lightning bolt.

"Stop, Ricardo," I implore. When he doesn't, I straddle him, my hands grabbing at his wrists. "Please, don't."

Before I understand what's happening he's thrown me down

173

onto the bed, fiercely pinning my hands to my sides. He's naked, covered in a sheen of sweat, and brimming with rage. I flinch, almost expecting to be struck, and we hang there, trembling and breathing hard. Without my mind giving the directive, my knee draws up his thigh. I don't understand the emotions coursing through me, but I know I want to help him through this darkness.

When his mouth drops to mine, he's holding everything back with trembling self-control, but the kiss quickly turns wild with anguish and need. His mouth crashes into mine, lips crushing me, tongue stabbing into me with hard, dominating strokes. I barely have time to respond before he's rolled me onto my stomach, his hand guiding him inside me in one savage thrust. I tilt my hips up until he's pressed in as far as possible, and a moan rises out of the darkest, primal cave of my emotion.

The sound sends him into a fury of movement. He releases a cry of his own while relentlessly jackhammering me. I absorb every reverberation, every shockwave, the totality of pain and pleasure, control and surrender, all indecipherably tangled together. I let him possess me, brand me, push me to the edge and throw me over. I cry out his name repeatedly in one long mantra, as he lets loose inside of me with a fierce, thundering growl. I feel the heat of his release flooding my channel, pulsing again and again as shudders rack his torso.

Finally, his fingers relax their bruising grip and he collapses on top of me, chest heaving. I lie on my stomach beneath him, scrambled and liquified, brain trying to catch up. Never, ever, have I experienced anything like that. Which is fortunate, as it would have terrified me before now. But Ricardo has already blasted my heart open and claimed it as his own.

He rolls off to my side and studies me silently, as if worried by what he might find.

"Well... I wanted to know what it was like when you let go of control..." I run my fingers down his cheek, sleek with sweat, and lick his salty brow. His eyes register surprise at seeing mine smiling. "So now I know... that it's intense as all get out... and unbelievably hot."

He lifts his head to look at me, seemingly amazed at my willingness to travel to that place we just visited. "You rock my world, Sirenita."

"Likewise, Pak Riko."

A profound calm follows, though not fully restful, as one question still hangs thickly in the air. I touch his face tenderly and eventually have to ask if he will tell me the rest of his story.

Quietly Ricardo describes the aftermath of Herman's departure. "Our lives became more difficult without him helping pay the bills. And there was this unspoken…accusation, I guess, that I drove away my mother's lover."

I arch my brow. "Who happened to be an alcoholic-wife-beating-pedophile."

"But it's never that simple, you know? He was also funny, and often protective of my mother. He would play with his kids, and they loved him, missed him when he left. Suddenly we were eating plain rice three meals a day and wearing clothes we'd outgrown. And I was left with this feeling that if I didn't exist, they might all be together like one happy family."

A hush follows, drenched in a pool of sorrow from the past. The snarled weight of words long held and never spoken begins disentangling in the telling, the charge gradually dissipating. As I embrace Ricardo in my arms, something greater holds us both, invisibly rearranging all the particles.

"I wish I could wind back the clock so that never happened to you. So you never came to those conclusions about yourself." I can see a part of him is still buried in self-reproach and my heart reaches out to him. I want to set him free.

Spotting the bottle of coconut oil on the bedside table, I reach across and pour a drop in my hand. Ricardo's eyes follow as I stroke the back of his thigh, tenderly moving over the slope of his smooth, perfectly-rounded buttock and up to his lower back. "Ricardo, you told me we're reclaiming our innocence together." My palm massages him, returning again and again to his muscled arc, seeking to replace the violence with love. Yes, I admit to myself, love. I was born to love this man, to help pull him out of the same darkness he's pulling me from.

With each return I let my fingers slip deeper into the crevasse and, although his body tightens, I also feel his arousal stirring. When my finger rests on his soft, tight circle of flesh, he tenses.

"I've never let anyone touch me there since."

"Will you let me?"

He eases into his confident smile. "I'm yours."

My free hand takes hold of his cock and squeezes the length of his shaft, breasts pressed to his heartbeat, while delicately the tiniest tip of my finger dips inside him. He is clenched and I move carefully, pulsing my finger as my other palm rolls up to the head and back down to his balls. My finger eases in a bit more, and his hips thrust his cock into my hand.

A song stirs, lifting inside me, and my desire to bring Ricardo comfort is so great that I dare to let the crystalline tones out to travel where they will. Gradually Ricardo's body relaxes, allowing me in, and my finger strokes him more deeply on the inside, this flesh as sensitive and alive as the rest of his body. He surrenders himself to my hands — no careful control or contained release — and I milk him onto my stomach in steady, rhythmic convulsions.

"Love. Only love," I whisper, slowly withdrawing my hands.

Dusk has darkened the room, but Ricardo's eyes are shining like sunbeams. Within his vulnerability he is noble, radiating strength, and my heart bursts to look at him. It feels like my chest is physically splitting open. This is the real open heart surgery, healing that can't be found in a bottle of pills or under a surgeon's scalpel.

"I love you," he mouths to me lower than a whisper, and although I've known it all along, it still radiates through me like a revelation.

When we kiss it is a prayer, wide-open, sunshine love, without agenda, without hunger, only appreciation. Heart to heart, soul to soul. Every touch is a merging. Every single moment tastes divine. Timeless. Mindless. Breathless. The reverberation of a single tone held into infinity.

A fter a long, cool shower, I am staring into the backpack.
"Did you forget something?" Ricardo asks, watching me
from the bathroom.

"Yeah, my sexy, elegant wardrobe." The clothes I packed for my
work trip a lifetime ago no longer suit me, and I need to save my new
white dress for the final ceremony.

Ricardo emerges from the bathroom, towel wrapped around his
midsection, and runs his palms down my body. "This is your sexy,
elegant wardrobe. The rest is accessories."

With that I put on a pair of cutoffs and a camisole. Ricardo tosses
on a casual pair of loose cotton pants and a gray tee, and manages to
look like a million bucks.

"Ready to face the world?" I question, though I'm really asking
myself.

"Now I'm ready for anything."

D inner and conversation at the mile-long table is already in full
swing.

Talia's voice rises above those around her. "I hear men call their
wives 'the boss' all the time, or say 'she wears the pants.' They seem
to accept their woman is in charge." As we approach the assemblage
hand in hand, Talia ceases her train of thought to take us in. "Ah, the
glowing couple returns from the Isle of Bliss."

I have no doubt the release and relief of the last few hours are
beaming out from us like floodlights, but in this gathering, with my
lover by my side, I do not feel the need to stifle the glow or shut it
down.

"I'll have whatever they are taking for dessert," someone says to
laughter all around, and just like that the tension breaks.

Talia, the premiere hostess, escorts us to the buffet, a sumptuous spread of salads and Indonesian dishes presented on a terrazzo counter. Behind us, the discussion continues.

"In the relationships I see, the women often hold more power."

"But are those women earning as powerfully as the men? Do they have as much opportunity to advance in their career?"

"And you're talking about women in New York. What about in Lagos, or Denpasar?"

"I think it's shifting everywhere, just more slowly in some places, more accelerated in others."

Pirate speaks up. "We've been talking about the feminine as if it's superior. Isn't that just reverse sexism?"

From nowhere, my voice joins the conversation. "I think the solution is the harmonious balance of the masculine and the feminine."

Talia extends her hand towards where Ricardo and I are sharing a bench at the end of the table, enjoying the feast. "Looks like the harmony of masculine and feminine is breaking bread with us tonight."

Ricardo beams, "And it's delicious as always, Talia. Thank you."

Switching gears, Talia taps on her tablet and scrolls through listings. "How about dessert, popcorn, and a movie or two."

Movies, my favorite. Talia sings out title after title, from *Dirty Dancing* to *I'm No Angel* with Mae West, placing her hand on her hip and giving it a shake.

"They're classics," I exude. "I could watch them all in one sitting."

"Says the filmmaker among us," Talia smiles. She points to the screen, "Let's start with *Sex and Lucia*, the obscure one."

I have already seen the film several times, but this is by far the best viewing yet. We shift into an air-conditioned screening room behind the dining area, filled with upholstered couches and oversized beanbag chairs. Ricardo settles into one of the cushy seats and I squeeze between his legs, leaning against him as his arms encircle me.

Ricardo has a distinct advantage as the film is in Spanish. I read the subtitles, occasionally distracted by his mouth on my neck or his lips around my earlobe. Pleasantly distracted. The way he keeps the connection between us active thrills me.

Halfway into the film, I notice his body becoming increasingly relaxed. His hands drop to my sides. "Ricardo," I whisper and he stirs awake. I ask him if he'd be more comfortable in bed, and he agrees, only to snuggle into me more.

Abruptly the room turns pitch black, a power outage interrupting just as the film approaches its denouement. "Noooo..." come a dozen groans in unison, awakening Ricardo.

Just as suddenly the generator kicks in, power returns, and Talia cues the film to where we left it.

Ricardo kisses my cheek, whispering, "See you upstairs," and takes himself to bed.

After the credits roll, the women select *Roman Holiday,* and although it would be fun to see Audrey Hepburn and Gregory Peck on a Vespa, it has been a day full of potent surprises, I am sleepy, and I have my own superstar upstairs waiting for me in bed. A wave of gratitude rolls through me as my tired legs navigate the retreat staircase. Ricardo and I haven't even spent a full week together and already our union has rewired my circuitry.

Approaching the second floor, a memory returns of watching another Hepburn film, *Breakfast at Tiffany's,* in the loft with Jorge. He had fallen asleep on the couch in the middle of the movie, and as I sat there alone a meteor of longing, a craving for something more, shot from the center of me into the lonely night sky. Trudging upstairs to bed, a sudden and uncommon certainty soothed my emptiness, sensing somehow, someday I would share genuine love with another.

Standing outside the bedroom door, I can tangibly feel the shift from longing into belief, as if the sad version of me on the loft stairs is receiving a signal from me right here, right now. My grateful tears reach back through time, saying, "Hang in there, the most beautiful love imaginable awaits you."

The sweetness of sliding into bed with Ricardo, his muscles heavy with sleep, his body unguarded. The comfort of wrapping into his arms which embrace me even from dreamland, as I nuzzle into the warmth of his chest. I know I could easily kiss him and jumpstart the sublime union again, but I give way to sleep in the safety of his arms.

After a quiet breakfast, Ricardo leads me down the hill, past numerous freestanding bungalows, to a spacious, circular bamboo structure jutting above a swiftly flowing river. A life-sized statue of a dancing goddess stands in the far corner, surrounded on multi-tiered shelving by smaller statues of feminine deities from various cultures. Talia, seated on a cushion in the middle of the polished wooden floor, looks rather like the statues, her eyes closed in silent meditation.

Sensing our arrival, Talia's eyelids flutter open and she invites us to join her, stretching her arms as if just awakening. Ricardo opens a cabinet and brings me a cushion, but I notice he hasn't grabbed one for himself.

As I sit, he kneels beside me and brushes a kiss across my cheek. "I'll leave you goddesses to speak privately." I watch him walk away like a child abandoned on the first day of preschool. Why does he keep springing things on me without warning?

"I always include seated meditation in our program," Talia begins without preamble, "but I've been wanting something..." she swivels her shoulders in a rolling, sensual wave, "more feminine. I asked myself what meditation might have looked like in an ancient priestess temple." She pauses to give me a warm smile. "Then yesterday Ricardo described to us the meditation you do, and when I saw it myself it was my fantasy come to life."

I nod, unsure what to say. My dancing meditation is almost as new to me as it is to her. When the silence grows long I try to fill the space. "I've never been very good at sitting in meditation. My mind races. Motion works better for me."

"Can you step me through your process?"

She moves to her feet, and I follow self-consciously.

"I usually do this barefoot in the grass or at the beach. But this space is lovely."

"We call this yoga shala our temple. It's round like a womb and the top is breast-like." I crane my neck at the conical ceiling, several stories high, made of overlapping, thatched segments with a circular skylight at the tip. When I drop my gaze back to hers, she is waiting.

"What I do is simple," I swallow, spreading my feet hip distance, lightly bending my knees, one palm holding my heart, the other my belly. Once I close my eyes and rotate my hips I grow more confident, and describe how through the undulations I dial in the sensitivity of the moment. "When I find it, I want to stay on that channel. Exaggerating the slowness quiets my mind." My wrists join in, moving as if through thick jelly, hands conducting an inner symphony. When I check on Talia she is following me, and I instruct her to reverse her movements, now taking her body in the opposite direction. We continue without further instruction, until after several minutes we both settle.

"Do you go into a trance?" Talia peers into my eyes.

"I'm not sure." When she tilts her head, I feel like apologizing. "Sorry I'm not more articulate. It's still new for me."

"You just articulated the process quite well, Sirena. How would you feel about assisting the women in this meditation each morning?"

"I think I could do that," I smile, but questions immediately bubble up. Who am I to lead these women in any kind of spiritual exercise? A few weeks ago I was filming fish. What if they see right through me, or worse, I embarrass Ricardo?

"Then welcome to the Harem," she says, embracing me. She informs me of her shared resources plan, as she calls it, which effectively means I am getting paid to stay at her swank retreat center with Ricardo, eat opulent buffets, and participate in the rest of the festivities. The difference between my last job and this one is striking, enough so that my eyes glisten.

I blink back my tears and look away. "Sorry..." I did not used to cry this easily or often, and certainly not in front of people.

"Darling, that's the second time you've apologized in as many minutes. There is nothing wrong with expressing genuine emotions."

Talia doesn't ask questions or try to make the tears go away. She stands there with me as if she has nothing else to do, holding the space for me, allowing me to be with my feelings. An invisible doorway stretches wide, and another stream of silent tears roll down my jaw and fall to my chest, words tumbling out, too, explaining the recent events in my life from the film shoot in Flores to my heart experience. "Basically I died and came back again. And everything has been different since then..." I pause to formulate, and more tears spring forth.

"I sense those tears are full of gratitude for the circumstances that brought you to where you are now." Her voice is gentle, knowing.

I nod, wiping my eyes. "I was in such a pit before, full of cobras and scorpions, but something oppressive has lifted off of me. The scorpions don't have a grip on me and the cobras have become my friends. It all brought me to Ricardo—" a little gasp comes out with his name "—and he brought me here to you."

Like a great mountain accepting whatever stormy tempests blow across it, she calmly receives and holds every word. And something else; at the core of the mountain is a reverence.

"You'll have to meet Gwendolyn," Talia tells me. "Don't ask, you'll see."

Feeling blasted open and sensitive, I slowly climb the stone pathway. When I spot Ricardo from the back sitting on one of the couches, my feet quicken their steps until I get closer, and what I see stops me cold. Two of the women from crew are kneeling before him, each massaging a foot in her lap, while another kneads his shoulders. They are laughing playfully, but jealousy overtakes my ability to reason. Immediately I am breathing cactus needles.

He must sense something because he glances over his shoulder and sees me there, immobilized. With a goofy smile he motions to me, as if I just discovered him with a litter of puppies. I will myself to be calm, but equilibrium is not something I am good at faking. I wave stiffly, then climb the stairs, throat on fire, seeking refuge in our room.

Sitting on the edge of the bed, I am biting a cuticle, wishing I could still the throbbing at my temples. I know I am overreacting, unfairly projecting my past onto Ricardo, and now I've made a fool of myself in front of his little entourage. This isn't Jorge sneaking around with his sinewy blonde from the dojo, so why does it feel the same? Is it unreasonable to expect that Ricardo wouldn't allow other women to touch him, given the out-of-this-world passion we've shared, or am I being narrow-minded? With each question I plummet farther down a frightening rabbit hole.

The door swings open and Ricardo steps in, stopping mid-step when he sees me. Worry splashes across his face. I look away, unable to face him, too angry at the both of us. I long for him to hug me and restore the connection between us, but I have lost my voice and anyway, I don't want to have to ask.

"They were giving me reflexology," he offers, "that's all." He sits beside me and nudges me with his shoulder. "Don't be trippin'. You can trust me."

"Really? Because you sure are making it hard to do that."

He frowns, and his voice now carries a sharp edge. "I didn't do anything to betray your trust."

"Is that so?" I can feel my face twist into something bitter, but I don't fight it. "You talk about energy exchanges, so what the hell was that? Calling it reflexology doesn't change the fact you're exchanging energy," I pretty much spit the word, "with other women."

When he doesn't say anything, I can no longer contain myself. "Is this what your celibacy was like? And your work in New York? Do you have yoga groupies in every port? Do you even know how to interact with women without having them want to climb all over you?"

I blurt the words, harsh and accusatory, and he flinches like I've slapped him. I want to say that to be this wide open with him I need to feel safe, but instead of admitting my vulnerability, I lash out. He doesn't say a word, but I sense his defensiveness rising and with it something tough, something of the streets of Brooklyn.

"You're using what I shared with you against me." His voice is hard.

"I wasn't the one sitting there with members of the opposite sex fondling my body parts." I grip my hands in my hair and groan. "Sometimes I wish you were uglier just so I could relax for a damn moment."

I'm waiting for him to shout and rage, to vent the frustration I know he's feeling. Instead I am met with an eerie silence that rattles me more. Then he walks away.

"I need to be with this. I'm going for a run," he says without a trace of his usual warmth, turning away from me and digging in the backpack. He changes his clothes in stoney silence and heads to the door without deigning to even glance my way.

"I thought only one of us gets to have an emotional reaction at a time," I call to his retreating back. I might be antagonizing him, but it's also a plea for him to be the wonderful Ricardo who makes everything right.

"You're gonna have to hold this one, Sirena," he responds, speaking into the hallway, and the bang of the door slamming jolts me like a gunshot.

I die a million deaths in those first few minutes. After pacing around the room, energized by anger, I end up sobbing on the bathroom floor. Did I actually think the depth of our connection would prevent us from all hurt? I know there is no such thing as the perfect relationship, yet the reality of that fact is wrenching. I want to blame Ricardo for this devastation, but am well aware that my own lack of self-esteem is a tinder box. More than anything I want to be able to trust him. I just can't tell if the problem is that he is untrustworthy, or that I do not know how to trust.

Flattened on the hard bathroom tiles, I hear an echo of Ibu Iluh's voice asking me if I pray. If ever there was a good time for prayer, this is it. I remember the grace that surrounded me when I left my body. I don't feel it right now — at all — but I ask it to return. I reach out to the sweetness of the love Ricardo and I have shared, and I ask it to guide us. *Love, please show us the way. Love, my heart cries out to you.* This is as strong a prayer as I can muster.

Through the sticky mess of tears comes a flicker of self-preservation and a hint of self-respect. I need to pick myself up. On a hunch I pop the macro lens onto my camera and meander through the retreat grounds keeping to myself, discovering hidden plots of fresh herbs, vegetables, and flowers. I shoot close-up abstractions of hibiscus and zucchini blossoms, gnarled bark and banana leaves. An image of swirling, pink rose petals seduces my eye, and I spend ages hovering over a single bloom.

When I return to the room Ricardo is sitting on the bed freshly showered, only a sarong tied around his waist. When our eyes meet we exchange such unadulterated regret that I think we both might burst into tears. He reaches out a hand, and I sit beside him, neither of us speaking.

"Can I show you a photograph?" I finally ask.

When I share the image of sensual, unfurling rose petals, he whistles softly. "It's beautiful. You have talent, Sirena." He stares at the photo for a long while, then adds, "I'd call that a self-portrait."

We sit silently side by side, with much to say and uncertainty about how to say it. Already our skin is melding where our legs touch, our bodies longing to merge, while our minds aren't budging.

"I'm sorry for the way I spoke to you, Ricardo."

"And I'm sorry for betraying your trust."

I look at him, surprised. "Did you?"

"Without jumping into bed with anyone, I have still been playing with the energy. You're right. I see how that hurt you and I don't want to do that again."

I sit there, upset by the confirmation that he was in fact flirting with those girls, but relieved by his awareness and acknowledgment. We sit some more, neither of us satisfied that we have bridged the gap.

Ricardo rubs his chin and takes a deep breath, clearly struggling. "It's no accident this comes on the heels of what we did yesterday." He looks at me, his eyes calling out to me. I watch the set of his jaw soften. "That was huge for me." He looks down. "I guess I couldn't hold it all." Then he turns directly to me, "I will, Sirenita. I promise you I will learn to hold this with you."

I let his vow sink in. He is admitting his vulnerability while I am hanging back to see what he does. If this is going to work, I need to also venture out bravely. "I can't handle being this wide open with you unless we are exclusive with each other. It's a deal-breaker for me."

"Come on, Sirena," he says with frustration. "Hooking up with those girls wasn't even a thought in my head. Point. Blank. Period." He leans back against his hands, looking at me a long while. "I told you, I've been waiting for you. I'm not looking around."

"I'm sorry," I concede. "I shouldn't have said it like that."

He drops his head, and I can tell he's fighting to stay open even in the face of my insecurity. "During my run I saw it from your perspective. Then I started catching how subconsciously I had brought in a situation that would interrupt the extreme intimacy from yesterday."

His honest self-reflection touches me, but something is still bothering me. I have to ask. "Have you ever been in a monogamous relationship, Ricardo?"

The silence that follows rips a hole in the tenderness. "No," he answers quietly. That single word drops like a two-ton anchor. I recoil, and he can feel it. He turns to me, "But I want to make that commitment with you."

"You want to, or you are?"

"I am."

I want to believe him, but every alarm bell inside me is ringing. I can't move or utter a sound.

"Please don't judge me by my past behavior," he tells me with a hint of sadness and some bitterness, too.

I am standing at the abyss, no middle ground to be had. It's all in, or all out. He has pledged loyalty and admitted he ran from our intimacy. What more do I want? I can't keep blaming him for a trifle, fearful of what might happen in the future. If I have to walk away then I will, but not before I've laid it all out before him. I need to come clean on my part.

"I'm not judging you, Ricardo. I'm terrified that you're going to break my heart beyond repair." I stand up and run my hands through my hair, suddenly wanting to rip the feathers out. "I'm already completely in love with you," an audible gasp punctuates the words, "and I'm so afraid I'm not enough for you. That I'm going to lose you."

I am shaking, and my calculating, protective mind has shut off, a torrent of undiluted emotion pouring out of me. I throw my arms around him, knocking my fists against his back. I can't stand feeling this way and am furious with him for turning me into this lunatic.

He grabs me in his arms and pulls me so tight I can barely move. "Let it go," he says, his voice and grip uncompromising.

When my body relaxes slightly he pulls back, hot liquid eyes locking onto mine. He doesn't move, doesn't break the gaze and it's like we are suspended midair. "I know I'm a gamble. And guess what, you're a gamble, too. But we have too much to gain not to risk it all. Do you get that?"

We hold there, immobilized, looking in and through each other. His lips part, but he doesn't say anything for the longest. When he finally speaks, the words are naked and direct as a sword. "I've never been monogamous, Sirenita, because I've never been in love before now."

A world of understanding passes between us.

We have survived a land mine. I can only hope the gods continue bestowing such generosity.

T he following morning is steamy, and patches of sweat soak our clothes as we wander through the nearby village. Approaching a hole-in-the-wall barbershop, I turn to Ricardo, my finger tapping my chin, then pointing to him. "Let's shave your head."

He gives me his raised eyebrow, then nods his comprehension. "The full effect."

Once the young man is finished with his razor, Ricardo's close-cropped cap is a mere dark shadow on his perfectly-shaped skull. I survey him from all angles, rubbing his newly-shorn head and kissing the scar now revealed at the back.

"Like it?" he asks without checking the mirror, waiting for my reaction. The smoldering look on his face takes my breath away. How does he keep getting sexier? I run my tongue over my lip, wondering what might happen if I jumped him right here on the rickety barber seat. Arrest? Deportation? Totally worth it.

When we return to the retreat center, the set-up crew has swelled in size and is in overdrive with preparations. A team of women unload box after box of food supplies into the kitchen, others hang strands of glitter lights from the ceiling of the main gathering area. They have already been hard at work: interspersed among the lights are Vietnamese silk lanterns in red, hot pink and orange, swaying in the breeze; endless meters of billowing magenta fabric drape down the corner posts from ceiling to floor; hanging flower pots overflow with orchids; and clusters of hot-pink pillows adorn the couches.

"Is this a retreat or a wedding?" I murmur to Ricardo under my breath.

He laughs. "They probably see it as marrying their inner self."

"Welcome to the party," Talia gushes, a clipboard and phone in her hands. "Ricardo, how on earth do you keep getting sexier?"

I have to laugh, having thought the same thing only minutes earlier.

Talia raises her phone to photograph Ricardo. At first he waves her away, but when she begs him to play along he crosses his arms and gives her a serious look, projecting into the lens, and right away I'm transported to a catwalk.

"Lunch is at one," Talia shifts back to business, "followed by a team meeting after lunch for both of you. And Sirena, we didn't get an email response from you. Check in with Rosalie to give her your account details."

I haven't had the time or inclination to communicate with the outside world and can only imagine the small mountain of mail sitting in a virtual box somewhere. "I can handle being bossed around by her," I whisper to Ricardo. "Reminds me of a film shoot, only girlier and happier."

"Just wait till you see it in action."

Upstairs I realize I have enough time for a bath. The first plunge all the way under is always my favorite. Resurfacing, the sound of Ricardo strumming his guitar in the distance has me bathing in thankfulness. I am fortunate to be here at this retreat, with this remarkable lion of a man.

How strange, leaving my passport in Ubud. Ricardo says we'll pick it up after the retreat, but it's unsettling being in a foreign country without the ability to leave should I need to. Something else slips into the water with that thought, a serpent of fear that circles around the tub, glides over my midsection, and squeezes tight.

When my visa expires, I will have to go back to Los Angeles and face Jorge. I picture returning to the loft to box up my belongings, without a clue as to where I am going next. The runways of New York? The mountains of Jamaica? A nunnery for the broken-hearted? A bigger question looms behind them all, taking the face of my uncle. What if he is still harming other children, and every day I leave him unchallenged is another opportunity for him to hurt someone else, someone voiceless, just like I was? Now I am steeping in a tub of swirling apprehension.

The sound of the guitar approaches, and soon Ricardo is leaning against the sink serenading me. I dip under the surface of the water, not wanting him to see me stewing in fear about the future, but of course as soon as I come back up, he takes one look at me and reads everything.

"Whatcha thinkin' about?" he asks, still plucking his guitar.

I love that he reads me like a book, yet sometimes I wish I could snap the cover shut. "I have to go back to LA. Eventually."

He doesn't say a word, but his face drops.

"I cut Jorge off abruptly, and I haven't tied up all the loose ends."

He looks like I just slugged him in the gut. "Are you wanting to see if you can work it out?"

"No way. It's completely over with him, has been for ages."

I read relief on his face. "What are the loose ends?"

I describe the loft and the rental property we own together, and share my solution of Jorge taking over ownership, how that would give me time to recreate myself. "I suggested the buyout to him, but he just kept telling me to come home. He doesn't know about you. And I doubt he'll be very cooperative once he finds out."

"Have you considered just walking away?"

"I did walk away," I reply, nonplussed.

"I mean from the property. Money. Stuff. What if you just left it to him?"

A gasp rises up my throat and my chin hits the water in shock. Those properties are all I have. I poured everything I made into them, and I'm in no shape to start hustling for film work right now. That money needs to buy me some breathing space. "Seriously? How can you even suggest that?"

Ricardo places his guitar on the vanity and raises his hands as if standing at gunpoint. Then he walks to me and kneels beside the tub, forearms leaning on the bathtub edge.

"Come with me to New York. We'll make it together, Sirenita."

I look at my toes, swishing the water around the tub. "My agent's in LA. So's my work. How?..."

"I'll support us. I'll find a way. I want to." His words are scrambling to get out of him at once, his mind moving faster than his mouth. "Doing the fashion thing would feel a whole lot better knowing it's for us."

He's shocked me into silence again. For years I've had my own career and income, and fought hard to keep it that way. With Jorge we always strived to have everything equal, and while I appreciate that Ricardo wants to soothe my fears, he's provoking new ones. First off, can he actually support us? If he can somehow, I am already risking my heart and happiness on the guy, do I have to add my livelihood and freedom to the equation? Something prickles through me and I grab it by its slippery tail: Is this a way for him to exercise more control over me?

"I'm afraid."

Ricardo climbs in the tub, clothes and all, and the water level rises, spilling over the top. He takes my face into his hands, and kisses me. "Please come with me to New York. I'll jump full force back into the fashion world. I want to take care of you. I want us to be together."

"I have to admit those are very, very sexy words," and I kiss him back. "But…"

I'm not sure how to say it, but I don't want to find myself living on a moldy mattress and eating beans between his modeling jobs. He's a free spirit, but I need security to feel safe. As usual, he reads my expression perfectly.

"Look, I'm not rich, but I'm not slumming. I have my bread and butter work and I'll get more. I made it big before and I can do it again."

He watches me closely, waiting for my confirmation, but I'm not leaping. A two-ton elephant of fear is sitting on my chest.

"Don't you see?" he implores. "I've been holding back because of what happened before. Now that you're here, everything is different. I'll rock it for you, Sirena, in every way. I'll kick the fucking door in," he says with absolute conviction, with every shred of his masculine energy. "Tell me you'll come with me."

He's wide open, reaching out to me with all that he is, extending a hand to pull me into his world. The power of his persuasion has lassoed me, but I don't want to be dragged all the way to Manhattan. I want the green light to come from my own authentic go-ahead without his influence. I am so newly intoxicated it's hard to know what is real versus fantasy.

When I don't say anything he pushes himself up and out of the tub, drags off his waterlogged clothing, and leaves the room. I stare at the soggy pile of cotton feeling just as flattened. I can't work out what I am still holding onto; I have already left everything I've ever known. Even my precious career looks beyond lackluster from my new perspective.

I get out of the bath and wrap a towel around my dripping body. Ricardo is quietly meditating on the bedroom floor. Although he is sitting completely still, the tension in his face and shoulders gives him away. Sheepishly I approach, and sit soundlessly nearby. When he opens his eyes to look at me, I see the stark sheen of rejection.

"I hurt you?" I ask, knowing the answer.

"Fuck yeah." His words shoot at me like passion and anger-filled darts, his look an intense laser beam that forces my eyes closed. I take in a breath, hold it, and let it out slowly. When I raise my lids, I am as open as a blossom with all my outer petals stripped away. He is burning through my resistance.

"Tell me what this thing is, Sirena?" he demands, jutting his jaw at me like a karate chop splintering wood. "Why are we together?" His eyes are wildfire, his voice rough with insistence.

I swallow, daring to say what is engraved on my heart. "Love," I whisper in delicate counterpoint to his tone.

"So why are you walking away from it?"

When I speak, each word is as soft as chiffon, yet the syllables drop heavily with the density of a neutron star. "You've been preparing for this, but even though I longed for it in every secret corner of my soul, I wasn't getting ready in the same way. I need time to catch up." I take a few more breaths, listening to my truth, eyes closed. When I open them, his attention is still riveted on me. I continue, my tone powdery, "It scares me how powerfully I'm drawn to you. And I'm afraid that what happened yesterday will happen again. Except next time I'll be alone in New York, no job, no cash, no…"

He stares at me, accused. "It was a foot massage." I hear him struggling to contain his defensiveness. "And I promised you in all sincerity that I would learn to hold the intimacy with you."

"And I appreciate that," I say, my hand lifting to my chest, "so much. But you can't change who you are. You send out a signal like a microwave tower, and women are drawn to you."

He shrugs. "I like attention. I like a lot of stimulation."

"I'm not stimulating enough for you?"

He throws his head back in frustration. "Give me a break, Sirena." The huff in his voice insists I stop whining from insecurity. "You are mindbogglingly stimulating for me. It's not about you being insufficient." He looks away and when he speaks, his voice breaks. "It's about me being an addict."

"Still?"

"Evidently."

"And you want me to commit to a life of this?"

"I'm working on it." He backs off his hard edge for the first time. "I'll dig deeper. I already let go of dope. I gave up sex for five years. I can give this up, too."

"What if it's deeper, more subtle?" I know I'm pushing him, but I can't stop.

"What if it's just as fucking deep as the belief you're incubating every single day that you're not good enough? That nobody really cares about you?" he shoots back at me.

We stare each other down until I bite my lip, acknowledging he has me. I have been running that storyline most of my life, and it's just as detrimental as his flirtation, maybe more so. I offer him a hint of a smile, and he grins bigger.

"Work on it with me." His eyes are serious, yet glowing with a strength drawn from a deep well. This man is willing to travel into the most loathsome cobwebs of my psyche with me and shine light there. I love him more than ever in this moment, but am still not ready to tell him I will move to New York.

"Ricardo, you are powerful and smart and kind. And I love the way you drive things forward..."

"There's a great, big, fat *but* hanging there."

"I need you to give me space about this decision. I don't want to feel overpowered," I say softly. "It has to be my own genuine yes."

His shoulders drop as my words sink in, but he pulls himself up again. "Take your time." His jaw softens. "You know, Sirenita, with a love this powerful we are going to be sandpaper for each other's rough edges."

He stretches an elbow up to his ear, hand dangling down between his shoulder blades, and reaches the other arm behind his back until his hands clasp. "This is exactly why I need to practice yoga." His hands, holding tight, pull hard against each other. "It takes strength to form the poses. That's my default way of moving through life." He inhales deeply, leaning into the stretch, sighing the breath out. "But it also requires holding a softness, an allowing, on the inside. That's the part I especially have to work at." He lets go of the hold. "Thank you for the yoga lesson, *amorcita*." He unfolds his legs and reaches his toes to touch mine as a dragonfly flutters into the room, lands on the floor between us, then flies away.

Lunch is a loud, lavish affair, the excitement palpable. I think this must be the definition of abundance, but Ricardo says, "You ain't seen nothin' yet." Following a dessert of Indonesian-spiced apple pie and vegan coconut ice cream, the presenters walk down the hill to Talia's villa.

The various specialists deliver verbal run-throughs of the daily schedules, and discuss sequencing, logistics, props, and musical cues. When the group disperses, Ricardo kisses me goodbye and heads out for a run. I am nearly out the door when Talia calls me over.

"This is your first retreat, so I want you to dive into the activities with the participants." She stretches out her toes, painted fuchsia to match the theme. "Darling, after what you've been through, this will be perfect for you. Just what the doctor didn't order," she laughs.

I bow my head in thanks. I wasn't sure about Talia when I first met her, but have come to see her as a fairy godmother, and tell her so.

"Hmmm... you've already been kissed by the prince, so what's next?" She raises her eyebrows suggestively. "He whisks you off to his castle?"

"Possibly. He wants me to move to New York." I don't exactly sound enthused, and instantly she picks up on it.

"Is he that bad at housekeeping?"

I laugh at the thought; he is far more orderly than I am. "No. I'm just afraid of what happens when we leave the breezy little island where we met and find ourselves in the middle of New York Fashion Week."

"He probably shares your trepidation. He's had one foot out of that world for awhile now."

"Actually, he says he's ready to jump back in full force."

Talia's head tilts as if she's about to impart some wisdom. I find myself leaning forward. "You've inspired him to climb onto his horse. Now you must let him do battle for you. He has to slay the dragon, or hunt the buffalo, or have his gorgeous mug photographed all around the world to be worthy in his own eyes of being your man."

I take that in, gazing across the brightly-colored canna flowering in her garden. She's right, but why does it feel like New York will be the beginning of the end of us?

"You know Ricardo is meant to be a king. If he doesn't step into his manhood, the relationship will falter."

If only the alternative didn't seem so dangerous. "It's like my old life is three sizes too small," I say. "I don't want it any longer, but I have no idea what comes next. And I don't want to be Ricardo's tag along."

"Thus you have landed in my lap."

"You're going to wave your wand and make me a new career along with my ball gown?"

"You'll have to trust the process," she winks. "I'm about empowering women and I mean business."

Wandering the grounds alone is a welcome breather. Every day with Ricardo is beyond intense, and I'm still wrestling with the impending move to New York. Dad's skeptical voice echoes through my thoughts. "Reni, be realistic for once…" But what is realistic at this point? Returning to the film industry? Working both coasts? I entertain the idea of finding jobs in New York as a still photographer, then dismiss it as fantasy. Every second person in that city has a camera hanging around their neck. Although I sense a conveyor belt transporting me from Indonesia to Manhattan, I am not ready to jump in headfirst. Everything is happening too fast.

Following the footpath down the hill past the temple, I find myself beside the river and immediately sense a quickening. I just love a river. The waters sighing over glistening stones excite the mermaid in me, and when she is happy some otherwise fastened doorways fling open. I take off my flip flops and wade along the bank, water trickling at my ankles, the high-pitched, electrical hum of insects surrounding me.

Eventually the ravine grows steeper and narrows, and the river divides itself into two smaller rills. I pause at the fork, unsure which path to follow, and something about the place captivates me. Then I see it: sequestered into the rock wall of the ravine is a cave. Stretching just above the river, a long, shallow, ancient-looking rectangle that could only be used for reclining seems to summon me.

"A dream cave," I whisper to myself.

I weave around rocks through the knee-high water, then drag myself inside the opening. Lying down on the cool rock floor, I shut my eyes and listen to the rushing stream. Neither fully awake nor asleep, I drift into the dreamtime.

My mind floats, untethered from its habitual worries, images like clouds drifting before me. An overgrown jungle materializes, leaves, flowers, and roots murmuring secrets, each with its own botanical melody. A large pink bud blossoms before me in full song, unfurling one satiny petal at a time. I find my limbs have become the petals, my fingers stamen and pistil reaching out to the sun. I am sticky filaments collecting pollen. I am the yearning of life itself to bloom and grow, the longing to ripen and split with seed aching through every molecule.

The landscape shifts, and my four padded paws strike dry, red clay, muscles contracting and elongating, fur brushing tall grasses, senses stinging on high alert, telepathically communicating with my sisters bounding beside me. The ecstasy of the pursuit, of the pounce, of teeth tearing flesh. I taste passion on my tongue, and it surges through my veins.

Someone once told me lions spend much of their lives sleeping because they are strong in the dreamtime. Right now that begins making sense to me. In dreaming, the path reveals itself before me and grows clear. It's in waking that things become more complicated.

When I return to our room, Ricardo is still away. Despite anxious pinpricks, I find the nerve to call Mom. She picks up immediately.

"Sirena, I was hoping you'd call."

I am about to sit on the bed and ask how she is, but pause in mid-motion, frowning.

"Sirena?"

"I'm here. I was just wondering… why don't you ever call me?"

"Well I know how busy you are, and…"

"Mom, I'm recuperating in the tropics. C'mon, be honest with me."

The silence that follows is awkward and I fight the impulse to fill it with nervous words.

"I suppose I've felt pushed away by you for so long," she finally says. "I just wait for you to come to me when you're ready."

"I know I do that." And now I know why, but I can only broach that subject in person, if at all. "And I'm sorry. I have a lot to tell you, but I don't know where to start."

"The beginning usually works," she offers.

My pulse quickens. I don't think she's ready to hear the whole story, and I'm definitely not ready to tell it. While explaining about my call to Jorge at the airport, I wander onto the balcony, seeking the support of the tranquil, green vista. "I pulled the plug, but our relationship had already died a long time ago," I admit. "He was having an affair, by the way."

"Jorge did that?" She sounds more surprised than I was by it. "I'm so sorry, honey. That must have been weighing heavily on you."

"It was devastating at the time, but I've grown since then. And I'm glad I moved on because…" I take a huge breath to prepare myself, settling into one of the rattan chairs and overriding my tendency to keep things to myself. "I've met someone. Someone wonderful."

"Wow," she breathes. "I'm happy for you, but it seems awfully soon."

I knew that was coming. "It is. I didn't plan this, believe me." *Keep being brave*, I coach myself. "But I think he might be the best thing that's ever happened to me."

"Does Mr. Best Thing Ever have a name?"

"Ricardo." I grimace at the cliché-holiday-fling sound of it. "He was born in the Caribbean and grew up in New York."

"You seem to like exotic men with Latin names."

"I noticed."

"What does Ricardo do for a living?"

Now I really want to curl up and hide. "He's a model."

"So he's the best thing ever and attractive, too?"

"Magnetically." Here goes the clincher. "And he wants me to move to New York with him."

"What?" It's more chirp than word. "You're moving to New

York?"

"I don't know. I'm contemplating it." I pull my feet onto the chair, wrapping an arm around my knees. I've never shared my most real thoughts and fears with my mother, but I want to. I need to. "Moving scares me. But mostly I'm afraid of how much I love him," I say softly. "It's deeper than anything I've ever had before." That is the most honest thing I have ever told her.

"That…" she's searching for the words, "sounds special, Sirena. Like a gift." I hum in agreement, while catching the clunk of our bedroom door closing. "When do your father and I get to meet Ricardo?"

"Soon. I'll let you know." The subject of our conversation finds me on the balcony and sits on the ottoman facing me. I smile as he places my feet in his lap. "I'll keep you posted."

"Thank you for calling, sweetheart. And thank you for telling me. I love you, Reni."

"I love you, too, Mom."

When I hang up, he leans forward. "How's Mom?"

"I told her about you."

He waits with curiosity, but without prodding. His restraint in these moments is enviable.

"She called you a gift."

He grins, running his thumbs along my arches. My spine stretches in response. "You're the gift, *amorcita*. You just haven't realized it yet."

That afternoon the women begin arriving for the retreat, individually and in groups, some wilted with jetlag, others sporting tans from extended stays in Asia. The opening banquet begins at sunset. On the far, ravine side of the swimming pool, a fire pit sends dancing flames high into the shifting night sky. Ricardo and I venture into the party atmosphere, past servers in traditional sarongs passing glasses of bright-red iced rosella tea, to the extravagant buffet color coordinated with the theme; spiced pumpkin soup, lemony dal, carrot and beet salads, and bright turmeric and jackfruit curries sit alongside slices of fuchsia dragonfruit drizzled with tamarind sauce, and handwoven Balinese baskets brimming with red rice. Thirty attendees plus all the presenters and crew eat in buzzing anticipation, getting to know new faces. The women are of varied generations and cultural backgrounds, not easy to peg, and I detect a variety of accents. After a dessert of Algerian orange cake and mango sorbet, the retreat staff peel away. I am finishing the last sips of lemongrass tea when a staff member requests we all form a single-file line.

Ricardo draws close. "I'm going to hang out with my first love tonight."

"Hmm?" I question, crossing my arms and raising an eyebrow sternly.

He hugs me tightly. "What does it say about me that your jealousy actually turns me on a little?"

I laugh at his earnestness. It seems I am constantly challenging Ricardo's spiritual evolution. "What does it say about me that I'm turned on just by you saying that you're turned on?"

He leans into my ear, longing and anticipation in a single hot breath. "I'll see you later. Gladys awaits."

He walks away, and a slew of eyes follow. I'm sure the attending women have noticed there is exactly one man on the property, and he's sex personified. Fortunately Gladys is a guitar. I can handle sharing him with inanimate objects. For now.

Excited chatter gives way to hushed silence as the line of women descends the stone path. The ceremony has begun. In the distance I hear rhythmic clapping and voices raised in song, electrifying the night air. Lining both sides of the pathway to the temple are the presenters and crew, all wearing flowing silk robes in shades of pink, their hands coming together percussively as they chant.

Love before you, love behind you.
Love above you, love beneath you.
Love surrounds you, love within you.
You are light, you are love.

We pass through the human birth canal and into the arms of Talia, our midwife, who greets each woman at the temple entrance as if meeting a long-lost friend. As I enter I am stunned to see how the atmosphere inside has transformed. Shimmering candlelight pools from multiple storm lanterns. Swathes of hot-pink fabric drape down giant bamboo support beams, surrounding a circle of lipstick-red cushions in the middle of the room. In front of each pillow is a lotus-shaped holder containing a flickering votive, and in the center of the circle an ornate mandala made of multicolored flower petals rests on the floorboards. Ricardo was right, these women know how to put on a show.

I tiptoe slowly toward the back of the room where the altar rests under a fragrant, blue cloud of incense smoke, taking in each statue, now wearing leis of fresh, fuchsia orchids, marigold buds lining their bases. Most special of all, beside the deities sits a female string orchestra — harp, lute, sitar, kora, violin and guitar — setting an angelic tone that transfixes me as I settle onto a cushion.

After the circle is complete, the final musical notes reverberate into a potent silence. Talia welcomes us, affirming the unique magnificence of each woman and announcing the theme for our time together: Love and Courage. With a booming voice and the cadence of poetry recitation, Talia declares the retreat a safe haven for our transformations yet to come.

The presenters, standing with dignity, form an outer ring around our seated circle. They call out the names of goddesses from cultures across the globe, creating something between performance art and prayer. Goosebumps tickle down my arms as each new voice soars.

"I am Aphrodite, Greek goddess of love. Awaken to me and love your body, your sexuality, yourself."

"I am Bast, Egyptian goddess of independence. I am the ability within you to choose your own path."

"I am Coatlicue, Aztec mother of all deities. I am the power that creates worlds and I am the creativity within you."

"I am Diana, Roman archerer, taking aim and hitting my mark. I am the focused intention within you."

"I am Eguzki, Basque goddess of the sun. I am your protection in the dark of night and through the dark night of the soul."

The invocation continues with Feng Po Po, Chinese goddess of the wind, riding the winds of change; Gabija, Lithuanian goddess of fire and hearth, the warmth of maintaining home within ourselves; and Hani-Yasu-No-Kami, Japanese goddess of clay and earth, our ability to remain grounded. The pirate stands as Inanna, Sumerian goddess of fertility. "I am your ability to give birth to your dreams," she projects solemnly.

Names from every continent — I had no idea this many goddesses existed — palpably whirl through the room, thousands of years of feminine wisdom, strength, and perseverance filtering through each reverent call. Around the circle, eyes glisten in the dancing candlelight. If this is how the retreat begins, I cannot imagine where we are going.

Eventually the repetition of names concludes. Talia's voice booms as she circles slowly around the perimeter, locking eyes with the women. "All of these goddesses exist within each of us. They are aspects of the one Holy Presence woven through all of life. Let us add our own name to this eternal lineage, and proclaim the divine quality we are embodying during our time together." She brings her hands together in prayer. "I am Talia, the embodiment of compassion."

We follow suit, each woman affirming her name and intention. When it is my turn, my heart pounds and hot prickles stab my armpits, but I speak out steadily, "I am Sirena, the power of love." And I believe it.

The evening continues with a fire ceremony where sheaths of paper listing our fears, traumas, and negative beliefs dissolve into smoke and ash. A foot washing ceremony cleanses us of stress and exhaustion, and an anointing of our foreheads with frankincense, myrrh, and sandalwood oils awakens awareness of our inner beauty. By the time the etheric music rises again, every woman in the room has opened like a flower and our eyes glow like gemstones. Joining hands, we sing the chant from the opening once more, personalizing it. "Love before me, love behind me, love above me, love beneath me…' The crew members toss handfuls of petals over our heads in farewell, and I follow the harem up the stone path, half-drunk from the emotion of the past two hours.

I dream I am drifting weightlessly underwater, held safely in a dark chamber. A translucent bubble surrounds me, womblike, and constant drumming like a heartbeat pulses through the current. I emerge from a clamshell as a pearl in the hand of a radiantly-beautiful woman with long, flowing tresses. The Goddess Aphrodite lifts the pearl to her luminous lips, and it sparkles with iridescence like an opal.

My eyes flutter open with a start as the sun is just beginning to paint the world the color of a pale peach. I have a job to do. The bed beside me is empty, but I am glad for the solitude. I dress quickly and am about to scoot out the door when my eye catches the blank art pad on the writing desk. I tear out a page and draw a spiral in the center. My message starts small and tight and expands along the curve, radiating outwards.

> *Pak Riko,*
> *You fill me from my center to the outer reaches and beyond.*
> *Every moment with you is a treasure.*
> *I love you,*
> *Sirenita*

I leave the note propped atop Ricardo's tablet and make my way down the hill. The temple is empty, swept clean of every last flower petal, and someone has arranged yoga mats in a circle for a fresh start. I sense cradled in the room's quietude the reverberation of last night's ceremony. At the far end, I stand on one of the mats and begin my morning practice. Doubts arise and I question if anyone will show up at this early hour; none of the retreat events are compulsory. Circling my hips in unhurried rings, peace comes to me gradually. While my wrists decide to twist towards the roof, my mind sinks downward, into a subterranean state, body occupied, thoughts slowing.

I hear footsteps and muffled voices, but remain grounded within myself. When I suppose it is nearing time for the session to begin, I open my eyes and to my surprise it already has; seven women are on their mats copying my movements. More women arrive, following suit, and soon without any instruction whatsoever a growing circle has joined in the meditation. I am trying to decide whether to stop and verbally address the group, or simply continue, when the sitar player arrives with her graceful, long-necked instrument and seats herself behind me. The sitar's otherworldly strains elegantly spiral us into a contemplative state, words irrelevant, and just like that the room is full, thirty women swaying before me. I want to remember this sense of ease, let it seep into every pocket of anxiety I have held.

After twenty minutes the final note of the sitar stills, and I thank everyone for joining me in meditation. My eyes meet Ricardo's, holding Gladys at the entrance to the temple. He is leaning against one of the columns, and soft light falls across his shoulders, body still and composed, one of his hands caressing the guitar. My lungs seem to stretch like rubber and my every hair rises as he strides to where I stand and takes me around the waist, not minding if the women milling about are watching.

"You're already the center of my world, *mi tesoro*," he murmurs, leaning into my ear. "The center, the middle, and beyond the beyond."

His lips graze my neck in the briefest touch, but it's enough to convince me to make a habit of note writing. His intense heat radiates through me, and if there weren't so many witnesses I have no doubt I'd now be pinned between his body and a yoga mat.

Unfortunately he has a yoga class to teach, the violinist and lutenist arrive to accompany him, and the women wait expectantly. I take to a mat, absorbing the luxuriousness of the live music. Ricardo asks us to engage our muscles while gently allowing our breath, the synthesis of hard and soft, ha and tha, sun and moon, in every move.

The days of the retreat unfold gracefully, artfully, the sagacious exercises and ceremonies peeling away one layer of our defenses after another, and the group coalesces into sisterhood. Talia and her team lead us through guided meditational journeys and free dance, breathwork and trust-building activities. Some practices have us giving ourselves to stream-of-consciousness writing, uncensored thoughts sprawling across the pages without lifting our pens. During other segments we translate our inner realm into color and shape, pastels, pens, and crayons visually interpreting our emotional world. Talia's compassionate voice assures us throughout that our full emotional spectrum is welcome. Whatever happens we can tell ourselves, "I am where I am, and it's okay." The sharing is profoundly honest as we work in pairs, small pods, and the entire circle, learning from each other through both laughter and tears.

After yoga in the morning, I rarely see Ricardo throughout the day. I can tell he doesn't want to interfere with my immersion into the feminine environment. When we do spend time together he refrains from discussing New York, not even mentioning it once, but the question hangs heavily between us.

At dinner, seated beside each other, we are involved in separate conversations. A woman next to me asks where I live, and I respond, discreetly, I am from Los Angeles. I feel Ricardo listening with his every pore, sense him seeking to magnetize me into his world, even as he laughs at someone's joke.

Lounging in our bed that night, Ricardo describes a yoga book he is reading. I'm pretending to follow along — while actually thinking about the afternoon exercise of writing out our fears — when he playfully pulls me on top of him. I think he's just trying to get my attention, but then he clasps my hands, slips his feet under my hips and extends his legs. Suddenly I am hoisted up and suspended in the air, flying atop his feet, laughing in surprise.

"Trust me?" he asks, bouncing me lightly on his soles.

"Should I?"

He rolls his eyes. "Let go of my hands."

It feels precarious and my fingers grip his more firmly. "My head will bounce into the wall."

A memory flashes from childhood, inching my toes to the edge of the high diving board, crippled by fear. Looking down, the swimming pool sparkles seemingly miles below me. I have jumped off this board countless times, but in attempting my first dive it has suddenly grown to monstrous proportions. My teacher encourages me from below, but her voice sounds remote. Eventually, I back away and climb down the ladder, defeated.

Ricardo slowly lowers me down to the bed, and, without moving, we retreat to separate corners. His expression is closed, sullen. I missed the moment and suffocated the fun.

"Give me time, okay?" I finally ask.

"You said that already. I'm trying."

"Do you want me to jump off a cliff with you without any hesitation?"

"No, I want you to soar with me without hesitation. Not falling, flying."

He gets out of bed, and starts walking away, but then turns to face me. "I don't know why I'm upset… there's no other way for this to play out. You can't even trust your own heart, so how could you ever trust mine?"

He walks into the bathroom and closes the door, hard.

The following morning Ricardo's yoga class focuses on leaning into trust rather than succumbing to fear. He guides the group through a series of balance poses, encouraging us to move beyond our comfort zone.

"Don't worry about executing the poses perfectly, just play along the edges of equilibrium."

Balanced on one foot in tree pose, he suggests we close our eyes, facing our fear of falling. He doesn't make eye contact with me even once.

During lunch a woman slips into the empty chair beside me. "I want to thank you for your dancing meditation, Sirena. I've struggled for years with seated meditation, but your method is something I'm going to take home. It's become a portal for me."

"I'm glad it's helping," I say, genuinely surprised. The meditation is not something I claim ownership of; it was a gift meant for re-gifting.

"I have a question for you, Sirena." A Puerto Rican woman with spiked hair leans her elbows across the table. "Why did you bring Ricardo here?" Suddenly all nearby eyes are on me. "He's a great yoga teacher, but they could easily have found a woman. This is a women's retreat after all."

At last it surfaces. I am only surprised no one asked sooner.

The honest answer is probably found in exploring Talia's warped sense of humor. Why not take a tantalizingly handsome, spiritually-conscious man living essentially like a monk, and toss him into a harem on the brink of feminine revolution? The mischief maker in Talia must have had a belly laugh, while her expansive soul knew this would be a way for everyone to release their judgements.

"Well..." I start off, trying to find words that explain the situation while honoring the validity of the question. "I didn't bring Ricardo here, he brought me. He's been teaching at this retreat for years. It's Talia who invited him and keeps asking him back." She waits for me to elaborate. "I know it's odd," I admit, "but he really just teaches yoga and lays low the rest of the time. Maybe Talia wants us all to face our gender beliefs in a gentle setting."

She seems to accept my explanation, and everyone moves on.

The retreat team calls our afternoon session The Activation. Blending ceremony and theater, the musicians beguile us in front of stunning visual images of nature projected across a large screen. Crew members dressed as angels in feathered capes spellbind us with their dance of flight through the temple.

"Remember, remember," they beckon, flapping their fabric wings. "Awaken, awaken."

Talia swoops in wearing a diaphanous gown and enormous wings of iridescent silk. Her words and movements fuse into dance poetry, every shift of arm, every bend of knee, every tilt of head expressing a subtle message. Evoking the power of thunder, lightning, and the volcanic soil we are sitting upon, she guides us into a journey of remembrance. "Recall your holy origins and remember the mission written on the fibers of your soul."

Somewhere along the way her voice fades away from me, and the musicians retreat into the distance. Traveling on a prophetic chord, I witness myself in another time and place. Ricardo and I lounge on a plush bed, but his skin is lighter, his body thinner. I am different as well, long and lean, a lute nestled in my lap. I sing to him, looking out at walls covered with rich tapestries. My rough flax clothing drapes over a chair beside his fine linen.

One of the angels whispers quite near my head, "Let go, let go."

Jungle vines creep in, smothering the earlier image. I am slashing through foliage into an urban cityscape. Present-day Ricardo strolls along a Midtown Manhattan sidewalk at dusk as city lights spring to life. His head turns and he smiles at someone. Is it me? I move toward him, but he walks straight through my body.

"Arise into the authority of your true self." Talia's voice draws me back into the room. "Dance your body alive. Dance your dreams into form."

Pirate pulls me to my feet, and the angels entice us into movement.

"Claim the power of your word," Talia continues, while on the screen behind her, lasers burst into intricate geometry. "Let truth roll off your tongue. Speak words that rouse us from slumber, and awaken the world."

Some dance ecstatically while others sway from foot to foot. A microphone circulates the room. Woman after woman pouring her spontaneous words into the collective field, affirming truths about herself, about all of us, about life itself. When the last has spoken, Talia concludes, "The word is made flesh."

She clasps hands with the two women nearest her, and they raise their arms above their heads. The rest of us follow, taking the hands of our neighbors, limbs lifted to the heavens. The activation is complete.

The women filter out of the temple and climb the hill in bubbly conversation, but I duck away and slip down to the river. I need time alone. Sitting beside the flowing stream, I draw spirals in the wet silt with a stick. My eyes close, and the vision of Ricardo in Manhattan returns. Was I about to step into the picture, or someone else? A flurry of goosebumps run up my spine and across my shoulders. Without giving my doubts room to reemerge, I drop the stick and run the entire way up the stone steps and the staircase to our room.

The door swings open and I pause, breathless, taking in Ricardo at the writing desk. He snaps his tablet shut and turns towards me with a funny half-smile.

Instantly my excitement deflates like a balloon losing helium. "Did you need some privacy?" It's offered politely, but we both hear the accusation in my voice.

A flicker of confusion passes over his eyes, followed by a stab of hurt that has me wishing I could start over again.

"Would you like to know what was actually going on when you came through the door?" he asks. "Or should we jump into a discussion about where your mind just went?"

My organs are twisting. He is not Jorge. "Can I walk out and have a do-over, please?"

A wry smile ghosts across his mouth. "As you wish."

I leave, closing the door behind me before reopening it. He watches, amused, as I humbly approach and touch the side of his face, tenderly holding my hand there.

"Ricardo, I haven't seen you all day." My fingers travel down his neck to his collar. "Have you had a nice afternoon?"

He receives the apology with grace and takes my hand, leading me to the bed. We sit together on the edge, legs touching.

"After you cut off my locks I sent a photo to William. He's been suggesting, cajoling, and practically begging me to cut them for years, promising all the work I'd get without them. I knew he was right, but the dreads were kind of a buffer. Now..." he tilts his head at me, "everything has changed." He makes his hands into paws and growls at me. "I'm ready to pounce."

"What does that mean exactly?"

He takes my hands. "Not sure. We'll see what kind of magic William can work. But he says he'll get a heap of campaigns for me. Big ones."

"So you took a selfie, emailed it to your agent, and now he's going to make you a celebrity?"

He laughs, then says in all seriousness, "The bigger the better. More money, more freedom, more time."

My expression must not be overly enthused, as he nudges his shoulder against mine. "Don't you see, Sirenita? It's for you, for us." He is giving me that look of unmasked honesty, the same one that makes him such a remarkable photographic subject.

All I can manage is, "Wow."

He takes hold of my hand. "I mean it."

"I know. And I want to support you in whatever you desire, Ricardo."

His shoulders relax. "Good." He opens his eyes up wide. "Now about that other thing..."

I was hoping he would forget my blunder in all the excitement of becoming America's Next Top Model. No such luck. Feeling like a little kid in trouble, I pull away from him.

"What did you think I was doing?"

"Nothing." I shake my head. "Nothing at all." Squirming, I make my getaway towards the balcony.

"Confess."

I glance at him sheepishly. "Gaming?" Pausing at the balcony door, I turn to find him leaning forward on his knees, all seriousness and determination. There is no way he's letting this one go. In a split second he lunges for me, moving in for the tickling and rendering me helpless.

"Okay, okay. I give up," I gasp, leaning into the wall for leverage to free myself. "I thought you were watching porn." When his eyebrows shoot up, I cross my arms. "Hey, most women would suspect the same if a guy suddenly closed his tablet like that."

"I thought I was being respectful."

"I get it. You were."

I stand there nodding, my mind tracking backward. I have a reason for leaping to conclusions, but of course it's rooted in the past with Jorge.

Early one morning Jorge slips into bed beside me, having just completed his shift at the station. I was shooting a promotional film while he was off duty, and we haven't seen each other for a few days. He wakes me up delicately, with uncharacteristic sensitivity. Still half asleep, I respond to his touch more readily than usual. We glide into union with an effortlessness we do not often find. Afterwards, I hum to myself while baking cranberry scones, adding vanilla extract to freshly whipped cream, and dicing peaches and apricots for a fruit salad. From across the loft I notice Jorge at his desk, staring at his computer. What I see next causes me to slice ever so slightly into the fleshy part of my third finger. Jorge's computer screen, reflected in the mirror behind his desk, displays large breasts heaving up and down. When I ask him why he would need porn after the beautiful morning we just shared, he responds, "I wanted to keep the vibe going."

"Jorge liked porn," I explain, wondering why that makes me feel like I failed him. "Sometimes I watched it with him. It was arousing for sure, yet disturbing." I think of the coldness between the actors, the waxed, hairless genitalia. In light of my recent revelations, the thought of adults looking like prepubescent children is shudder-producing. "Whenever I caught Jorge watching it, I felt betrayed."

"Those days are over, *mi cielo*. It's me, right here, looking at you."

I absorb that. What a shift. "I'm sorry I jumped to the wrong conclusion."

"Nothin' to be sorry for. I need you to be honest with me." He kisses my forehead. "Just another opportunity to go deeper."

We fall into a contemplative moment, and I know it's the perfect time to make my announcement. Instead I waffle, studying the jungle view, stalling. I sidelined my initial inspiration and have to reclaim it. The words I need to say reveal my most naked feelings, requiring absolute surrender. When I look up, the atmosphere in the room feels charged and Ricardo's eyes are pools of liquid light. He waits for me to speak, and I open my mouth, but at first nothing emerges.

"I… think…" is what comes out, tripping over my own words. "I want to go where you go," I finally whisper. "I'll go with you to New York."

I'm expecting Ricardo to pounce on me as he's prone to do, but he hangs back, his eyes searching mine, invisible beams shooting between our pupils.

"You're sure?

I nod.

Then he goes for me like a spring-loaded coil, grasping me in close, seemingly trying to see how many surfaces of his body he can press against me at once. He lets out a long, heaving sigh as if he has been holding his breath all these days, in limbo.

"You-made-me-wait," he releases in one breath into my ear. Each word rings from his chest like a gong, his voice burning with dragon fire, searing through my skin, into my cells, showing me how deep he had to dig to find patience.

We sink to our knees, pressed together. "Thank you for waiting," I whisper. "I didn't want to feel pushed and later resent you for it."

We roll on top of each other on the floor, kissing and talking. I describe my vision during Talia's ceremony, leaving out the first part about the couple in the opulent bed which I don't understand. I hope the New York mystery is now resolved. I just needed to make up my mind.

"You have integrity, *amorcita*. I respect that." Standing up, he reaches for my hands and pulls me to my feet. "I knew you'd come around." With a raised eyebrow, he flashes his sunburst smile. He would seem arrogant if I didn't know how hard he works for that confidence.

Ricardo leads me to the bed, then stands completely still. I had thought my announcement would spur something wild and frenzied, but instead every little thing is now remarkably delicate. I unbutton his pants, and they tumble down his legs. He stretches out on the sheets, and I kneel beside him. Opening the doorway into our future together has weighted the moment with significance, and I am worshipping at the sacred altar of masculinity in a way I have never done in the past. Taking hold of his shaft, I run my other hand up the beautiful length to the head. What my body is doing with his is familiar, but the respect and the surrender with which I am doing it is new territory. I was not willing to humble myself to this degree in previous relationships; male strength was terrifying, if a turn on. The way Ricardo holds his masculine nobility with genuine tenderness allows me to sink into the dark mystery of my femininity. The eroticism embedded within this honoring of Ricardo's manhood startles me, and I see how much I was simply going through the motions at other times in my life, wanting this and yet keeping myself from it at the same time.

I lower my mouth over the head of his thick, rock-hard cock, sucking all the way down to the root and he lets out a low roar. My tongue licks a line up the shaft, wet mouth creating suction at the top, over and over again, refusing to stop — even when he thinks he wants me to — until he fills my mouth and I take all the way in every drop he has to give. It feels like a consecration and my lion deserves this.

After a sumptuous dinner buffet, Ricardo and I are chatting with Talia and a smattering of other women still remaining at the table. Focusing on each creamy bite of raw vegan carrot cake on my fork is how I attempt to ignore the way the women constantly pull Ricardo into their conversations. His thumb lifts up to dab a bit of cashew frosting from my lip, and someone sighs.

"Let's all go dancing in the temple," a woman beside Talia suggests. "Ricardo, Sirena, join us."

"I only enter the temple during yoga practice," Ricardo deflects, leaning into the back of his chair. "The rest of the time it's off limits, for women only."

"Why not be Krishna tonight?" Talia suggests. "With a thousand gopis dancing around you." I stare at her in horror.

"Doesn't violate Harem privacy?" he questions, and I almost have to laugh at his earnestness.

Talia has made up her mind. In fact, she feels a dancing Ricardo is exactly what the women need before the final ceremonies tomorrow. I could bow out, saying I'm tired, or go watch a movie, but sending Ricardo and his groupies off unchaperoned will leave me squirming until he returns.

"Sounds fun," I shrug casually.

I think my delivery is convincing, but Ricardo's hand squeezes mine under the table, and I know he's seen right through me. He could make apologies and lead us both back to our room, but I sense he wants us to do this, if only to prove he is worthy of my trust.

The temple lighting is low key, only storm lanterns lining the perimeter, but I recognize Aurora, the manicurist, across the room doing double duty as DJ, sending bass notes vibrating through the wooden floorboards. Some women dance alone, eyes closed, while others stream long silk scarves. A few lean into one another maintaining direct contact in a continuous push-pull, subtle cues directing who leads and follows, their movements startlingly intimate and spontaneous. I hover near the entrance watching, fascinated but intimidated.

Through the open side of the temple, I focus on the waxing moon sprinkling silver across the river. I am trying to find my sea legs with Ricardo in this kind of environment. I don't want to be suspicious around other women, clamping onto him like an old barnacle. With resolve I dance toward the moonlight, venturing into the center, leaving Ricardo near the entrance.

One of the contact dancers is the woman who thanked me for my meditation. As she approaches I smile, realizing too late that she wants to engage me in her improvised movement. She dances increasingly close, unaware of my discomfort, until her arm is brushing against mine in fluid, serpentine waves, her ribs leaning against my side. It doesn't feel sexual, but is still intense, and I start wishing the floor had an escape hatch.

As if hearing my plea, Talia sways over to us, something thick, shiny, and golden draped across her shoulders. The something moves, tensing and sliding, and I realize it is alive.

"Time for you to meet Gwendolyn."

She laughs at what must be my utterly startled expression and offers me the albino python. I am stuck between shock and denial as she carefully places the heavy serpent body across my shoulders.

Gwendolyn is one solid muscle, her skin cool and slick, her every movement scintillatingly sensitive. My initial wariness dwindles, soon transforming into delight as Gwendolyn and I establish a communication of wavelike movement, a conversation of sorts. Her sensual body evokes my own sensuality and I come alive, my motion as fluid as Gwendolyn's. Talia beams at me and dances away while I laugh at myself; I am more comfortable doing contact improvisation with a snake than another human.

As caught as I am in the serpentine moment, Ricardo's presence tugs. Attempting subtlety, I peek and find him dancing in the same spot where I left him. Several women encircle him. He interacts with detachment, but regardless, my muscles tighten.

"Help me, Gwendolyn," I silently implore of my new friend, closing my eyes. The beat picks up and Gwendolyn grows more active, her head sliding downward between my breasts and around my hips, before climbing my back. My arms follow her lead, transforming into snakes, each one of my fingers shape-shifting into a serpent, and my jealous thoughts fall away like so many old scales.

Someone slips behind me, pressing into me, matching my rhythm. Wordlessly, body to body, Ricardo conveys his understanding, showing me his support. I lean into him, protecting Gwendolyn high on my shoulders.

He turns me around to face him, and I let myself gravitate into the erotic cosmos we stir up together. Without touching, I dance my feelings for him. My movements liquify and my mood elevates. He is getting into a warm groove himself, but the song slows, the volume decreases, and the dancehall closes out of respect for our neighbors in the village. We shift into complete stillness, just standing there staring at each other as shadowy bodies disperse around us.

At the entrance I find Talia bidding goodnight to the departing dancers. "Talia, I think I'm in love," I say, reluctantly returning Gwendolyn to her owner's shoulders.

"She likes you," Talia winks.

Grateful to have passed through another ring of fire unscathed, Ricardo's soft breathing lulls me to sleep and soon I slip into a dream. A feather quill in my hand, I am a troubadour seated at my desk, composing music. My long robe does little to stave off the chill in the room, but a fire burns within me. Feverishly, I transcribe the love of my life into prose and melody. The parchment beneath my hand stretches long into a fallow field, and suddenly I am walking outside Florence, my poems in a satchel over my shoulder and a lute knocking against my back. Dark clouds are gathering, the wind howls, and I must lean into the gales to move forward.

Up ahead looms a palatial estate. After brief questioning the servants allow me entrance. Inside is a festive celebration, the gentlemen and ladies elaborately dressed in layered finery and glistening family gems. From the hallway I notice a man seated in one of the rooms, and although the high-backed chair obscures his face, my heart stutters in my chest as I recognize him.

A servant guides me away from the boisterous dancing in the main hall to a small drawing room. A gathering of guests take their seats and I begin singing, knowing if they are pleased by my offering I will eat and sleep well tonight.

Near the end of my second song, the man enters the room. Our eyes meet. He is the longing of my heart, Ricardo not as I know him now, but as a nobleman long lost to time. Behind the pattering of polite applause, my lover behaves as if I am a stranger.

I begin singing my newest song, the anthem of our love, but he walks out before I finish. I cannot continue, forsaking meal and shelter to return to the windswept fields. A gust lifts the top of my satchel and a dozen parchments sweep across the pasture, beyond my grasp. I let them blow away.

It is the morning of the last, full retreat day. At my request, Ricardo is playing guitar for the dancing meditation, our final session. After all the women arrive in the temple, I ask them to follow me to the river, and we climb down the stone pathway in a venerational silence. Ricardo is already sitting on a flat boulder, improvising a soulful rhapsody. The women form a meandering line along the riverbank, bare feet in wet silt. Wanting to take in the serenity of their bodies oscillating in the early light, I wade across to the opposite side of the river. As we sway, I sense the group click together like the vertebrae of a snake, molten, effortless, synthesized with each other and the motion of water, the chirping of birds, the chords of Ricardo's guitar.

The morning is beginning to warm when we return to the temple. Ricardo's yoga practice today is yin style, every pose on the floor, either seated or lying down. We hold each position for many minutes and they also are a meditation. The lyrical kora coaxes our muscles and the web of fascia surrounding them to surrender any tension into the wooden floor. Ricardo moves quietly around the room, squatting to gingerly adjust our bodies into deeper stretches. He speaks about letting go into trusting that everything, absolutely everything, is happening for our benefit, which gives us a lot to wrap our minds around as we wrap our arms around our knees for a twist.

Talia opens her morning session with a discussion about most of us having a beauty wound. We tend to habitually criticize our body, in detail, not accepting or appreciating ourself as we are. The group moves through artistic explorations of our beauty, ending with a dynamic verbal exercise in pairs, mirroring beauty to our partner. "There is nothing broken in you to fix," Talia insists. "Explore the powerful woman you already are. Let go of needing to improve yourself and just be yourself."

I skip lunch, eager to share my dream with Ricardo, and find him reading on the bed. After showering off the sweat of another hot, sticky Indonesian day, I join him. Resting my head on his chest, I feel the fullness of the moment exactly as it is and want to luxuriate in it, but I know I only have so much time before the afternoon workshop.

"I had a dream last night, about us. But something was different..."

Ricardo's finger strums up and down the tender place between my breasts. "Do tell."

"We were in the Middle Ages. I was poor and you were a nobleman." I describe my songwriting and my longing for the serious, aloof man at the estate. "When I saw him in the dream I felt the same surge through my body that I do when I see you." I squeeze his arm for emphasis. "It was you, Ricardo, only he didn't look like you. Do you think it was a past life?"

He tucks a lock of hair behind my ear, taking in my words. "Could be. For sure I've known you longer than two weeks. I feel it in my bones."

I nod, but can't shake the memory of walking through the fields, broken, lost, and forlorn. My throat starts closing tight. "There's more."

His fingers dance down my arm. "It's okay, tell me."

I want to say, 'It's just a dream,' but the word just catches in my throat. How can I explain that this experience changed the fabric of my soul? All my romantic notions of love were lost in that storm, scattered by the wind. That feeling of danger, of love being a terrible liability, has followed me to this day.

I swallow and maintain his gaze. "If I say something crazy, will you promise not to have me committed?"

His eyes are dark and unreadable. "You don't need to say it. I know. This is why you've been afraid of stepping into my world. And why I've been worried about hurting and losing you. We're chapters in a longer story."

Awestruck by his understanding and acceptance of something this seemingly farfetched, I only nod.

A series of emotions flicker across Ricardo's eyes until an inner determination takes charge. "Whatever may have happened before, we're making new choices right now and that's what matters." He takes my hands in his, gripping firmly. "I want us to love each other without limit until the past becomes irrelevant. I'm loving you with everything I have to give, Sirenita. Just give me a chance to show you, here, New York, Italy, anywhere."

I know he means it. With a faraway look out the glass doors, I silently commit to letting my old stories blow away. I do not want them papered across my experience any longer, calling the shots. I am ready for happier tales. I know that doubting Ricardo is a contraction that hurts me and trusting him feels like anything is possible.

Free-standing full-length mirrors beside multiple racks of clothing line one section of the temple, looking like the backstage dressing room of a theatre. Baskets, duffel bags, and suitcases overflow with saris, sarongs, bolts of lace and velvet, costume jewelry, belts, scarves, shawls, sequined brassieres, gloves, hats, and all manner of lingerie. Talia suggests dressing as the empowered woman we truly are, be it flowers and feathers, or spiked leather. Aurora pumps the music, and in the festive atmosphere we prance our way through costume selection, accessorizing, manicures, hair and makeup. Some women choose the tribal belly dance costumes from my first day, others drape themselves in the togas of antiquity, goddesses sprung to life. An older group laces up Victorian corsets and burlesque garters, while Pirate struts around in nothing but a pair of gold nipple tassels and matching thong. I settle on a glamorous, silvery forties gown with a fitted bodice and full skirt brushing my ankles, a pair of stretchy, silver gloves that rise above my elbows, and pile my hair high on my head, finishing off my movie-star persona with a multi-strand rhinestone choker. *If only my old film crews could see me now*, I laugh to myself, searching around for a pair of pumps.

"Sorry, we draw the line at shoes," Talia sighs. "Nothing screams vixen like a heel, but we have too many sizes to contend with."

A photographer has set up various backdrops, and as each woman takes her turn posing, the harem exuberantly encourages her to step into her beauty. I ask the photographer if I can use her spare camera to snap more candid shots, losing myself in red lips, glittering bosoms and fleshy hips. I am about to return the camera when several women decide to pose together nude, bolstered by the uproarious cheers of the group. Two of them have had mastectomies as cancer treatment, and within the embrace of the harem they are radiant. Hiding behind the lens, I brush the tears from my eyes.

The final dinner banquet is the most sumptuous yet. A giant ice carving of a goddess adorns the center of the buffet, with watermelons and papayas sculpted into flowers set around her feet. Ricardo is already seated when I arrive, looking more scrumptious than the feast. I glide toward the table, taking in his black dress shirt, unbuttoned to his chest, sleeves rolled up to his forearms. His lips are moving in animated conversation, but they slow as he sees me. He rises to greet me with a gentlemanly bow, twirling me around, and pulling out my chair. He has never seen me dressed up like this — neither have I, for that matter — and I love his old world charm. My reborn self needs a ballgown.

After dinner Talia stands and clinks a spoon against her glass. "Magnificent women, tonight is not only the full moon, but the blood moon, a total lunar eclipse amplifying all the intentions we have been setting. In every temple across this island people are holding ceremonies. We will have our own ceremony beside the swimming pool this evening with music, dancing, swimming, and copious amounts of chocolate."

As cheers go up for chocolate, Ricardo makes his way over to Aurora, set up poolside with the DJ decks. He leans close to her ear and confers a moment, before returning to me with a smug little smile. When the speakers suddenly swell with ballroom music, I realize what he was up to.

"May I have this dance?" Ricardo reaches for my gloved hand, and I almost swoon then and there. He formally takes me in his arms, maintaining a polite distance, one hand set firmly upon my waist, the other clasping my palm. As we swish across the terrace I can't help laughing up at him.

"How does a Brooklyn street kid know how to waltz?"

"I don't," he smiles, teeth bright in the moonlight. "Just good at faking it."

Aurora shifts the tunes to Latin dancehall. If I thought Ricardo was smooth ballroom dancing, now he moves as naturally as he breathes air. He pulls me in close, mouth tucked into my throat as he lays the Spanish accent on thick. "*Merengue* was born in the Dominican Republic, like me."

I have no idea what I'm doing, but I let my hips loose and follow him step for step. The song changes, and his eyes glow even brighter. "Here's the *baracha*." He spins me out and whips me back into his chest.

"Wow, you must have really sweet-talked Aurora."

"Only so I could dance with you."

I am still teasing him when Talia places a hand on my shoulder. "May I cut in?"

I bow out as the DJ segues into salsa. Talia and Ricardo move like seasoned pros, hips and shoulders swinging, feet in constant motion, teeth flashing, clearly enjoying themselves. When they pull in close, I notice Talia whispering intently in Ricardo's ear. I don't want to spy, but can't help myself.

Bountiful trays of handmade chocolate arrive poolside. Amid the cheers, a shout breaks out announcing the first noticeable shadow of the earth cast onto the surface of the moon, followed by a tremendous splash. Pirate has jumped into the pool, dragging Aurora in with her. Laughter fills the air as the rest of us plunge in, hand in hand, costumes and all. In no time the water is a writhing mass of wet fabric and running mascara.

I'm a soggy mess by the time Ricardo appears at the pool's edge, offering his hand. Instead of lifting myself out of the water, I spontaneously push my legs against the wall to pull him in. He doesn't expect it, and I throw him off balance for a moment, stumbling forward, but he quickly catches himself, dropping my hand like it burned him. I was just being playful, but as Ricardo jumps back it's clear he is not pleased. I haul myself out of the shallow end, and he tosses me a towel from a stack on a lounge chair.

"Let's dance somewhere private," he says, voice low and gravely, "like our balcony."

In our room I peel off my soggy gown, feeling guilty but not understanding why. "I was just goofing around," I say, worried when he won't look at me. "It wasn't mean spirited, I promise."

"You didn't do anything wrong." He is leaning against the wall, looking miserable.

"But?…"

There is a beat where he struggles with deciding what to tell me, before straightening his shoulders and marching forward. "I don't know how to swim."

My lips part in surprise, his words dropping like concrete shoes in water. He was born on an island. I met him on an island. He seems to be a master of just about everything. "No one ever taught you?"

"Who would have?" He shoves his hands into his pockets. "I'm an inner city kid, Santo Domingo, Brooklyn. No swimming pool in the backyard. No lessons at the country club."

The deprivation in his voice leaves me acutely aware of how privileged my background was in comparison. Under his pain is something else I cannot interpret, but want to soothe. "I can teach you, Ricardo." He is having a hard time meeting my eyes, so I know this is delicate. "Please, let me teach you."

He waves a dismissive hand at me. "It's fine. It doesn't really matter any more."

It is not like him to bow to fear in this way, and I catch a glimpse of the side he doesn't like to show. The trapped addict. The fighter with a chip on his shoulder. The little boy still afraid of his own power.

But the water is my element, my stronghold, my friend. "You've helped me with so many things. Please let me help you."

He doesn't say anything for a moment, then looks at me with resignation. "Alright," he shrugs.

I towel off and dress. Ricardo hasn't budged from where he's holding up the wall. His eyes stare at the floor, but he's looking inward.

"What happened to our private dance?"

We sway on our balcony, heart to heart, cheek to cheek, watching the earth's shadow bite into and gobble the moon until it puts on a surprising show, turning blood red and looming large, setting fire to the dark void.

L ater in my dream a lion's haunches pound the grasslands, frantic, hounded. His broad, noble head whips back, zeroing on poachers encircling a lioness and cub. He pivots in a single, graceful bound and storms directly at the hunters. A ferocious roar fills the air. The lioness makes her escape with her young, but a tranquilizing dart hits the lion's flank. He stumbles while running away, rolling across the dust. The lion awakens to find himself locked in a cage onboard a ship. Everything is foreign; the tight confines, the putrid smells, the heaving motions. A violent storm releases the fury the lion is unable to express. When a rogue wave crashes across the deck, ropes snap and the cage tips, sliding into the inky depths.

I awaken early, Ricardo still asleep. Carefully I slip out from under his arm and tiptoe to the glass doors. Thick, moist clouds blot the sky, descending all the way to touch the earth. The veil between the worlds feels thin.

Soft, early-morning daylight filtering through the windows caresses the contour of Ricardo's supine body. A sudden inspiration has me quietly reaching for my camera. The diffused lighting is perfect and won't last. *Click.* Close ups mostly, many looking abstract; the shell of his ear, the curl of his lip, the slope of his ass. I lean back for some wider shots of the delicious muscles along his arms and back. Even without conscious participation, I can see how remarkably photogenic he is. From every angle, the camera loves him.

I tease the sheet away, exposing more skin. Clouds shift, sunlight pours in, and I notice one brown eye observing me.

"You know I charge by the hour," he grins, still sleepy.

"You'll be paying me. The lighting was exquisite."

I shoot a few more, his liquid-mocha eyes unmasked, reaching through the lens.

The day is overcast and dreamlike, the mountainous region enshrouded in milky-moist shifting clouds. At the top of the stairs I spin in circles, clutching to my chest the Empress Bag with the chrysanthemum print. My white silk dress lifts as I turn, whirling around my legs. Pirate, also sporting a circle skirt, joins me. The twirling feels like reclaiming my carefree youthfulness and unspoiled sexuality.

We descend the stairs for our final ceremony as if stepping out from heavenly mist, every participant cloaked in white. The presenters and crew, in flowing white robes, line both sides of the path, chanting as we pass. Talia greets each and every woman with a hug at the temple entrance, and an elegant splendor from the musicians fills the space. Each cushion, set in a circle once more, has an accompanying pink canvas tote. Inside is a flash drive with pictures from our photo shoot and a silk scarf embroidered with *Love and Courage* in glittery script. As the circle fills we meet each other's gaze with glowing eyes. We have become a harem.

The music stills. In turn around the circle we share our retreat experience, focusing on the love and courage we have gleaned from our time together. The quality of seeing and being seen is exquisitely reverential. With hugs, tears and laughter the women make their final goodbyes, then hop into minivans leaving for the airport or new destinations on the island.

In the dining area Ricardo and I thank Talia, then climb the stairs to finish packing. I am rolling my new dress when I venture, "How about getting in the pool with me before we go?"

"Not here," he answers quickly, words clipped and acidic, jaw tight, not the least bit pleased I have raised the subject.

"I'll be with you. We can stay in the shallow end."

He gives me a sharp look, a glimpse of the inner-city streets, and I go to him, my fingers soothing his temples. "I don't mean to push you. Just offering."

"I'm not ready."

"Okay. Can I ask you when we're back on Nusa Dewi?"

"Yeah," he sighs.

"Are you wishing I'd let this go?"

"If it's up, it's up for a reason."

As he zips the backpack, I ask, "What did Talia whisper to you last night when you were dancing?"

He turns to me fresh-faced, as if the swimming conversation didn't happen. "She wanted to be the first to let me know about a dinner invitation." He pauses with a crooked smile. "With Cora Lezar."

That stops me in my tracks and I fumble the room key in my hand. "You're having dinner with the design queen of the fashion world?"

"We are, I hope. But William hasn't confirmed it yet."

My mind is reeling from the magnitude of what he just told me. A campaign with Lezar could be big, red carpet big.

"Talia and Cora are close," he adds. "I've worked with Cora before, but just the runway. She's expanding her men's line, and Talia sent her those pictures she took on her phone."

"What does dinner mean?"

"An erudite interview?"

"You don't waste time, do you?"

He gives me a cocky, told-you-so sort of look. "It's just a dinner party."

I give him half a laugh. "Sure."

The bike bumps down the road, backpack resting on the front footrest, and Gladys strapped to my back. Children run beside our scooter waiving to us as we breeze along, and a man seated on the side of the road offers us a smile so warm it seems to melt any reserve I have ever held. Passing vistas of flooded rice fields looking like terraced reflecting pools, I thrill to see a flock of heron, white wings spread, gliding in for an insect meal.

Leaving behind the higher elevations, we descend into more congested villages. Traffic comes to a complete standstill under the blistering sun as a procession passes en route to the local temple. It seems the entire village, young and old, parades past carrying ceremonial umbrellas and banners, all in matching sarongs. Tall, tiered, offerings of fruit and roasted chickens balance gracefully on the women's heads. Some of the men clang cymbals decorated with pompoms or strike large brass gongs hefted upon their shoulders, reverberating down the road.

Movement provides the relief of a cooling breeze once we are rolling again. We stop briefly in Ubud where I am happily reunited with my passport, including its new visa extension. After a few moments to stretch, we return to the road.

The further south we drive the more densely populated the streets, a sea of motorbikes interspersed with cars. The scooter in front of us carries a colorful cloud of inflated foil balloons. Out of nowhere, a tiny child barely old enough to walk, totters onto the road between parked cars. Ricardo's body tenses as he catches sight of the child, positioned directly before our front tire. I watch the chubby hand point up at the brightly-colored toys, and in that moment everything becomes elastic, as if happening in slow motion. All is eerily silent and then, without a shout or even a thought, the world is tilting, the bike sliding. In front a man rushes in, snatching up the toddler and whisking him away, just before we collide with something — it must be another bike — turning the squeal of braking wheels into something wilder, more chaotic. In that elongated moment I know we are going down. What comes to my mind is Gladys on my back, and I manage to swivel, avoiding my full bodyweight crashing down upon her. I sense a collision of forces coming together; mine, Ricardo's, the other driver's, the child's, intersecting in this weirdly-odd perfection.

The unforgiving solidity of the street is a jolt back into normal-time reality. My left foot is painfully wedged underneath something hard. Instantaneously three or four Balinese men are by our side, lifting the motorbike to free us.

"Sirena, are you okay?" Ricardo's eyes are wide with concern. He pulls the guitar from my back, dropping it quickly and rather roughly to the ground.

"Hey, I didn't save her just so you could throw her around."

The men wheel our motorbike out of the road and a crowd of a dozen more forms around us, spectating. The driver we collided with does not appear to have suffered injury, but the molding over his exhaust pipe has bent. Ricardo pulls bills from his wallet for repairs, they shake hands, and the other driver speeds away.

I hobble over and pick up Gladys, realizing I am limping. My foot is rapidly swelling. Ricardo shifts into emergency mode, and it seems like only seconds later we are in a car, my scarily-focused lover firing a stream of rapid commands into his phone. He calls Talia, requesting her medical contacts, and the motorbike rental company, explaining where they can collect the bike. Ricardo is jabbing another number into the phone when I notice his left arm is scraped, a scarlet bloom spreading through his cotton shirt. When I draw his attention to it, the way he shakes it off lets me know he is internally berating himself for what happened.

"You're great in a crisis, Ricardo. Master of efficiency."

"Had a lot of practice. I'm great at messing stuff up."

"Is that what you're thinking?"

It might be unreasonable, but my veins fill with indignation. The powerful emotion spreads through me like watercolors across a wet page, and I can't hold it back. I don't want to. After years restraining myself, I'm starting to find my voice.

"Stop it," I say, words steeped with passion. I catch the driver glancing back at my outburst in the mirror, but barrel on. "Don't take my power away, Ricardo," I say with a certain fierceness. "You did not create this situation all by yourself. We did this together, you and I. And that little child, his father, and the other driver. You don't get to own this. We all do."

Ricardo gives me a slow nod, but he seems taken aback.

I soften my voice a little. "You think you messed things up for your mom — I think you helped her more than you hurt her, by the way — so now you're going to destroy everything precious for the rest of your life. Well you can't. I won't let you. It has to be time for a new concept of yourself, or I can't live with you."

Oh my. Did I just say that? Yes I did, and I meant it.

"What actually happened just now is that you protected the child and that is valiant. And I protected Gladys, out of love for you."

He is still speechless, but listening with both ears. Now that I am on a roll, the words continue spilling from me. "I'm responsible for my own body. I am not some weak victim of your supposed disasters. I used to feel that vulnerable, but I can't go there any more and that's because of you. So if you want to take credit for something, take credit for that." I finally give him a hint of a smile. "Well, not all the credit, but some of it."

We sit in silence. Purged of my frustration, the mood shifts and I find my gentleness. "I've been hesitating, dragging my foot so to speak, afraid to take that big step forward into New York with you.

I have to take responsibility for that." I place my hand on his. "I'm joining your world, Ricardo, and drawing you into mine. That scares me big time. And it's the best thing I have ever done."

He places a kiss on my forehead, holding his lips there for a long time so that I feel all the way through his lips down to his heart.

"*Muchas gracias, mi cielo*. Thank you. And I hear you. Every word."

We pull into the emergency room of a modern hospital taking up one wing of a shopping mall, making it hard to understand where one stops and the other begins. Inside, the emergency room is packed with locals and tourists, and I fidget impatiently on my hard plastic seat. I'd like to go home and let my foot heal on its own, but Ricardo insists I get an X-ray. Barely a month in Indonesia and I'm already in another hospital, I groan to myself.

An orderly cleans Ricardo's scrapes and another pushes me in a wheelchair to the X-ray room. Eventually I see the doctor, a middle aged Balinese man as much priest as medical practitioner, who determines my foot is not broken, just a badly-sprained ankle. He sends me off with a pair of crutches and cryptic words of advice.

"Step forward with confidence," Ricardo translates.

B ack in Ricardo's hideaway on Nusa Dewi, I spend the rest of the day beside the fan, reading. My foot hurts and my entire body is in mild shock. Ricardo dotes on me and I let him. I want to savor every last drop of this honeymoon phase, knowing things will certainly change when we return to civilization.

He brings to the bed a bowl of mauve-colored passionfruit and a Scrabble board. We break open the skin of the fruit with our thumbs and feed each other the sweetly-tart membrane and crunchy, black seeds. I am surprised Ricardo plays Scrabble, even more so when he trounces me the first few rounds.

"This is ridiculous," I say, tossing my final tile on the board. "English isn't even your first language."

"Actually, English is my mother tongue," he corrects me. "Spanish was with the neighborhood, at school. Moms insisted on proper English at home to prepare us, someday, for America. But she'd break into Patois when she got mad. Still does," he grins.

The sly smile of competitive pride starts to fade after we play enough games for me to learn his Scrabble tricks and give him a run for his money.

At night, the steady beat of dripping rain drifts through open windows. Cozy in bed, foot elevated on a pillow, I am watching a movie on my laptop. Midway through, I notice Ricardo leaning against the doorjamb as if he has something to say, but he returns to the living room without interrupting.

The film was shot in Los Angeles and many of the locations are recognizable to me. When it's over, LA stays on my mind. The idea of signing the properties over to Jorge does have a stunning finality to it, but walking away was Ricardo's idea, not mine. Am I contemplating it simply as an avoidance of confrontation? I hear my accountant father's disparaging voice telling me to be logical and overcome my tendency for dramatic gestures.

Mulling it over without conclusion, I check email. Mom has invited me to bring Ricardo along to a special event: Uncle Carson is being granted an award — by the Children's Hospital, no less — honoring his years of service on the Board. The family is purchasing an entire table of seats for the expensive gala dinner, and I need to be there, she gushes, as they will screen the short film I shot about Carson. The thought of sitting beside Carson, applauding his moment of glory, is beyond revolting.

Ricardo returns to the doorway, sees the movie has ended and sits on the bed beside me. I raise my eyebrows in anticipation of his mysterious announcement without sharing my own. He doesn't say anything, just purses his lips with an I-have-a-secret expression. I shoot back a cough-it-up look, waiting.

"Sirenita," he finally says, setting his tongue on his lip, "you know when you said you want to go where I go?"

"Yes...?" I mime a drumroll.

"After Fashion Week in New York, I'm going to Milano." He bounces on the bed towards me, letting his excitement out, only to freeze and apologize for jiggling my foot. "Will you come with me?"

"Go with you to Italy? Um, let's see... I think I could manage that. My busy schedule is wide open."

"Good. Because mine is filling up."

"Do tell."

"William booked me on the runway in New York for Cora Lezar," he does a backward roll across the bed, "and Allesandro Vario in Milan." He pauses to see how that's landing with me. They are fashion royalty, and I tell him he was born to be a king. If he is not to rule a kingdom, then the fashion world will have to do.

His excitement is vibrating through both of us, even if anxiety creeps around the edges. "Does walking the runway pay well?

"The runway's prestige and positioning, not big money, but it can lead to the big money."

"And the dinner?"

"William hasn't breathed a word about it. He's friends with Cora, too. It's a tight circle. In the meantime, he booked me some catalogue work, my bread and butter."

I get still, knowing I need to elaborate about my discomfort. The financial insecurity is only part of my concern. "I have fear about what it will be like for me in New York," I tell him quietly. "I wonder if I'll feel invisible. I don't want to be a little puppy following you around."

"You are no one's little puppy, *mi tesoro*. You're a lioness. An artist. A medicine woman." He puts his palm on my chest, letting his hand fall to my breast and leaves it there. "So you want to know if I'll still be there for you?"

I twist my lip, feeling silly and young, but unable to shake it.

Ricardo takes both of my hands, masculine strength and gentleness in one gesture. "Okay, I'm gonna cut to the chase." He looks into my eyes with such absolute directness that I hold my breath. "We're life partners. This power between us isn't going away, it's only going to grow. I'm telling you what I know."

I am speechless.

"I haven't wanted to overwhelm you, at least not any more than already I have."

We both know this is no ordinary romance, but he has made a huge statement for such a new relationship. How does he know that so soon, and with such certainty? I was with Jorge for years, unsure. Maybe it doesn't have anything to do with time. Hearing Ricardo's proclamation, I realize how much I have yearned for this level of commitment. We gaze into each other's eyes, allowing the fragments of the past to drift away and the startling newness of the present to sink into our bones.

In the morning I am stretched on the couch, foot propped, and Ricardo brings me a mug of green tea. After a hot, juicy kiss goodbye, he leaves for a run on the beach. With the space all to myself, I translate the time difference, noting it's early evening in Los Angeles. Grimacing at my swollen appendage, I tell it, "Alright foot, we're stepping forward, just as the doctor ordered."

The phone rings repeatedly, and I'm about to hang up when Jorge answers.

"Hello Sirena." I can hear his breath, slow and wary, on the line. "I didn't know if I'd ever hear from you again."

"I'm sorry I couldn't contact you sooner. I needed time."

"Needed, as in past tense?"

I ignore the question. "I'm returning to LA soon, but only briefly. I'd like to pack my things from the loft."

"I don't believe you mean this. Stop messing with me and come home. You've made your point."

"I don't care to make any points. Your opinion has long stopped meaning much to me. I just want to wrap up our lives and move on." The words are sharper than I intended, but he needs to understand I am serious.

When he responds it's obvious he has heard me loud and clear. "In that case you'd better get yourself a lawyer. I won't make this easy."

I have to laugh, though I am more outraged than amused. "On what basis? That I had an affair that ended our relationship? I think you're getting your stories mixed up, Jorge."

How bizarre that I would even contemplate giving him full ownership as an act of goodwill and liberation. I was already practicing the apology speech I would need to give my father. "Neither of us can afford legal fees, Jorge. And while I'm still angry about some things, I would actually like to see you better off, not impoverished."

A horrible silence ensues, but finally he asks, "When are you coming?"

I am about to say 'just before New York Fashion Week', but catch myself. "Around the end of the month."

"Are you bringing him?"

Oh my. Did I think I could avoid this? I want to tell him it's none of his business, but that would only throw gasoline on the fire. "I will be in LA with…" What do I call him? "My new partner."

"So you're having an affair of your own," he bites out with venom.

"Not at all. I ended my relationship with you properly before meeting him."

I speak the words calmly, but the hostility in Jorge's voice frightens me. He is a raging fire, and even with the world's oceans separating us, I am overwhelmed by the need to get away from his blaze.

"I have to go now, Jorge. Let me know what you think would be an equitable solution. I'll email you with the exact date and time I'll be at the loft."

"That's it? Just like that, you walk away?"

"We're done."

He is still speaking in a berating tone when I hang up. I do not sob this time. I am, indeed, finished.

As I sip my tea, Mila's exuberant voice calls out from the porch. Surprised, I shout for her to come in. "I thought you'd be off to Vietnam or Laos by now," I say as she crosses the room to the couch.

"How'd you find me?"

"I saw Ricardo yesterday running on the beach. Didn't he tell you?"

I shake my head as she gives me three kisses on my cheeks, Dutch style, and sets her bag down to take a closer look at my foot. "It's a size bigger than your other one."

"You should have seen it yesterday."

"I told Ricardo I'd like to give you a treatment. And you could use some turmeric to bring down the inflammation. Have any?"

I tilt my head toward the kitchen. "Feel free to check."

She pads off, and I hear the refrigerator opening and closing. After the whirling blender silences, she offers me a glass of something bright yellow and fizzy.

"Blended turmeric, tangerine juice, passion fruit, pineapple, soda water, lime and a bit of honey." To my surprise she grinds a dash of fresh black pepper onto the top. "Activates the turmeric," she explains.

I take a sip. "This medicine goes down easy. Thank you."

"Keep drinking the turmeric. It's anti-inflammatory." She lifts the bag at her feet. "I brought some needles with me. Would you like a treatment?"

I am slightly suspicious of becoming a human pin cushion, but I have heard people rave about the benefits of acupuncture. "Poke away."

"I practice the five elements technique," she explains, pulling out a box of fine needles. "They don't stay in long," she assures me, assuaging my obvious wariness. "I think you'll like the poetry of it."

Mila carefully takes my pulses. "I'll palpate the channel where the energy is blocked." While placing several needles in my foot and around my ankle she continues talking, distracting me. "This will release the constricted blood and chi." Another needle goes in closer to my toes. "Now I'll activate the Yin Tang at your third eye, the intuitive point called the Hall of Impression, and at the crown chakra, the *Bai Hui* or Hundred Convergences, where all the channels meet."

The needles are instantly calming. Mila is expounding about meridians, a thousand petaled lotus, and an empress, but I only vaguely hear her in the background as I float into a blank, peaceful state. Once I fully return to the room, the needles are gone, Mila has packed everything up, and is preparing to leave.

"Thank you," I stretch my arms. "That was relaxing."

"It's nothing," she says, pink cheeked. "I can see Ricardo is taking good care of you. You looked so tired when you first arrived on the island. And now, even with an elephant foot, you're radiant."

"He's opening me up in a zillion ways," I admit. "It isn't easy or pain-free, but it's…delicious."

Her eyes peer into mine, searching for something. "You're lucky. I want that more than anything."

"I'm here to say it can happen," I encourage her.

She nods. "Get some rest and keep drinking jamu with turmeric and black pepper. I left a jug in the fridge."

I thank her, feeling uncomfortable that my happiness only seems to make her more aware of the holes in her own life. I am trying to think of some way to support her when she stops at the door and adds, "I almost forgot. Some other Dutch people are staying at the hotel and we're having a party tonight. Drop by, if you can move around."

The day is still young and, newly refreshed, I wonder what other tasks might be ready to come out of avoidance. Gregor needs to know I'm switching coasts, and I have to figure out how to send my boxes to New York. Something else surfaces, bobbing like an inflatable toy suddenly released from underwater.

"*Selamat pagi*," Joko exudes. "Good to hear from you."

I greet him in return, but am too excited to fluff around with niceties. "I want to repay my loan, and I have another big request."

"If you want to go diving, I'm ready."

Joko's clearheaded perceptivity brings a smile to my face. "I have to get underwater before I leave Indonesia. Can you possibly come to Nusa Dewi?"

236

"I have some time off at the end of this week. I'll make the arrangements."

This time I'd like to make things easy for him. "I met a friend who has a dive boat. I'll take care of it."

"Up to you. Are you headed back to LA?"

I explain that I need to tie up loose ends there before moving to New York. Do I venture into the personal? Something compels me. After all, it was Joko's recommendation that brought me to Ricardo's island in the first place.

"I... I fell in love with someone, Joko."

"I'm not surprised. I hear happiness in your voice. I'm glad for you, Sirena." He is quiet for a moment. "I did hope it would be me."

Oh no. I didn't see that coming. I think of Joko more as the good uncle I never had. The disappointment in his voice brings to mind Mila and all the lonely hearts in the world waiting to find their beloved. When I tell Joko he is one of the kindest men I have encountered and the next woman to marry him will be very fortunate indeed, he thanks me.

"Do you still want to dive with me?"

"Absolutely. Still want to dive with me?"

He promises he does, adding he'll let me know when he has booked his flight. "*Terima kasih*, Sirena. You woke something up in me that I thought was dead."

Something in me was dead, too, I muse as I hang up. It took dying, and Joko's resuscitation, for me to awaken. With every step forward, the weight of my past seems to crumble behind me, leaving only a sense of awe.

On a roll, I phone Mom. Her voice is light and airy as she asks me how I am. I inform her I plan on returning to LA, but only to pack up the loft. Ricardo will be joining me initially before he has to work in New York. When I give her the dates, she exclaims gleefully, "That couldn't be any more wonderful, darling. Bring Ricardo to the family brunch, and we have an extra seat for him at Carson's award dinner. Libby is hiring you to photograph it." She breathlessly adds the last point like it's the cherry on top.

I am stunned. My family rarely included Jorge, and now she is extending invitations to Ricardo sight unseen. I want to tell her I cannot possibly attend the gala, but she sounds so happy, and I cannot explain — not now, maybe not ever — that I am refusing because her revered older brother molested me. Although at the moment I feel ambushed, what if life is conspiring to bring me a perfectly-crafted moment to face Carson?

"Hmm... well, okay," I stutter.

"Fabulous." Before I can absorb what I have agreed to, she switches gears. "So... how is Jorge taking all this?"

Shame splashes up like a belch. Judging myself through my family's eyes, I look impulsive and quixotic. My parents, aunt and uncle, and most of their friends have stayed together for decades. My brother is married with two children. As usual, I am the loose wire. "Jorge is not exactly pleased with me."

"I guess that's to be expected, sweetie," Mom says without a trace of the judgement I just heaped on myself. "I trust you've made a good decision for yourself."

"Thanks for having faith in me."

"I've always had faith in you." She seems to want me to digest that. I suppose it's true; I simply haven't had faith in myself, or anyone else. "I'm happy Ricardo will meet the family. How special."

Special would not be my choice of adjective given the company, but I assure her I can't wait and make my goodbyes. Whew. I am swirling, but with only one more call I'll be finished. I start to dial Gregor's number when Ricardo returns, and I put the phone down. I haven't budged from the spot where he left me on the couch, but somehow the world looks different.

"Pak Riko," I sing out, "so much happened while you were gone." He sinks onto the couch beside me. "*Que onda?*"

I tell him about confronting Jorge, Mila's visit, and the alignment of our trip with the family brunch and gala dinner, all in rapid, run-on sentences. I leave out the part about Joko, I guess because of his new disclosure. I am not sure how Ricardo would handle it, but know I wouldn't like if he planned on spending the day out with an admirer.

"Facing these things I was avoiding is so energizing I could run a marathon. On crutches."

"*Asombroso.*" He is giving me his undivided attention, eyes glowing with adoration. "When you're all lit up like this I feel like I'm falling for you all over again."

"You look happy, too," I say, shy all of a sudden. "Major endorphin release with all the running?"

"It's you, Sirenita, telling the important people in your world you are coming to New York with me. Running's whack compared to this high."

"Come closer so I can kiss you without moving my foot."

I lean towards him, but he pulls back. "I'm super sweaty…"

"Let me verify that." I draw him in with my arms, kissing his beautiful, damp cheekbones, his strong, salty jaw, his succulent mouth.

"Don't move. I'll shower off and be right back."

"It's unlikely I'll sprint off anywhere."

When I hear the sound of the water running, I decide to slip in the final call. It's late in Los Angeles and Gregor is probably already drinking his supper, but I'll give it a go.

He answers immediately. "You're a mind reader."

I laugh. "Do you represent carnival acts, too?"

"I was literally just about to call you. When did you get back?"

Sure, I haven't heard from him since I left LA, but now that I call him, he says he was just about to dial my number. "I'm still in Indonesia."

"Book a flight home."

Geez. Maybe he really was about to call me. "What have you got up your sleeve?" Nervous prickles tingle across my shoulders.

"A rabbit, a top hat and a showgirl to boot. But first tell me this: how's your health?"

"Never been better."

"For real?"

I tell him my ankle is currently propped up on the couch with a sprain, but will be better in a week. He responds by saying he's glad I'm already sitting down. He has news. Big news.

"Spit it out, Gregor."

"I landed your dream come true," he spills. "Feature film. Ample budget. Shooting in LA. Largely female crew, with a feminist script. You can sleep in your own bed at night and it'll keep you happy for at least the next six months. Come on back and meet with the producers. They already love you."

I slump into the couch. I should be jumping for joy, but I am not. If anything, I'm angry and confused. Why now, when I've called him with the express purpose of taking a break? The very thought of accepting this project makes my stomach wrench, though it's everything I ever thought I wanted.

"Well?" Gregor has never been especially patient. "Why are you not screaming in my ear right now?"

"It's wonderful news, but I'll have to get back to you, Gregor," I finally say.

"Sirena, I wrestled this thing to the ground for you. I had to get on my knees for this one."

"Thank you for your efforts," I scowl. "But give me a day."

"Half a day. They think they're meeting you tomorrow."

"Right."

When he hangs up I stare at the phone in my hand like it's a grenade about to go off. He has not offered me just any job, but my dream job. My career is as important as Ricardo's, isn't it? I have worked hard to get a pushy agent who can score gigs for me as a cinematographer. I've taken every scrap of work that has come my way to climb the ladder in a field still completely dominated by men. And now what? I walk away from it all to become Ricardo's personal assistant?

My lover's honey-coated tenor wafts from the shower. Reason tells me to take the job, but my heart instructs me to scramble under that shower head and jump the man, foot be damned. Quickly, before doubt can overtake me, I call Gregor back.

"We're on," he breathes a sigh of relief. "I was worried you'd lost your senses."

"About that," I say tentatively. "I, uh, already made the decision to leave LA. I'm in a new relationship and I'm moving to New York."

"For a guy?" he groans. "Seriously? You're killing me…"

"I know," I interrupt, "and I appreciate everything. But I can't take this one."

"Honey, I think you're wonderful, but I can't find jobs for you if you aren't available to take them. I have to eat, too. If you walk away from this one and change coasts, I've got to let you go."

I should have expected this, but it still smacks me like a random punch to the face. "Of course. I understand." My voice cracks, and I tell myself to pull it together. With steadier words I thank Gregor for all he's done, and hang up.

And just like that, I'm all in.

Ricardo sings his way from the bathroom to the living room, a towel tucked around his hips. I sit on the couch in stunned silence, watching as he tips forward onto his hands, feet gracefully balancing over his head. The towel gathers at his waist, offering a tantalizing glimpse of caramel skin. He is not the only one who's world has turned upside down.

Ricardo flips onto his feet and slides one arm around my back, the other under my knees. I find myself gently lifted from the couch and floating through air as he carries me to the bedroom. I can't bring myself to interrupt the mood as he tenderly places me on the sheets and removes my clothes, careful not to knock my foot. He whips the towel off with one efficient tug, then he is spreading me open, his face between my legs, his tongue softly stroking. He hits just the right spot, with just the right pressure, until the melting spreads outward in steady ripples. My fingers rake the stubble across his scalp as stronger waves build, mount and subside. I sink back into the pillows, panting, hungry for more of him, and pull his shoulders to bring him up, but he tells me it is time for yoga.

"What about you?" I ask, my hand straying.

"Later," he says with that million-dollar smile. "Do you want to wait here? Or can you do the class if you take it slow?"

I can't be sure if it's the acupuncture, the turmeric, or the orgasms, but a close look at my left foot reveals my appendage is now looking more like mine, not a rhino's. "I want to come with you." I scoot off the bed. "And Mila invited us to a party on Crystal Beach, by the way."

"Yeah, that's right." He's gathering his yoga gear, pulling on a shirt. "Slipped my mind."

That seems uncharacteristic, but I have no time to dwell on it. We head into the late afternoon sun, Gladys up front, me clinging to my crutches, and Ricardo driving like an old man.

A Chamber of Om, the entire room chanting the ancient syllable repeatedly at their own pace, begins the class. Ricardo's teaching style is gracious and generous, adjusting a foot here, a spine there, shifting someone's ribcage, offering me alternatives that relieve the strain on my ankle. He connects with each person as he navigates the room, saying we are "twisting our bodies in order to untwist our minds." I follow him with my eyes, enjoying his mastery, his fluidity, even as an unease brews within me.

I passed on a feature.

After class, the usual swarm of students mill around Ricardo. Mila, missing from today's class, must be busy with party preparations. Knowing it will be slow going on the crutches, I begin my journey to the beach alone. The drummers are already pulsing their throbbing tribal conversation before the choppy waves as I swing myself the full distance across the beach and sit on the sand. Something deep and baffling that I cannot name is rumbling beneath the surface, reminding me of the warnings before my heart attack. The similarity frightens me and the disquiet in my chest grows tighter.

Two guitarists arrive with a trumpet player, and the music swells. Tourists strolling along the beach stop to listen, silhouetted against the burnt-sienna hues. By the time Ricardo and a few yoga students join the circle, agitation has overtaken me. Should I call Gregor back? Ask Ricardo to join me in Los Angeles after he has finished his shows?

I don't need to think about it too long. The reality is film productions consume the crew's every waking minute, barely leaving time for a few hours of sleep. My current fragility and our budding relationship would be compromised, at best. I choose Ricardo, I remind myself, reaching to feel at peace.

He sinks beside me and rests his chin on my shoulder. We listen to the music, but he doesn't lift his guitar from its case. "Let's go home and finish where we left off," he breathes into my ear.

"Can we go to Mila's party first?" I think of her sad expression as she walked out today. Making an appearance is the least I can do. "She won't expect us to stay long."

A look flickers across his features, a tightening of the eyes so quick it could be easily missed. "Sure, if you want to."

We make our way across the beach. The crutches sink into the sand with every step, but I congratulate myself on an excellent upper-body workout. In the distance, the trumpet blares.

At Crystal Beach we find a hopping poolside party already in full swing, cocktails flowing, cigarette smoke rising, pop music blasting. Clusters of conversations are mainly in English, some in Dutch. We spot Mila at her improvised bar, set up at a table covered with bottles of duty-free liquor.

"Hey, Ricardo, Sirena," Mila calls out to us, tottering slightly. We cross through the crowd and she throws an arm around us both. "Glad you came to my party. What are you drinking?" She looks at Ricardo, eyes glazed.

"Nothing for me, thank you."

"Oh come on, not even a beer?"

"I don't drink."

"That's no fun," she scowls. "Sirena, what about you?"

I accept a beer so she won't be offended. It sits on the table beside me, beading in the heat.

When the conversation lags, I show her my foot, telling her the swelling has come down. "It worked," she squeals. "The wonders of turmeric."

"That and your needles. I wouldn't be upright tonight if you hadn't visited."

"And we would have missed you," she smiles.

Some partygoers sidle up to the table beside us, and Mila returns to her role as barmaid, cracking jokes and sloshing generous shots into each glass.

"Running dry already," she says, holding up an empty vodka bottle. "We'll have to switch to beer. Ricardo, can you help me carry a couple of cases?" She stretches her arms above her head. "If I'm not careful, I'll throw my back out."

"Sure. Where are they?"

"In my room. I'll show you."

As they walk away, Ricardo gives me a small wave. A French couple pull the last of the beers from the cooler, and we fall into a long discussion about diving. When they meander off, I stand alone, armpits aching from the crutches. What is taking Ricardo and Mila so long?

I could sit down and wait, but instead I drag myself through the crowd, toward the huts. Mostly I use the crutches, but experiment with putting weight on my foot. Not bad. Every few steps I try again.

At Mila's room I knock on the closed door, but no one answers. I am about to turn back when I hear Mila's distinctive laughter ringing down the path. She must have switched huts, I realize, hobbling my way towards her voice.

This door is wide open. Mila is lying on the floor, laughing uncontrollably, her arms crisscrossed over her chest, while Ricardo hovers above, feet straddling her, leaning into her arms with his hands. Mila lets out a long groan of satisfaction.

"Do you want more?" he asks, his face now just inches above hers.

"More," she implores.

Bent over her torso, his long fingers on her arms, he presses his weight into her. Laughter sails out of her again as she tells him how

244

good it feels. I watch her knee draw back, her toes slowly tracing the full length of his calf. My heart is pounding and I grip onto the doorframe as the room begins to tilt. Ricardo looks up over his shoulder, and we lock eyes for a moment. I don't stick around to see what comes next. I bolt as fast as I can on crutches.

The path before me wobbles beneath a film of tears and my ankle screams in protest with every stumbled step, but that is nothing compared to the suffocating rage that is exploding in my veins and ripping through my organs like shrapnel. I hear a shout but it seems wrapped in wool, and without thinking I have somehow passed the pool and reached the steps down to the beach. Disbelief and fury fuel my muscles, propelling me forward, away, refusing to let me stop. I cross from dry sand to wet, its firmness allowing me greater speed, even as my temples throb, threatening to implode. And through the angry-red haze is a whisper: why isn't Ricardo following me?

Darkness blankets the world. The sun has long sunk into the ocean and the moon has not yet risen. I knock into an unseen object with my crutch and stagger, catching myself and continuing on at my furious pace, perspiration pouring from my brow. I could run for weeks, months, years, all the way back to LA.

The thud of footsteps on wet sand joins my puffing breaths, but I don't hesitate even one second.

"Sirena."

With his call I look over my shoulder to see Ricardo running behind me. He is moving far faster than I can and will soon overtake me. My frenzy pounds even harder then, ignited at the sight of him. I'd like to tear him with razored claws, spit dragon fire at him, envelope him in flames, scorch him with a taste of the hurt wringing me inside out.

In no time he catches up with me, reaching out and grabbing my shoulder. I shrug off his hand with undisguised rancor and keep moving. He runs in front to get me to stop, but I maneuver around him. Hand on my elbow, he blocks me.

"Get away from me," I shriek, startling a pair of young Indonesian lovers sitting near the palms. They watch, astonished, as I flail to free myself from Ricardo's grasp.

When he doesn't let go, I snap. My anger and pain, layered through the years like striations of granite on a mountain wall, explode. I have hidden this dynamite my entire life and now I cannot, will not, contain it any longer. In fact, I am running full speed straight into it. My uncle's abuse, my parents' detachment, and Jorge's cruelty coalesce, irrefutable proof that Ricardo's addictive personality is now just one more repetition of the pattern. But good little Reni is quiet no longer.

"I'm done with betrayal," I scream at the top of my lungs. The words boil upwards through my throat, thunder out of me, and I swing one of the crutches at him. He catches it, holding the lightweight aluminum in the air, not moving a single muscle. The hand at his side balls into a fist, and I sense he wants to strike me, but all he does is let the crutch fall to the sand.

"Sirena, it's not what you think. Yeah, you saw something. But your imagination is blowing it up."

The words are spoken slowly and clearly, but I cannot really hear them. The forest fire is burning out of control, incinerating my ability to reason. Rage has overtaken my senses. Rage owns me. I wrest my arm from his grip and hobble farther down the beach. He lets me go.

When the ache in my foot and under my arms becomes too acute to ignore, I sink into the sand, utterly depleted. I wail at the stars until my weeping grows into loud, gasping-for-air sobs that shudder through my body. How could I have fallen into this trap of believing Ricardo would be different? How could I ignore the warning signs and set myself up for disaster? It was too good to be true, but I threw myself at his feet anyway. I cry until I have nothing left, seething at myself more than him.

How absurd that I ever considered giving Jorge the properties. And forfeiting the director of photography position on my first feature film. Far more humiliating than those mistakes is giving my heart to someone who could discard me for a silly, brief flirtation. Smashed and broken, I kick my feet fiercely into the sand. Sharp pain shoots through my injured foot, but it barely registers. What a fool I have been, reckless and irresponsible. Who knows, I could at this very moment be carrying his child. There is no way I can go to New York with this man. What on earth was I thinking? He will be cavorting with naked supermodels every time he goes to work while I do diapers. I kick again, sending sand flying into my face, and swipe it away angrily, sitting alone on the beach, bereft, pulverized, smashed into bits of sand.

Eventually, with great effort, I pull up to my feet and begin swinging myself back to Crystal Beach. Lights flicker in the distance and the journey grows monumental. The skin under my arms where the crutches rest has rubbed raw by the time I slink past the dregs of the poolside party. Stragglers sip drinks, laughing together on lounge chairs, and I pass without making eye contact, a bad-tempered alien lizard creature from Planet Misery. Ricardo is gone. Good.

In the reception area, I encounter Mila returning from the parking lot. "Ricardo's been waiting for you," she says, her face exuding relief at finding me, mixed with a strong measure of trepidation. "He just borrowed somebody's bike to drive down to the other end of the beach to find you."

The last thing I want is notification of Ricardo's whereabouts from Mila. I just stare at her, then make my way around her toward the front desk. I need to reserve a room, and remove myself from the foyer before I do something I will regret.

"Sirena, we didn't do anything," she insists to my back.

I ring the bell at the desk, ignoring her. I hope the staff are still around at this hour or I'll be sleeping on the beach.

"Whatever happened, it was my fault," Mila continues. "I asked him to adjust my back, and…"

I pivot, exploding on her, "I saw it, Mila, so save me the blow-by-blow."

"You're upset, but try to understand. I just wanted…" her voice cracks, "to feel what you're feeling," she spills softly, full of pain.

Some compassion filters through, even as I grip the crutches to stop myself from scratching her eyes out. "You won't find it that way."

"I know that." Her eyes attempt to connect with me. "Really, he was just being kind. Ricardo's not interested in me. He loves you."

Tears come again. My throat is sore from screaming and my nose is running. Mila tries to hug me, but I back away. No staff have appeared, so it looks like I will need to make a lounge chair my bed. I am about to head to the pool when I come up with another idea.

Mila follows, trying to find out where I am going, but I insist I'm not interested in speaking one more word with her. I shuffle away through the parking lot and down the dusty path leading to Wayan's compound.

It is late at night to be arriving as a guest. A pair of dogs jar me with their barking. A middle aged man I don't know greets me at the entry gate. When I ask for Wayan he steps aside, revealing Wayan already standing in the background.

"Ibu," Wayan says softly, surprised. "Are you okay?"

"Yeah. Sorry." I can only imagine what I look like, tear-stained, sweaty and covered in sand. "It's been a long night. Is your room available?"

"Yes." His eyes rake up and down, settling on my foot. "You are hurt."

I just nod, and he quickly realizes I am not in any mood for chatting.

"Follow me."

Wayan leads me to a simple room with a bed and a dresser. He wants to explain about the shared toilet and breakfast in the morning, but when I fail to respond, he finishes with goodnight and makes a quick retreat. Alone, I sob quietly into the pillow, caught between the sharpest pain and numbing disbelief. All is lost.

Emerging from the room in the morning, I find my young friends are excitedly waiting on the porch steps. Joining the boys on the stoop, I compliment them on their blue-and-white school uniforms, and the smallest one climbs onto my lap. The absolute relaxation of his body is a revelation and the longer we sit, the more we melt into each other. I used to think I didn't like small children, but today these kids are the only people I can tolerate. I put my arms around his little tummy and breathe him in.

A young woman with hair to her waist gracefully serves me a fruit plate, scrambled eggs and stiff white toast. I offer it to the boys, but it is time for them to run off to school.

"Not hungry?" Wayan joins me.

I shake my head and ask him if he can take me in his boat somewhere secluded. He says he knows of a small, uninhabited nearby island. I don't have anything with me other than my crutches and the clothes on my body, but he trusts my promise to pay him later.

The wind is up and our boat bounces over rough water. The overcast sky hangs heavy with humidity. I stare at the ocean without seeing a thing until Wayan tells me, "This is the place."

He anchors the boat near the shore. Carefully I pick a path on my crutches through shallow waves, over rocks and broken bits of coral, to a small, sandy cove. Tucked in beside wild jungle growth is a ramshackle fisherman's hut. I cross the sand and peak in the window, finding within the dilapidated walls a woven-palm mat across a rustic wooden floor.

"I'll take it," I say to myself with a joyless smile.

After a bit of convincing, Wayan agrees to leave me here until early the following morning. He is concerned about me staying alone, without food, and insists I take the two plastic bottles of water he has onboard. When I thank him for delivering me to my temple, something registers and he seems to understand.

The sand is hot and rough against my feet as I watch Wayan's boat disappear from sight. Waves come in and retreat, the sea a dark barrier beneath heavy gray sky. The breeze tosses my hair and it sticks to my face. I listen, but do not hear a single whisper from the voice of my heart.

A lone seabird swoops overhead. How I long to join it, freed from the density of my human existence. I watch sand crabs burying themselves near the shoreline, and a community of ants freely crawling up the wall of the shack, then wander the border where sand meets thick jungle, brushing against leaves like an animal sensing with my pores. I roll in dry sand, scooping up handfuls, fervently scrubbing my arms and legs to exfoliate the misery. I lie at the water's edge letting one mild wave after another crash upon me, then drench myself in the ocean, holding my breath beneath the surface until my lungs want to burst. I stand in the shallow water and shake all my body parts at once, quavering forcefully, fierce grunts, cries and moans springing from my mouth, until I collapse, dog-tired. None of it relieves my heartache.

Of their own accord my arms rise from my sides and I hold them straight out, shoulder high. Minute after minute passes and I refuse to let them drop. Beads of perspiration form above my lip, the sun burns my shoulders, my neck muscles complain loudly, but I refuse to budge, my resolve only strengthening. Tears trickle down my cheeks, joined by a waterfall of sweat now pouring from my forehead, but I grit my teeth and continue, arms rigid and upright, surrendering into the pain. I cannot, will not, lower them until something shifts. My rage rises and I want to strike out like a boxer, but I burn through my wrath until all that is left is pervasive sadness. Something clicks.

Arms still spread wide, I pad in circles using both of my feet, round and round, cautiously at first but speeding up as I go. My voice rises to the clouds in shrieks and cries and grunts, the sound spreading fissures that crack through my despair. A whiff of freedom teases my attention. Eventually my circling slows, coming to a stop, and gradually, incrementally, my aching arms lower. When they reach my sides, I sit in the sand, utterly static, staring out to sea, watching the sun drop lower on the horizon. A knowingness emerges out of the stillness: I cannot carry this darkness any longer. I must find a better way.

Using a crutch and my fingers as shovels, I dig a grave in the sand. When it feels deep enough, I collect rocks from the shoreline.

One at a time I hurl the heavy stones into the pit with every bit of intensity I can manage, naming each as I throw it. Victimization, I bury you. Jealousy, smash. Insufficiency, pound. Betrayal, blast, shatter, crumble.

It isn't until dusk begins hinting its arrival that I finally sip from a water bottle, allowing liquid to soothe my scorched throat. Lying in the sand, tinted clouds drifting above, Mila's voice sifts through my head. "Really, he was just being kind…"

The sun, subdued by clouds, sends blushing streaks low across the sky. My mind echoes questions. Is Ricardo's sexual magnetism something he manages, or an essential part of him? Is my requirement that he give himself to me fully an impossible demand? If it's foot rubs and spinal adjustments now, will that graduate into full-fledged affairs once our honeymoon period is over? Isn't it disastrous to enter a relationship on the basis that someone might change? That is exactly what I have done.

As darkness descends, I contemplate returning to Los Angeles. My dream job has become the booby prize, but Gregor might be able to work some magic and get me back into the crew. I no longer have a place to live, and if I stay in LA I cannot sell my car. Until I start pulling paychecks I will have to live with my parents. Grimace.

Beyond that reality is one much harder to swallow: a life without Ricardo. Looking out for his campaigns in magazines and wondering each day what he is doing. Returning to the dating scene and holding every new beau up to Ricardo's impossible standard.

The cloud cover shifts, stars becoming visible in the gaps. My heartbeat synchronizes with the steady lapping of the waves and I let myself acknowledge the truth. I love Ricardo more than I have ever loved anyone. I admitted to Mom I was afraid of how much I love him. Have I drummed up this drama out of fear? Ricardo said we are life partners; I bet he's questioning that tonight.

The breeze chills my sunburned skin and I shiver. Time for bed in the shack. Stretching out on my back, I stare at the ceiling in a prison cell of my own creation. My empty stomach grumbles. No direction feels conclusive. I toss and turn on the hard floor, without mattress, sheet, or pillow, dreamless.

A rapping jolts me awake. My eyes open, but nothing is decipherable in the pitch black. The sound comes again, and I realize someone is knocking at the cabin door. As I open it, a flashlight blinds my eyes and I startle back, but Wayan quickly tips the light up to his face. When he said he would pick me up early I didn't realize he meant before sunrise. He explains he has a full day of scuba diving booked. We wade to the boat and glide swiftly across the placid surface of the water in silence. Other boats are fishing with nets in the predawn stillness.

We dock at daybreak, and Wayan helps me arrange a motorbike taxi. I sit sidesaddle on the scooter, holding my crutches and bumping along the road to Ricardo's house, nerves jumping. I cannot avoid him forever.

The stepping stones over the pond are slippery with dew and I wobble my way carefully, apprehensively, bone-tired. On the veranda I pause. The early morning is quiet, punctuated only by the chords of a string instrument filtering through the open doors. Each note is achingly sad, plucked from the ether with devastating finality, a melody of mourning.

The driver is waiting behind me and I know I need to enter, but my muscles have become unstable, shaky. When the music falters, I know Ricardo has either heard or sensed my arrival, and I must continue.

At the doorway I halt again, leaning on my crutches, catching sight of Ricardo seated on the living room floor, his mandolin cradled in his arms. When our eyes meet the world stands still. His jaw is tight and his eyes look empty; I doubt he has slept. We stare wordlessly at each other, neither of us budging.

Eventually Ricardo sets down the mandolin. Rising to his feet, he seems to regain his presence and the stature of his full body overwhelms me. His face is hard, unforgiving, and I do not like seeing him angry; it makes me afraid. I have been furious and blaming him, yet in this moment I feel terribly guilty. I have caused this reaction in him.

"I can't do this," he says coldly and calmly.

I lean into the doorjamb for support, dizzy, weakened. I knew it. He is done with me. Through everything I have somehow known this moment would arrive, that he would finally realize I was too much trouble, too watery, too reactive. I have exposed the worst of myself to him and, as if I am three years old again, here comes the punishment, chastised for my strong emotions. Fear and shame drip through me and all I can do is stand there, head bowed, waiting for the guillotine to fall.

"You cut my feet out from under me," he continues, the words cut so fiercely he may as well have accused me of castrating him. That is the last thing I would ever want to do. I grip my crutches, desperate to escape his hostility, and glance back at the driver, now smoking a cigarette only a few short steps away. I am tired of hurting us both, and am sorely tempted to leave my things and make a dash for Wayan's compound. It would be better if I left.

Ricardo's eyes narrow. "That's right, run away. That's what you do, isn't it? Whenever things get tough, you just…" his hand spirals vaguely, "disappear."

Shellshocked by his hostility, I remain silent, but basically the answer is yes. A jumble of thoughts clamor inside me, defenses and accusations, curses and appeals, a mass of contradictions that leave me wordless, motionless, staring at him.

"I'm guessing you're here for your things. Go ahead then. Go." He nods at the side of the room where I discover he has stacked my luggage. "I packed for you."

The irrefutability in his voice leaves me nearly catatonic. He doesn't want me. I had expected him to be upset about my disappearing act, but thought he would have some remorse, apologies even, not blame me for the entirety. To pack my bags and kick me out… I am staggered.

I could acknowledge, maybe, that his interaction with Mila was within the bounds of his work as a yoga teacher, but the way she was touching him — and the way he allowed it — would not have happened had they been aware of my presence. That alone makes it a betrayal. Somehow amid all his annoyance at my eruption, he's forgotten that fact.

"Your words are like punches. You're all blame and no responsibility. You hurt me, as a result of your own weakness," I spit. "And I've had it with weak men." I swing a few steps towards my bags, then turn and add, "I know you wanted to hit me on the beach. Is that what comes next?"

Now he's the one who can barely meet my gaze. I turn away from him, moving towards my belongings. Behind me I hear him say, "I didn't."

I pause, looking at him over my shoulder.

"I had the impulse to strike because that's what all the men I grew up around would have done. But I didn't do it. You had the impulse to swing, and you swung. You had the impulse to run, and you ran. It's cowardly and it's beneath you." His voice is like steel. "Two nights. You didn't come home..." I hear a small crack in the tough tone and it slices deeper than the anger, "...or tell me where you were."

Now I feel his anguish. He looks as devastated as I was in those first few hours of utter desolation. Ricardo betrayed my trust, but I went and severed the intimacy between us. I turn to face him again and, barely above a whisper, I mouth, "I'm sorry."

We stare each other down, moving below the anger into the pain. Flushes of emotion spread like dark ink through my torso. He takes a step, but halts. "You took one trigger that rocked your boat and you blew it up big. You focused only on that, like everything that came before it didn't mean anything. Like all that beauty was just irrelevant."

I watch our chests heaving up and down at opposite ends of the room. "That beauty is the reason it destroyed me, Ricardo."

I am starting to see things from his perspective, but my own outrage is alive and well. A flash of Mila's foot brushing up his calf makes my eyes sting.

"What you've said about me is true," I continue, embarrassed by the hot, fat tears that have started rolling down my cheeks. "I do run away from conflict. I'm used to working through everything alone and sometimes I have to be by myself to get clear." I try to control them, but deep, shuddering breaths break my words. "Yes, I'm responsible for going ballistic and bolting, but I'm not the one who kickstarted this event. All you've done is attack me. You haven't said a word about what started this whole thing. I know what I saw. And I know the look of guilt that flashed in your eyes when you discovered me standing at the door." My voice is dripping with sixty-three emotions at once.

Ricardo's face softens, the truth in my words reaching him. "You were there when Mila asked for my help. I think she did have ulterior motives, but I didn't."

Ugh. He is giving me a classic, lame, guy response. "Oh, poor Ricardo. The innocent male lured into the sticky female web of seduction." My hands are dramatic in their sarcastic gestures, but I am not holding back. "I think the strongest impulse you have is to see how many women you can draw in and you generate it like a forcefield 24-7. I can't live with the playboy way you're going about life."

He has nothing to retort and looks down. "How's this any different than sneaking away to a bar every chance you get," I continue, "saying 'I don't really take a drink, just have a habit of licking the glass'?"

Hurt and shame splash across his face and he looks away again, scowling.

"Why do you do it, Ricardo?" I pursue a bit softer, needing to know.

"I, just…" He scrubs his hands over his eyes. "I've been acting this way so long, I can't work out if it's a choice or just part of who I am."

"Dig deeper," I fire.

His body immediately tenses. "I'm trying."

"Not hard enough."

"What do you want to know, Sirena?" He stalks toward me, and I lean away, against the wall. His eyes are dark, intense, and aggressive, sucking the breath from my lungs as he stops just inches from my face. My eyes dart to the door at my side, and two strong arms rise on either side of me, caging me against the wall and barring my escape.

"Would you like to hear how neglected I felt growing up?" he growls. "The churning need I had to be noticed? What a fucking tonic it was to finally become a man and feel desired?"

The heat radiates off him, and I can see self-control shivering through his muscles. "Isn't that the biggest addiction of all, to be wanted? I almost let a guy suck my cock once, just because of how much it turned him on." His laugh is short, and bitter. "I pose for cameras, adored for what? Some bone structure and brawn they think will sell product? I can do all the meditation and grounding in the world, but I crave that attention. I live for it."

His words are filled with loathing, but even as he speaks them I am caught by how remarkably beautiful he is. Not for the warm brown of his eyes framed by thick lashes, nor the powerfully-muscled arms on either side of me, but the raw vulnerability that trembles beneath every word. Ricardo is a book full of dark secrets, but I want to know each one. I want to draw every shadowy hurt into the light, but to do that, he needs to understand the heart I am placing in his palm.

"Don't you see, I agreed to walk away from everything to be with you? The city where my family lives, my properties, my career… Do you get that?" Something in him relaxes slightly, even as he continues fencing me in. "I just turned down the job of my dreams to follow you to New York, and I lost my agent in the process." His eyes widen in surprise, and with a deep breath his arms drop to his sides. "That's right. A feature film. It would have meant staying in LA, so I passed." I look into his eyes as directly as I possibly can. "To be with you."

"You did that?"

"Uh huh. And just a few hours later I find you leaning into Mila's body asking if she 'wants more.'"

We stare at each other again, but he can't hold it and shifts his head away. Something hit home. I inhale deeply now that there is some breathing room between us.

"I called my sponsor last night." His voice is flat, but there is something else there, a softness that begs me to try and understand. "He said I've been single for a long time, behaving like a single man. That I need to mature to be in relationship. And I want to. I'm willing to change."

I want so badly to believe him, but he has already said the same. My silence speaks volumes.

"I didn't betray you." His eyes are glassy, which makes my eyes fill again with tears. "I know how it looked, and I know I should have found a way not to fall into that situation." He pauses, then adds, "But I would never willingly hurt you. And if I need to quit teaching yoga, or modeling, or whatever to prove that to you, I will."

I blink up at him, repeating his words in my head, but convinced I've heard him incorrectly.

"I will, Sirena. I'll follow you to LA, and help on your film set. I'll be your one-man support team. All that matters is that we're together and you trust me. The rest is background detail."

The generosity of that gesture astounds me.

He takes a deep breath and his Adam's apple bobs as he swallows. His eyes close, and when he opens them again the toughness has receded. "I'm in, Sirenita. All the way.... even though you swung one of those crutches at me." We both allow a hint of a sad smile. "I've always been all in, from the first moment I saw you."

I'm still reeling that he packed my luggage and told me to leave. Now he's turned around and laid his world at my feet. The reversal has left me with whiplash. When I try explaining my confusion, he reaches out his hand and touches me lightly with his palm as if I am a delicate bird.

"I never wanted you to go. You know that, don't you?" His voice is gentle as his temple brushes mine. "But I needed to let you go, if that's what you wanted."

I shake my head no at him, slowly, unable to express just how much the thought of leaving him destroys me. With just one single glance into my devastated eyes he pulls me in tight, and the world begins to right itself once more. Oh, to be wrapped in his arms again, to nestle my face into the crook of his neck.

This time when my cheek turns wet, I realize the tears are not my own. "I thought I lost you," he says quietly.

His hands pass gently over my head, stroking me, as I relax into his body. The crutches fall to the floor. I feel his cheek stretch against mine. A smile.

"You have sand in your hair."

"I have sand in my everything."

We are beginning to walk toward the shower when there's a cough at the door. The driver is standing there, looking completely embarrassed. Before I can remove my purse from my suitcase, Ricardo has paid the man and apologized for the delay, returning from the door to sweep me up into his arms.

He carries me into the bathroom like I am his queen and places me gently on the bench. I am transported back to the moment he first stood before me, proud in his nakedness and heated with desire. This time he turns on the shower with careful, solemn motions. Sand sprinkles out of my clothing as I remove it, and my resistance falls away with it, as does my fear. Nothing is broken. This is another face of love revealed, a difficult maneuver in the dance of intimacy, but we are still dancing. Just as my heart experience was truly a heart opening, this explosion has not shattered our bond but revealed how deeply we both desire it. As far as we had pulled away, we now spin that much closer together, letting the trauma wash down the drain. Wordlessly we bathe in each other's forgiveness, allowing our bodies to melt back into each other.

My crutches are still in the living room. Ricardo carries me to the bed, and sets me down, then slides beside me. Pressed together side by side, the only motion is our mutual rhythm of in-breath and extended, synchronized out-breath. We have both been beaten and tenderized, now every nuance is made new again. We caress each other first with our gaze, then with our fingertips, adoring cheek and nose, hip and thigh. Each sensitive micro-movement is an apology and a promise, aware of what we have lived through and who we must become.

Linking our fingers together, we kiss our relief and our pledges. Slowly reassurance gives way to savoring. I raise my knee to his hip, offering myself to him, opening to the whirlpool he inspires within me. I want to wrap every part of me around him, to bond my being with his now that my heart believes it may actually be safe to love him this much. I can almost see fine, threadlike tendrils emerging through our skin, weaving us into each other.

When he rolls me onto my back, we spiral into something thick and trancelike. I am slippery like jelly and it is easy for him to pull nearly out and continually plunge back inside of me, our eyes locked, breathy moans escaping us with every stroke. Beyond the damp aroma of our mingled bodies, I catch a whiff of exotic perfume, and my mind's eye momentarily flashes on a mysterious flask, stashed since antiquity, suddenly uncorked. Available, unshielded, liquified, invisible doorways are unlocking. Around Ricardo's body, suspended over me, I see a glimmering outline, an early morning glow of light like an illumined cloak.

His hand stretches out, grasps a pillow and slides it under my bottom. My ankles hook over his shoulders, his hips roll faster, leaning in, my thighs pressed back beneath the weight of his torso. Hot tongue on my neck, he drives in deeper than ever before, up against my cervix, all the way in. The intensity is nearly overwhelming, but I allow it, I open to it, I give way to it, I let him take me.

"You're… my fucking… gravity," he groans into my ear, punctuated by his thrusting hips.

Those words are a hotline direct from his heart through his magnificent cock, searing into every level of my being and I know nothing will ever be the same after this moment right here. He is mine, I am his, that's the way it is.

When I close my eyes, my entire body quaking with emotion, two serpents rise up my core, twisting, flipping on power switches as they climb. Every part of me is humming like a live wire, electrically charged; even my teeth are buzzing. An intense pulsing echoes through every thrust, a shimmering that spreads, and I let the passion mount. Ricardo is my anchor, my rock, the ground that allows me to fly. He is the safety net that catches me as the vibrations rocket through every cell. Tears stream down my face, nothing held back, every gate thrown open to new territory of trust. I am crying out, and Ricardo's voice joins mine, laughter erupting, both of us tossed in the surging waves. We find ourselves bobbing in a sea of immeasurable beauty, love inundating every corner. One single word drifts into my mind: bliss.

Afterwards we are sticky and the bed is soaked, but we stay, holding each other. The taste of heaven is still sweet upon our lips.

"Sirenita..." Ricardo starts, but his voice trails off, something ticking through his mind. "If you want to take the feature, I'll go with you to LA. I mean it."

I kiss him all over his face. What a kind offer. "I know you would follow me to the ends of the earth." My fingers brush the high planes of his cheeks and his lips, swollen from my kisses. "But shooting a film means months of absurdly long days and sustained stress. I'm ready for something new, and you're ready to dive back into your scene."

"Speaking of which..." His voice tapers off again. I can practically see the thoughts ricocheting through his brain. "William called early this morning. I sent him the photos you took of me."

I think of the ridges of his abdomen in the soft morning light, the dark patch of hair glimpsed behind the edge of the sheet. Those photos were not meant for public consumption.

"I didn't send them all," he grins, drawing a finger between my breasts to my navel. "He dug 'em, big time. Said they are refined and lyrical, and he doesn't hand out compliments for the sake of it. He wants a meeting with you when we get to New York."

"Really?" A tremor of happy anticipation wriggles through my stomach. "Does he rep photographers?"

"No, but he knows every agent who does. And every top photographer." He shifts onto his elbow, gearing up for something. "It's something we can discuss at Cora's dinner."

"So it's happening?"

"Done deal." He leans in conspiratorially. "I think your photos clinched it."

I am so proud of him I'm bursting. "You did this yourself, Ricardo. You're magic."

"Really, *amorcita,* it's us. Together."

We look into each other's eyes, taking in the mighty approaching changes.

Stroking his leg where the lion tattoo is, I explain to Ricardo about Joko saving my life and his offer to dive with me. "I've been uneasy about it, but I don't want to leave Indonesia without going underwater again. He's coming to Nusa Dewi in a few days to join me."

"I didn't realize you'd become afraid of diving." He nudges his nose playfully against my jaw. "So we both need to face some fear about water."

"I hadn't thought of it that way."

"I'll go first. Today's the day."

In the late afternoon heat, we drive the motorbike to Crystal Beach. Ricardo pays a small fee at the desk for us to use the pool. Gratefully, it is empty.

While he reclines on a poolside chair feigning relaxation, I take a few photos of his smooth, brown skin warming under the full sun. I have just captured an alluring shot of his hard, flat stomach when he abruptly announces, "I'll jump into the deep end."

That is not how I pictured this. I thought we could start on the steps together, moving into progressively deeper water until he is ready to take a dunk. "Are you sure?" I crinkle my nose, checking to see if he's bluffing.

"Completely."

"Let's talk it through at least." I sit on the edge of his chaise. "Think of it as yoga in water. Inhale and hold your breath. Jump in, your weight pulls you down to the bottom, and your body pops up to the surface by itself."

"I can do that."

"Then what?"

"I don't know."

"You take a breath and dog paddle, or thrash around a bit," I smile.

"Sounds important." He flashes a quick smile, but mostly his expression is serious.

"Do you want to practice the swimming first before taking the plunge?"

"Nope."

He is casual and decisive. I would wonder if he's been pulling my leg, but when he stands at the side of the pool, I can feel the courage he is summoning. I hop-walk to the edge, the lifeguard on duty, and dangle my feet in the water. His eyes are closed, his concentration pulled inward, his body still. After one particularly long, deep breath, he jumps over the side of the pool into the water, sinking down.

When he pops to the surface his face is smooth and calm, with a look of discovery as if he was experiencing the element of water for the first time. With a few strokes that are somehow both awkward and graceful, he is holding onto the edge where I am sitting.

"I did it," he beams, face stretched into an exuberantly proud, even youthful, smile.

"Are you sure you never swam before?"

"First time."

He pulls himself out of the pool in a single, effortless move, stands by the edge, and jumps again. And again. I witness firsthand

Ricardo's focus, how he can zero in on something and hone it. This is why he is good at so many things, and also how he became an addict. He doesn't believe in half measures.

Holding onto the side, he splashes water in my direction. "Come on in."

I slip in and under, resurfacing beside him. As I glide against his body in the cool slickness, a shimmering awareness filters through me. Ricardo has allowed himself to fully enter my watery world. For once he is the fish out of water.

He asks me to show him how to do the crawl. I demonstrate, and he practices the short length of the pool. Some things are difficult to learn as an adult without looking like a buffoon, but Ricardo is in tune with his body and his physical agility is quickly extending into swimming. Before long he is doing a handstand poolside, walking on his hands to the very edge, and flipping into the water.

An outbreak of giggles expose my young Indonesian friends spying on Ricardo's water circus over the low beachside wall. I invite them in, and they descend with shouts of glee.

"I was like these guys when I was a kid," Ricardo tells me, "running around with my crew."

I ask the boys to swim with us, but their initial response is to refuse. While they back away laughing, Ricardo tells me they don't know how either. Once again I am baffled; their uncle is a scuba instructor and they live by the beach. Ricardo explains many of the island people traditionally fear the ocean, believing it full of spirits.

I offer to teach them, but they are shy. Pointing to the pool and then the cafe, I say, "Es crem," with enthusiasm. The bribe works.

We start with the boys splashing on the steps, putting their legs into the cold water and wildly pulling them out. Eventually I lure them in up to their chests. Before long Ricardo is doing handstands in the water, and the boys are trying to emulate him, falling over and laughing uproariously. They turn Ricardo into a ladder, climbing onto his shoulders and jumping off. At one point all three children are hanging on him at once, and I can tell from Ricardo's glowing eyes that he has become enamored.

Just then Mila emerges from the beach, dripping wet, observing from a distance. She remains in the background; we don't make direct eye contact. The boys spot my camera on one of the chairs and ask if they can take photos of Ricardo flipping into the pool. Afterwards I request a shot of the two of us jumping into the air, holding hands, capturing the moment just before we hit the water. After several failed attempts, Mila steps in as coach, and the oldest boy clicks a memorable image of us in mid-flight, leaping together into the realm of conquered fear.

While we move to the restaurant for one more vanilla ice cream party, I notice Mila slipping away down the footpath. Now that the storm has passed, my anger towards her has receded. I don't want to vilify her; I want to make peace. Motioning to Ricardo that I'll be right back, I follow her into the garden and call out her name. She turns, surprised.

"Hey," she says warily as I approach. I almost laugh, wondering if I am scarier than I realize. "I'm glad to see you two made up," she hedges.

Our eyes meet and hold. We both have remorse for our behavior. "I think it was something we needed to go through."

She mumbles another apology and starts walking away, cheeks scarlet. Before she gets too far I ask, "Do you want to have ice cream with us?"

She studies my face cautiously, and her uncertainty warms into a partial smile. "Alright. Thanks."

Ricardo shoots me an astonished, but admiring glance when I return with Mila. While I photograph the rambunctious boys eating their ice cream, jostling each other and wiggling their silly arms in constant motion between spoonfuls, Ricardo asks Alit to blend the flesh and water of coconuts into creamy, white smoothies for the grown ups. We sip our drinks together, watching the gentle swells of the ocean.

Days later when Joko arrives at our house, we greet him like a visiting dignitary. Ricardo thanks him for saving my life, and the two men form a natural bond. Joko invites Ricardo to join us, but he bows out, unready for an ocean swim. He doesn't seem to have any qualms about me spending the day with Joko.

At the seaside dive shop we fill our tanks, then load our equipment onto Wayan's outrigger, including a picnic Ricardo helped me prepare. "You look happier, Ibu," Wayan tells me, and I just smile.

Zipping along the surface of the ocean, the breeze blowing back my hair, I feel as if my soul is skipping alongside the boat. Our first stop is the cove with the desolated shack where I spent the night. In the shade of ancient, towering, white mango trees, the three of us spread sarongs on the sand and share the picnic feast created in Joko's honor. He shares freely about his wife's long battle with cancer, and I describe more of the journey I took in leaving my body the last time we dove together. My words seem to soothe him, and he drinks in every detail.

It isn't until we arrive at our dive point and Wayan kills the engine that I face a flush of apprehension. Suited up from our fins to our toothpaste-washed masks, Joko seeks to put me at ease. "I will watch you every moment, Sirena. If you feel even a little discomfort, signal me."

"Thank you, Joko. I think I'll be fine."

His smile is enigmatic. "I think so, too."

We flip backwards off the side of the boat, bob back up to the surface and signal to begin our descent, slowly sinking. I have no trouble clearing, so the pressure on my ears is only slightly stronger than on land. Submerged in a foreign landscape that is somehow also home, we float along a reef teeming with life, vibrant with rainbow colors and textures. Through crystal-clear water, Joko points out giant brain coral, spiky lion fish, and funny faced clown fish with orange stripes. I am rediscovering my childlike wonder at being able to breathe underwater, a mermaid in her lair.

When we drift into deeper water, out of nowhere the distant flapping of dark wings announces the arrival of mantas flying directly at us. I count seven as they approach, gracefully encircling us. Their bodies undulate as they pass, flapping then coasting, watching us curiously with huge black eyes on the sides of their heads. Immediately I sense their affable intelligence. The mantas bring delight and a cascade of realizations like pearls strung on a necklace.

It has taken actually submerging to realize I am not afraid. Fear cannot have the same grip on me any longer. The grace is always with me, even when I think it has left, and fear cannot exist in its presence. I am not worried about diving or leaving my body and, most importantly, I am not afraid of remaining in it. I can trust the pathway of rose petals my heart trails for me. I can embrace moving to New York and I can even face my uncle. I have dived into the ugliest, most terrifying parts of myself and survived. Even if I were to die this day, I would only feel appreciation for the time I have spent in my body, especially each and every moment with Ricardo. I am no longer afraid of living fully, living largely, full spectrum, full-speed, ahead living. I know I am not leaving today; I have much yet to do. I hear the subtle drumbeat, the throbbing of my own life force beckoning me, calling my name, telling me the doorway is open. Here in the depths, I am receiving its signal, beaming inside of me and flashing everywhere around me. It is the call of the new world Ricardo and I will build together, a life anchored in honesty, in intimacy, in an ever-deepening love. From underwater, mantas dancing elegantly around me, the ineffable is offering me a beauty shining brighter than the sun, the moon and the stars, and my heart sings out, "Yes!"

The End

Let's have a dialogue about Girl Submerged!

Please offer your honest review on Amazon.

Visit the website: www.girlsubmerged.com

Please sign up to receive the blog.

Check out the events and retreats.

You can even purchase the Empress Bag and the silk dress described in the book!

Book Two, *Melting Snow,* will be coming your way soon.

ACKNOWLEDGEMENTS

I offer my most genuine appreciation to my editor, Cate Hogan, for her wise and fiercely honest notes with each of this book's many drafts. I am a better writer and a better person due to the inner chiropractic adjustments I had to go through with each major revision.

Deep thanks to my book cover designer, Kelly Carter, who condensed the emotional complexity of Girl Submerged into a single, jarringly beautiful image.

I bow to my photography angel, Alina Vlasova, whose uncanny sensitivity behind the lens creates magic again and again, aided by the masterful graphic skills and artistic eye of Spoonci. You are a team made in heaven.

Gratitude to Rex Sumner who took the time to painstakingly format each and every detail, responding to my notes even when attending a ceremony with headhunters in the Borneo jungle.

Endless love to my children and friends for your patience as I focused unceasingly on letting this story pour through me and onto the page.

Avara Yaron is an entrepreneur and an artist with a lifelong passion for tropical islands. She particularly enjoys a coconut cappuccino accompanied by deep conversation and belly laughs.

A periodic shapeshifter, Avara has earned a film degree, a spiritual counseling license, and has explored life as a painter, filmmaker, designer, counselor, group facilitator, retreat leader, chef, and nutritional educator.

For more than two decades Avara has had a romance with the island of Bali, initially as the manufacturing hub for the line of fine jewelry and handbags she designed. After traveling back and forth 24 times, she finally packed and moved to Bali. There she dreamed up two cafes serving plant based cuisine.

In the midst of all that food preparation, this story took over Avara's life and she gave birth to the Girl Submerged trilogy of novels. The series merges two of the great loves of her life, the islands of Jamaica and Bali.

Avara has a biological son, a daughter adopted from China, a wild dog and an abandoned cat. She wrote a food column for Inspired Bali magazine, and it should come as no surprise that this book has descriptions of food in it.

girl SUBMERGED

Avara Yaron

girl SUBMERGED